James Robertson is a poet, short story writer and essayist, as well as an acclaimed novelist. His five novels are *The Fanatic*, *Joseph Knight*, *The Testament of Gideon Mack*, *And the Land Lay Still* and *The Professor of Truth*. *The Testament of Gideon Mack* was longlisted for the Man Booker Prize and picked by Richard and Judy's Book Club. *Joseph Knight* received both the Scottish Arts Council Book of the Year Award and the Saltire Society Book of the Year Award in 2003–2004. *And the Land Lay Still* also received the latter award in 2010.

365

stories

James Robertson

PENGUIN BOOKS

PENGUIN BOOKS

Published by the Penguin Group
Penguin Books Ltd, 80 Strand, London WC2R 0RL, England
Penguin Group (USA) Inc., 375 Hudson Street, New York, New York 10014, USA
Penguin Group (Canada), 90 Eglinton Avenue East, Suite 700, Toronto, Ontario, Canada M4P 2Y3
(a division of Pearson Penguin Canada Inc.)
Penguin Ireland, 25 St Stephen's Green, Dublin 2, Ireland (a division of Penguin Books Ltd)
Penguin Group (Australia), 707 Collins Street, Melbourne, Victoria 3008, Australia
(a division of Pearson Australia Group Pty Ltd)
Penguin Books India Pvt Ltd, 11 Community Centre, Panchsheel Park, New Delhi – 110 017, India
Penguin Group (NZ), 67 Apollo Drive, Rosedale, Auckland 0632, New Zealand
(a division of Pearson New Zealand Ltd)
Penguin Books (South Africa) (Pty) Ltd, Block D, Rosebank Office Park,
181 Jan Smuts Avenue, Parktown North, Gauteng 2193, South Africa

Penguin Books Ltd, Registered Offices: 80 Strand, London WC2R 0RL, England

www.penguin.com

First published 2014
001

Text design by Claire Mason

This is a work of fiction. Names, characters, places and incidents are either the product
of the author's imagination or are used fictitiously, and any resemblance to actual persons,
living or dead, or to actual events or locales is entirely coincidental

Set in 9.6/12.45 pt Legacy Serif ITC
Typeset by Jouve (UK), Milton Keynes
Printed in Great Britain by Clays Ltd, St Ives plc

ISBN: 978-0-241-14686-6

www.greenpenguin.co.uk

At the beginning of 2013 I began an experiment. Could I write a short story on each day of the year? The stories would all be exactly the same length: 365 words. By the end of the year, if the experiment was successful, there would be 365 365-word stories.

Despite some anxious moments on days which seemed reluctant to reveal or release their stories, I completed the task. Then, throughout 2014, the stories appeared, one each day, on the website of my publisher, Hamish Hamilton (www.fivedials.com). Now they are collected here in one volume, their third life. I hope they have more lives to come.

James Robertson, 2014

January

The Beginning

Before the beginning there was nothing. And nothing came from nothing, since nothing can. But something, somehow, did, and that was the change. Was it a moment or an aeon – and who among us is bold, clever or foolish enough to define the difference? Well, anyway, there was a time when change happened – and *that* was the change, the first pulse or tick or fractional movement that signified the arrival of time. *Chronos*. And the *how* of that change has ever since been the fuel of legend, faith and science, and arguments among them. In the end – which is itself a subject of similar contention – everything is theory and speculation. Priests, shamans, physicists, philosophers, evolutionary biologists and natural historians are as one on this, though they might vigorously deny it: nothing they can offer us is much more than informed guesswork.

Ahead of these pretenders came the mother and father of them all – the chronicler, recorder, teller of tales. One day the mist rose from the ground, and the thought was, *What is this?* The mountain rose in the sunlight and the thought was, *How did it get there?* The river ran, birds chatted and sang, animals bellowed and grumbled, and the thought was, *What are they saying?* And hard behind that one came others. *Who am I? Who are we? What is this strange mystery in which we find ourselves?*

The night came down – or up – as it had done before, the moon was in the night or it was not, the stars were there or they were hidden, and – something was different. The storyteller saw a pattern and began to trace it. Or there was no pattern, it was just guesswork. And this was the beginning, before which was nothing (and of that 'before' nothing was or could be known). This was the beginning, when fire, that had burned dry grass or leaves outside, was brought inside, to a circle of stones, and was fed through the night. And our ancient forebears gathered round and looked at the flames, and held out their hands to the heat, and waited for the dawn.

The beginning was when the storyteller first said, 'In the beginning . . .'

Story

for Jamie Jauncey

What is a story? A writer friend tells me that if he said he went on a train from Perth to Doncaster, changing at Edinburgh, that wouldn't be a story, but if he said it was only when he got to Doncaster that he realised he'd left his bag in Edinburgh, that would be. Something has to change for it to be a story, my friend the writer said, something has to happen.

A boy goes out to the shop and doesn't come back.

A boy goes out to the shop and doesn't come back for seven years.

A boy goes out to the shop and when he comes back seven years later he is a girl.

These are stories, if I am not mistaken.

Here is another.

A boy goes out to the shop for a pint of milk but coming home he turns left instead of right, and walks through the woods. In the woods he finds a strange mound covered in thick, soft, green moss, and he sits down on it, and he falls asleep. And while he sleeps, out from a door in the side of the mound come the fairies, who drag him away to their underground world. They beat him and starve him and make him their slave, and put a spell on him so he forgets who he is. After seven years' hard labour they let him go, and he wakes on the soft green mound with a confused memory of that terrible time. And the pint of milk is there on the ground beside him.

So he hurries home and in through the door, and in tears he tells his mother and father what happened. How sad and worried they must have been all the years he's been away. They smile at him. That's a good story, they say, but you've only been gone twenty minutes. And he sees that they are no older than they were when he left, and he looks in the mirror and neither is he. But when his mother opens the milk it is shrunken and solid, like cheese, and – according to the stamp on the carton – seven years out of date.

At the John Bellany Exhibition

What are these rooms full of? What are these pictures about? You walk past blood and fish-guts, unspeakable horrors real and imagined, unremitting toil, raw sex, turmoil, violence, and the symbols of a religion that goes beyond sect or creed in its relentless chess-game of life and death. There is something local about this ferocious art. When a Scottish Calvinist goes round the back of the world into darkness he will meet a Scottish Catholic coming the other way. And Hell may be there, but what sign of Heaven, or God?

This art has no peace. Even in the late landscapes of Italy the sky looms over towns and villages, threatening destruction. Through all these rooms you feel you are following a man who still, at seventy, can only wrestle and grapple with life.

But in one small section you do find tranquillity. Addenbrooke's Hospital, Cambridge, 1988. Bellany's liver has packed in under the abuse he has dealt it. He is admitted for a transplant. The operation, like so much that has happened to him, is a challenge. He comes through it. The new liver takes to him. Regaining consciousness, he cannot yet believe he is alive. He asks for pencil and paper and starts to draw. His hand. Himself. Self-portrait after self-portrait. He draws and paints himself back into life. He stares out at himself, at the place he is in, at life returning. And because he is still weak, at the mercy of tubes and wires and the healing process, there is a kind of peace, a kind of acceptance, and something else – a bright, clean, heavenly light.

You remember these hospital images from when you first saw them, a quarter of a century ago. You were a young man then, and the Bellany you were looking at was in his mid-forties, younger than you are now. But you had thought you were looking at an old man, at the resurrection of an old man. It is a shock to realise how young he was, how much more life he had in him.

And you too. And still have. Here you are today, his paintings and you, on this grey Edinburgh afternoon, alive.

The Glack of Newtyle is a long, narrow, twisting defile between the hills of Hatton and Newtyle in Angus. It runs south to north from the high ground of the Sidlaws down to the rich, fertile land of Strathmore. The Glack has always been a place of uncertainty, and sometimes of danger for the unwary. Today, especially on early winter mornings when the sun has not penetrated its gloomy bends to melt black ice, or at night when deer haunt the trees that line its many bends, it catches out drivers who have their minds on something other than the road – the over-confident, the careless or weary. Broken fences and the debris of smashed vehicles in the ditches are testimony to these not infrequent mishaps. But centuries ago, according to legend and chronicle, the Glack harboured perils of a more horrific kind.

A cannibal and his family had their lair nearby, and would lie in wait for travellers making the journey from Dundee northwards. Men, women and children alike were taken and devoured – the younger the victim, it was said, the more tender and sweet did they judge the flesh. At last these depredations could be tolerated no longer, a force was assembled and the 'brigant' and his wife and offspring were captured and burned, with the exception of a daughter who was only one year old at the time. She was brought to Dundee and raised and fostered there till she came to womanhood. Then she too was condemned to be burned, though whether for having participated in her family's crimes as an infant or because she had reoffended is not clear.

A huge crowd, mostly of women, cursed her and spat on her as she was led to the place of execution in the Seagate. The lassie turned on them angrily. 'Why do you chide me so, as if I had committed some unworthy act?' she cried. 'Believe me, if you had experience of eating the flesh of men and women, you would think it so delicious that you would never forbear it again.'

So, says the chronicler, without any sign of repentance this unhappy traitor died in the sight of the people.

The Executioner

I take a log from the pile, position it on the block, adjust my stance, swing the log-splitter. The log divides under the blow and the halves fall like toy buildings. I throw them into the creel.

My father taught me how to do this. Method, not strength, he advised. 'Feel the weight of the head,' he said. 'Let it do the work.'

I place another log, swing the splitter. The log seems to separate an instant before contact, as if it self-destructs to avoid what's coming. As if it could know.

At my parents' house over Christmas, I did various tasks around house and garden that they can no longer manage. The strong, practical, hands-on man who taught me how to split logs is now so slow, stiff and unsteady that it's not safe for him even to put one on the fire.

He was an outdoors man. Now he can't walk to the paper shop without running out of breath or falling. Cold air kicks off his angina. But one mild, calm day I got him into the wheelchair and pushed him to the beach where he used to sail his boat and walk his dog – both now gone.

We parked the wheelchair by the cars and made it down the wooden steps onto soft sand littered with clumps of weed left by a recent storm. With him gripping my arm, we reached the flat, firmer sand on which the waves were breaking, sullen and regular. A family was playing with two dogs. Dad's distance sight is better than mine. He watched the joyous energy of those children and dogs for a long time.

On the way home he was talkative – more than in the house where competing noises make it hard for him to hear or be heard. I leaned down to his ear and found we could communicate pretty well.

Back by the fire he sat glaring at my mother, as a prisoner might at his warder. 'I'm having another dog before I die.'

An impossibility, but we didn't deny him it. A few minutes later he was asleep.

I take another log, position it, adjust my stance. Swing the splitter.

He saw her first among the trees, flitting like a deer, or the ghost of a deer. With her long black hair and pale face, and her lack of fear, she wasn't like a deer at all, but that was how he thought of her. She stopped, looked at him as a deer might, but then unfroze and moved on, careless of the cracking of twigs under her feet.

She was from the big house. He had heard about her.

He reached the stone wall with the gate set in it. This was as far as you could walk in the glen: the wall marked the policies around the big house, and the gate was usually shut and bolted. But today it was open.

The house and the people who owned it were nothing to do with him or his kind. Money had built it, and the memory of money sustained it. The girl's parents were hardly ever there, he'd heard, though he couldn't recall who had told him this. Her father was in London, her mother in France. They led separate lives, so the story went, and neither of them worked. They didn't have to. That was what made them different.

He was just a boy from the village. She had been sent away to school, so they had never met. That was not supposed to happen.

The house was old-looking, but not as big as he'd expected. He'd expected a castle. How could he have walked these woods for so many years and never seen the place? Because of the high wall, he told himself, but it wasn't that. The house was like the ghost of a house. If he went away now and came back in the morning, would it still be there?

There was a doorway with a low lintel. The door was of thick, rough wood with iron studs in it. It was open, as the gate had been.

He thought, *If I go in here, I may never come back out.*

He heard the girl's voice singing, the clink and clatter of food or drink being prepared. For him?

He said to himself, *What do I have to lose?*

Luggy

There was a fisherman in Shetland, called Luggy, who went to sea with his companions in a long, narrow boat with a mast and a sail. They might be out for days at a time if the fish were not present. Sometimes a terrible hunger would come on them. Luggy had a basket in which he kept a line with a wee lead weight on it, and when they were starving and not a fish was to be had in the whole wide ocean he would drop this line over the stern of the boat and let it out to its full extent. When he pulled it in there would be a cod or plaice, fresh-grilled and steaming, on the end of the line. He would unhook the fish and share it with his mates. None of them knew how the fish came to be cooked like that, and they did not care to ask. They were famished, and the smell was irresistible.

Luggy had another trick he liked to play in stormy weather, when he couldn't get out to sea. His house was on the edge of a moor and he would go to a place where there was a deep, dark hole in the peat and let his line down through it, and pull up a smoked trout or salmon and take it back to his wife. She preferred a rabbit but she didn't complain. Apart from anything else, there were no pans to clean.

This all happened a long time ago. Nobody would believe you if you told such a story nowadays, but back then people were ignorant and believed all kinds of nonsense. Had Luggy told them, however, that there were billions of gallons of oil at the bottom of the same sea he fished, and that the oil could be brought to the surface and used for cooking, heating, manufacturing, powering vehicles and many other purposes, they'd have shaken their heads at him. 'No, no.' Especially if he'd gone on to explain that it would all be used up in less than a lifetime, every last drop. 'Aye, that'll be right,' they'd have said. 'Fetch us another fish supper, Luggy.'

Thanks, but No Thanks

for Michael Marra

As I was out walking the other day, I met a man who looked familiar. We passed, nodding and glancing as we did, and then, when we'd gone a few paces beyond one another, we both turned.

'Is that you, Michael?'

He seemed to weigh this up for a few seconds.

'Aye,' he said. 'That's what I thought, too.'

It was his voice all right. The unmistakable gravel of his songs, of his phone calls: *Are you going to be in later? Can I come round? Have you got time?* I always had. And round he'd come.

'What are you doing here?'

'Well,' he began – and then wasn't there.

I stood looking at his echo, the empty space six feet away. I thought, *If I go home and sit in at one side of the kitchen table, maybe he'll be there at the other side.* He always took an age to drink his coffee. No need to rush.

I wished I could remember everything he ever told me across that table. *If it was easy it wouldn't be worth doing,* he'd said, more than once.

'Did they send you back?' I said. 'Like Frida Kahlo?' But that was unfair; it was what *he'd* imagined, in one of his songs. I had no right.

I told him a story once, something that had happened after a death, and he listened but he was being polite, or kind rather, because that's what he was, kind. 'That's okay,' he said when I'd finished. 'But I don't want metaphors.'

I could see how you wouldn't, in his shoes.

I carried on along the road, but I couldn't stop myself imagining him telling me something, and it went like this: he'd arrived at the gate, and it was open, with no one on duty, so he'd just put his head in to have a wee look, in case he wanted to slip away without bothering anybody. All was fresh and neat in there, very meticulous decor, but he didn't like how they'd applied the paint. They'd been mean with it. There wasn't enough boldness of colour. *And I bet,* he thought, *there isn't a piano.*

So he didn't go in.

How is it that dogs understand instinctively that the best way to alleviate their stomach disorders is to eat grass? It's not as if their mothers can have taught them this. Most dogs are taken from their mothers when they're barely off milk. Yet in later years, afflicted by constipation or just a bit bilious, they start tearing at the long green stuff. They *know*. How come?

Perhaps a kind of canine folk medicine is in play, passed from generation to generation when older dogs meet young ones in the woods or in the park or on the street.

One dog to another, sniffing its arse: 'You're smelling a bit bland, son. Bunged up, are you? What you need's a good clump of grass.'

Other dog: 'Grass? What? You're having me on!'

'No, I'm serious. I know, it sounds weird, and none of us wants to be mistaken for a cow let alone a sheep, but grass is the thing, believe me.'

'Not for me! I like my meat – fresh off the bone, or straight from the tin at least.'

'We all do, but you can overdo it. No roughage, son, that's your problem.'

'Well, since you mention it, I am pretty tight.'

'You're like a drum. It's hard work too, having to do your business in two minutes when you're in that condition. Stressful. And they always bloody watch you. Anyway, give the old grass a go, that's my tip.'

'Right, I will.'

'Mind you, don't overdo it, and don't look like you're enjoying it. Sends out the wrong message entirely. I hear some poor sods are getting fed nothing but a kind of dry vegetarian biscuit mix, day in, day out.'

'It's a bloody sin, imposing that on a dog.'

'Then of course they go crazy at the first opportunity, hoovering up road-kill, a rotten seal on the beach, anything with some flavour. But their systems can't handle it. Back it comes, all over the best carpet. *Then* they get a leathering.'

'There's no justice, is there?'

'None. Well, can't stand around sniffing your arse all day. You take my advice and eat some grass. This time tomorrow you'll be feeling brand new.'

On his arrival in Samarra, Death's first thought was to track down the man who had thought to evade him in Baghdad, and settle their score. But something made him pause. What was the hurry, and why the need to hunt for him deliberately? After all, had he not always expected their meeting to take place here? Furthermore, he knew from the man's master that it was to Samarra that the servant had fled, so fate had obviously decreed that this was where their paths would cross.

Nevertheless, Death was not entirely at ease. What had been worrying him all day was his own reaction on first seeing the man in the marketplace in Baghdad. Why had he been surprised? And why had he let his surprise show on his face, even if the servant had misinterpreted that look as threatening? Was he losing his touch? He did not think so, but the affair had upset him.

He took out a small mirror which he always kept about his person, and practised expressions. No, he did not think anyone could easily mistake a look of surprise for one of malevolence.

As he pondered thus, he heard a commotion in a narrow alley just off the street where he was walking. Two men were grappling with a third, apparently trying to rob him. Death saw the blade of a knife glinting in the moonlight. He shouted a warning as he advanced, and the robbers, horrified at the sight of him, ceased their attack and ran off into the night.

'What good fortune that you came by at that moment, sir,' the victim said, 'for if you had not, those villains would undoubtedly have murdered me. How can I repay you?'

'I have no need of a reward,' said Death.

'Well, I am doubly grateful,' the man said. 'Especially as this is the second time today I have narrowly avoided death.'

Now Death was thoroughly confused. He quickly took his leave of the man, who it was clear did not recognise him, although the two robbers had.

Death found a quiet, dark place to be alone, and there he stayed for several days. He needed to think.

Jack was setting out to seek his fortune. 'You take care, Jack,' his mother said, 'and keep an eye out for yer twa brithers that went ahead of ye. We've never heard onythin frae them, and I'm feart they've got intae trouble. They might even be deid.'

'Dinna you fash aboot me, Mither,' said Jack. 'I'll send word back aboot how I'm gettin on, and if I find ma brithers I'll let ye ken.'

After a few miles he came to a town, and he stopped at an inn. And his two brothers were inside, drinking and laughing and singing with a crowd of other folk. 'I'm glad tae see ye're weel,' said Jack, 'but ye might at least hae got word tae oor auld mither. Ye ken whit a worrier she is.'

'Ach, we're that busy,' they said. 'Tell her yersel if ye like. We hivna the time.'

So Jack went on down the road, and things turned rough for him. First a giant tried to eat him, then he had to get through a forest of thorns, then he was robbed of his money. He'd just about had enough of fortune-seeking when he met a man coming the other way. 'Will ye take a message tae ma mither?' Jack said. 'I will,' the man said. So Jack described all that had happened to him. 'But I'm still alive,' he said. 'And so are ma twa brithers, but they're too busy enjoying themsels tae tell her.'

So the man went on, and he came to Jack's mother's house. There was a big party going on, with an old woman at the heart of it. He said to her, 'Are you Jack's mother?' 'Aye, I am that. In ye come, sit doon and get yersel a drink and a bite tae eat. Now, whit was it ye were sayin?'

'I've a message for you from Jack,' the man said. He could hardly make himself heard. 'He's had a bad time, but he's alive. And his brothers, they're alive and well too, but he said they were too busy to get in touch.'

But the woman had turned away and was already speaking to someone else.

The girl climbed the stairs to bed, carrying a much-loved book, a collection of fairy tales. Even before she could read, that book had gone everywhere with her. She would insist on the stories being read to her, or she would look at the pictures and tell the stories to herself. Later she read them out loud, and now she was able to read them into herself. The book was part of her, and a part of her was in the book.

Her father cycled to his work every day, five miles there and five miles back. More than two thousand miles every year. If you are familiar with Pluck's theory of atomic exchange, you will understand how, over time, some of him became bicycle, and some of his bicycle became him. Yet despite this interaction it was still quite easy to tell them apart.

Often the girl would sit and watch her mother sewing and patching a favourite pair of jeans. She had had these jeans for many years, and there were so many repairs in them that it became impossible to discern where the original material stopped and the repairs began. But as far as the mother was concerned, they were still the same jeans, *and* they still fitted her.

The girl's grandfather had spent his life at sea and now liked nothing better than to potter about in his wee wooden boat. It was an old boat. It had been his father's, and before that *his* father's, back and back through the generations. And the boat was like the jeans. Everything in it had been replaced at some time or other – boards, mast, tiller, oars, sails, ropes. But it was still both the grandfather's boat and the boat his ancestors had sailed.

Then there was the grandmother, a fine, youthful woman, but with new hips, new knees, new toe-joints and various internal organs that had not originally belonged to her. Yet when her granddaughter cooried into her she was still soft and warm and smelled just the same as she always had.

And soon the girl would be a woman. But where would the girl in her end, and the woman begin?

'The implications of this are quite appalling,' the Minister said.

It was clear that he spoke for everyone round the table. They sat in silence, contemplating the implications. Sunlight streamed in through the windows behind the Minister, half-blinding the Chief Food Safety Officer, the Chief Medical Research Officer and the Chief Agricultural Officer. The Minister's Chief Political Adviser let them suffer for some minutes, then rose and lowered the blinds.

'How can you people have got this so wrong?' the Minister said.

'I wouldn't go so far as to say we got it wrong, exactly,' said the Chief Food Safety Officer.

'The science is very complex,' said the Chief Medical Research Officer. 'We can only base our recommendations as to what constitutes a healthy diet on the latest available evidence.'

'There is nothing the matter with fresh fruit and vegetables *per se*,' said the Chief Agricultural Officer. 'It's just that they're not as good for us as was once thought.'

'Not as good for us?' the Minister said. 'They're really *bad* for us. We've been banging on about five portions a day for years and it turns out we've been advocating poisoning the entire population.'

'That's pitching it a bit strong,' the Chief Food Safety Officer protested, but without conviction.

'Well, what about these cancer-risk figures?' said the Chief Political Adviser. 'What about these heart-disease estimates?'

'I don't suppose the results could be inaccurate, could they?' the Minister asked in a pleading tone.

'Biggest survey of its kind ever undertaken,' said the Chief Food Safety Officer.

'Flawless methodology,' said the Chief Medical Officer.

'The proof's in the potatoes,' said the Chief Agricultural Officer.

There was silence again. Then the Minister turned to the Chief Political Adviser.

'Clive,' the Minister said, 'this time tomorrow morning, when we reconvene, I want a full strategic action plan in place. Gentlemen, we must not sidestep this issue. We must face up to our responsibilities. Immediate, decisive and effective action is required. I take it we are all agreed? Very good. It is absolutely imperative, then, that not a word of this is permitted to enter the public domain for a period of at least – shall we say – thirty years?'

The Assassin (1)

The writer hit the alarm clock, switched on the bedside lamp and thought about the day ahead. He intended to begin a new story that morning, and this was a disquieting prospect. However, he was always nervous at this stage of the process, so he also felt strangely calm.

He brought his arm back under the covers because the room was cold. He remembered that he had woken at some point during the night and seen his wife standing at the window.

'What's the matter?' he'd asked.

'Nothing,' she'd said. 'It's snowing. Come and see. It's beautiful.'

But he had been very comfortable where he was and had declined her invitation.

His wife was asleep. He fitted himself against her back and put his arm round her.

He decided to sketch out the opening sentences of the story in his head before getting up and going downstairs to his desk.

The writer hit the alarm clock, switched on the bedside lamp and thought about the day ahead. His wife was asleep. He fitted himself against her back and put his arm round her.

Outside, a character from his new story was walking through the snow. Glancing up at the house he saw a faint light through a gap in the curtains at one of the windows. He imagined a bed in that room, with a man like himself lying in it. Perhaps there was someone there with him, a wife or lover. The man would not want to face the day, cold and snowy as it was. He'd prefer to stay in bed, warm and safe. But he'd have to get up, because he was a writer and he intended to begin a new story that morning.

The man outside was not a writer. He did not yet have a name, or an occupation. These were things over which he had no control: he might turn out to be a farmer, or a policeman, or a tramp, or even a hired assassin. This was a disquieting prospect. However, he was always nervous at this stage of the process, so he also felt strangely calm. If he was required to kill someone, he would do it.

The Assassin (2)

When the postman came out onto the street, the man with the umbrella was just going in. The postman hardly glanced at him. Later he would have only a vague recollection of anyone having passed him. He would feel some guilt, but not much: it wasn't his job to stop people going into buildings. He would also feel a thrill, knowing he had been so close to what happened.

The man with the umbrella climbed the stairs. People, he thought, didn't realise that they were always on the edge of life, that something was always happening in the next house, in the next street.

The man with the umbrella did not feel guilt. He was past that. And he didn't feel much of a thrill either, just a slight quickening of the pulse, caused mainly by a concern to make sure he left no trace of himself anywhere along the route.

He had a moustache, a hat, glasses and a scarf. Later he would not have any of these. Nor would he have the umbrella.

The flat was on the fourth floor. He paused briefly on each landing, to catch his breath and to listen. Below him he heard a door being closed and locked. He waited while the woman – he could tell from her walk – went downstairs and out. When the street door slammed and all was quiet again, he proceeded to the fourth floor.

It was dry outside, but it might rain later. Many people were carrying umbrellas that day, as a precaution.

There were three doors on the fourth floor, which was also the top floor. The door he wanted was at the far end of the landing. He did not particularly like this situation, as there was only one exit route. On the other hand, there was little likelihood of his being disturbed.

He thought, if after I give the password he does not open the door, I will simply walk away. He will be too frightened to come after me. If, however, he opens it . . .

He unscrewed the cap on the tip of the umbrella. He was careful not to let the blade touch the ground.

He rang the bell.

The Disenchantment

The observatory tower, now an empty, roofless shell, stands as a landmark on the hill, visible for many miles in all directions. People from the area, returning after a holiday or even years of absence, say that as soon as they can see the tower they know they are home.

It was built some two centuries ago for a local laird with an interest in the stars. It was not long before it fell into disuse – perhaps because the amateur astronomer found that he could see little more of the night sky from that lonely spot than he could from a room at the top of his own house. There might, however, have been another reason for its abandonment.

One summer's night, studying the moon through his telescope, the laird found that he could see the lunar surface in the most remarkable detail. As he swivelled the instrument something astonishing came into view. He called to the servant waiting below with their horses.

'Come up here and look through the glass!' he shouted. 'Tell me if you cannot see what appears to be a building of some kind on the moon.'

The servant had long ago concluded that his master was mad, yet through the telescope he too could see a tower, very similar to the one on which they stood, perched on a ridge of the moon.

'You're right,' he said. 'What's more, there are two figures on the ramparts, and they are mocking us.'

Frantically the laird pushed the man out of the way, and peered again.

After some minutes, during which time the laird's whole demeanour became less and less animated, and more and more disconsolate, he stepped back. 'No,' he said. 'It was a delusion after all, doubtless caused by shadows on the moon. Go back to the horses. I will be with you soon.'

The servant never again visited the observatory with his master. But years later, with a drink inside him at the fireside, he would recall what he had seen through the telescope: the men on the moon, their backs turned, their breeks dropped, their coat-tails flicked up, and their large, pale hindquarters gleaming at him across space.

Democracy

A lioness one day lay down in the shade of some trees to escape the afternoon heat. While she slept some elephants came wandering among the trees. One elephant was about to step on the lioness when she woke up, and roared to alert him to her presence. His front foot rested on her body, trapping her, but he had not yet applied his full weight, which would instantly crush her to death.

'Spare me,' she said. 'You and I are the strongest, proudest, fiercest beasts in the land, yet we coexist peacefully enough. Lift your foot and I'll leave this cool spot to you and your clan.'

'It is nothing to me whether I kill you or let you go,' the elephant replied. 'You are no use to me dead, since I cannot eat you, but you lions, working together, will sometimes attack an elephant on its own, kill it and devour it. Why shouldn't I reduce that future risk by killing you?'

'If you ever find yourself in such circumstances,' the lioness said, 'I will tell the others that you spared me when you had me at your mercy.'

The elephant weighed up the arguments and decided to release the lioness, who hurried away and rejoined the pride.

Not long afterwards, on a night hunt, the pride surrounded a solitary elephant. Despite his size and strength, gradually they exhausted him, and he realised that he was in grave danger. Just then he recognised the only lion who up till then had not been clawing or biting him.

'Traitor!' he cried, as he sunk to his knees and the lions mauled him ever more ferociously. 'I thought you were going to put in a good word for me.'

'I am no traitor to you,' the lioness replied. 'I already pleaded your cause, but I am only one among many, and was overruled. The most I can do now is not participate in your death. However, since I accepted the majority decision, I will be allowed to share in the coming feast. You probably now wish you'd killed me when you had the chance, but it wouldn't have made any difference to your fate. Sorry.'

They stopped at the bealach* to share a bar of chocolate, and tea from the flask.

'I don't like the look of that,' he said, nodding westward. 'That's an awful lot of snow up there.'

They both considered the thickening sky. Behind them the broad white shoulder of the ridge they had just descended hid the first summit from view. The ridge looked much steeper from below. The thought of climbing back up was not appealing.

'What are you thinking?' she asked.

It was still only one o'clock. Neither of them was keen to retreat.

'In distance it's almost as far to go back as it is to go on,' he said. 'But there's another three hundred metres of ascent if we carry on. Won't be much fun if the snow gets really bad.'

The sensible thing would be to err on the side of caution. Come back another day for the second peak. But they were both fit, experienced hill-walkers, and they had all the right gear. They were not reckless people.

They had seen nobody behind them. Whichever way they went, they'd be the last ones off the mountain.

'You know what will happen,' she said. 'If we turn back the sun will come out and it'll be blue skies all the way to the car.'

'Whereas if we go on there'll be a blizzard and we'll get lost, and the mountain rescue boys will say we were bloody idiots, and it will be very embarrassing. Assuming we don't die.'

'Let's not do that,' she said. 'Not yet.'

They watched the western sky a minute or two longer. 'More tea?' she asked. 'No, thanks,' he said, and she shook out the lid, stuck the flask in her rucksack and loaded up.

'There's certainly no point in hanging about here,' she said. 'The light's good for another three hours, but it's a long walk out.'

A few snowflakes were falling. 'Well,' he said. 'It's decision time.'

'What the hell,' she said. 'When are we going to be here again? Not for years.'

He thought how good they would feel if they completed the route. They smiled at each other.

'Let's do it,' she said.

* mountain pass (Gaelic)

Jack and the Tin of Beans

Jack was driving his cow home from market. He was fed up. Yet again, he had failed to find anyone prepared to buy the beast, at any price. He was not looking forward to telling his mother this depressing news.

So when a man coming in the other direction stopped to inspect the cow, Jack's hopes were raised.

'How much will ye gie me for her?' he asked.

'Oh, I've no money,' the man said. 'All I can give you for that old cow is this tin of beans.'

It was just an ordinary tin of beans in tomato sauce, but Jack thought this was better than nothing. The deal was struck, the man went on his way with the cow, and Jack bore the tin of beans homeward.

When his mother heard what he'd done she went berserk. 'Ye're naethin but a pure eejit, Jack,' she said. 'Whit use is a tin of beans? We canna even plant them so they grow intae a beanstalk. And noo we dinna hae a coo.' And she took a broom and beat him with it till he was covered in bruises, kicked him out of the house and flung the tin of beans at his head.

'That's aw there is for yer tea,' she yelled, 'so if ye want tae eat, away and open it!'

Well, Jack tried every way he could to break into that tin. He used a tin-opener, knives, a hammer and chisel, he smashed it off rocks, he even took an axe to it. But after all his efforts, there the tin was, without so much as a dent or a scratch on it.

'Tae hell wi this,' Jack said, wiping his brow. 'That tin's no right. I'd have mair chance gettin at thae beans if I shouted "Open sesame!"'

No sooner had he uttered the magic words than an enormous genie dripping in tomato sauce stood before him.

'I am the genie of the tin of beans,' this being intoned, 'and your every wish is my command, O master.'

'Aye, well fuck off, will ye?' cried Jack. 'And gie me back ma fuckin coo.'

And in an instant these things were done.

The Crow

The metal pole had once had some road sign or other at its top, but now a crow was perched there instead, cawing angrily at every passer-by. Against the snow lying on the pavements the crow looked exceedingly black, and in the quiet of a Saturday morning his cries echoed loudly round the surrounding buildings.

Nearby, a man in orange overalls was at work picking litter into a black bag. The crow seemed particularly to direct his rage at him.

'Och, shut it,' the street-cleaner said.

A middle-aged man and woman were strolling arm in arm along the pavement. They could not ignore the crow's raucous display.

'What are you making that racket for?' the woman asked it.

The cleaner pointed his litter-pickers at the creature, provoking another round of corvine abuse.

'There's something spooky about that bird,' he said. 'I was in Melville Street five minutes ago and he was there, behaving just the same. Then I come round here, and here he is again. He's following me.'

'They're intelligent creatures, crows,' the woman said. 'People can train them to do all kinds of things. My mother used to have a jackdaw that sat on her shoulder. She wasn't bothered by it at all, even when it pulled her hair. She liked birds.'

'Well, I don't like that one,' the cleaner said. 'It's like Dracula or something. It's got an evil way of looking at me.'

'She's reading *Dracula* at the moment,' the man said. 'My wife, I mean, not her mother.'

'My mother's dead,' the woman said.

'You see?' the cleaner said. 'Spooky.'

The woman frowned. 'You're depriving it of its breakfast,' she said. 'It's saying feed me, feed me, and you keep putting last night's chips and things in your black bag.'

'Well, why doesn't it go ahead of me, and save us both some trouble?' the cleaner said. 'But it won't. It'll follow me, just you watch.'

And the crow did follow him, cawing ceaselessly as if he might at last relent and empty the contents of his bag out onto the pavement. Every so often they stopped and eyed each other malevolently.

'My money's on the crow,' the woman said.

A Wintry Tale

It's snowing again, hard. You wonder how it cannot be snowing everywhere else. How can the sun be toasting people lying on beaches? How can there be a dry wind blowing sand across deserts? The snow is falling, thick and steady and constant, and what you can see of the sky is full of more snow – so much that it must surely fall for days, burying pavements, benches, bushes, bicycles, cars, trees, houses. You look through the window and it is hard to imagine it ever stopping.

Yet a man came by this morning who lives six miles to the north, and he scoffed at the paltry depth of what's lying here. 'Call this snow?' he said, and boasted of eight-foot drifts around his house. After calling on you his job was going to take him up one of the glens. He might not make it, he conceded, if the ploughs had not been up that road, and perhaps even if they had. The folk in the glen would scoff at the snow *he* has.

You are reminded of a story written by a famous writer, set in one of those glens. It was the last story he ever wrote, and it had a subtitle: *A Wintry Tale*. The narrator, a minister, is keeping a diary, a record of his life during the weeks in which the glen is 'locked', by which he means when, because of the snow, no one who is in the glen can get out, and no one who is out can get in. That phrase, 'the glen is locked', has always appealed to you. In the story, this is the prelude to doubt, delusion and madness.

Six pigeons and a blackbird are sitting in the naked branches of the birch tree in the garden. Earlier they fed off crumbs and seeds on the bird-table. What are they waiting for now? Their shapes are silhouettes in the afternoon light. Are they waiting for it to stop snowing?

You go back to the screen, type and shape these words; ponder whether you are saying anything of any use or interest. When you turn back to the window, all the birds have gone.

The Wee Man

The queue shuffled forward a few feet, stopped, then moved again. The folk in it turned their collars against the cold rain. They hoped the lecture would be worth the wait.

A man and a woman emerged from a taxi. They were important people. Their clothes were expensive but not very waterproof.

The important man smiled confidently at the wee fellow with the beard who was taking the tickets.

'Good evening, do we go straight in?' he said in one important breath.

'Not without a ticket you don't,' the wee bearded one replied, barely glancing up. 'And the back of the queue is down there.'

People nearby had recognised the important man: a politician, a former leader of his party, now ennobled and with his lady beside him. Immediately life was interesting again.

'I understood that the lecture was free.'

'It is,' the wee man said. 'Free, but ticketed. Hence the queue.'

'Well, the speaker and I have been friends for years. I told him we would certainly be here.'

'You certainly are,' the wee man said, tearing tickets and letting others past. 'But you still need tickets.'

'This is ridiculous,' the important man said. 'Don't you know who I am?'

The wee man paused, looked properly at his interrogator for the first time, and said, 'No.'

'Well, I think you're being excessively . . . I mean, for heaven's sake . . .' The important man was dismayed to find he could not complete a sentence. He glanced uneasily at the faces of people now eager to stand out in the rain a minute longer, if there was going to be a scene. They could tell their friends about it.

The wee man was tearing tickets again, as if he could happily do it for ever.

The important man's lady was, unlike her husband, still a politician. 'The queue's moving quite fast,' she said, taking him by the elbow. 'Perhaps we'll be lucky.'

'Yes, perhaps,' he said. As they moved away from the wee bearded man, he muttered, 'I don't believe for a minute that chap didn't recognise me. He'd simply got himself into a corner, and couldn't back down without losing face.'

'Yes, dear,' the important man's lady said.

After three weeks of bloody chaos the Bishop arrived. Horrified, he called an immediate halt to the civilisation programme and summoned the generals for urgent talks.

'There will be no further civilising until we have established the true nature of these creatures,' the Bishop declared. 'I'm shocked that you have permitted your troops to act in such an irregular and unjustified manner.'

The assembled gentlemen looked abashed. One or two hung their heads.

'From what I have learned,' the Bishop continued, 'these creatures are quite unlike us. They enjoy eating spiders and ants, the noises that come from their mouths are utterly unintelligible, they fornicate without restraint or censure – indeed, a promiscuous female is held in high esteem among them – and they wander about without a stitch of clothing on. However, strange though all this is, it does not necessarily mean that they are not human and that we should not treat them as such. So before we proceed, I want you to suggest arguments, in relation to each of these habits, in favour of their being human.'

'Well, the French like eating frogs,' one general remarked. 'The Muslims refuse to eat pigs. Yet we agree that, for all their faults, the French and Muslims are human.'

'Have you ever heard a Scotsman speak?' asked another. 'Or a Hungarian? Despite their barbarous tongues, we allow that they are human.'

'To have sex with anyone except one's wife is of course a grievous sin,' a third general said. 'As for loose women, they are an outrage to God and good society. Nevertheless, though we detest such immorality, who here can say that he is above reproach? And do we not accept that even the worst trollop in the basest brothel is human and not beyond redemption?'

'You have all spoken wisely,' the Bishop said. 'But what about this business of going around in the nude?'

Despite deep concentration, nobody could think of a single example of humans voluntarily and without shame or care wandering about displaying their nakedness for all to see.

'Very well,' the Bishop said. 'Let the slaughter continue.'

And it did – with increased ferocity, for now it had the blessing of the Church.

Off the motorway and onto the short cut, over the hill: almost as soon as he'd made that decision he was doubting its wisdom. The motorway, gritted and salted, had been black, but on this narrow road there was a fresh white dusting even before it began to climb from the carse.* Perhaps he should play safe, drive the extra ten miles to the city and out through its suburbs to reach home. But there was no easy place to turn the car. Anyway the snow wasn't that deep. Fifteen uneventful minutes was all he needed.

At the first bend he felt the tyres spin, grip, spin again. He braked, not heavily, and the car lurched sideways. He steered into the skid, and brought the car to a halt. He let go a deep breath. Okay. Still no room to turn, so he set off again, slipping into second gear but no higher, balancing his efforts to turn the wheel as little as possible against the need for enough speed to cope with the incline. He took corners in the middle of the road. At least at night there was some warning from headlights if someone was coming the other way.

There was no moon, but his own lights illuminated the snow lying everywhere, giving the landscape an eerie brightness. He was suddenly aware of the loudness of the orchestral music he'd been playing. It filled the car, but he hadn't heard any of it these last intense minutes. He hit the *off* button, turned the heating down. He wanted to be alone, to be just himself on the road, to concentrate on the drive, to get home without incident.

Round the last tricky bend, he crested the summit. *All downhill from here.* As he thought this, a flickering movement to his right distracted him. On the bank above the road, level with his window, a roe deer was running, its eye full of fear, its lean, brown body shining in the weird light. Such near grace, such wild, white-bummed beauty, and he the only witness. And the deer, outpacing the car, skipped down onto the white road, crossed into the trees, and was away.

* stretch of low-lying alluvial land beside a river (Scots)

A Hero of Mine

i.m. Angus Matheson

'Heroic', that was a favourite word of his. Anybody or anything that he admired could be heroic: a stoical philosopher, a daring shinty player, somebody managing to survive in extreme poverty, or perhaps a bird or cat that showed resilience, defiance. All these were heroic in his eyes. He was a teacher of history, and history was full of heroes as well as those who did not come up to the mark. But if this was part of his thinking – that he assessed heroism from an academic viewpoint – it was neither the beginning nor the end of it.

And although he used the word often, it would be wrong to think that he overused it. When he said it, he meant it. There was weight in the word, and measurement. He came from a place and time that produced heroes, and he recognised and acknowledged them. Against the brutality and dishonesty of the world and the general failings of humankind, heroism mattered to him. When he remembered a heroic person or witnessed or read of a heroic incident he did not want it to pass unnoticed. Even people with whom he disagreed – staunch adherents of a certain bleak religion, for example – could display heroic tendencies, and he would not see them diminished.

And he was, himself, a hero. He had multiple sclerosis, and he suffered from that cruel disease long enough, and fought it and rode it and swore at it – he was a man of Skye, a Gaelic speaker, and I never heard anyone swear so heroically in English as he could – and it in turn trampled on him yet he was still there after it had done its worst, unbeaten. Gradually the disease wore him down but still he resisted and I think it was he who decided when it was time to go. I remember the last time I saw him, some weeks before he died, and when he said goodbye he said it as if he would not say it to me again.

'Goodbye,' he said, and I did not register the tone in which he said it at that moment, but later I did, and I hear it now. 'Goodbye.'

The Rules

Outside the restaurant I paused. It was cold on the street – not much above zero – but I wanted a little preview, so I pretended to inspect the menu in the window while taking a look inside. The glass was quite steamed up but I could see figures in there, their heads and hands moving as they talked and ate. It seemed busy, but that was understandable: it was early evening, people had finished work and were having a drink or a meal before whatever was going to happen next in their lives.

I could see my girlfriend, sitting at a table about halfway back. She was waiting for me, as agreed. She wasn't alone. Kieran, a guy from her work, was with her. I liked Kieran, I'd met him a few times and we'd played football together once or twice, but why was he with her now? What was going on? Probably nothing. They'd finished work and were having a drink before I turned up and Kieran went home or somewhere else. That was all, probably.

He was an attractive man, Kieran. I kind of admired him but he worried me too. My girlfriend was an attractive woman. Probably I didn't need to be worried but that wasn't the point. You can't just tell yourself not to feel something. They worked together all day and after work they went for a drink. Couldn't they get enough of each other's company?

You're not supposed to feel jealous. It's not considered civilised or adult. But when you have a girlfriend you really want to keep, and you remember how you got her but you don't know why she's still with you, it's hard to stick to the rules. I could feel myself boiling up inside. I wanted to burst in there like a tornado, asking no questions and accepting no explanations.

But I knew what I was going to do was slide like a snake into the jungly heat of the place, give her a loving kiss, then clasp hands with Kieran and say, 'How are you, Kieran? Good to see you.' Because that was the civilised, adult way to behave, even if it was killing me.

Related Incidents

for Emily

Five bags of sugar. No small weight to carry inside you, but now she has arrived in the world, her first day out. Here, the thaw is on, green appearing as the snow retreats, the sound of water running everywhere. Fifteen miles away, across the hills, across the firth, she is home. New daughter, sister, niece, grandchild, great-grandchild. Only hours old and already she is all these things and more.

Much further away, an old man is trying to get his clock to go. It is a grandfather clock. He wonders, *Is there such a thing as a great-grandfather clock?* It's always been temperamental, but after being moved recently from the corner of one room to the corner of another (a necessary relocation) it has taken to stopping every twenty minutes. The secret is to have it sit on the floor just right, so that the pendulum swings with a regular tick, like a strong heartbeat. Every morning he taps another coin into place under the base, and starts the pendulum. Twenty minutes later the clock stops ticking. But he does not give up. Sometimes it ticks for half an hour. One day it will decide to keep going, as if it has been in that corner, in that room, all its long life.

One day far into the future, the baby will be an old woman. Her mind will be full of the life she has led, the people she has known, the love she found or lost, memories that bring smiles or tears, a world that has changed beyond anything she could possibly have imagined when she was a little girl. One day, but not yet. For now, her life is unlived, unremembered, unimagined, unwritten. She wakes, she cries, she feeds, she sleeps. Every other discovery awaits her.

The old man watches the second hand tick round the clock's face. If he keeps watching, the hand may keep moving. If he turns away, takes up his newspaper or switches on the television, it may not. He knows there is no logic to this hypothesis. Some say that a watched kettle never boils. He thinks it possible that a watched clock may never stop.

Man and Beast

Off the bus, she overtakes them making their way towards the High Street. It's the dog that first attracts her attention, a sprightly black and white beast with alert ears and bright eyes. The man, grizzled and weathered and using a stick, is probably much younger than he looks. He is wearing several layers and has a pack slung over his shoulder. The dog stays close to the man's side, on an invisible leash of – it's clear at a glance – utter devotion.

'What a bonnie dog,' the woman says as she falls in with them. 'What is she?'

The man eyes her – suspicion followed rapidly by appreciation. Years have made him expert in assessing the motivations of people who engage with him.

'Collie and Jack Russell and a bit of Staffie and something else, no sure what,' he says. 'D'ye like dogs?'

'Oh yes,' she says. 'Is it all right to clap her?'

'Aye, she's fine.' At the corner of the street they pause and the dog lets herself be stroked, but always with an eye on her master: *I'm only doing this for you*, the look says.

'She's lovely.'

'She's my darling. And clever, tae. Goes everywhere wi me. I'm a traveller, ken.' He assesses the woman again, then adds, 'A Gypsy. No wan o thae New Age travellers.' His hand goes towards the dog, who lifts her head to him. Only a true Gypsy, the woman understands him to mean, would have a dog like that.

They go their ways. She glances back at the man and his dog, her heart lightened by the encounter. She is thinking of how, sitting at the back of the bus, she'd had to admonish a young lad for having his feet up on the opposite seat. Grudgingly he'd removed them, but without looking at her, his attention focused on his phone. Three, four times after that, she'd seen his legs twitch, seen the shift in his slumped posture preparatory to the feet going back up. But each time he'd remembered, kept them on the floor, like a puppy learning. He was still on the bus when she got off. She wonders where his feet are now.

All Will be Well

for Alice Marra

A man of quiet genius passed this way last night. He didn't want his name in lights, he wanted it in brackets, that's what he said. He wanted others to sing the songs he wrote – in their own way because nobody could sing them his way. And this happened, in a big hall in a big city (not his) for which he once wrote a big non-anthem. (Trust Michael to give the place something it didn't bargain for. Listen – that's the sound of high-heid-yins sucking in their cheeks.) So the stage was set, and onto it came wonderful musicians, singers – among them his son and daughter, his brother, others who had been his oldest friends and cronies, and none untouched by his special craft and gift – to play and sing his songs in their own ways. And two thousand of us there to listen, and we were (the ones) in brackets.

What left me high and dry and stranded came at the end. After his daughter had stood centre-stage, alone but not really alone, and sung the song he'd told her was his finest – and she did it with such bravery and love, you could hear him give his proudest affirmation, 'Good girl!' – they came back on, those *compañeros* of his music world, and finished the night with the only song they could. And all his wise humanity came flooding in, and pouring out, and nothing to stop the tears from falling. Two thousand rose, to applaud the one who wasn't there, and that provoked another, final song, and I felt a lightness where just before there'd been such heavy weight. I thought of the osprey nest he used to watch, his solicitude for the chick, his pleasure seeing it lift from the nest for the first time, learning flight, its sudden knowledge that it could be done. And Michael – gone yet with us still, as long as we have ears to hear and breath to sing.

To rise above his loss is fitting tribute. No houseroom for the notion that we can't. To rise like the bird that lives, and flies, and knows itself alive.

All will be well, they sang. And it will.

In the Middle of the Wood

for Gavin

It is a frightening thing to be lost in the middle of the wood. All your ghosts and fears went there before you, and you thought they were away for good – childish childhood fancies banished by reason and common sense and the need to show the world an adult face. You told your own boys about the middle of the wood, led them there like Hansel and Gretel, but always brought them home again. To have left them would have been a betrayal of everything you were in their eyes: their strong, loving, protective father. But now they are grown and somewhere else, and their mother whom you love so much, you can't hear her calling you any more. You're alone, defenceless, a man unmanned. The wind has dropped to a sneer among the trees. And those ghosts and fears crowd in with their mockery and poking fingers.

It was daylight not so long ago, and you believed you'd enough time and stamina to make it. But then the track ran out, the briars thickened and the dark came down like blood. You thought you'd just about get through, but no, some cold malignity had it in for you. It took your map and compass, your food, your wine and cigarettes, your clothes and sturdy shoes, and left only yourself to you. Looking around to see where you were, who you were, you no longer knew.

Bits of you are scattered on the forest floor, hanging ragged from the trees. You scrabble about but it's hopeless, as quickly as you gather them you fall apart again. You've never had to do this before – put life back together. You're a child, you want to cry, you want a hand to hold. The trees hold out theirs, whip them away again. Trust, certainty, the promise of daylight – wiped. Nothing, any more, is guaranteed.

People did this to you and strolled away, ignorant or careless of the chaos they left behind. You are the wreckage of their hard ambitions. I've left you messages, but I cannot reach you. I hope we meet again, though, and soon – if you find a way out of the middle of the wood.

CHAIRMAN: Mr Humbelby, these are serious matters. You have not been summoned before this committee in order to avoid answering the legitimate questions that we have to put to you.

WITNESS: I am not avoiding the questions.

CHAIRMAN: You are treating these proceedings as a game, as if we are trying to catch you out and you are trying not to be caught.

WITNESS: It certainly feels like that. Like you are trying to catch me out.

CHAIRMAN: Mr Humbelby, let me ask you again. When your company paid this very substantial amount to your agent, did you or did you not know who would be the ultimate recipient of that payment?

WITNESS: We did not know.

CHAIRMAN: Did you try to find out?

WITNESS: That was a matter for our agent. It was down to him to seal the deal.

CHAIRMAN: You didn't care how that was done?

WITNESS: We are not talking about a contract to supply library books here. This is tricky negotiating territory.

CHAIRMAN: Involving enormous sums of money and the delivery of sophisticated, lethal weaponry, which your company was introducing into an extremely volatile political situation.

WITNESS: The political situation was not of our making. We did nothing illegal in fulfilling that contract, if that is what you are implying.

CHAIRMAN: I am not implying anything. You must admit, though, that it seems strange that you, as CEO of a very large organisation, having responsibility to the board and your shareholders, should have neither knowledge nor curiosity as to where several million dollars of the organisation's money should end up.

WITNESS: I don't admit that at all. It was good for business, good for our shareholders. In that region of the world, you have to cut your middlemen some slack. We knew where the money was going.

CHAIRMAN: I don't understand. A minute ago you said you did not know.

WITNESS: I mean, we knew in a general sense. We made the payment. If you have to make a payment to secure a contract and the payment is made and the contract is secured, well then, you needed to make the payment. Which part of that do you not get?

February

Coping with It

Biology had not been one of his strong subjects at school. In fact most of his understanding of how the brain and body worked was based on 'The Numskulls', a cartoon in *The Beezer*, which he had read avidly as a boy. He thought the Numskull approach to neuroscience was really pretty sound: it made sense to him that a bloke in the eye department controlled whether he bumped into walls or not. Nor was it beyond his comprehension to think of workers in overalls shovelling food down his throat while he was eating. In fact, to make their lives easier, he used to eat slowly, taking only very small mouthfuls, and chewing well before swallowing. If he showed them respect, he reasoned, there was a fair chance they'd reciprocate.

As a boy he had also believed that when he put a record on his parents' gramophone miniature musicians would start playing behind the fabric of the loudspeaker. These guys were very versatile. They could play the Beatles or Beethoven with equal accomplishment. But if you opened the lid you couldn't see them. They were down there in the workings of the machine but they were shy and modest.

Of course, he didn't believe that about the gramophone any more. The advent of smaller record players, followed over time by cassette recorders, CD players, iPods and digital downloads had pretty much put paid to the notion of tiny guitarists hiding in big wooden music chests. Pure fantasy. But the Numskulls, well, it was harder to shift them from his thinking. So when the surgeon said, 'I'm really sorry, but there's not much we can do, it's so advanced,' it was easier, rather than listen to the surgeon's technical information, to picture a whole section of the brain department having to close because of dry rot or concrete failure or something. He thought of energetic wee men becoming lethargic, wheezing and coughing, stretching their aching backs, taking longer and longer tea breaks. Not being able to function any more. Sick-building syndrome. Conceptually, he could just about cope with that.

That was it then. Sick-building syndrome. What a bastard. He felt so sorry for the wee guys.

The garage door ajar, the van backed up to it. Something was not right. I walked up the drive. My shoes made no noise on the gravel. It was my parents' house even though they did not have a drive or a garage. Even though it did not look like their house.

My mother was not at the window. My father did not come to the door. The van had its rear doors open. I walked down the driver's side and looked in the back: a lot of old furniture, junk mostly, as far as I could tell. They were having a clear-out, and why not? They had collected enough over the years, but would they not have told me, asked me to help? It was not inconceivable, however, that my mother had organised it, although 'organise' was not a word I associated with her of late. The previous week she had been about to post a wad of £10 notes to some animal charity when I arrived. I'd said, 'If you want to give them something, that's fine, but let me send a cheque for you.' 'But I want them to have *this* money,' she'd replied.

'Hello?' I called. A man emerged from the garage, rather quickly. A bulky man, middle-aged, unshaven, in dirty overalls: he looked a bit shifty, but he smiled pleasantly enough.

'What's going on?' I asked.

The man said, 'We're clearing the garage, like the old lady asked us to.'

'This is my parents' house,' I said. 'Where are they?'

A second man appeared from the garage. The first man might have been his father. The younger one had a mean, devious face.

'I'm not sure that they really want to get rid of all of it,' I said.

'Have a look yourself,' the older man said. 'If there's anything that shouldn't be going, it's no problem.'

I turned to inspect the van's contents more closely. There was a lot of wood. The furniture seemed all broken. I saw a pile of my father's sweaters.

Something was definitely not right. Just as I was thinking that I should not have turned my back on them, the blows began to fall.

The Brownie

'In the daytime he lurked in remote recesses of the old houses which he delighted to haunt; and, in the night, sedulously employed himself to discharging any laborious charge which he thought might be acceptable to the family, to whose service he had devoted himself.' So wrote Walter Scott of the Brownie, that strange, thin, shaggy, domestic spirit, who loved to stretch himself by the fire when no one was about, but did not perform his drudgery for that or any other recompense. In fact, if anyone sought to reward him with comfort or food, he immediately took offence and disappeared from the place for ever.

That was in an age when such superstitions found ready believers in young housemaids, old menservants and credulous farm labourers. I am not so sure, however, that the Brownies have altogether departed. There is one, at least, in our house, who tidies away so thoroughly at night that in the morning pairs of spectacles, keys, pens and suchlike are impossible to locate. And he is active during the day too. Put something down for a minute when distracted by the telephone or doorbell or a song on the radio, and when you come back it will be gone. Then the hunt begins. You retrace your steps, carefully re-enacting the last five movements you made, but the thing is away. Hours or sometimes days later, it reappears, either in the most obvious place, where you looked ten times already, or in some obscure location – in a drawer you never open, inside a book you've not read for months – where somebody must deliberately have hidden it. It cannot be proved, but suspicion must fall on some reincarnated species of Brownie.

But why the switch from drudge to idle mischief-maker? It's obvious. There's nothing left for him to do. Domestic appliances have made the Brownie redundant. So he wanders the house, cunning and evasive, lifting something here, putting it down there. It's not housework any more, it's a game. He is beset with lack of purpose, with *ennui*. His ancestors, if they could only see him, would be dismayed at his delinquency. The truth is, he no longer knows why he exists.

'Jack, I'm aye runnin efter ye and I've had enough,' his mother said. 'Away and find yersel a wife.'

'Och, Mither,' Jack said. 'I could never get a wife that would look efter me like you.'

'Nae doot,' she said, 'but ye'll need tae try. Whit ye need's a wife that can spin, and that'll dae ye.'

So Jack goes out and he finds a spider spinning a beautiful web, so he catches the beastie and brings it home. 'Mither,' he says, 'I've found masel a wife, the finest spinner I ever saw. Will she dae?'

'Jack,' she says, 'she can spin but she canna gie ye yer breakfast every mornin. She'll no dae.'

So he goes out and he sees a hen that belongs to his neighbour. 'Can I borrow yer hen?' he says. 'I've a notion tae marry her, tae please ma mither.'

'Aye, on ye go, Jack, ye daft bastard,' the neighbour sighs. So Jack takes the hen home. 'Mither,' he says, 'I've found masel a wife that'll gie me a egg for ma breakfast every mornin. Will she dae?'

'Jack,' she says, 'she can gie ye a egg every mornin but she canna gie ye a blanket for yer bed. She'll no dae.'

So he goes out and takes a sheep off the hill and brings it home. 'Mither,' he says, 'I've found masel a wife that'll gie me a blanket for ma bed. Will she dae?'

Just then the laird's man comes to the door. 'Jack's been stealin,' he says. 'He's taen a yowe aff the hill and I'm here tae arrest him.'

'Jack, steal a yowe?' says his mither. 'Dinna tell such lies. They've been courtin, that's all, but she's no guid enough for him, so ye can hae her back.'

Well, the laird's man doesn't fancy taking on Jack's mother, so he grabs the beast and hurries away.

'Mither,' Jack says, 'I've tried and tried, but I canna seem tae please ye. I doot I'll just need tae stay single.'

'Jack,' she says, 'ye're right. If ye took a wife she might gie ye a bairn, and there isna room in this world for anither eejit like you.'

The Ethical Dimension

CHAIRMAN: The last time you came before this committee, Sir Richard, you eloquently described some of the practical and ethical issues surrounding the negotiation of defence contracts in certain parts of the world.

WITNESS: I am sure I said nothing about ethics.

CHAIRMAN: Well, it was some time ago.

WITNESS: I reread the transcripts only yesterday. I am quite clear that I did not talk about ethical matters.

CHAIRMAN: Do you not think that there is an ethical dimension to the making and selling of armaments?

WITNESS: There may be an ethical dimension when it comes to the *use* of armaments. If we are discussing ethics, every country has a right and indeed a responsibility to defend itself, its interests and its citizens against aggressors, would you not agree?

CHAIRMAN: With respect, Sir Richard, we are asking the questions here.

WITNESS: Ask away, but I doubt I can help you with your ethical dimension.

CHAIRMAN: So you don't see your company's activities ever being limited by any moral sanctions that you or your Board might choose to impose?

WITNESS: If a man wants to protect his house by installing a burglar alarm, is the man's morality of any concern to the hardware store where he buys it? I think not.

CHAIRMAN: Surely you are being disingenuous? Would you not agree that a burglar alarm and a gun are two quite different devices? You cannot take a burglar alarm from the house and go down the street and kill somebody with it.

WITNESS: Neither can a gun kill anybody unless somebody fires it. There is no ethical dimension to a gun.

CHAIRMAN: So, in short, you don't care to whom you sell armaments?

WITNESS: It is not a matter of not caring. We are bound by law. If the law does not allow us to sell armaments to certain countries or in certain circumstances, then we do not sell them. Your ethical dimension is covered by statute and by government policy. Do not look to me for moral guidance on this issue. Look to yourselves.

CHAIRMAN: Thank you, Sir Richard. We appreciate your giving up your valuable time to be here.

WITNESS: You are very welcome.

There is life in the margins of all our lives – life moving in light and shadow. And sometimes it grants us a view – the blackbird taking a bath, the toad in the herb garden, owl calling to owl in the moonlit trees of the park, the mouse scurrying for cover.

But what is it, that life? Why should it bring such glad beatings of the heart, such tears to our eyes? What can those creatures possibly have that stirs our love, our envy, our grief?

Imagine this: on the phone one night, a woman in a block of flats in the middle of a city, talking to one friend about another who was found dead only that morning. He has gone out of the world far too early, this man, and in circumstances unnecessarily sad and painful. As she is speaking, the woman looks out of her kitchen window, down into the parking area in front of the building. A hedge borders the car park, and between the hedge and the building is a shared garden, composed of a lawn and some flower-beds. Suddenly she sees, running along behind the hedge, a big, healthy-looking fox. It crosses the lawn, slips between two cars, trots across the car park illuminated by streetlight, and gracefully leaps over a fence into the darkness.

Nothing special about that, you might say: there are urban foxes every-where. But the woman has only ever seen a fox here once before, months earlier, and on that occasion she was also on the phone, speaking about *another* friend who had died *that* day. And because of this coincidence – which is in all probability no more than that, a coincidence – she cannot help but tell her friend on the phone what has happened, and ask aloud, but also into herself, what the significance of seeing the fox might be. What can it possibly mean?

Maybe just that: possibility. To be the fox in the streetlight, the owl in the moonlight. To be the toad beneath the sage bush, the mouse running for its life. Nothing else. To be the blackbird, most beautiful of singers, and not know of what or why we are singing.

Simon of the Peat Bog Moor

Simon Stoblichties was not like other men. Some said he was mad, others that he was the only sane man in a world of madness. Whatever the truth, Simon retreated from society and went out onto the peat bog moor to commune with God, if He was there, and with the mystery of the Universe if He was not.

An old tree that had been struck by lightning stood on the moor, stark, solitary and without its crown. Aided by a carpenter from the nearest village (three miles away), Simon built a small wooden platform. They hoisted it to the top of the tree and fixed it there, and then Simon climbed up, to 'wait out the bad times' as he put it.

The carpenter, impressed by Simon's single-mindedness, promised to send his son to him every few days with food – whatever scraps could be spared. The boy duly came, and Simon would lower a rope and pull up a basket containing the gift, and also send down a bucket containing his waste, which the boy disposed of in a deep part of the bog. Water Simon would not take, relying on heaven for his supply, which meant that for ten months of the year he rotted and during the other two almost died of thirst.

Day after day, through all the seasons, Simon stood on his platform, facing now north, now south, now east, now west. He habitually turned towards the most inclement weather, from whichever direction it came, and seemed glad to suffer its depredations. Only in the very severest conditions would he wrap himself in some old blankets and animal skins supplied by the villagers. Usually he eschewed all coverings, and stood naked before rain, wind, hail and snow. But he never complained, not even on rare summer days, when the scorching sun combined with ferocious biting insects to torment him.

For thirty-seven years, Simon Stoblichties watched sentry-like over the moor. His beard grew to his knees, he outlived the carpenter, and the carpenter's son was a middle-aged man before Simon died. But whether the bad times were past by then, and whether he ever communed with God, nobody could be certain.

'See that Simon Stoblichties,' the villagers said, 'he's aff his heid, a total bampot.'

The carpenter said, 'Maybe, but he does us no harm, and he's three miles away. Let him be.'

Some of the village children went to throw stones at Simon. But it was a long walk, and no matter how often or how hard they hit him they could not make him cry out. He received their missiles as he received the weather, almost joyfully. The children grew bored and went home.

Then came the minister. He was not happy having Simon in his parish. He saw him as a rival, a trespasser, a mad vagrant who should be moved on. Or he might not be mad, but a servant of the Devil. The minister consulted with his elders, and they decided to put Simon to the test.

'We will go out to the peat bog moor,' the minister said, 'and I will order him to come down from his perch and acknowledge my authority. And God's, of course. If he refuses, we will chop down his tree, and drive him from the parish.'

'What if he obeys?' one doubter asked.

'That is unlikely,' the minister replied. 'We'll take an axe anyway.'

So he and five elders picked their way across the moor like six black crows in a line, and when they reached the place where Simon was, the minister called up to him.

'Simon Stoblichties, in the name of the one true God, I command thee, come down from thy perch and acknowledge my authority. And God's too.'

To their surprise Simon, having tied a sheepskin around his waist to make himself decent, came down the tree like a squirrel. Without hesitation he said, 'I acknowledge the one true God and His minister. Will there be anything else?'

'Oh,' the minister said. 'Well, no, that's grand, thank you very much. Goodbye.' And the six crows hopped away, confused and disappointed.

However, by the time they were back at the manse, refreshing themselves with tea and whisky, they were congratulating themselves on their triumph.

'It's as well he submitted,' the doubting elder remarked. 'The blade on this axe wouldn't chop butter.'

The Tolerance of Simon

The village was proud of Simon Stoblichties. He might be a bampot, but he was their bampot, and what was more he was valuable. As his fame had grown, so had the crowds who came to gawp at him. To them he was some kind of prophet, even though he hardly ever uttered a word unless alone with the carpenter or the carpenter's son. People treated his tree as a shrine, tying articles of clothing to its bare branches and placing offerings of food, wine, jewellery and money at its base.

In the evening, when the pilgrims had trudged back across the moor to the village, where they would stop for a meal or sometimes stay overnight, the boy would come and take the donations away. He might send a loaf of bread or an apple up in the basket to Simon, but everything else went to the common good fund. So, what with the trade the pilgrims brought and the proceeds of their gifts, the village understood that Simon Stoblichties was the best thing that had ever happened in its history.

This did not prevent a lively ongoing debate as to his mental condition. The general opinion, which villagers were careful to keep from the ears of passing pilgrims, was that the wind must have rattled Simon's napper once too often. After all, even in a country with a pleasant Mediterranean climate you'd have to have a screw loose to stand on a stob all your life. But to do it in the middle of a Scottish peat bog, where all four seasons were flung at you in the course of one day and often in the space of an hour, well, *quod erat demonstrandum* as the Romans used to remark.

The carpenter alone dissented from the common view. 'Simon has always seemed sane to me,' he said. 'From where he stands, the rest of us probably look pretty unhinged. It's all a matter of perspective.'

'Aye, aye,' everybody agreed with good humour. The carpenter was daft as well, of course, although a very fine craftsman. It was amazing how tolerant you could be of lunacy when you had a financial stake in it.

One filthy day of driving wind and freezing rain, the Devil walked over the peat bog moor to lay a bit of temptation on Simon Stoblichties. Whatever Simon stood for, on this occasion he was lying down. He had wrapped himself in all his blankets and skins, not so much to keep warm as to prevent them blowing away. It was before the start of the tourist season, but in such foul weather nobody was about anyway. The Devil stood at the foot of Simon's tree and called up to him.

'Got a light, pal?'

Simon leaned over the edge of the platform to see who was asking such an idiot question. When he saw the Devil he groaned. He knew he was in for it.

'Forget it, I've got wan masel,' the Devil said, and he pointed his finger at a nearby rock and smashed it to bits with a lightning bolt. Then he lit an enormous cigar from the smouldering ruins.

'Chilly the day, eh?' he said, summoning up a bijou wee cabin with a peat fire and a triple-glazed picture window. He settled himself in an armchair with a twelve-year-old malt whisky, and scanned the wild scenery.

'Want tae come doon for a heat?' he shouted.

Simon shivered and groaned again. He said nothing.

'Come on,' the Devil chatted on. 'Just hop doon for five minutes, get a heat and a dram – oh, and a wee bowl of soup – and then away back up again. Naebody'll ken.'

Simon crawled to the far side of the platform.

The Devil chucked another peat on the fire.

'Look, I ken ye're no the Son of God,' the Devil said. 'I'm no wantin ye tae take a heider so His angels can swoop in and save ye. I'm no gonnae ask ye tae turn stanes intae breid, or tell ye this shitehole can be all yours if ye worship me. I'm just sayin, gie yersel a break. Whit difference will it make?'

Simon's brain was too cold to think of an answer. He didn't know if there *was* an answer. He did know that it would be fatal to argue. His only hope lay in silence.

The Salvation of Simon

Simon Stoblichties felt as if he had been lying on the rough, cold, wet platform for many days. He also felt as if he had been away for the same length of time, somewhere else. *I have been sick*, he thought, *or perhaps I even died. But I am back now*. For all that it left him exposed to the elements, for all that it would never be a place of comfort or safety, the platform felt pleasingly familiar. It felt like home.

A little rain was falling. He crawled to the edge and peered over. The Devil was not to be seen. Surely he had been there? Had he not tempted Simon with all manner of food and drink? Had he not proffered heat, a soft bed, clean linen, warm clothes, books, music, art? Had he not appeared in the guise of a white stag, an angel, and various beautiful, alluring women, promising in turn purity of thought, eternal rest and unimaginable sexual gratification, if only Simon would descend from his tree and abandon his mad asceticism?

Well, he had resisted the Devil and sent him packing. What about God? In all the years he'd spent out on the peat bog moor, there had been no sign of *Him*. Not a shout in the wind, not a blessing in the rain, not a glint in the sunshine, not a whisper in the snow. Simon had come to commune with God, and God had failed to show. So if all this wasn't for God, then for whom, for what? For the Universe? The Universe didn't give a damn. He wasn't even a speck of dust to the Universe. So what was he?

He was alive. Slowly, painfully, he got to his feet. His legs and back were so sore that he could not straighten them. His beard was a tangled mass of grey and white. But as he stood, the last spatters of rain died away, and blue patches began to appear in the clouds. Light was filling the sky, a new day beginning. He turned to the east. In the distance, a small figure was trudging across the moor towards him, carrying a basket.

CHAIRMAN: Lord Humbelby, may I conclude this session by asking you a more personal question? We are all familiar, of course, with the term 'military-industrial complex'. There is sometimes a rather negative perception in the popular imagination of the relationship between arms manufacturers and the armed forces, and of course governments. Does that bother you? After all, your entire career has been in the defence industry.

WITNESS: Actually I suspect the popular imagination of which you speak is quite relaxed about that relationship. Do not forget that the defence industry employs many thousands of people, often in highly skilled jobs, and earns this country billions of pounds in exports. As for the armed forces, well, they are held in the highest public esteem.

CHAIRMAN: We don't forget any of that, Lord Humbelby. We are acutely aware of it. And I agree that in addition to appreciating the jobs and earnings that companies such as yours provide, the people of this country have a very strong sense of national pride. Nobody in their right mind could deny that this country punches well above its weight in the world, and that that is a good thing. That it should do so in a decent and principled way is what this committee exists to ensure. We may have had our differences of opinion with you in the past, but not on a matter as fundamental as this. Which is why I asked the question.

WITNESS: What was the question again?

CHAIRMAN: Does it upset you that the so-called 'industrial-military complex' is sometimes regarded negatively?

WITNESS: No.

CHAIRMAN: It would upset us if it upset you.

WITNESS: It doesn't upset me in the slightest.

CHAIRMAN: Your feelings aren't hurt?

WITNESS: Not a bit.

CHAIRMAN: Well, that is a relief to us all. Lord Humbelby, for some years now we have benefited from the wisdom of your experience whenever you have come before us, and I would like the record to show that this committee is grateful for the insights into the workings of the defence industry that your expert evidence has given us.

WITNESS: As I think I may have said on a previous occasion, you are very welcome.

Sometimes you just don't know someone. You think you do, but no, it's a mirage. They're right in front of you, you can reach out and touch them, and the next thing they're gone. What happened? Nobody can tell you. It just happened. That person stopped being who you knew. They just stopped.

I'm only saying this because what trust can you put in another human being? You live with them, eat with them, sleep with them, you watch TV and go drinking together, you sit together at the pictures, in the park. Everything. You wash their clothes, you smell their shit, you know every noise their body makes. And they know you. There isn't a thing they don't know about you, that's what you believe.

Then one day, out of nowhere, they say, *Sorry, it's over.* You say, *What?* They say, *I can't do this.* Do what? You have no idea what they are talking about because you never heard this before, not from them, not a distant rumble of it, but then you understand, you understand precisely, because this isn't the first time for you, far from it, and they're staring at you as if it were you who spoke, you who broke the spell, if it was a spell. Then you hear a voice, yours: *Don't you want to be here?* And you know the answer before they say it. *No. Not with you. It's no good any more.*

You cry, inside, outside, one or the other or both. Maybe they don't go right then, or maybe they already went in every way except physically. They already packed their belongings and this is them signing off. So this isn't the start of a fight, or of trying to mend what's broken, it's the end, the parting shot, and you didn't see it coming, just like before.

For a while after they've gone there are little wisps of them hanging about, and then nothing, like they were never here. But they were. You know because you look in the mirror and you're different without them. You're still here, solid as life. But in every way except physically, no, it's not you at all.

Jack and the Puddock

'Whit's love, Mither?' Jack asked.

'Mair o yer daft questions,' his mother said. 'Who's been tellin ye aboot love?'

Jack held up a tattered old book. 'There's a story in here aboot a lassie that faws in love, and I wondered whit it was,' says he.

'Weel, ye'll no find it in a book,' she says. 'Away ye go tae the well and hae a look for it there.'

So Jack's away to the well and he draws a bucket of water and up it comes with a puddock* in it.

'I'm lookin for love,' Jack says. 'Is it doon that well?'

'It might be,' says the puddock. 'There's water doon there, and that's whit puddocks love maist, so aye, ye could say that.'

'Weel, I'm tryin tae find oot whit love is,' says Jack, 'but I dinna think it's water. Maybe for a puddock, but no for me. Ony ither ideas?'

'Weel,' says the puddock, 'sometimes in stories a lassie finds love when she kisses a puddock.'

'But that's the very thing that happens in this book I was readin!' says Jack.

'Aye, weel,' says the puddock. 'That proves it.'

'Dae ye think it would work for me?' says Jack.

'Dinna ken,' says the puddock. 'Ye could try.' So Jack puckers up and closes his eyes and lands a kiss on the puddock's mouth, but nothing happens.

'Sorry, Jack,' says the puddock. 'Wrang puddock.'

'Maybe it's because I'm no a lassie,' Jack says.

'Aye, weel, maybe,' says the puddock. 'I suppose if kissin a puddock works for a lassie, kissin a lassie might work for a laddie.'

'Ye could be right,' says Jack.

Just then this bonnie young lassie comes to the well to draw some water. So Jack says, 'Excuse me,' he says, 'I'm lookin for love,' and he plants a big kiss right on her lips.

As soon as he's finished she wallops him, a really hard slap on one cheek, followed by another slap on the other. Then she gets her bucketful of water and marches off, leaving Jack in a daze with his ears ringing.

'Is this me in love noo?' he says.

'Naw, Jack,' says the puddock. 'Wrang lassie.'

* frog (Scots)

'Hang on,' he said. 'Something's happened.'

He put down the phone and went into the front room, where the noise had come from. He'd heard it as she was speaking. Like a stone dropping into thick mud. He'd known at once it wasn't from within the house.

The shutters were open, the lights on. In one of the big windowpanes a web of cracks radiated out from a central hole. Traces of snow were sliding down the glass.

'Fuck's sake,' he said. It was half past ten at night. He went back to the phone. 'I'll call you back.' Outside, the path from the front door was slushy, and immediately his slippers were soaked. He looked up and down the street. Everything he did seemed seconds too late. Had he really heard running feet, stifled laughter? He peered up the dark lane across the way, but could see no one.

From the pavement the room was a bright and tempting target. A scoop of snow was missing from the roof of his car.

Fucking kids. It wasn't the first time either. There'd been a football once; ended up in the back of the television. And earlier that week he'd yelled at a group of them after a snowball had thunked against the bedroom window. It wasn't malicious, he was pretty sure. It was just stupid.

He returned inside and pressed redial. He explained the situation.

'Call the police,' she said. 'Right now.'

'I'm just going to.'

They didn't go through all the stuff they would go through later: how it was only a snowball, nobody was hurt, it was overkill getting the police involved. What else could he do – except nothing? But he was angry, and the wee bastards had run off and even if he knew where or who they were he couldn't go after them like some vigilante. Anyway, without the police he couldn't make an insurance claim.

'Don't get stressed,' she said.

'I'm okay,' he said. 'I could just do without this right now.'

A cold draught was blowing through the hole in the window. It was a kind of violation. He felt it against his face, the chill invading the house.

Incredible. You know when I was born? Eight years, not even a full eight years, after the war. I'm talking about the first war, not the second. The Great War we called it when I was a boy, but that didn't last. And now it's one hundred years since it *started*. Incredible. Imagine being around that long, of having gone through all that time. Or maybe time goes through you, like sand through your fingers. Maybe that's a better way of imagining it.

What is it, time? It's nothing. It marches on whether you're wearing a watch or not. Good times, bad times, you get plenty of both when you're here this long. That's not a moral thing. Time makes no judgements. It just keeps going. You can't touch it, you can't stop it, you can't stretch it out a second longer than it is, it's immune to you. Nothing, that's what time is. I'll tell you, it may be nothing but it kills you in the end.

People talk about 'bad' language but that's just people talking, there's no morality in language either. I didn't always understand that but I've had time to consider it. People think because I don't use 'bad' language that makes me quaint or something. What do they know? They use language like it's throwaway stuff but it's precious, like time. There was plenty of 'bad' language when I was in the army, in the second war. I could swear like the best of them if I chose to. Or the worst of them. Some of the finest men I ever knew had the foulest tongues, and scented soap came out of the mouths of liars, thieves and hypocrites when they opened them.

People think there's nothing much going on inside this old shell. The lights are on but nobody's home, that's what they think. But there's more in here than in all their little lives put together. They think they get the same stories over and over from me, and it's true, that's what they get. They're the stories I let out in the open, the ones I slip off the leash. The others? None of their fucking business.

A True Likeness

It was the day of the great unveiling. The Princess had been sitting for her portrait, hours and hours over several sessions, but finally the artist had declared his work finished.

No one but he had seen it, not even the Princess. The artist was considered the finest in the land, and the Princess was of course the most beautiful woman, so the painting, if a true likeness, would be indisputably wonderful. The King therefore ordered its immediate public display.

The Princess was nervous. She instructed her most trusted servant to mingle in the crowds and report whatever he overheard.

First to view the portrait was the royal family. Next, the lords and ladies of court came to admire it. Finally, the common people were allowed into the gallery.

The Princess heard only positive remarks throughout these proceedings. She retired to her quarters as soon as she could, to await the servant's report.

'You need not flatter me,' she said, when he arrived. 'I want only the truth. What do the King and Queen *really* say?'

'Your Highness,' the servant replied, 'they say that the portrait captures the beauty of your person, the dignity of your position and the strength of your heredity.'

'I noticed, however,' the Princess said, 'that they hardly looked at the painting itself, and seemed more impressed by the richness of the frame. What of the lords and ladies?'

'They,' the servant continued, 'think it shows you as the finest diamond in a necklace of fine diamonds.'

'By which they mean themselves,' the Princess said. 'Their views are worthless. What did the common people say?'

'Ah now,' the servant said. 'They looked at the portrait very closely. Some commented that you looked tired, others that you looked old. Several thought that you seemed to be an ordinary person, just like them.'

'This is very bad,' the Princess said. 'I feared just such a response.'

'Do not concern yourself,' the servant said. 'I have already organised an accident which will result in the painting's total destruction. As for the artist, he will never be heard of again.'

'Thank you, loyal friend,' the Princess said. 'I knew I could rely on your honesty.'

Shade

i.m. Vernon Robertson

We were undertaking a major study of the Upper Diyala that year. In Kurdish its name means 'shouting river', presumably because of the noise it makes going through the narrow gorges. The river valley is an ancient trade route between Iran and Iraq. Everything is ancient in those parts, or was back then. I'm talking about the late 1950s, a lifetime ago.

We were looking at irrigation, land use and conservation, and so Duncan was invaluable. He was an ecologist when most people had never heard of ecology. Even then, some of us could see what was coming, that the price of progress would be devastation of some of the most beautiful places on Earth. And we had no illusions, we were part of it. Our survey work would inform the decisions of governments, but at least we could warn them in advance of the possible effects of what they wanted to do.

Well, Duncan and I took a weekend off and drove up into Kurdistan, through the Rawandiz Pass to Haji Umran near the Iranian border. It was late spring and the flowers were magical. On the way we stopped at the little town of Shaqlawa, in the centre of which is a huge plane tree, said to be the one under which King Xerxes rested. An unlikely story – the tree would have to have been thousands of years old – but when we saw its great spreading branches we could almost believe it.

Duncan and I were opera buffs. We stood under that plane tree and sang the aria 'Ombra mai fu' from Handel's opera *Serse*, in which the King praises its shade. All the local people stopped what they were doing and watched us, these two white Europeans in shorts. They must have thought we were insane, but we did not care.

The weather was perfect. We got to Haji Umran that evening, ready to spend the following morning searching for alpine flowers. However, it snowed heavily overnight, and it was pretty chilly, botanising in the snow in our shorts, and not very rewarding. But what I remember is not that, but the plane tree, the aria, and Duncan and I singing it.

He'd stayed out too long, walking on the shore in the gathering dusk. Now, as he came back through the rotten gate and under dripping trees, he could hardly see twenty yards ahead. The rain was ferocious. He kept thinking of the large whisky he'd have in the residents' bar as soon as he'd changed his clothes.

The hotel grounds went on for ever. He was in a confusing network of paths with dark, looming hedges on either side. Occasionally there'd be a circle of lawn with a statue in the middle, then more paths and hedges. The place was completely overgrown. The hotel, which had been so prominent from the seashore, was not visible.

Somebody was up ahead, a woman. The moon breaking through the clouds cast a strange glow upon her. She wore a long white dress, and was dancing in a swaying motion back and forth beneath a tree.

He called out to her. 'Hello!' But there was something odd about her movement.

'My God!' He started towards her. She was hanging. She was in her night-dress and her feet were clear of the ground. 'Help!' he shouted as he ran.

Then he was cursing his own foolishness. His heart pounded even as he made himself laugh at the old plastic sack caught on a branch.

'Did you call?'

An old man in overalls and a tweed cap was standing close by him. He had the weathered cheeks and big hands of a man who worked outdoors. He was carrying a spade.

'Oh, hello, yes. I seem to be lost.'

'Where are you trying to go?'

'To the hotel, of course.'

The man pointed to another path to the left. 'That way. You'll see the lights as you go round the next corner.'

'Thank you, thank you.'

'You are welcome.'

A few minutes later, standing in the lobby, he wiped the water from his hair. He could almost taste the whisky on his lips. He'd have one now, before he went up.

'Terrible weather,' he said to the receptionist. 'I got caught out. Luckily I bumped into the gardener and he gave me directions.'

'What gardener?' she said. 'There is no gardener.'

Where did he come from, that man with the shining smile? He came in a long dark coat, and dark was his face beneath the broad brim of his hat, but when he lifted that hat and gave his smile, if my heart had been of ice it would have melted in the warmth of it.

We had had the news of his coming from Oban, and we had had it from the fishing boats of Barra, and all up the long road from Lochboisdale to Gerenish the word of his approach came to us like the tap of his fine black boots.

Whiter than lambs in May were his teeth, and his hands like two brown trout from the loch. When he showed me his wares and I saw the length of his fingers I wished to bring them to my lips and make them wet with my kisses.

Then he sat down across from me and drank his fill of tea. And Peigi Mhor was at the drying green, but I did not invite her to join us. And though it was not proper, I fetched a little whisky from the press, and even if it was against his faith, did he and I not drink it?

And on the bed he laid the clothes he had brought all the way from Glasgow. Such beautiful things I hardly dared touch them, nor could I look at him when asking their price, knowing they were too dear and too delicate for such as I.

So he folded them all away save one, and that one he gave to me. Deep it is in the bedroom kist, still in its tissue paper, and never will I wear it. And he spoke of the land of his people, and how at nights he dreamed of returning there.

Where did he go, that man with his shining smile? He came in a long dark coat, and lovely was his face beneath his hat, and when he put his fingers to my lips it was to stifle my cries of joy. And Peigi Mhor was at the drying green, but I did not invite her to join us.

That braggart has it coming to him. Take the cork out, Hamish, and throw it away. We will not be needing it again, unless perhaps to stop up his flatulence and send him tight-lipped and tight-arsed back to where he came from.

Who does he think he is, strutting about as if he owns the place? Repulsive is the way he twists his lip when he gives an order. Pour me three or four fingers, and a splash of water in it, and I'll tell you what he can be doing with his orders.

No, no, we have had quite enough of his insolence. In my father's day it would not have been tolerated. Then you would have seen the claymore fetched from the hayrick, and the targe, metaphorically speaking, from under the peat stack. Aye, go on, another will not go amiss.

Soon enough he will know the reward he will get for sticking his nose in where it is not wanted. A bloody nose it will be. We may be hard to rouse, but once we are up we do not readily sit down again. Is a dram not the very spark to set the heather blazing?

Have you seen the nose on him? Like a turnip, it is. I could lop it top and bottom and it would not be much diminished, but the sheep would still reject it as fodder beneath their dignity. He is an apology for a man. Ten of him would not make one of us. Tip it up, man, tip it up.

The arrogance in his voice is enough to stir me to violence. Last night I heard him braying through in the lounge bar. He thinks he is better than us, but we are better than him. If it had not been for the women present I would have told him to his face.

If he turns up tonight I will settle with him in the car park. The tyres of his Range Rover will be flat and if he wants to know who let the air out I will not be the first to deny it, no indeed. Yes, Hamish, I will, since you ask.

We did not think we would miss the unlocked doors, the neighbours who knew the details of your day before you did. Nor did we expect to lament the streaming kitchen, the wet clothes always hanging about our ears, the rank smell of boiled mutton.

When we boarded the ferry it was without regret for Sundays, for the endless sermons of hatred and the thunderous God of our forebears. Sweet was the music in our headphones, and glorious our schism from that dour old bastard in the dog collar.

Cutting the peats till your hands were raw with blisters, your back was broken in five places, the sweat ran off you like mud and the cleg bites were like a range of low hills on your arms – this was not labour we were sad to relinquish.

Winter days without light, horizontal rain, an absence of shopping malls, cinemas and phone signals, hardly a stretch of road straight, long and wide enough to get into fourth gear, the slowness and predictability of island life – gladly we exchanged these for adventure.

And I am not saying I would want to go back, but six years in this shite-hole is enough to make the most cynical of men reach for the pen of sentimentality, the guitar of nostalgia and the bottle of fond memories.

What beauty is there in concrete? What peace sounds out in sirens? What sanity in the ubiquity of handguns and assault rifles? What humanity in unaffordable health insurance? We have arrived in the Promised Land, but a hundred years too late.

An eight-lane motorway is all very fine, nor can it be denied that sky-scrapers have a certain grandeur, but I am three months without work and there is nothing left in the bank. And back there you never came home to find that the place had been turned over.

I am spared the constant tears of Morag but only because she has taken up with someone else and moved out. It is not for me to blame her. I leave the radio on all night now, to drown the neighbours' shouts with country music. Those singers know me better than I know myself.

Everything was proceeding normally. The dentist probed and scraped, calling out numbers, and his assistant recorded the condition of each tooth as it was checked. Bob Cruikshank had his eyes closed, but he knew that this was what she was doing.

'Very good,' Bob heard the dentist say. Assuming that he was being addressed, Bob nodded slightly and made a reciprocal approving grunt.

'Hang on,' said the dentist. He seemed to be in the lower-left region. 'That's interesting.' More probing and scraping. 'Have a look at this.'

Bob felt Muriel leaning over him.

'Wow,' said Muriel.

'Quite,' said the dentist. 'Relax, please, Mr Cruikshank. I want to go just a little deeper.'

There was a brief silence, then a kind of plughole gurgle. 'Whoah, whoah, whoah!' the dentist shouted, and in an instant he and Muriel were in amongst it like a SWAT team. A quick, professional-sounding exchange followed. Bob, unable to speak with his mouth full of equipment, was more than a little anxious.

'Bring that over. Cap it. Right, clamp on. Secure? Good.'

'This tank?'

'Yeah, I think that's wise. Where's the uh . . . Oh, thanks.'

'Pressure's up to max now.'

'Okay. Open that valve about a half-turn. Great. Now, Mr Cruikshank.'

Some, at least, of the equipment was removed from his mouth.

'What's up?' Bob asked with some difficulty.

'Nothing to worry about. On the contrary, it's your lucky day. Our lucky day. Know what this is?'

Between his thumb and index finger was a plastic phial, in which a viscous-looking black globule was floating in some clear liquid.

'I hope that didn't come out of me,' Bob said.

'Oh, but it did,' Muriel said. She clapped her hands. 'It absolutely did.'

'Oil,' the dentist said. 'That's a big field down there. Nearly blew the tooth right out, but it's safe now. Mr Cruikshank, I don't think you'll be paying any dental bills for a long time.'

'Oil?' Bob said. 'Are you mad?' He tried to sit up but the dentist held him down.

'Mad? No,' the dentist said. 'Not mad, but rich – yes! You, me, Muriel – we're going to be rich as Croesus. Muriel, off you go, girl. Fetch the big rig!'

Stone

This morning you take a stroll out to the Pictish stone, two miles from home. A good walk to a good place. Up onto the high road, which runs along and over the Sidlaws down to the Tay, and which gives commanding views of the Grampians to the north; past the castle and four neat cottages, and then to the stone. An old road, this: once a path, then a track, five hundred feet above sea level, avoiding the worst of the low-lying bogs. There would have been more trees on the hillside then, protection from the weather to which it is now exposed. A place from which to look north and not be easily seen. From here you'd see them coming, whoever they were.

A neighbour, who was out at the stone two days ago, remarked that the mountains, though still white, were looking contented, as opposed to saying *Fuck off*, their usual mood at this season. But perhaps this is a ploy, to lure you to them, and once you are lured they'll say, *Fuck off* now, *if you can*. The King of the mountains is Death.

Who brought the stone, ice or man? Around here the ice moved from west to east. However it arrived, this six-foot slab didn't originate in these parts. Different kind of rock. The carvings are only on the south side, and very faded. Two discs linked by a Z-rod: a frequently occurring symbol with a meaning lost to us. Below this, a mirror, and maybe a comb. At the top, an animal, camouflaged by the lichen, with a curved back and open mouth. Dog? Wolf? Boar? Bear? At this distance, this close, it is impossible to be sure.

But you trace the lines with your finger and you know that men, if they did not transport it here, stood it upright. Why? To mark the land? To leave *their* mark? It is not hard to imagine them imagining you imagining them. The mirror of time. And they would have seen, as you do looking north, that this is what there is, earth and sky, and that the stone will outlast its carvings and all of us too.

Some stories are so good that they deserve repeating in every generation. This one I have stolen, shamelessly, from the folklorist Robert Ford's book *Thistledown*, published in 1891. It concerns Henry Mackenzie, author of *The Man of Feeling*, a novel which Robert Burns said he prized 'next to the Bible'. It was Mackenzie who used the misleading phrase 'this Heaven-taught ploughman' in a review of Burns's first volume, the Kilmarnock edition of 1786, and thus helped to secure the poet's reputation among the Edinburgh literati, who were stirred to their stockinged soles by the notion of rustic genius coming among them from the far reaches of Ayrshire.

Years later, in 1814, Walter Scott dedicated *his* first novel, *Waverley*, to Mackenzie, calling him 'our Scottish Addison'. Mackenzie's famously sentimental novel was published in 1771, the year of Scott's birth, and though twenty-five years separated the two writers Mackenzie would predecease Scott by little more than eighteen months. In old age Mackenzie was described by Henry Cockburn as 'thin, shrivelled and yellow, kiln-dried, with something, when seen in profile, of the clever, wicked look of Voltaire'. Now *that's* a description worth reproducing, accurate or not. And so is this story, as related by Ford.

In houses of quality, as late as the end of the eighteenth century, it was the custom to keep a sort of household officer, whose duty it was to prevent drunk guests from choking. Mackenzie was once at a festival at Kilravock Castle (home of his cousin Mrs Elizabeth Rose) in Nairnshire, towards the close of which the exhausted topers sank gradually back and down on their chairs, till little of them was seen above the table but their noses; at last they disappeared altogether and fell on the floor. Those who were too far gone lay still there, from necessity; while those who, like the *Man of Feeling*, were glad of a pretence for escaping, fell into a doze from policy. While Mackenzie was in this state he was alarmed to feel a hand working about his throat, and called out, when a voice whispered, 'Dinna be feared, sir; it's me.' 'And who are you?' 'I'm the lad that lowses the graavats.'*

* loosens the neckties (Scots)

Close

A boy went down to the shop but not the nearest one. He went well past that, until he reached an unfamiliar part of town where he was not known, where nobody would recognise him and stop to chat. 'Aye, Kenny, how's your mither? How's your faither?' All that Kenny shite. He needed to be away from that.

He hung about for a while, watching people entering and leaving the shop. Just a wee corner shop but it was doing a good trade in milk, bread, crisps, juice. Drink and fags. All ages, coming and going. He got his money into his fist and went in.

The man behind the counter had a sleepy, careless expression on his face. The boy reckoned it would be all right, he'd turn a blind eye, but when he asked for a packet of ten the man looked at him hard.

'How old are you, son?'

'I'm eighteen.'

'Any ID?'

'Eh, what?'

'ID, son.' The man shook his head. Hopeless. As the boy started his retreat he shrugged, as if it didn't matter. *No skin off my nose*, was a phrase his dad used sometimes. It was no skin off his nose.

Outside he stopped two or three youngish people in whom he thought he might find sympathy. 'Gonnae buy us some fags?' he said, holding out his money. But they shook their heads, laughing at him. One stuck-up cow lectured him on the evils of smoking.

He hung about in a close entrance. He didn't fancy walking all the way home without getting what he'd come for. It was dark now. The shop would close in half an hour.

A couple of men were approaching. 'Gonnae buy us some fags?' he said before he could see them properly. They came right up to him. Then he saw that they weren't men at all, more like his own age, but different. They had older, harder faces.

'Who the fuck are you?'

'Want a smoke, dae ye?'

'Aye,' he said, but then added, 'No, it doesnae matter.'

'Shouldnae fuckin ask then, should ye?'

They pushed him further down the close. He didn't call for help. What would be the point?

FEBRUARY | 26

62

Daft Davie

I remember Daft Davie standing at the top of the hill where the sign with the name of the village on it was. He must have stood there a lot, out in rain or sun, or why would I have such a strong image of him? A tall, thin man in a dirty anorak, and with a bad lean, as if over many years the wind had forced him to grow like that. Day after day he was there, leaning, and staring down at the houses. I used to think he had walked all the way up and forgotten what for, and that was him staring back down trying to remember.

Guys in cars would wind down their windows and yell abuse, or chuck an empty can at him as they roared past. Sometimes I was in one of those cars. I'm not proud of the way we behaved, but we were stupid kids. If Davie'd been a statue we'd have treated him the same. I don't know if he even noticed us. He just stood staring back down the hill.

Beyond where he used to stand the road flattened out and headed off into the rest of the world. Davie always had his back to the village sign. You could read the name of the village if you were driving in from outside, but not when you were leaving. There wasn't a sign that said THANK YOU FOR DRIVING SAFELY. COME BACK SOON or anything like that. We didn't expect visitors and we didn't get any. It was a seaside village but not that kind. Sometimes you'd see strangers turning their cars at the bottom of the hill and that was all you'd see of them. They knew right away they'd made a mistake.

I haven't been back in thirty years. Most of the guys I hung out with never left. They died of drink or in car accidents or maybe they're still alive. I wouldn't know.

But one day Daft Davie was gone. Maybe he'd been gone a while, but this one day I was on my own and I noticed his absence. I took it as a sign, and I got out.

Another time – any number of other times – she might turn around and nothing would be there. Nothing would have happened. Because that was the thing, it was always over, she never quite saw *it*. What she saw was the ripple, the vibration, the aftermath. And this was why the experience was never complete. She understood this. She was an unreliable witness, because what she saw was not what she saw but a visual echo of what she *might* have seen.

She looked through the dining-room window and it was as if a gust of wind, on a day entirely still, had waltzed across the grass and flowerbeds. Along the route of the old brick path that had been there before they re-designed the garden. No cat or bird moved like that. And no gust of wind either, because there was a gauzy kind of shade to it, and a shape. And *waltz* wasn't right after all, for something so straight, so pedestrian.

She thought, *Did I ever see her when the brick path was still in place?* And that was odd, because until that moment she'd never thought of it as female, but there it was: *her*.

She thought, *A day does not exist unless we say so, and even when we say so it requires collective will and individual imagination to sustain its existence. The next day, it's gone. You cannot capture time and hold it. A date in a diary proves nothing.*

She thought, *I will go to my grave believing that I saw whatever it was I saw.* She was quite shocked at this betrayal of her own scepticism, this undoing of reason, but not as much as she might have been. Because it was not the first time.

She didn't have a 'gift'. She absolutely didn't believe that about herself. It wasn't about her, it was about the garden, and who had been there before.

One year in every four, she thought, *there is a day after this one that does not exist in the other years. We accept that: it's an invention.* But this was different: a real, unreal thing that had happened, somehow, just before she, somehow, witnessed it.

March

Freedom

A fox and a hound met early one morning on a hillside. It was a beautiful spring day: the sun warmed the earth, daffodils stood around in groups smiling and nodding, and everywhere were the sounds of birds and insects at their work. Nothing was further from the fox's mind than being torn to pieces by a pack of hounds, and nothing less desired by the hound than to be part of a frenzied mob murdering a fox.

'How is it,' the fox asked, as they lay on the grass together, 'that we are such enemies? Although we are genetically distinct, it's surely only chance that made you a friend of humans, and left me here in the wild.'

'I often wonder about that,' the hound replied, 'awake at night in the kennel, or when the keepers bring us our food. Whether it's chance or design, we can't undo it. Yet, for all my comfort and security, I envy you your freedom. Sometimes at night we hear you barking, and that sets *us* off. *They* think we're simply desperate to get after you, and at one level they're correct. But what we really want is to *be* you, not hunt you down.'

'I've heard you howling,' the fox said, 'and often laughed at the thought of you stuck in your pen, but other nights I've wished I was there too, with a full belly and a warm bed. But if I were, you'd gang up and kill me in seconds.'

'Sadly, you're right again,' the hound said. 'Our forebears made a pact with men, and we must live with it.'

The fox was suddenly nervous. 'How did you get out here?' he asked. 'Is this a trap?'

'Not at all,' said the hound. 'I found a hole in the fence last night. In fact I must get back or it'll be mended, and then where would I be? I've enjoyed our chat, but next time I see you I'm afraid it'll be business as usual.'

'Of course,' the fox said. 'Goodbye.' And he sat on alone, thinking of the hole in the fence, and wondering if there was some way it might not be mended.

A Moment

Some moments never go from you. They're like rocks sticking up out of a river in spate. The water churns round them but they don't shift. Once maybe a route existed, a way of stepping between one bank of the river and the other, but you can't see it any more. You used to make that journey back and forth without thinking, hardly conscious of the rocks you stepped on, but now the fierce water has submerged some of them, and your courage, or foolhardiness, isn't as great as it once was. So you're left looking at the ones that remain, clear as they ever were even though you can't reach them.

A bunch of you after work, Friday night, knocking back the beers, reliving the comedies and frustrations of the day. You should be getting home, but you stay for another. Home is where the heart isn't. Your wife is waiting for you but the pain of going in through that door is not bearable, not without more drink. The bar is hot and loud, everybody's talking, laughing. Some of you will be back at work on the Saturday shift, but who cares, who's even thinking about that? And *she's* there, so why would you leave? You smell her perfume, you are inches away from her hair, her cheekbone, her mouth. She's laughing at your jokes, which are funny *because* she's laughing: some signal has passed or is passing between you. And that moment comes when everybody in the bar is somewhere else, it's just you and her, and her hand is in your hand. You have no idea how or when that happened, but it did. It's as if you've been holding hands for ever. You know that it means something, but what? And some voice, not hers or yours, suggests going on to another bar, and the others come back into focus and still your hands hold, out of sight in the crush, but it's going to end soon, that hold, it has to end, because it has nowhere to go. Hold it, hold on to the fit of your two hands. Neither of you will ever feel this again. Not ever.

Jack was passing an inn and fancied a pint of beer, but he'd no money. The innkeeper said, 'If ye dae a wee job for me ye'll get a pint for yer trouble. Away tae the cellar and fetch some coal for the fire.'

So Jack takes the coal scuttle and opens the trapdoor to the cellar and starts climbing down the ladder. After a while he thinks, *This is an awfie deep cellar*. And a while later he thinks, *And awfie dark, tae*. And some time after that he thinks, *I'll just away back up and forget aboot the pint*.

But at that moment he reaches the foot of the ladder. He's in a cave piled high with heaps of loose coal, and he can see this because there's a red light glowing, round a corner. He keeks round the corner and sees a huge roaring furnace, being stoked by the Devil, and inside it are the shapes of people burning in eternal agony.

Jack thinks, *I'm no hingin aboot, but I may as well take some coal since I'm here*, so very quietly he fills the scuttle, then starts back up the ladder. It's hard work with the full scuttle but he's doing fine till a big lump of coal slips out and falls to the bottom with a terrible crash. So now he can hear the Devil coming after him. Jack climbs faster, he can feel the weight of the Devil on the ladder below, and now he's catching at his heels, spitting and cursing, but Jack makes it into the inn, slams the trapdoor down and staggers up to the bar.

'There's yer coal,' he says, peching and sweating.

'And here's yer pint,' says the innkeeper. 'I was wondering where ye'd got tae.'

What Jack's wondering is if he's just woken up from a nightmare. 'That's an awfie deep, dark cellar ye hae,' he says.

'Aye,' says the innkeeper, 'but I'll tell ye something I never hae ony bother wi, and that's *damp*,' and he gives Jack a diabolical wink. And Jack knocks his pint back in a oner, and runs for the door, and never goes near that inn again.

The Hand

He looked at his right hand. He brought its pink fingers and trimmed nails closer to his face. Was it this hand? How many times had it made the sign of the cross or been raised aloft as he blessed individual men, women and children, whole crowds and congregations of them? Was it really this hand that had held the host for fifty years? He turned it this way and that as if it were not attached to him but an object to be inspected, inquired into. And yes, that was what he was doing: asking questions of the hand, of himself.

He tried to remember it younger, himself as a young priest. The certainty of faith that he had felt – or that he seemed to remember feeling – was so far away now that he almost laughed. He thought of all the great and petty men he had met – politicians and statesmen, leaders of business or war or other faiths. That hand had shaken so many other hands, and sometimes, away from the public gaze, he had wiped or washed it thinking of the deceit, cruelty or hatred it had touched. It was easier to forgive in public than it was to forgive in one's heart.

It had touched women's hands too, that hand. He had never understood women. They had loved him, the devout ones, but he had given them nothing in return – nothing, at least, of essence. They had said he was courageous, but he knew himself better than they did. If he could pray now, he would pray that the women might forgive him.

But he could not pray. He stared at the hand. It would not join together with the other in prayer again. He was beyond prayer.

If thy right hand offend thee, cut it off, and cast it from thee.

He was quite alone. *I will now spend the rest of my life in retirement.* As if it could be that easy.

He wished he was dead, a sinful wish, but it was the one thing he felt that was clean and true and without doubt. If the hand could act without his will, he would not resist it.

'Is that what brought you all the way up here?' the interviewer asked. 'An uninterrupted view?'

The older man said, 'I thought we'd finished.'

'We have, but there are always more questions.'

'Is that thing not switched off?'

'It is now.'

The interviewer put the machine in his briefcase, which he snapped shut with a show of finality.

His host reached for the whisky bottle and refilled their glasses. From the smeary jug the interviewer added some water.

'I was speaking metaphorically, but yes, absence of interruption was the motivation. Space to think in, silence to write in. When I first came to the islands I thought I'd come far enough for those. I hadn't. So I came to *this* island. But it was no good down in the village. Worse, in fact.'

'Worse?'

'Worse than the city. Oh, it may seem quiet, but it's close quarters. Any noise, however slight, is amplified tenfold. When the ferry arrives it's unbearable. Speaking of which, you have one hour. So when this place came up for sale, it was the obvious solution.'

'It certainly is a splendid location, but I imagine the track must be difficult in winter.'

'Impossible. I don't mind that. One has to keep replenishing supplies, that's all.' He nodded at the bottle. 'And I have a freezer.'

'You seem to cope admirably.'

'Don't patronise me.'

'What I mean is, most people would have given up after one year, let alone twenty.'

'Most people are soft.'

'And do you really think you'll stay? There must be a lot of physical work, especially for someone on their own. What if you're ill, or . . .'

'Or what? Too decrepit? Is that what you're too polite to say?'

'We all have to face it eventually.'

'Then I'll retreat, as far as I must. Actually, if it comes to it I'll go straight from here to the city. One move. Game over.'

Through the window lay the vast, flat, deceiving sea, and other islands floating on it.

'I'd better be off,' the interviewer said, but he did not move. His glass was not empty. He estimated that if he walked fast he need not leave for another ten minutes.

Lying awake in the middle of the night, he suddenly thought of a dog his grandparents had kept, when he was very young, and how it used to turn and turn in a circle in its basket before settling down. That anxious flattening of the blankets, that spin into a tight, self-protecting coil, had fascinated him. 'Why does he do that?' he asked once. And the answer came: 'Well, long ago, when dogs lived in the wild, they had to make a new bed every night, so they'd turn like that to make a nest in the grass or leaves or wherever they were, to be as safe and comfortable as they could. And they still do that, even though they've forgotten why.'

It had seemed a reasonable explanation then. It still did. And when he wondered why that image of the dog had come to mind now, out of nowhere, and so vividly, another reasonable explanation immediately asserted itself. Because of his father. Because what had woken him was another memory, or a dream, of getting his father to bed the last time he visited. Supporting him as he shuffled through to the bedroom, to the twin beds disliked by his father but which gave his mother at least a chance of a decent night's sleep. Turning back the duvet before his father lowered himself. Helping him shrug off his dressing-gown. Bending to ease first one slipper, then the other, from the old white feet. Lifting those feet and swinging the legs onto the mattress. Pulling the duvet over him. Kissing the bald top of his head, and smoothing the wispy, baby-soft hair down behind his ears. Without his hearing-aid his father was already half in a world of slumber. He smiled up from the pillow, all the mental frustrations, bodily inconveniences and physical obstacles of the day receding, perhaps forgotten already. And he, the son, looked down on the father, a big man yet small somehow, a child again, exhausted, ready for sleep.

And the dog was long ago, years and years away. He lay awake, seeing it so clearly, but no matter how hard he tried he could not remember its name.

Death went to the doctor, complaining of constant lethargy, stress and an overwhelming sense of doom.

The doctor listened carefully. 'When was the last time you had a holiday?' he asked.

'I've never had a holiday,' said Death.

'Well, that's the first thing,' the doctor replied, 'before we even consider medication. Take a week off, go somewhere quiet and relaxing, and don't think about work.'

Death packed a bag and headed for a seaside resort. He'd been there before, though not for a holiday, and remembered rather liking the place. He booked into a discreet hotel and spent the first three days avoiding people, exploring the coves, bays and beaches of the coastline. The weather was glorious. He warmed his bones in the sun, filled his lungs with fresh air. *This has been the problem*, he thought: *too much work and not enough light*.

On the fourth day the sky was grey, threatening rain. He stayed in town, and as he wandered from shop to shop, café to café, his mood, too, began to darken. He had not noticed before, but the place was full of old people, tottering and querulous, their faces lined with pain and weariness. Not all of them, of course: some bubbled annoyingly with *joie de vivre* and loud optimism. But even these, when he observed them closely, were not doing so well. The women wore a lot of make-up, and the men, when they thought no one was watching, slipped off their happy masks.

In a little park overlooking the sea, he sat on a bench to contemplate. Why was nothing simple?

A woman on the next bench was speaking into her phone. Her face was wet with tears. 'I hate seeing him like this,' she was saying. 'It's awful for him, awful for everybody. He wants to go and he can't. Day after day I think this will be it, and it isn't. But he's had enough. He's really had enough.'

Death looked away, embarrassed. It was his fault. Here he was, sitting about idly, and for what purpose? It wasn't even sunny. How dare he feel sorry for himself?

He stood up and walked briskly to his hotel.

First to go was the television. That wasn't hard. It was mostly rubbish that came out of it anyway. And the news was better on the radio. No, not better, weightier. Yes, that was part of what she craved: substance.

Next, the computer. The daily wade through emails, the fatuous chatter of so-called friends on social networks – gone. She had to cancel her online banking facility, and arrange to receive bills by post and pay them by cheque, and this would be dearer but she didn't care, there was something civilised about slowing down. She found her old typewriter in a cupboard but the ribbon was dry and the keys stiff, so she took it to the charity shop, and rediscovered the pleasure of writing with a fountain pen. Her first correspondence was with the TV licensing authority, who assumed she was either mistaken or lying.

The mobile phone went. One last text went out to everybody – *AS OF NOW I AM NO LONGER AVAILABLE ON THIS NUMBER* – and, once she'd chopped the SIM card up with the herb cutter and recycled the dead phone, she wasn't.

For six days she lived in blissful tranquillity, sleeping, gardening, making soup and reading Anthony Trollope.

On the seventh day her daughter arrived, puce with rage. 'So you're not dead or lying helpless on the floor,' she said.

'It would seem not.'

'And how would I have known? All my messages have bounced back and your answer-machine's not working.'

'It was, when I took it to the charity shop.'

'What's going on, Mum?'

'I want to go back,' she said. 'I hate this world of gadgets. I hate that word "connectivity". I don't want that, I want human contact. And look, here you are. You've come to see me for the first time in months. I'll make some coffee.'

'This is pure hypocrisy,' her daughter said. 'I bet I know how you spend your days now – with your nose stuck in a book and your mind so far removed from reality that you don't hear the phone ringing. What kind of human contact is that?'

'You have a point,' she said. 'Come in and let's talk about it.'

Closing Down

The store had never been busier. You could call this ironic, but there was no irony about it. It's what happens when you have a closing-down sale. If we hadn't been dying, the vultures wouldn't have gathered. There'd have been the usual trickle of customers, and Ken, Jim and myself (we were the only ones left by then) would have been fighting over who was going to serve them. Yes, it was a bit depressing, but we were heading for the dole queue anyway, and at least with it being busy the last days went fast.

It was, weirdly, quite touching, the way people coming up to the tills with armfuls of CDs and DVDs kept apologising. They were sorry about our jobs, sorry about the shop closing, sorry they were picking up such bargains. (I'm lying, they weren't sorry about that.) It was like hearing people saying nice things about you over your deathbed. 'You'll miss us when we're gone,' Ken told them. And they said they would, but they won't. They'll buy everything online, or download stuff for a fraction of what we used to charge. 'Miss us?' Jim said. 'They won't even remember our faces.'

'Is there really another twenty per cent off this?' one old guy asked, dumping a boxed set of Westerns on the counter. 'It's so cheap already.'

'I know,' I said, managing a smile. 'But when we finally shut the doors on Saturday, we don't want John Wayne still hanging around. Everything must go.'

'Including us,' said Ken, beside me.

'Saturday?' You could see the old guy's cogs turning. 'So it'll be even cheaper then?'

'If it's still here,' I said.

He started to say something else, but bottled it. 'Okay, I'll take it,' he said, handing me a twenty, and I put the sale through and gave him his change and he toddled off with *Fort Apache*, *She Wore a Yellow Ribbon*, *The Searchers* and all the rest.

'That old cheapskate was going to ask you to keep it aside for him,' Ken said.

'Shameless,' I said.

The queue snaked round the display units. You couldn't see the end of it.

'Can I help someone?' Ken shouted.

They were passing the end of a particular street when he said, 'See that old tenement? I went to view a flat in there once. Must be thirty years ago.'

'When you were with Martha?' she asked.

'Yes. We'd been looking for a while, and it sounded promising, so we made an appointment to see it. Didn't I ever tell you this?'

'I don't think so.'

'Everything else in the street is new,' he said, 'so it looks different, but that building hasn't changed.'

They stood hand in hand on the corner while he talked.

'After we rang the bell there was a silence, then this weird hissing noise behind the door. An old bloke let us in. He'd been spraying the place with air freshener, so much you could hardly breathe. The bloke was probably only about fifty, but he seemed old to us. Very neatly dressed, jacket and tie, but it was all wrong, kind of spivvy. The jacket was yellow corduroy, and the tie was a bow tie. And he had this music, cha-cha-cha stuff, going right through the flat, big speakers in every room. And instead of turning it down while he showed us round, he turned it up. We couldn't hear a word he was saying.

'Then he showed us the bedroom. It was all pastels and frilly curtains and a satin bedcover, and on the bed, I'm not kidding, there were dozens of teddy bears, ranks and ranks of them. And he didn't explain, he didn't apologise, he just said, with a kind of flourish, "And this is the bedroom." And all we could see was teddy bears.'

'I think you did tell me,' she said. 'I remember now.'

'Well, we got out of there fast. It was like, where are the bodies buried? It was a nice flat, but we couldn't have lived there, not after that. Funny what sticks in your mind. If I'm ever in this part of town, it's that flat and those teddy bears I think of.'

'And are you?' she said.

'What?'

'Ever in this part of town?'

He looked at her strangely. 'No,' he said. 'I don't suppose I am, not often.'

The Abbot

It was the savage boys watching from the cliffs who warned the Abbot that they were coming. He thanked the boys, stilled their excitement, and calmly made his preparations. To the violence that was about to be unleashed he would offer no resistance, hoping thus to neuter it. *One day*, he thought, *the blood lust will drain from these men of war, and remorse bring them to the God of those they have butchered.*

With the books, the holy relics, the silver chalices and whatever else they could carry, he sent the younger monks and the savage boys deep into the hills. Although trembling with fear, the brothers at first refused to leave him, so he explained patiently why they must. 'When they arrive, they will need to kill. It is who they are. If you remain, they will kill you because your youth and strength make you the nearest we have to warriors. But you must survive because you are the future. By killing us old ones they kill only the present.'

He kept with him Blind Eoin, and Osseine, who was deaf and so crippled that he could not have fled anyway. The Abbot blessed the young ones and kissed them goodbye. 'Bury us on your return,' he said. 'Then begin again. Rebuild what they have destroyed, restore the precious things that speak of God, and prepare for when you too must die, perhaps in the same manner. Now go.'

Later, he led Eoin and Osseine down to the beach and helped them to kneel in the sand. He placed Eoin nearest the water, since he would not see death wading towards him from the boats. Further back he placed Osseine, who would not hear Eoin's cries. At the high-water mark, he himself knelt. He would see and hear all, and know what was coming to him. Yet to die in this beautiful place of white and blue, of solitude and storm, where he had lived a pure and penitent life, was not the worst thing. And from here, so he faithfully believed, he would go to God; to whom, as the oars and sails approached, he made one last prayer for forgiveness.

The Skull

for Ange

'Now,' the old woman said, 'before you go up there I want to introduce you to someone.'

She moved to the shelves lined with bits of stone and bone, the fragments of prehistory. She moved slowly, not because she was sore or stiff, but because she had passed the age of hurrying, for anything. Her face was like a pencil drawing, cross-hatched and grey.

'Here,' she said. 'Meet the ancestor.'

Her thin, strong fingers lifted it, the small brown skull like a helmet. The mandible missing, but five long teeth hanging from the upper jaw. The nasal cavity where a mouse might have made its nest, the eye sockets deep and sulky, and in their recesses tunnels back to where the brain once sat, sending and receiving messages, taking on and defeating the world day after day and storing its victories away. The mottled crown, pitted and smoothed, a stone rolled by a million tides.

It wasn't an archaeological site, it was a croft with a tomb, and the house was not a museum. In a museum the curator wouldn't be an old woman in a cardigan, inviting us to feel, to touch the past. Rain battered the window behind her.

'Take it,' she said, 'she'll not bite. Hasn't bitten anything for five thousand years. Bonnie, isn't she?'

And she was – that half-mouth's grin, that cranium map of however many years she'd lived, that stony vault from which she'd seen an island of stone. I held the skull and felt someone's breath on my neck, but there was only you and me and the old woman.

'Follow the path along the fence,' she said. 'When you get to the entrance you will see a flat board on wheels, like a big skateboard, and you will lie down on that and push yourself in, then send the board back out for the other one. Lie flat and you will not bang your head.'

'You're not coming too?' you asked.

'Och no, I don't go out these days, not in weather like this anyway. But you'll be fine, it's dry inside. Cosy, it would have been.'

She held out her hands for the return of the skull.

Insignificance

From an early age I was conscious both of my own insignificance and of the infinite nature of the Universe. One source of this sense was a game that my brother and I shared. It consisted of a road layout around which you had to manoeuvre a plastic vehicle without striking any objects, such as a pillar box, telephone kiosk and bus stop. There were also some pedestrians whom you were supposed not to knock down.

Each vehicle had a metal band on its base. By means of a magnet under the board, controlled by a joystick, you could jerkily negotiate your car or motorcycle round the corners and through the junctions of the roads. The idea was to avoid hitting any of the objects or pedestrians, but the cars and especially the motorcycles (which tended to fall over and travel on their sides) were difficult to control, so my brother allowed two collisions or one fatality per round before elimination. It was a good game, but it required concentration, which my brother had more of at eight than I did at five.

I found the box it came in at least as fascinating as the game itself. On the lid was a picture of two boys playing the game, and next to them lay the lid of the box, on which was a picture of the same two boys playing the game. Logic persuaded me that within that picture, though too small to see, must be another lid with the same image on it. Extrapolating outwards from this progression, I speculated (aloud) that my brother and I might be portrayed on the lid of a box larger than ourselves, and that somewhere outside our sphere of consciousness two enormous boys were playing the same game . . . and so on.

My brother did not like my theory. He grabbed the lid from me, accused me of always spoiling his fun, and punched me in the face. He then pointed out that the smaller boy on the lid did not look like me, nor did he have a bleeding nose. I admitted through my tears that this was true, but secretly I knew I was onto something.

Birthday

He heard the toilet flush and then her feet padding back from the bathroom. It was very dark. He sat up and drank some water. When she saw that he was awake she began to sing.

'Happy birthday to you, happy birthday to you . . .'

'What time is it?' He was hot. He pulled off his T-shirt and dropped it on the floor.

'Three o'clock,' she said. 'Were you born yet?'

'Aye, I think so. I should ask Mum, in case I ever want to get my horoscope done or something. They need that, don't they? The exact time of birth?'

'Who?'

'Astrologers.'

'You're never going to go to an astrologer.'

'I might. It might be interesting.'

She gave a little snort of disbelief as she settled herself back into bed.

'Aye, you're probably right,' he said.

'So you reckon you were out by now?'

'Well, I know it was during the night anyway, because she had me at home, and Dad was camped in the other bedroom with my sister and brother. And when they woke up in the morning and heard me crying he told them there must be a chicken in next door with Mum.'

'And that was you, a few hours old.'

'That was me.'

They lay side by side in silence for a while. His eyes having adjusted to the dark, he could make out the familiar shapes of wardrobe, chest of drawers, chair. A little moonlight seeping round the shutters made the cracks in the ceiling plaster seem to move, as if across shell.

He touched her hand and said, 'Fifty-five years ago, I was naked, just like I am now, pushing myself out of her, into the world.'

She laughed. 'You were a lot smaller.'

'And not so hairy.'

'It's incredible,' he said after another silence, 'to think of that baby being born, and me here, and all that time stretching between us. And we're the same person.'

'Creation is incredible,' she said. 'Life is incredible.'

'You couldn't make it up,' he said.

She laughed again. 'That's ridiculous.'

'My point.'

A few minutes later he wondered if she was asleep, but he didn't say anything, in case she wasn't.

The Last Elephant

Nobody could be a hundred per cent sure about the last tiger. There were pockets of forest in Indochina and Sumatra so dense and inaccessible that they might hold a few specimens as yet undetected by poachers or zoologists. Unlikely though it was, most conservationists conceded that the survival of the last two subspecies of tiger could not be disproved beyond all doubt. But with the African elephant, no doubt remained. You cannot hide an elephant.

A TV comedian made a few feeble jokes along those lines: the elephant in the room, the elephant in the cherry tree, the elephants in the telephone kiosk. ('What's a kiosk?' younger viewers asked.) It was like watching someone kicking a corpse.

After a day or two, the headlines changed and the world moved on. It wasn't, after all, as if anyone could do anything about it.

A politician keen to show what a tough, realistic guy he was said, 'Listen, things become extinct. Languages die out. Civilisations collapse. There are ten billion people in the world, nearly two billion of them in Africa. What are we supposed to tell them, that they can't have that land because elephants matter more than they do?'

Others said it was a tragedy, a disaster, a wake-up call to humanity – all that guff. An online farewell documentary received millions of hits, but somebody did the analysis and found that after three visits most people never came back. Wildlife porn, some smart commentator called it. You get off on it once or twice, then it stales. What were you watching, really, when what you were watching didn't exist any more? Elephant ghosts? Whatever they were, they were never again going to do anything different from what they did on that film. So how long did the baby have to swing its trunk in boredom before you too got bored? How many times could you watch the big bull desperately trying to mount the female that was just too small, too young, before you switched off? You felt dirty, ashamed. You wished you didn't recognise what you were watching. You wished you didn't know that such a creature as an elephant had ever existed.

Jack and the Witch

Jack was an easy-going lad who mostly lived without a thought of Death, but sometimes that thought would pop up like a big black question mark right in front of his eyes.

He went to see the local witch. The witch's cottage was low and dark, and unpleasant smells issued from the pots on the stove, but she herself was friendly enough.

'Aye, Jack, whit can I dae for ye?'

'D'ye hae a spell so Death canna kill me?' says Jack.

'Och, that's a hard one,' she says. 'I can cure most aches and pains and fevers, but I canna stop Death gaun aboot his business.'

'That's a shame,' says Jack. 'It seems tae me he must be a right bad character. He causes nothing but trouble and grief. Even just thinkin aboot him makes me feart. Is there nothing tae be done aboot him?'

'Did ye ever see him?' says the witch.

'Naw,' says Jack, 'but I've heard a lot aboot him. They say he's a terrible fierce strang fella, so I widna like tae see him.'

'Well,' says the witch, 'I'll let ye hae a wee look at him, and then ye'll no be feart. Because he's no as bad as ye think.'

So she tells Jack if he goes down to the millpond and bends right over the fence he'll see Death at the bottom of the water. It's a very still day, and she conjures up a special gust of wind to blow across the millpond. When Jack gets there, the water is as flat and still as a mirror, and he bends over the fence and peers down into it, and along comes the witch's wind and runkles up the water just where he's looking. And what he sees down there is a wee, wrinkled, auld man with a crooked back looking back at him with a worried look on his face.

'Is that Death?' Jack says to himself. 'That auld bodach* couldna hurt a flea! I'm no feart frae him.'

So he went home happy, and of course, because he was just a young lad, it would be many, many years before he saw Death looking at him again.

* old man (contemptuous, Scots from Gaelic)

Self-Control

At the interval, as the applause dies away and people begin to make for the exits, the woman in blue turns and smiles nicely at the young man behind her. He and the girl beside him are the last to stop clapping.

'Did you enjoy that, then?'

'Oh yes, it was very good. Wonderful.' His hair is black and unruly, his jaw unshaven. He has some kind of foreign accent. She already knows this because, before the concert started, he leaned forward and asked if he could see her programme. She felt exploited but as she and her husband had only glanced at it she felt she couldn't refuse. He took it eagerly. 'Thank you, thank you.' After a few minutes he returned it. 'Thank you,' he said again.

'You liked the pianist?' the woman says. The pianist, along with the conductor and orchestra, took three bows.

'He is genius,' the young man tells her. 'This is why I must hear him. It is hard to come to this concert but I must.'

'You've come a long way, you mean?'

'No, I mean expensive.' He laughs. 'I am student. I do not eat for two days, but is worth it.'

Obviously he must be exaggerating. It fits with his borrowing her programme.

The woman in blue's husband says, 'Shall we get a drink?'

'In a minute.' To the student she says, 'It's a shame that the *andante* was spoiled.'

'Spoiled?' He looks astonished.

'By the sniffing.' She nods at the girl. 'Your friend sniffed all the way through it.'

The girl says, 'I did not sniff.'

'It was very distracting.'

'No,' the student says. 'She did not sniff. She only cry a little, when the movement finish. She cannot help it.'

'It was so beautiful,' the girl says.

'You should learn more self-control,' the woman in blue says. She is still smiling nicely. 'When you come to a concert like this, to a place like this, you should be more considerate of others.'

'It was the music,' the girl says. She looks as astonished as the boy.

The woman in blue stands. 'Yes, gin and tonic, please,' she says to her husband. 'Shall we go?'

The Man on the Bus

I used not to be able to read on buses. It made me feel sick. But recently I've found I've got over that. Maybe it's a benefit of maturity. I'm glad, anyway. There is so much still to read, and not much time left. Or maybe there is, but how would one know?

I was deep in a collection of stories by a writer new to me, recommended by someone whose opinion I respect. The stories were powerful. They told of a section of society about which I knew nothing, yet I found the characters completely convincing.

I was hardly aware of the man in the seat next to me until I heard him say, 'Excuse me,' twice, and realised he was addressing me.

'I'm sorry?' I said, looking up.

'Are you enjoying that book?' he asked.

'Yes, I am,' I said, slightly annoyed.

'I'm glad,' he said, smiling. 'I wrote it.'

I looked at him more closely. His claim seemed unlikely, judging by his dishevelled clothing, malodorous smell and bloodshot eyes. But as soon as I thought this, I realised how flawed my reasoning was. He was, indeed, not unlike some of the very characters I had been reading about.

'Well,' I said, 'if you did, I congratulate you. It is excellent.'

'You don't believe me?'

'You must admit,' I said, 'this is not something that happens every day.'

He smiled again. 'On the contrary, I meet characters from my stories every day of my life.'

'That's not quite the same thing.'

'It is if you are me,' he said. 'Of course, the people I meet don't usually know it, especially if they have yet to appear in one of my stories. Well, this is my stop. I hope you continue to enjoy the book. Goodbye.'

I watched him make his way to the front of the bus and get off.

It was only then that I remembered that on the inside back cover of the book was a photograph of the author. The picture was grainy and distant, and showed a much younger, neater man than the one who had been sitting beside me. But that, I understood, did not prove a thing.

The Fabairseidh Thistle

for Joseph Bonnar

'And how did you come by it?'

'It was my grandmother's. I inherited it when she died. She was born in Scotland but fled when she was nineteen, at the time of the revolution. Her father was a lawyer. They escaped with absolutely nothing, just the clothes on their backs. Oh, and a small trunk packed with jewellery.'

'And do you know where they lived?'

'Yes, Edinburgh. In the old Georgian quarter.'

'Which of course was terribly damaged in the revolution. Well, that all fits perfectly with this beautiful item, because the Georgian quarter was the redoubt of the old moneyed class – the aristocrats and oligarchs and, crucially, the legal establishment. And so what we have here is a rare survivor from that age, and we know exactly its provenance not only because of your story but because it's in its original box with the jeweller's name and address printed on the silk interior. An address, sadly, that no longer exists.

'Do you recognise the central motif? The purple top rather gives it away, doesn't it? Yes, it's a thistle. In pre-revolutionary Scotland it was customary for people to give each other thistles. In the countryside they plucked real thistles, in the housing estates they exchanged cheap plastic ones, and in high society they traded incredibly ornate variations on the thistle theme, such as this.'

'So was the thistle some sort of love token?'

'No, it represented antagonism and deep loathing. But a piece like this was designed with, as it were, a postmodern knowingness, and would have been given as an expensive joke. "Darling, I detest you," that kind of idea. It's 24-carat gold, and the diamonds are charming, but it's the exquisite enamelling that is really impressive. And the little mark on the back? Well, that denotes a name we're all familiar with, doesn't it? There was quite a fashion among the upper classes for using Gaelic orthography even though none of them could speak the language. It's a lovely thing, and rather poignant in the light of your family's history. As to value, well, I can see this easily fetching €150,000 at auction. Thank you so much for letting us see it.'

The Experiment

I was an experiment.

I knew this suddenly and intuitively. How old was I, seven, eight? Lying on the floor, playing with some plastic soldiers, I saw the shadow of my hand pass over them. I moved my hand back. This time I did not so much see the shadow as feel it, as if I were one of those soldiers and a dark, terrible force – of which he was ignorant but had, just then, some imperfect perception – had disturbed the air he breathed.

Those soldiers were inanimate, I understood this, yet alive to me: I could and did make them live. And somehow they – or one of them at least – had become conscious of my life-giving, my power.

The next thing I understood was that I was being watched. I picked up a man with a rifle slung on his back, about to throw a grenade. His face betrayed no knowledge of me: he was intent only on the act of throwing. I replaced him, and continued to play studiously as if nothing had changed. I learned from that soldier not to let them see that I knew.

Them. Yes, there were several, wherever or whoever they were, and I was their experiment. Years later I would see the film *The Truman Show* and recognise in its artificial construct something like the world as I began to perceive it at that moment. But my situation was not an entertainment for millions of viewers, nor would I be able to find an exit, a door out of that artifice into reality. This *was* reality, and I was in it. My bodily functions, my behaviour at home and at school, my sleep patterns and mood changes – everything was being captured and analysed. But could they access my thoughts? I didn't think so. I chose to operate on the basis that they couldn't.

I am an adult now, and have put away childish things. I have also become so skilled at the game of bluff which commenced that day that I often completely forget about it. But then some small thing reminds me. The experiment continues. They think they are still running it, but they are wrong.

To the Airport

Amid the fumy, head-pounding traffic, on the other side of the glass, upside down almost, a tangle-haired, grinning face. Hand making a winding signal. What was he saying?

She reached for the button, depressed it. Nothing happened.

'Don't look at him,' the driver said. 'Look in front, please.'

'What?'

'Don't make eye contact.' She saw only his dark glasses in the rear-view mirror. He had his hand on the master switch, preventing her from opening the window.

'It's just a boy,' she said. 'Is he selling something?'

'No boy. Bad man,' the driver said. He revved the engine, jerked the car half a foot forward. The lights stayed red. Horns blasted around them. The boy slipped. She thought he was going under the wheel.

'Careful!' she yelled at the driver.

The lights changed. The car shot forward, crunching over potholes, braked, moved again. The boy was gone. She felt sick. The last twenty minutes had been like this. Crowds spilling off the pavements at every junction; trucks, scooters and cars jostling for space on the hot tarmac. Engines backfiring, she hoped.

She saw the white silhouette of an aeroplane on a blue road sign.

'Don't worry, soon be out of here,' the driver said, but the set of his mouth was not reassuring. It was the mouth of a man who hated everything outside his car – the other vehicles, their drivers, the road surface, the beggars, kids on the make, women under their huge loads, women selling fruit, selling themselves. Most of all he hated the flurries and eddies of young men, smiling till you denied them, then suddenly banging on your roof, shaking fists at your windscreen, yelling abuse in whichever of five languages they thought matched the look of your passengers.

And she knew all this. She'd been warned often enough. If she'd let the window down a crack, the boy's fingers, his hand, his whole upper body would have been inside in seconds. The grin would have vanished. He wouldn't have been a boy any more. He hated her, wanted everything she had, whatever it was.

'I'm sorry,' she said. She clutched her bag. All she wanted was to be somewhere else.

'You'll need to sign a declaration,' the woman behind the post-office counter said.

'Declaring what?' asked the man who'd handed over the parcel.

'That you're not sending anything dangerous.'

'What constitutes "dangerous"? There's a letter in there containing some pretty inflammatory language.'

'Anything that's in this,' she said, pushing a leaflet under the glass.

He looked at the various images depicting firearms, aerosols, dustbins, rodents and human remains. He pointed at one. 'Is that a horseshoe?'

'I think it's a magnet.'

'So I could send a horseshoe? A horseshoe could be dangerous, in the wrong hands.' He opened the leaflet. 'There's even more inside.'

'It's supposed to be comprehensive.'

'It's certainly that.' He continued reading. A queue began to form.

'What's in the parcel?' the woman asked.

He looked up. 'That's between me and the recipient.'

'If you could tell me what's in it, I could tell you if it's a prohibited item.'

'I'm checking that now. That's why you gave me this, isn't it?' He read some more. 'Has anyone ever actually admitted to you that there was a rocket or a consignment of heroin in their parcel?'

'That's not the point.'

'That's exactly the point. Normal, law-abiding people are being asked to declare that they are not idiots or criminals. If I'm posting a submachine gun to an accomplice in Virginia I'm hardly likely to admit it, am I?'

The woman looked again at the parcel. 'This *is* going to Virginia,' she said.

'That's right. Virginia is where the CIA has its headquarters. Does that make you suspicious?'

'Look, I'm just doing my job.'

'We've heard that one before.'

'Come on,' someone in the queue called. 'This is ridiculous.'

'I concur with the voice from the stalls,' the man said. 'However, so as not to delay the transactions of my fellow citizens, I will step aside in order to read this document more closely. I would be grateful for the return of my parcel.'

'You don't want to send it?'

'Oh yes, I do. I will be back.'

The woman passed the parcel through the hatch. 'I think you're making rather a meal of this,' she said.

'You started it,' the man said.

'It's me again,' the man with the parcel said.

'So it is,' the woman behind the post-office counter said.

'Interestingly, according to the leaflet you gave me, I may not send ammunition in my parcel, except air-gun pellets. Yet I am prohibited from sending an air gun. Where is the logic in that?'

'I don't make the rules,' she said.

'Clearly not, for you are not an imbecile. Have you seen this bit? This symbol, of acid being poured onto someone's hand, represents corrosive products, which the leaflet says are classified as dangerous. But a product marked by this symbol along with the words "Danger – causes serious eye damage", is apparently *not* classified as dangerous. So. Burns your hand: prohibited. Blinds you: safe to send. According to this leaflet.'

'Do you want to send the parcel or not?'

'I do.'

'Well, would you please sign the declaration at the bottom of this label.'

'Another document!' he exclaimed gleefully.

'This one goes on the parcel.'

'And proves what? Since you haven't inspected the contents, you have no idea whether my parcel is safe. You are taking it on trust. Do you trust me?'

'It doesn't matter whether I trust you or not. You just have to sign the declaration or I can't accept the parcel.'

'My point being, if I am intent on sending something dangerous, I'm going to sign anyway, am I not? Would you like to see some ID?'

'No, that's not necessary.'

'Then I shall sign as John Smith. Is that all right?'

'Is that your name?'

'Why do you ask?'

'It sounds like you just made it up.'

'But it's one of the commonest names in the world. You see, you don't trust me.'

'Just sign the bloody thing,' a voice said loudly, from behind the rack of greeting cards.

The man bent over the label presented to him. 'Robust advice from the gallery,' he said conspiratorially.

'Thank you,' the woman said. 'Mr Smith. That will be £3.86.'

He smiled at her. 'Is that all?'

'It's not bad, is it?' She sounded relieved.

'So little to send utter devastation across the Atlantic? It's terrific. Thank you for your excellent service. Good morning.'

Just Go

The tiny bus shelter had a pungent, animal smell, tolerable only if you took shallow breaths. Usually Todd waited outside, but the snow-laden wind was bitter, and the bus was not due for ten minutes. Numbed already by the walk from the farm, he went in.

There was a small, glassless window, through which you could watch for the bus. On the outer side of this stood a man, hunched, the collar of his thin jacket turned up.

'Aye,' Todd said.

The man barely nodded. Todd did not recognise him from any of the nearby cottages.

'Mair bloody snaw,' the man said. The ferocity loaded onto those three words was impressive. Todd wondered what he'd sound like if he had a grudge against anything more than the weather.

'Well, ye ken whit they say, in like a lamb, oot like a lion.'

He was only trying to show solidarity but the reaction was as if he'd told a downright lie.

'Who's *they* when they're at hame?'

'Just folk,' Todd said.

After a minute the man spoke again.

'He's haein a laugh at us, eh?'

Todd gave a non-committal grunt. If it was theology they were getting into, he wanted none of it.

Suddenly the man let out a shout. 'Think winter's over, dae ye? I'll show ye, ya wee shites!'

Todd saw the bus coming. *On time, thank God.* He came out of the shelter and raised his hand. The man gave no sign of moving.

'Here it is then,' Todd said. The snow was heavier now, thick bursts whisking in the wind like egg white.

The bus pulled up. Still the man didn't move.

'Are ye comin?' Todd called above the engine's din. 'There's no anither yin for an oor.'

The man scowled, a look of pure hatred.

Todd shook his head. 'Suit yersel,' he said, and stepped onto the bus. 'Christ, it's cauld oot there,' he said.

'Whit aboot yer pal?' the driver asked.

The man was shaking his fist at the sky. Snow boiled around him. He seemed to be in the middle of his own personal storm.

'Just go,' Todd said, as if he had the authority. The door hissed shut.

Craig

I was scraping a living in those days. I had a job in a warehouse, on the back shift. The wage covered my rent and a few drinks, that was it. I don't remember eating much. I was thin as a whip, strong, hungry. My whole life fitted into four plastic bags.

There were eight of us in a three-bedroom flat. My room was the kitchen. When everyone else had gone to bed I put a mattress on the floor and that was me. In the morning people stepped around the mattress to get their breakfasts. It wasn't ideal.

Then someone left and I moved into one of the bedrooms. It cost an extra fiver a week but for that I got a bed I could go to when I liked. I was sharing with a guy called Craig.

Craig was a lump of lard. He was supposed to be at college but all he did was watch TV and eat junk food. I certainly never caught him reading a book.

The first morning, Craig's alarm went off. It played 'Yankee Doodle' on repeat. The third time through I advised him to hit it, before I hit him. After that, nothing happened.

It was still dark.

'What time is it, Craig?'

'Six o'clock.'

'What are you getting up now for?'

'I'm not.'

'So why did your alarm go off?'

'I like to wake up early.'

'What for?'

'So I can think.'

'What about?'

'Stuff. What I'm going to do today.'

'That'll be fuck all then.' I thumped the pillow, turned over.

Craig started snoring. He'd been doing it all night.

I got out of bed, crossed the room and ripped the covers off him. 'Get the fuck out of there,' I said.

He went into the foetal position. 'It's cold,' he whined.

'I'm going to count to three.'

He rolled off the bed, grabbed the duvet and fled.

I lay for another hour, but it was hopeless. I got up and made a coffee. When I went into the living-room Craig was on the sofa under his duvet, snoring again.

I moved out a week later. It was either that or the jail for murder.

The phone rang just as she'd got the children to the table.

'Stay there,' she said. 'I'll be with you in one second.'

'No you won't,' Chelsea said.

It was a recorded message about mis-sold insurance. She hung up and went back to the kitchen. She counted out the fish fingers, four each, the less brown ones for Sam.

'Who was that?' Chelsea said.

'Wrong number.' She couldn't be bothered explaining.

'What's a wrong number?' Sam asked.

'It's when someone phones someone but they make a mistake and get someone they didn't mean to.'

'That was a lie,' Chelsea said.

'What was?' She put peas on Chelsea's plate and baked beans on Sam's because if you put peas on his he wouldn't eat anything else they'd touched, which would be everything.

'You couldn't have been. You hadn't even gone by then.'

'What are you talking about, Chelsea?'

'You said you'd be with us in one second but you already were with us and you couldn't get away and come back that fast. So it was a lie.'

'It wasn't a lie, it was an expression. It meant I'd be back very quickly.'

'But you didn't know that. You didn't know it was a wrong number. It might have been Harry.'

'It wasn't Harry.'

'But it might have been and then you'd have been away for hours.'

She slid oven chips from the baking tray onto the plates.

'No I wouldn't.'

'You would and our tea would have got cold or gone on fire.'

'Can I get red sauce?' Sam said.

'You've got baked-bean sauce,' she told him.

'That's not red, it's orange,' Chelsea said.

'It's tomato. It's the same thing.'

'That's another lie,' Chelsea said.

She slammed the tray on the hob. In the tiny room it sounded very loud.

'That's enough, Chelsea. I don't lie to you. I never lie to you. Don't you dare say I do.'

'Sorry.'

'I should think so. Eat your tea.'

The phone rang again. She made herself not go for it. The children didn't eat, waiting for her to move. Eventually it stopped.

'Was that a wrong number too?' Sam said.

'No,' she said. She started to cry.

Hypnophobia

Awake isn't good. Awake is almost as terrifying as not being. The world is full of anxieties. Traffic, weather, electricity, gas, food, disease, dogs. People (dealing with them). Work (if he ever has any again). Sex (ditto). Religion (ditto). What hope do you have, really, if you think about it? And that's the thing: other people can shut off the possibilities. Not him. It drains him. He looks out of the window at the wind whipping the naked trees, the rubbish blowing down the street, and he sees danger everywhere. Being inside, door locked, windows closed, basic food in fridge, is better than being out. Not good, but better.

It's when he starts to succumb, the weariness narrowing and blurring his vision like a screen closing down, that the real fear kicks in. That other zone looms, where what little control, what vague belief he has in being able to keep stuff at bay, disappears. He can't go there. Mustn't. Never lies down on the bed nowadays. Bed is a place of terror, not of safety and comfort. He sits in the armchair, television on – thank God for 24-hour TV – and treads around the edges of sleep. A combination of the TV sounds and his own fear brings him back every time. No wonder he can't hold down a job. Staying awake is a full-time occupation.

Anything can happen if you go there. You can choke, burn, the building might collapse, war break out, anything, and it's no good saying the chances of any of this are infinitesimally small. The point is being asleep and not knowing. The point is not waking up again. Ever.

How do people trust sleep? Believe that they'll come back? Because the odds against doing that shorten every time. One day you won't. You'll go into the zone and that will be it. Over. Lost for ever. That's what sleep is. Permanent loss. You won't even know you've gone. It is too horrible to contemplate.

His head jerks again, returning him to full consciousness. He is utterly exhausted. But he's back, he's put a foot in and come back. So long as he can keep doing that he'll be okay.

Indian Country

You forget more than you retain, and that's the truth. Great desert stretches of time, and memories blowing across them like tumbleweed. Or maybe the tumbleweed bumps up against an old tree, a fencepost, a ruined homestead, and *that's* the memory. I'm thinking of a night in Arizona, nearly forty years ago. I don't know why I still feel it because it was nothing really, it wasn't the Grand Canyon or Monument Valley or any of those magnificent places, it was the very opposite of magnificent, but I do, I feel it.

I was in a sleeping-bag on hard, unforgiving clay, under some scrubby, spiky bushes and the night sky's dome, black studded with silver. The moon glowed like a spotlight. It was high summer, but the nights were chilly. Fifty yards away was a highway, with trucks going by in both directions. In the intervals you could almost imagine yourself alone.

'We're not the first happy campers here,' said Frank, six feet away. 'There's a collection of beer bottles by my feet.'

There were other signs too – cigarette butts, and a single, tattered, canvas gym shoe. Old-fashioned, not like a modern sports shoe. It could have been there a month, or a decade.

'This is Indian country,' I said.

I don't recall, now, how we'd got there. We were miles from any town. Whoever had given us our last ride of the day must have turned off the highway, heading for a ranch or homestead. In the morning we'd walk the fifty yards and start hitching again, before the sun was high.

'So am I supposed to panic or what?' Frank said.

'I'm just saying. The Navajo reservation isn't far up the road. Some Navajo guys were probably trying to get home and stopped here for the night, same as us.'

'So long as there's no snakes,' Frank said.

'There's bound to be snakes,' I said. 'Zip up tight.'

I always sympathised with the Indians in Westerns, always wanted them to win.

A truck approached, roared by, faded.

There was no give in the ground. We were both filthy from days of travel. We had no money. It felt good. That's what I remember.

Sometimes he felt he could live permanently in a hotel, like someone in a 1950s American movie: a detective, or a man the police might be looking for. Something about the idea of living like that appealed to him, something about coming and going at odd times of the day or night, eating in diners or drinking alone in dingy bars where other men also drank alone. The hotel room would be clean but simple, sparsely furnished, with a hard bed and a closet where his suits and shirts would hang. The hotel lobby and reception would be seedier, a little tired and faded, and the proprietor, a woman in her fifties, would be tired and faded too, a woman who had seen better days, and who was sustained by memories from those days. She and he would understand each other, she would know he always paid his rent and he on the other hand could tell her things she'd keep to herself, but then again there was a line they would both know not to cross. The hotel wouldn't offer much comfort, it was in the wrong part of the wrong town for that, but it would provide a man like him with what he needed, a place he couldn't call his own.

Whenever he stayed in a hotel in a big city, or just in a town he didn't know well, his imagination would run along these lines. People hardly noticed him, he had a boring job in a boring business, but this meant he had to go away sometimes, and he could make something of that. He and his wife didn't have much left to say to each other, so it was hardly surprising that when he was away he fantasised. He chatted up the receptionist without intending or expecting anything to come of it, and nothing did; he walked the familiar, unfamiliar streets, he stopped in a dull little bar for a whisky and felt conspiratorial. It was as if he were waiting for somebody, as if he were caught up in something mysterious and potentially dangerous, the kind of thing that was never, in his life, actually going to happen.

'Do people still do this?' she said. 'Have affairs in hotels in the middle of the afternoon?'

'We're doing it.'

'Yes. But it seems . . . I don't know . . . it doesn't feel real.'

He laughed. 'It felt real enough just now, didn't it?'

She laughed too. 'Of course.' But that wasn't what she meant.

While he was in the shower she dressed, then went to the window and drew back the curtains. She did this surreptitiously, not making herself too visible even though no one could possibly know she was there, no one who might recognise her would be down in the street looking up accusingly or in surprise. And so it was: the street was deserted. It was a grey, nondescript view, which in a week or a month she would struggle to recall. Unless they came back, but they wouldn't, not to this hotel. If they came here again the excitement, the pleasure, which *had* been real enough, would not return with them. She felt this very strongly.

There was a block of flats, a terrace of identical houses, a brick-built factory or warehouse where nothing seemed to be going on. There were trees in a tiny park with railings, a bench and flowerbeds. A woman she'd not noticed at first was on the bench, while a small white dog sniffed the flowerbeds and the sad patch of grass they surrounded.

This is nowhere, she thought. *I'm looking at one of those empty, vague, precise, dreamlike scenes painted by* . . . but she couldn't remember the artist's name. *It will never look like this again*, she thought, *because I won't be here to see it*.

The shower stopped. She heard him whistling. He was trying too hard to whistle tunelessly. It might have been endearing but she thought it ludicrous. He would know she was listening and would be assessing, wrongly, the effect his unmusical whistling was having. She considered leaving right then, before he came back into the room, but she didn't go. She stayed at the window, watching the white dog and the woman on the bench. She thought they must belong to each other, but she could not definitely conclude that this was so.

Ye want tae seen it, man. This suit gets oan the bus, looks like a lawyer or somethin, but he's big, ken, ye widna mess wi him. He's goat wan o thae suitcases like a dug on a lead, and he pits it in the luggage rack and he comes and sits doon at the back. And we're headin up the toon and the bus comes tae a stoap, folk are gettin aff and suddenly the guy's chairgin doon the bus like a fuckin bull, yellin at the driver tae haud the door. So whit it is is this boay's liftit the suitcase and he's awa aff the bus wi it, but the driver hauds the door and the guy's oot efter him. Well, the boay hisnae goat a chance, has he, he's jist a wee skinny lad, a junkie, he mustae thoaht there wis somethin in the case worth chancin it for, ken, but it's that heavy the big man catches him efter aboot twenty yairds, he grabs the case wi wan haun and the boay wi the ither, then he draps the case and whacks the boay right in the mooth. And the driver's pulled up alangside so's we can aw see, and folk are gaun, well, that's whit ye get, and the guy hits him again, jist melts him, but he keeps at it, doof, doof, doof, and noo folk are gaun ooh and ah and driver, tell him tae stoap, I mean it wis brutal, man. So the driver shouts at him, that's enough, pal, eh? and the guy looks up, there's blood aw ower the junkie's face, and he lands wan mair punch oan him, probly broke his fuckin nose, then he picks up the suitcase and gets back oan the bus. I'll decide when it's enough, he says tae the driver, and he pits the case back in the luggage rack and gies the haill bus a stare, then he comes and sits in the same seat again. See at the next stoap, jist aboot everybody except me goat aff, and we wurnae even up the toon yet. Tellin ye, man, it wis mental, ye want tae seen it.

April

The Eejit

Jack was fed up with everybody thinking him foolish, so he went to the village schoolhouse and said to the dominie,* 'Will ye gie me an education so I'm no an eejit ony mair?'

The dominie looks Jack up and down. 'Even I cannot do that, boy,' he says, 'but come in and sit at the back of the class and see what you're missing.' So Jack goes in and the lesson continues.

The dominie is chanting numbers and the bairns are chanting them back. *What a daft cairry-on*, thinks Jack. There's a big craw sitting on a branch by the window. 'Caw, caw, caw!' says the craw. 'Caw, caw, caw!' says Jack. And soon they're newsing away fine till the dominie bangs his desk lid and tells Jack he's an eejit for not paying attention. (Actually he says 'idiot' but Jack kens what he means.)

'I wis peyin attention,' says Jack. 'I wis peyin attention tae the craw.'

Then the dominie has the bairns open their books and read aloud, going round the class. Jack has never heard a more boring story in his life. He dozes off. The next thing, the dominie is banging his desk and telling him he's an eejit for not staying awake. Then the dominie starts asking the bairns questions about the story, and if the answer's right nothing happens, but if the answer's wrong the dominie calls the bairn out and belts his hand with a leather strap. Then the dominie asks Jack a question. He hasn't a clue what to say because the story was that boring, so he decides to say nothing.

'Are you deaf, boy?' the dominie yells.

'Naw, I'm no deif,' Jack says, 'and that's the right answer so ye'd better no belt me for it.'

'That's impertinence, boy. Come out here and take your punishment like the rest.'

'I'll come oot,' says Jack, 'but I'm warnin ye, if ye hit me wi yon thing I'll hit ye back.'

'I'll not have that kind of talk in my school,' says the dominie. 'There's the door.'

'I'm on ma wey,' says Jack. 'Ma name's Jack, and if that's an education, I'd rather be an eejit.'

* schoolmaster (Scots)

'It's simply not fair,' the Minister said. 'Here we have an elderly lady, a widow, and because she can no longer look after herself, the family home has to be sold to *pay* for her care. That precious place with all its memories, which she had intended her children to inherit, is going to have to be disposed of. It's wrong, and that's why we are doing something about it. In future the maximum that lady will have to pay for her care is £75,000.'

It was an emotional interview. He left the studio with tears in his eyes.

On the street, between him and the ministerial car, stood a woman. She looked about sixty, but it was hard to tell.

'Could you spare a pound, sir?' she said.

'What?'

'You see, if you give me a pound, and if I can get a pound from thirteen other people this week, then I'll be all right.'

'What do you mean?' the Minister asked.

'They've changed the benefit system,' the woman said. 'I live in a council flat, and because I have a spare bedroom they're cutting my housing benefit by £14 a week. And if I can't make up the difference I'll have to move out, though God knows where to. But I just can't afford to lose that kind of money.'

'But surely you don't need the extra room?' the Minister asked.

'It was my daughter's room. She still comes and stays once a week, to help me out with things. It's been difficult since my husband died.'

'Your husband is dead?' the Minister said. 'Did you share a bedroom with him?'

'Oh yes, right to the end. We loved each other very much.'

'Then you not only have a spare bedroom, you yourself have a double bedroom, is that correct?'

'Yes, but if you could spare a pound that wouldn't matter.'

'Matter?' the Minister roared. 'Of course it matters. Out of my way, you greedy, thieving, idle woman. How dare you waste my time for the trifling sum of £14.'

This story is grotesquely exaggerated, crudely simplistic and politically biased. At the same time, however, not a word of it is a lie.

Imagination

There was once a man so old that most of his family, and all of his friends, had left the world long before him. He had been in 'the war', and when he spoke of that time it seemed to anyone watching that he was not only mentally but also physically reliving his experiences. Even when, overcome by the power of imagination, he lapsed into silence, his legs and arms would jerk and twitch, his whole body move as he refought battles. His young relatives, for whom 'the war' was only history, were thankful that they had not had to undergo such experiences.

Increasingly infirm, and having gradually but completely lost his sight, the old man had to move into a residential home. One morning the staff found his room empty, his bed not slept in. A search was undertaken, but without success. Then the telephone rang. A neighbour had discovered him outside his old house, cold but in good spirits. She was now giving him his breakfast. How, though, had he got there during the night? The house was five miles away, along a complicated route, and he was a blind nonagenarian who could not ordinarily reach the dining-room without assistance.

When questioned, he vigorously denied phoning for a taxi or having been given a lift. He had walked all the way with his comrades, he said – naming three men who had been dead seventy years – and whenever one of the party had tired the others had taken it in turns to support him as they went. He never wavered from this account, and no other explanation of how he had made that journey was ever found. A few weeks later he had a fall, and shortly after that he died.

It was the old man's grandson who told me of that last march. The story has stayed with me ever since. It makes me think of the dying Balzac, who looked at his doctor and cried out, 'Send for Blanchion!' When mere mortal physician could do no more for him, the author called for one of his own characters. And who can say that Blanchion did not come, and did not bring relief?

Skin

When I was still some distance from the village, I came upon two young boys playing beside the road. They took one look at me and fled, screaming, never before having seen anyone like me. By the time I arrived at the houses, word of me had spread, and I was surrounded by an army of children. The infants regarded me with a mixture of terror and astonishment, clinging tightly to their bigger brothers and sisters. The older children exhibited more curiosity than fear, and one bold girl, approaching me, licked her fingertips and rubbed them on my lower arm to see if I was painted. Greatly amused to find that I was not, she encouraged the others to check for themselves. A detailed investigation of my skin, hands, hair, ears, nose and lips ensued. I submitted to this with good grace, for it was a remote village, and it was clear that though tales or even pictures of men and women such as myself might have reached there, none of my examiners had ever seen the genuine article in flesh and blood.

The innocence of those few minutes was to me a delight I shall never forget. There was neither malice nor suspicion nor revulsion in their attitude towards me: I was simply different and therefore, for a while at least, exotic. But then the adults began to appear, polite and not hostile, yet infinitely more reserved. They shooed the children away, as if they were a nuisance to me, or I a danger to them. I saw doubt and mistrust in those adult eyes. I might have come bearing dirt or disease, or with a strange faith, or with moral standards that they did not share. The men might suspect me of coveting their women, the women might expect me to fight their men. I was different, and so I represented change, and most people are afraid of change.

And there was something else. I was only one. One might be tolerated. A few might be acceptable. But what if there were more like me – smiling, peaceful, apparently wanting nothing, but on their way in their thousands, their tens and hundreds of thousands?

The Man Upstairs

The bus is just over the bridge when a procession of folk comes down from the top deck – not to get off, but to find themselves other seats.

'There's a fellow up there being sick,' a woman tells the driver. He nods. It's obvious he doesn't want to know. It's his bus but it's not *his* bus.

She comes to the back and says it again, as if we can't hear the retching and the rattle of vomit on the floor above our heads. 'Oh, he's terribly sick,' she adds, after another volley.

'Is it drink?' an old man asks.

'I don't know,' she says. 'But he's not well.'

Trainers appear on the stairs. Is this him? No. It's a young fellow in a tracksuit, alert, buzzing, fresh-faced, who launches himself from the bus at the next stop. Surely our man would be sweaty and pale, shivering and feverish, not flying off like a gymnast? And nobody said, 'Better now, son?' Nobody said, 'That was him.'

The bingo halls are coming up. The women rise like a wave and head for the exit.

'*You'll* be sick if you don't win tonight,' the old man says, cackling.

The woman laughs back, shaking her head. 'I'd rather go home penniless than be the one that has to clean this bus tonight.'

So now the lower deck is half empty, or perhaps that should be half full. Upstairs everything has gone very quiet. All that was in him must have come out. What next? Maybe he's embarrassed, afraid, reluctant to show his face. I'm trying to picture the scene up there. Has he moved seats? Is anybody else still with him? Is he conscious? Dead?

The bus's tyres rumble over the tarmac, the wipers thud back and forth across the glass. There are just a handful of us now, all with our own thoughts, or not with them. And upstairs, some man – dead, or not dead. Somebody should go and check. I should go. But I don't move. I sit exactly where I am, anticipating two things – my stop, and his spattered shoes staggering down the stairs – and I am not sure which I want to see first.

The Blue Plaque (1)

Having wrapped up all his meetings by midday, Douglas could devote the afternoon to Aileen, who had come with him, desperate to enjoy the city after the long, hard, northern winter and the completion of her new novel. They saw an exhibition at the National Gallery, ate an early dinner in Soho, then decided to stroll back to their hotel in Bloomsbury for a nightcap before bed.

Aileen kept pointing out the blue plaques, commemorating musicians, athletes, philosophers, scientists, politicians, inventors and so forth, that were displayed on the buildings in which they had been born, or had lived or worked. To Douglas she seemed almost infatuated by the plaques.

'There's even one at 221b Baker Street,' Aileen said, 'although not an official one. I saw it yesterday.'

'What were you doing in Baker Street?'

'I went to the Sherlock Holmes Museum, I told you.'

'So you did. Sorry. Is that where it is?'

'Well, of course. That's where he had his rooms, at Mrs Hudson's.'

'Ah yes,' Douglas said. *Surely*, he thought, *Sherlock Holmes was an invention?*

They had entered a square, on the far side of which stood their hotel. He quickened his pace, but Aileen had homed in on yet another bloody plaque, on a narrow, brick-built house with a grey door and shuttered windows.

'Look how bright and blue it is!' she said. 'It must be very new.'

'There's the hotel, darling,' he said. 'Let's get that drink.'

'Wait a minute!' she called. 'You won't believe this. It's got your name on it! Your *exact* name!'

He returned nervously. 'Well,' he said, 'it's not *that* uncommon a combination.'

'It's *completely* uncommon! Look, it even says "Architect". How creepy! Oh!' Her tone suddenly changed, the frivolity draining away. 'It says you lived here from . . . four years ago to . . . last year. And, Douglas, the date of your death! You've only got two years left!'

'Darling, what are you talking about? That's not me. It's someone else with the same name.'

But she was staring at him as if the plaque told the truth, and he had uttered some ridiculous, betraying fiction.

He moved towards her. Even as he did, she rang the doorbell.

The Blue Plaque (2)

Douglas and Aileen stood in front of the blue plaque, together but separate, each trying to make sense of what they were seeing: his name on it, the authoritative statement that he had lived at that address for three years, and the unavoidable inference, from the dates given, that he would be dead in another two. Aileen rang the bell a second time.

'It must be some kind of joke,' Douglas said while they waited.

'So you keep saying. I don't find it funny, Douglas.'

'It's nothing to do with me,' he snapped back. 'I'm not amused either, by the way. Anyway, I thought you had to be dead before you got one of these things put up.'

'Not long to go, apparently,' she said.

'How many times do I have to tell you? It's not me.'

'It's you all right. Who else could it be? The only question is what you've been doing down here for the last three years. On your business trips.' She did not so much say the word 'business' as spit it on the pavement.

Douglas lost his temper. 'For Christ's sake, stop talking as if we're in the middle of one of your stupid paranormal novels. This is either a sick joke or a complete coincidence. And obviously, if it's the former, it's wrong on two important counts. First, I've never lived in this house, in fact until five minutes ago I didn't know of its existence. And second, I'm not dead, nor do I intend to be in two years' time. So will you please get those facts into your infantile little head?'

He felt infuriated, justified and terrified. What made him so angry was that it *was* just like one of her novels. If he could only hang on for another page or another minute, he would wake up and it would all be over. It probably was anyway, after what he had just said about her writing.

They heard steps behind the grey door. A woman, less glamorous than Aileen but considerably younger, opened it. Although she raised her eyebrows, she did not seem particularly surprised.

'Oh,' she said, 'it's you.' And then: 'And who's this?'

I don't know how he got up there – how *could* he get up there? – but one night I woke and heard his movements, and knew at once, by some instinct I cannot explain, what I was hearing. After that first time I used to listen out for him pacing the joists, testing the spaces in between. Heavier than a mouse, subtler than a squirrel, not panicky like a bird. He was clever, understanding that the plaster beneath the insulation material wouldn't take his weight. I would hear him in my dreams, sniffing and pawing at the dust. Then I'd wake, and hear him for real.

That summer, which began so dry, was one of the wettest on record. After three days of particularly solid, unrelenting rain I needed to check the roof. I didn't want to disturb him but it had to be done.

I poised the ladder, lifted the hatch and hauled myself up. Searching the underside of the roof for signs of leaks, I smelled his wildness. When my torch scanned the farthest shadows, I saw two diamonds flashing in the beam. The roof was sound.

Common sense told me that he could not stay there indefinitely. I placed a dish of water by the hatch, and left the hatch open and the ladder in position when I descended. That night I left the door into the garden ajar, and slept with my bedroom door and the doors into all the other rooms shut tight. I left biscuits at intervals along this exit route. And somehow I did sleep.

In the morning he was gone. He left a few auburn hairs on the rungs of the ladder, a dusty paw print on the stair carpet, and the crumbs of his hunger in the back lobby.

I closed up the hatch, put away the ladder and washed the empty dish. I felt sad but I had no reason to be. I consoled myself with thoughts of him running in the hills, in the woods, his tail a flaming bush of freedom.

I think of him often, even now. I miss him. I wish he would come again into my dreams, but he never does.

A voice came from the radio, then another, and another. Rich, old, rough. Regional voices: sounds made by working people of the not so long ago, from places broken and crushed, covered over and landscaped, or just left to rust and rot. Like voices from the early days of wireless, without the scratch and crackle. Men remembering, not the Thirties or the War, but the war of thirty years ago. Blink and you're back there. Like yesterday.

'She was a fighter, I'll give her that. She fought for her class. I don't blame her for it. She was against us and we were against her. When you pull on your boots and go down a stinking pit on a cold, dark, winter's morning, you go with other men and there's comradeship in that, solidarity. That's what we were, a community, and she attacked us. What could we do but fight back? It was our lives.'

'It's a mistake to make a monster of her. There are people holding street parties – I saw it on the telly. Most of that lot weren't born, it's just an excuse. I won't dance on her grave but I'll raise a glass to her going. If she was a monster does that mean the monster is slain? They'd have you believe it. Do you think when the tabloids print BEAST across the face of a child molester it'll never happen again? It's human nature, like it or not. She may be dead but what she stood for's alive and well.'

'You had to take sides. That was how it was. And nothing has changed, whatever anyone tells you. The only thing that's changed is all the politicians have gone over to the other side. All educated together, all sound the same, all with the same policies. Who represents people like us in that place today? Nobody I can see. Nobody I hear.'

They were there for a few minutes, those voices, then they were gone. And the tales they told were true, but truer still were the sounds they made in the telling. You don't hear them any more. You just don't hear them. It was like listening to ghosts.

Allison Gross

from an old ballad

Ah, well, she is dead at last, the old witch. I for one will not mourn her passing. By the end she was nothing to be afraid of, a tottering crone with a wandered mind, but once she was feared and hated in equal measure. Just to hear her voice made your gorge rise. To look on her brought blood to the eyes.

That time I was up at the tower – her place – I did not mean to go, but she beguiled me with her promises and I lingered. There was something fascinating about her, repulsive though she was.

'You can be rich,' she said. 'You can have anything you like and you can have it now, you can own everything and owe nothing. All I ask in return is that you be my lover.'

I couldn't do it. 'No,' I told her. 'Get away from me.'

'But you came to me,' she said. 'You must want something.' And she promised me more, the fat of the land, the jewels of the sea, and the secret knowledge that would conjure fortunes from the air. And I was sorely tempted.

Yet I refused her. Sure I did. I could never have kissed those ugly lips, not for all the gifts in the world.

Then her honeyed words turned sour, and she put a spell on me. I could do nothing to resist. My strength left me, and I fell senseless to the ground.

She made a monstrous worm of me, long and thick and foul – as foul as she was. I was sick and ashamed at what I had become. She laughed as she watched me drag myself about. 'You should have kissed me when you had the chance,' she said. 'You could have had it all.'

Later, the spell she'd cast was cancelled by the Queen of Fairies and I was restored to my proper shape. You can believe that if you like. I do. I have to. Rather that than the alternative, which is that I became so used to my new self that I stopped noticing.

Anyway, the witch is dead and can do no more harm. That's all that matters, isn't it?

The Wife of Usher's Well

from an old ballad

There lived a wife at Usher's Well, a woman of substance. She had three sons, big, strapping boys, and she sent them on a trip across the sea.

Barely a week had passed and word came that the ship they had sailed in was lost, with all aboard feared dead.

Two more weeks went by before the awful news was confirmed: never again would she see her boys.

Then the woman made a terrible wish: that neither wind nor flood should cease till her sons came home to her, in flesh and blood just as they had been.

All summer and autumn storms raged, both at sea and on land, till about Martinmas, when a calm descended; and home at last to the wife came her sons.

They wore hats fashioned from birch bark, a wood that is said to protect the dead from the living. But the tree from which that bark came grew in neither bog nor ditch on this earth, but at the gate to some other world.

Joyfully the woman ordered a feast to be prepared. The house was swept and cleaned, and fires lit. And there was a servant girl, shy and lovely, who had been fond of the youngest son, and he of her, and he caught her eye again as she worked, and again her heart was softened.

The mother prepared a bed for her boys, long and wide enough to take all three. And through the deep night, as they lay sleeping, she sat with her cloak about her, watching over them.

Weariness at last overtook her. While she dozed, the dawn broke. The eldest son stirred. 'Time we were away,' he said.

The youngest son sat up. 'Time indeed, brother,' he said. 'I hear the cock crowing, and the fretful worm turning in the earth. We must return to the place we came from, before we are missed.'

Softly they made their way from the room, out of the house and past the steading. And all three, as they went, cast a fond last look at their sleeping mother, and the youngest bit his lip as he thought of the girl who had kindled the fire.

The Demon Lover

from an old ballad

She wondered if her heart would burst. Seven years! Love, desire, grief and fear surged through her.

'Where have you been? After all this time?'

'Does it matter? I've come for you, for the promises you made.'

She was enraged. 'Promises? Who made promises? You left me! And now I'm a married woman.'

He turned as if she had struck him in the face. Tears welled in his eyes. 'I'd never have come back but for you. Never. But for you,' he continued bitterly, 'I might have had love in another land. I might have had a princess.'

'And it's my fault?' she cried. 'If you had the chance, you should have taken it. Fine well you knew no princess was waiting for you here.'

'I don't give a damn about princesses. It's you I want.'

The way he looked at her – she felt the old, fierce passion. She thought of her husband, kind and dull and bloodless, the children who exhausted her, the grinding poverty of her life.

'What can you possibly offer,' she said, 'that would make me leave my family?'

But she knew, as soon as she asked it, that she would go.

'My ship is in the bay,' he said. 'My crew and every comfort you can imagine await you.'

So she kissed her babies for the last time, and went with him, and he took her out to the beautiful ship.

No crew greeted her when she set foot on deck. The sails filled of their own accord, and he steered the ship unaided, and in cold silence.

The land faded from her sight. 'Who are you?' she wept.

'Save your tears,' he said. 'You'll have plenty to cry about soon.'

On the horizon – soft green hills bathed in sunshine. Hope rose in her. He saw her looking and shook his head, laughing.

Another mountain rose from the sea, vast, black, covered in ice. She turned to him, and he nodded, and laughed again.

Then with one push of his hand he toppled the topmast, and with his knee he cracked the foremast, and he broke the ship in two, and sank it beneath the shadow of that terrible mountain.

The Two Magicians

from an old ballad

There she stood in her finery, taking the air, tall, handsome, proud. *Think you're something, don't you?* the blacksmith thought.

She hardly glanced at him outside his forge, grimy, sweaty, thick as a bull. *Coarse brute*, she thought.

'Aye, lady,' he called. 'Red suits you. Are you waiting for a ride? I'll give you one.'

'Go to hell, pig.' She bent to the ground and came up with a pinch of dirt. Tossed it away. 'You're not worth that! I wouldn't go with a blacksmith for anything. I'd sooner be dead and buried.'

'And I wouldn't pay a button for you, and if I did it would be too much. But I'll ride you, lady, see if I don't.'

No ordinary souls, this pair. Sparring was their entertainment. The rest of the town kept well clear of them. Rumour was they were witch and wizard – magicians anyway. She threw him one last look, and turned herself into a turtle dove. Up she flew. *Ride me now if you can*, she thought.

Suddenly another dove was with her. They banked and wheeled as he tried to force himself upon her. *Enough of this*, she thought, diving rapidly. At the last moment she changed into an eel, and slipped into the burn with hardly a splash.

A speckled trout was at her side, herding her in under the bank. The blacksmith's glint was in the eye of the fish. *Still here?* she thought. She surfaced as a duck and flapped across to the millpond.

Seconds later a drake with a big red comb was lunging at her rump. *You're determined*, she thought, *but I'll be rid of you yet*. Swiftly she switched into a hare, and loped off up the hill.

She heard panting at her heels. A greyhound was after her, the same wicked gleam in his eye. *Right*, she thought, *that does it*. She transformed herself into a grey mare and gave the dog a good hard kick, sending it skyward.

Something thumped down on her back, a black saddle, with stirrups and pommel all pointed and gilded. She felt the girth tighten under her belly. *Bastard*, she thought. She took off at a gallop.

Orfeo and Isabel

from an old ballad

There is an old saying: *Where the wood greens early, there the deer goes.*

Long ago there was a King famed for his skill at piping. One day he went hunting, but while he was away a servant came looking for him.

'You must come back at once. The Lady Isabel is very sick.'

'What happened?' the King demanded as they rode. 'What is wrong with her?'

Nobody knew. One minute she was fine, the next she collapsed. The physicians were at a loss.

'They're saying it was the fairies,' the servant said. 'They're saying the Fairy King has wounded her with one of his little arrows.'

An ominous silence greeted their arrival.

'Where is my Lady?'

'She is dead.'

They had laid her out, as beautiful and unblemished in death as in life. The King's grief was terrible to see.

'They've taken her soul from me,' he said, 'but they'll not have her body.' So guards were posted to watch over her, but the guards slept, and in the morning her body was gone.

The King set off in pursuit, but the trail ended in the greenwood, by a great, grey stone. He sat down and waited.

Seven years he sat, and his hair grew and covered him over like moss.

Then he heard a great company approaching, some on foot, some riding, and among them the Lady Isabel. The grey stone opened like a door into the earth. In they went, and the King followed.

He brought out his pipes and began to play: first a lament, then a march, and finally a reel so wild and joyous it would have cured the sickest heart.

A servant approached. 'They're impressed. Come into the hall, will you?'

Deeper in he went. Strange, inhuman folk they were, the foremost among them not half his height.

'You played well,' the creature said. 'What will you have for your playing?'

'I will have my Lady Isabel.'

The one looked at the other. 'Take her. Go home. What's yours is yours, what's mine is mine.'

So he and she departed. And that old saying was ever in his mind: *Where the wood greens early, there the deer goes.*

That Face

You see that face everywhere these days. You know the one. The dead-set look that goes with the trudge. A woman – it's very often a woman – is making her way along the street, carrying two or three bags, and it seems every other person on the pavement is going in the opposite direction. So she has to lean, weave, shove her way against the tide, and each step is exhausting her. You can see this from the way her back is bent, her head lowered as if into a wind, but there is no wind. And the face is on her, the one sculpted by that invisible wind. *I have to keep going*, it says, *if I stop I'll never start again. If I think about everything that's looming up to hit me I'll collapse in a heap right here.*

A man – it's often a man – is pushing a buggy through the shopping centre. Everything about him looks poor: his clothes, his shoes, the pallor of his skin, the thinness of his arms as he pushes. He might be the father or the grandfather, it is hard to say, but he's got the child on a weekday morning and maybe you're making assumptions but you guess that this is his job, his only job, and that he's been doing it since the child was born. He has the same face as the woman: the one that says, *This is what I do, this is all I do, this is my horizon.*

And the child in the buggy is crying, fretting: not a cry of alarm or pain, just a constant, anxious fret. Already the invisible wind is having its effect, the hard climate of circumstance is shaping and sculpting.

It strikes you later, when you've seen the face a hundred times during the day, that it's nothing new. How could it be, when the face can pass so easily from generation to generation? It is centuries old. It's the face of resignation, of being on the receiving end, of being oppressed. The face of poverty. You feel the waste, but not the pity. You feel the shame, but not the responsibility. You feel the anger.

Then the sun came out. As if by accident, as if it didn't mean to but forgot itself. Twenty minutes earlier the sky had been a big grey leaking blanket and everything was wet. It had been like that for days, weeks: long enough, anyway, that you couldn't remember the last sunny day. Cold too – miserably so. Even when it wasn't raining the air had felt heavy, full of chill moisture. Damp eating into your bones, rotting your skin. But then, by miraculous chance, the sun came out.

Twenty minutes was all it took, and you felt that bone-destroying, skin-sapping process thrown into reverse. Bright blue holes appeared in the blanket, joining up to make bigger expanses. Soon there were just a few grey rags remaining up there. The roads and pavements were being steam-cleaned. Steel and glass on buildings gleamed and winked. People stretched themselves, pushed back hoods, lowered and shook and folded umbrellas. They smiled. Everything was going to be dry again. The heat on your shoulders – how soon you remembered the goodness of that! You wanted to be a lizard, flat out on a stone, absorbing, making the most of it.

You ate your sandwich on a bench in the public gardens. The wooden slats were dry and warm. An old man sat down at the other end. You glanced at him, but he was oblivious to you. He had a newspaper. He folded it carefully, brought his face down to within two or three inches of the page, and started to read. The intensity of his concentration was fascinating. When he reached the bottom-right-hand corner of the section of page he was on, he refolded the paper and started again from the top-left-hand corner.

You had to return to work. You sensed that the old boy wouldn't be shifting as long as he still had some news left to read. And you hoped that, for as long as he had, the sun would stay out. A favour to old age: *I'm here now so I'll stay*. You were envious of him sitting on, of his reading every word, even of his shortsightedness. You stood up to leave. He did not notice.

The Painter

Every morning she steps out of the back door and makes her way to the spot a few yards beyond the cottage, at the edge of the field. She likes the fact that she can get there without being seen. The route gives her that seclusion, that invisibility – no one knows she is there, so if someone knocks at the front door of the cottage and gets no answer he or she will assume she is away. This means she can paint all day, undisturbed.

Sometimes she catches herself in the middle of her work. What is it she is trying to grasp? A feeling? Yes. The feeling of the light, the sea, the earth – elemental things. She doesn't need to go anywhere else for this. She doesn't need grand subjects – in fact grand subjects would be a distraction. They would get in the way of what she is looking at, reaching for. Here, this unremarkable place by the sea, is enough. Nor, in truth, is it unremarkable.

One painting leads straight on to another. All day she's there. She leaves her paints and brushes and easel out overnight, a studio in the open air. While she works the wind blows things against the canvas – insects and bits of grass. They stick to the paint and she removes them or she leaves them but either way they become part of what she is doing. The tough, huddled wee tree buds, puts on leaves, loses them. She digs and scrapes at the paint with the pallet knife, the brush-end. Last year the field was barley, this year oats. She presses seeds into the paint. Wildflowers bloom and fade, grasses lengthen. Everything is the same, but every day different. It seems silly to shift about, so she stays put.

There is an urgency about that – staying in one place, capturing it over and over. Thoughts flock in like gulls, or one hovers like a solitary gull. She isn't well. She is in pain. She wants to write a letter to the woman she loves but more urgent is the need to paint. What is it so close within her grasp, so impossible to hold? It is life.

The Little Fever

Scott's heart burns a little this morning. He was out to dinner last night and it is probable that he had a glass or two more than he should have. Now middle-aged, and a man who seriously overworks himself, he knows he should drink only in moderation, and usually he does. (He remembers the old judges of his youth – no moderation on their part when a case before them was protracted! Strong black port and biscuits sustained them – and little attempt made to disguise the fact.)

He eases the discomfort with a dose of magnesia. While it settles he glances over his sheets from yesterday, and is pleased to find that the deadlock has released overnight, the tangled trap of incident and character he had written himself into has unknotted itself. All the threads and colours separated and ordered – as if by magic! How that happens he does not know, but it does, it still does. He goes to bed clueless as to how to extricate the plot and wakes up with a workable plan. God knows he needs that to keep happening!

It's as if, when the body sleeps, the intellect goes to work, unhampered by conscious effort or willed direction. He suspects this mechanism is triggered by the little fever an extra glass of wine produces. Can't prove it, of course – and excess kills the process stone-dead – but when he thinks back over all the novels he believes the theory is correct. Were there any that he wrote into the middle of with the least notion as to how he was to get out at the other side? None that he can recall. It's a perilous way to ride – not one he'd recommend to aspiring young authors – but it's the only way he knows. He prays for strength to stay in the saddle a while longer. Four thousand pounds for each three-volume novel. The account comes down – slowly, but it comes down.

He scribbles these thoughts in the journal. He could stay with the journal all day, but it is wageless labour. No, not labour, it is talking to a friend, the best he has. Writing novels is labour now, but it pays.

'How long have you known me, Brent?' Douglas asked, as he handed out the drinks from a silver salver. Malt whisky for them, gin and tonic for Aileen. They were in the conservatory. All very civilised. Brent relaxed into the big, soft armchair.

'Twenty years,' he said.

'Twenty-two, actually. And Aileen for seventeen. You were my best man, and you married the chief bridesmaid, Aileen's best friend. Isn't that right?'

'Statement of the obvious, Douglas,' Brent said. 'Yes, I married Sophie.'

'Poor dear Sophie,' Aileen said. She was staring out into the garden.

'Yes,' Douglas said. 'Poor Sophie. What I'm saying, Brent, is that we've been friends a long time, all of us. Haven't we?'

'Absolutely.'

'You probably know me as well as anyone does. Wouldn't you say?'

There was something tight in Douglas's voice. Brent didn't like it.

'Probably,' he said.

'You see,' Douglas said, sitting down at one end of the big sofa, 'we have a problem, which I'd like to sort out. The problem is, Aileen thinks I'm having an affair. She thinks I've been playing away from home.'

Brent took a mouthful of whisky. 'Oh,' he said.

'And I thought, because you know me so well, you could tell her how absurd that idea is.'

Aileen turned her head towards Brent, her face blank. *Help me out here,* he thought.

'You're my character witness,' Douglas said, watching Brent very intently. 'You know I wouldn't do that, don't you?'

'No, I don't think you would,' Brent said cautiously.

'Of course everybody's capable of doing stuff behind someone else's back,' Douglas said. 'And no doubt I've flirted with some stranger at a party now and again. But an affair? Why would I have an affair? I mean, look at her. My Aileen.'

Brent said, 'I don't know what to say.'

'I'm asking your opinion,' Douglas said. 'Do you think I'm having an affair?'

'No,' Brent said.

'Good,' Douglas said. 'That's settled then. Marital bliss is restored.'

Aileen took a huge slug of gin. 'Don't be such a prick, Douglas. Just say what you really want to say.'

Brent sat up. The room bulged with anger. He braced himself for whatever was coming next.

Piano

For about a month, every morning on my way to the paper shop, I heard a piano being played when I passed a particular block of flats. It was a 1970s block, worn and shabby, with a door at the common entrance that badly needed a new coat of paint. I had a sense, probably from the handwritten labels taped onto the entryphone system, that many of those flats were occupied by people who didn't stay long: students, maybe, or workers on short-term contracts. But for those four or five weeks, on a daily basis, I heard piano music drifting from an open window on the ground floor, and I thought this gave the building grace and grandeur, a kind of permanence and solidity that it otherwise lacked.

I have no idea who the player was, because although the window was slightly open there was a grubby blind that was always pulled down so I couldn't see in. But whoever it was, he or she was very good. Often I heard the same piece of music – not stopping and starting, but flowing with confidence and sensitivity, as if on each occasion the player was trying to extract ever more feeling from the keys. I didn't recognise the music and I still don't know what it was because I've not heard it again, even though I listen to a great deal of classical music on the radio. Such a lovely piece. It made me pause on the pavement every time.

One day I went by at a different time, and the window was shut but the blind raised. There it was, a glossy, black grand piano, squeezed into the room like a stallion into too small a stable. There wasn't space for anything else, apart from an unoccupied piano stool.

Not so long after that, a morning came when the music didn't happen. I looked: the window was shut, the blind up – and the piano was gone. That great, beautiful creature – vanished. I couldn't believe it. I felt bereft. It was like being in love with someone, who leaves without saying goodbye before you can tell them. It was like waking from a delightful, heartbreaking dream.

'Leon!' he called, not loudly. He bent the metal sheet back into place, let his eyes adjust to the dark. 'Leon! Where are you?'

He could make out the crates they'd turned into chairs, the blankets and bits of cardboard they slept on. He crawled a few more feet, dragging the sack, then was able to crouch. The sack would feel heavy and therefore, at least for a moment, exciting to Leon, who was much smaller than he was. But the haul from the hotel bin wasn't exciting: two bruised apples, a huge but yellowing lettuce, some overripe tomatoes and half a loaf of day-old bread. Still, he'd make it sound as good as he could. And then there was the special thing he'd lifted from the booth at the hotel entrance. He'd just run past and taken it. The man in the booth was too slow but the doorman had almost grabbed him. He couldn't go near that hotel for a week now, but it had been worth it. What a prize! A whole, untouched, unbroken bar of chocolate, still in its wrapper!

'Leon!' He'd been away longer than usual, and Leon sometimes got frightened, thinking he'd been caught or hurt and wouldn't be coming back. But he always came back.

He heard a shuffling sound at the back of the hide. Then a match was struck, and Leon's little face was there. Leon lit the stub of candle they kept for when they ate.

'Are you okay? I'm sorry I'm late. You won't believe what I've got.' He pushed the sack over.

'What?'

'Have a look. Nice bread, juicy tomatoes, apples – and something else. A surprise.'

'A surprise? Will I like it?'

'You'll love it.'

Leon took out the tomatoes and divided them, three each. He tore the bread into equal pieces. That was his job.

'What's this?'

'A lettuce.'

'Yuck. Is that the surprise?'

'No, but you have to eat it first.'

'It's like eating grass.'

'I know, but we have to eat it. Then the apples. Then you get the surprise.'

Leon felt around at the bottom of the sack. In the candlelight a huge smile broke across his dirty face.

Poison

Something was eating the poison in the woodshed, lots of it, after it had lain untouched all winter. One morning I discovered that the bait, which I'd put into jam-jar lids and placed at various points around the shed, had been either eaten or scattered across the floor, and all the lids moved behind what was left of the winter stack of logs. This was a distance of some ten or twelve feet. A mouse, a whole team of mice, wouldn't be capable of doing that – even if collecting jam-jar lids was normal mouse behaviour.

The timing didn't make sense either, although Eddie, my neighbour, said he'd once lived in a farm cottage so cold the mice used to leave at the start of winter and return in spring, like retired Brits with apartments on the Costa del Sol. Four mornings in a row I replaced the lids and replenished the bait, but whatever was eating it seemed immune to the poison. Eddie helped me pull the logs and everything else out of the shed, and we searched for corpses, a nest or some entry route, but found nothing, not even any droppings. Well, there was one round pellet – evidence of nothing really, except maybe constipation. I trawled the internet for images of different kinds of shit – mouse, rat, squirrel, bat, hedgehog – and none of them matched, in shape or quantity. Given how much bait was being consumed, I'd have expected heaps of the stuff.

'A fox?' Eddie suggested.

'No way in or out for a fox,' I said. 'Anyway, we'd smell it.'

'Well, all you can do is keep putting the bait down,' he said.

'I hate the idea that I might be killing off a hedgehog that's just woken up from hibernation,' I said. 'Or somebody's cat. It's weird. Why would any animal move all the lids like that? What's the point?'

Eddie shrugged. 'Maybe tomorrow you'll open the door and a huge rat will be standing there, wearing armour made from tin lids. And he'll be very, very pissed off.'

We both laughed, but Eddie laughed loudest and longest. He could afford to. He wasn't going to have to open the door.

Flight

Once, when I was about thirteen, I was standing in the middle of my bedroom, not thinking of anything in particular, when a hairbrush flew off the top of the chest of drawers, three feet away, struck me on the arm and fell to the floor. This was quite a surprise. I tried to reconstruct what had happened, looking for a rational explanation. Had I been close enough to knock the hairbrush accidentally? No. Had there been a gust of wind from somewhere, or had the hairbrush been positioned right on the edge of the chest? No. I was forced to conclude that it had indeed flown, propelled by no discernible external force.

Later, I read somewhere that adolescents, subject as they are to great physical, hormonal and emotional changes, may generate some kind of magnetic power that attracts objects. It's an interesting theory, but one, I suspect, with absolutely no scientific basis.

Yesterday morning, when I was opening the shutters in the sitting-room, I suddenly remembered this incident. I remembered the strangeness of it, the urge I had felt to 'explain' it, the mix of thrill and disappointment when I could not. I then indulged myself by carrying out a foolish kind of experiment. Concentrating my mind on a row of objects on the mantelpiece – a candlestick, a postcard, a small dish, a shell, a box of matches, another candlestick – I willed each of these objects in turn to fly from its position. Nothing happened. Could I persuade one of them to budge even a fraction of an inch? No. Recalling that I had not deliberately provoked the original incident with the hairbrush, I turned away and – without seriously expecting a result – considered, not those objects, but the fact that spring was finally here and that I might get out into the garden in the afternoon, to do some tidying up.

Nothing.

Ach well. I went through to the kitchen to make myself some breakfast. As I filled the kettle, something smacked against the window, then fell from view. I went outside. On the ground lay a blue tit – tiny, delicate and, though quite dead, warm with the life that had just left it.

The Call

for Alan Taylor

Two men are walking through a small town, very late at night, one a few paces ahead of the other. They are on their way home. Home is several miles away. Apart from them, the street is deserted. The town is a place they hardly know, except by reputation. It is not a good reputation.

It would take too long to explain fully why they have ended up where they have, but the chief contributory factors are: drink; a party; pursuit of, as it has turned out, unattainable women; a dearth of transport options, either public or private; and drink.

The men do not speak, but not because they are not on speaking terms. On the contrary, they are old and firm friends. They have simply reached that stage of proceedings when speech is neither useful nor easy. Silence, of the brooding, dogged variety, reigns as they trudge along the street a few feet apart.

In the middle of the town, outside the post office, is a telephone box. (These events take place in the pre-mobile-phone era.) As they pass the box, the phone inside starts to ring. The first man ignores it. The second man pauses, observes his companion forging ahead, seems to weigh up his options, and finally, going over to the box, enters it and picks up the receiver.

'Is that you?' says a male voice – a very hard, unpleasant and threatening voice.

'It is,' the second man says. Because it is.

'Stay there,' the other voice says. 'I am coming down there now, and I am going to kill you.'

The line goes dead. The man in the telephone box replaces the receiver. He steps out into the street. His companion is now sixty yards away. The second man listens – for the sound of footsteps, or a car engine – but hears nothing.

He starts walking, quickly. After half a dozen paces he breaks into a run. After fifty, when he is close on the heels of the first man, the latter hears him coming. He turns round and takes note of the look on his friend's face. Still not a word passes between them. The first man, too, starts to run.

The Total Eclipse of Scotland

On this day, the first recorded total eclipse of Scotland took place. Such events must of course have occurred before, but no one could say for certain when. Advances in astronomy and meteorology meant that for the first time the exact moment and duration of the eclipse could be accurately predicted. As a result there was mass observation of the spectacle.

Despite many scientific reassurances that the eclipse was an entirely natural phenomenon, it was an unnerving seven minutes for many Scots. As the sun, moon and Scotland aligned, the lunar shadow rapidly and ominously spread from west to east across the Outer Hebrides, the inner islands, Argyll, Galloway and Wester Ross, until the whole country was cast into utter darkness, and did not begin to re-emerge for some three minutes.

A not insubstantial minority was convinced that the event must carry some fateful meaning: some said it signified God's displeasure in a backsliding and licentious people, while others thought it heralded the dawn of a new age for the nation. Pagans, Druids and other practitioners of alternative lifestyles gathered at standing stones and similar prehistoric monuments. Several suicides and a number of never-to-be-solved murders took place during those seven minutes, in places as far-flung as Campbeltown, Cumbernauld and Arbroath, although no convincing evidence that the eclipse was responsible has ever been produced.

Civic Scotland responded in different ways. In Edinburgh, a fireworks display on the castle battlements marked the occasion. In Inverness, pubs were allowed, indeed encouraged, to stay open for twenty-four hours as refuges for the nervous or superstitious. Along the 96-mile border with England, relays of cyclists, runners and, in the Tweed, swimmers, 'raced' the eclipse from Gretna to Berwick, cheered on by thousands of spectators: those to the south, bathed in sunshine, enjoyed marvellous views, while those to the north, plunged in gloom, were unable to see a thing.

In a post-eclipse opinion poll, thirty-five per cent of the population said the eclipse should become an annual event; twenty-five per cent said they would prefer a total, and permanent, eclipse of England; and the remainder said they didn't care what was eclipsed so long as they got the day off work.

The new blocks of flats at the waterfront do not look to him, from half a mile away, like blocks of flats at all. They are battleships – vast, towering, grey, black, all plated sides and gleaming spars, bridges, walkways and projecting platforms, different faces of steel and armoured glass, and all with a lack of symmetry, as if the naval designers, keeping pace with advancing technology, couldn't stop adding extra layers of defence or methods to detect the enemy. In the sunshine and against the few swiftly moving white clouds these giants seem to lean into the stiff easterly breeze, straining at their anchors, ready to put to sea.

Between the flats and where he stands is an old dock with a decaying wharf, and beyond that a man-made spit extending far out into the water like a runway. Piles of rubble, concrete blocks and heaps of gravel punctuate this spit at irregular intervals. There, another two of the battleship blocks were supposed to be built, but they never were, because the property bubble burst. Their ghostly absence makes the ones that were completed seem very far away. He imagines people in them watching the shoreline from their windows, waving frantically, seasick, wanting to be brought back to land.

But they can't be brought back. At the peak of the boom the biggest apartments out there went for as much as £750,000. Now they can't be sold for half that. Their owners are becalmed, marooned, grounded – whatever marine terminology you prefer – by negative equity. And if it's grounded they are then the tide is out, and nobody knows when, or if, there will be another tide like it.

'More money than sense.' So said many, himself included, who both envied and despised the wealth that was poured into those apartments. He thinks of the old story that when James IV commissioned his warship the *Great Michael* it was said that all the woods of Fife were used in the building of it. And then came Flodden, and James's death, and the *Great Michael* was sold at a knockdown price to the French, who eventually left that mighty vessel to rot in the harbour at Brest.

Jack and the Shell

Jack was walking by the sea. The sea was a marvel to him. He thought of the strange creatures that lived in it. What was it like to be a flounder or a jellyfish, or one of the things that had lived in the shells he collected from the beach?

On the road home, he stopped to take one of these shells from his pocket for another look. It was shaped like a swirl of ice cream without its cone. He put it to his ear and heard the sea. How had the snail, or whatever it was, lived in such a narrow space? He put his eye to the open end, squinting at the inner spiral. He pressed his eye hard into the shell.

There was a nasty popping sound, and Jack suddenly found that his whole head was inside the shell. The sea was very loud. He tried to pull his head out, but the shell was too tight. *Weel*, he thought, *if I canna gang back I'll hae tae gang on.* So he squeezed his shoulders in, and his arms, and then, gripping hard with both hands, managed to pull his legs in too.

Noo I'll turn roond and get oot, he thought. But he couldn't turn. He was completely stuck. The constant roar of the sea was deafening.

'Help!' Jack shouted. 'Help!'

A passing gull, hearing his cry, said to itself, *There's a shell wi somethin alive in it.* It flew down, picked up the shell and dropped it from a great height. The shell smashed on the road, and Jack burst out, the same size as ever – far too big for a gull to eat. The bird flew off, but not before leaving a long yellow streak down Jack's back as a mark of its disappointment.

'Och, Jack,' his mother said when he arrived home. 'Look at yer jersey! Aw covered in shite.'

'But it's lucky when a bird does that, Mither,' Jack said.

'It's no lucky for me that has tae wash it,' she said. 'Gie it ower, ye daft gowk.'

But Jack knew how lucky he'd been. It's not every day you narrowly miss being a seagull's dinner.

'That place,' Mick said. 'Christ, what a hole.'

'Anyway, I was back up there last week, for work,' Tom said. 'First time in years. So I had to take a turn round the old haunts, didn't I? Well, half the street was gone. Our building – completely demolished. You know what's there instead? A health centre.'

Mick was laughing so much he had to put his glass down. There was something desperate about the way he laughed, Tom thought.

'That's brilliant,' Mick spluttered. 'Maximum points for irony, eh?'

When Tom went up for another round, Mick slipped outside for a fag. The pub was quiet but then it was a Monday. Tom checked his messages. Nothing from Geraldine. Not that he'd expected anything. Tom and Geraldine, for God's sake. What future other than one of continual strife could there be for a couple with those names?

Mick was a mess. Tom would have to sub him all night, so would be responsible for them both getting pissed again. He didn't know if he could go on meeting him like this, for the old times. What were the old times now? They were over. You either waded in alcoholic nostalgia or moved on. He wondered why he'd mentioned the flat. Why he'd gone back at all.

Mick came in again. He lifted his pint. 'Thanks, pal.'

'Good luck,' Tom said.

'Remember Paul?' Mick said. 'Who had the box-room for a while? Nobody ever went in. Just putting your head round the door was bad enough.'

'He cooked his meals in there, along with everything else,' Tom said. 'He had one of those camping gas rings.'

'Aye, his bed caught fire more than once. Whatever happened to him, do you know?'

'He died,' Tom said. 'I told you before.'

'Paul died? Bloody hell. Bloody *hell*!' Mick's astonishment was almost as forced as his laugh. 'How did he die?'

'Drink, drugs, everything,' Tom said. 'Actually, what happened was he stepped in front of a bus. I told you that. But it wasn't the bus that killed him, not really.'

'Bloody hell,' Mick said. He took a drink. So did Tom.

'A health centre, eh?' Mick said. 'That's a good one.'

'The technology really is amazing,' said the Minister for Defence Procurement. 'Once all our security teams are equipped with these devices, we will be able not only to save lives but also to speed up vehicle and body searches at checkpoints. It's a win-win situation. Actually it's a win-win-win situation because the Department will save money too, after the initial outlay.'

'Extraordinary,' said the Secretary of State for Defence. 'And you say the technology was originally developed to locate lost golf balls?' He chuckled. 'Perhaps I might be allowed one for my personal use.'

'I am afraid the golf authorities have banned them. They've ruled that they give an unfair advantage and encourage ungentlemanly conduct.'

'Oh, quite right, that never occurred to me,' replied the Secretary of State. 'Now, seriously, you've seen a demonstration of these detectors in action, have you?'

'I've seen the demonstration video, yes,' the Minister said.

'And how effective are they?'

'They are ninety per cent effective up to a distance of one kilometre. This means, to maintain one hundred per cent security, we will still need our people to carry out inspections on one in ten vehicles, and one in ten people passing through checkpoints will have to be physically searched. But naturally the high visibility of the detectors will itself increase confidence among the general public, and act as a further deterrent to any would-be terrorists.'

'Splendid,' said the Secretary of State. 'In your memorandum you advise buying six thousand of them. How much will that cost?'

'Forty million dollars, including the consultancy commissions.'

The Secretary of State gasped. 'That's an enormous sum.'

'Yes, but you must remember that once the equipment is purchased the only additional running cost is battery replacement. I estimate that the Department will save twenty million dollars on staff costs over the next ten years. Plus many lives, of course.'

'Which must always be our paramount concern. The consultancy commissions, are they clearly shown in the accounting paperwork?'

'No, they are what we call invisible earnings.'

'I see. And when would we expect to be in receipt of the first of them?'

'I have them here,' the Minister said, tapping his black leather briefcase.

'I must confess,' said the Minister for Wellbeing and Security, 'to having some doubts as to whether the technology really can deliver everything you say it can. Leaving aside the civil liberties issue, about which we can expect the usual fuss in the usual quarters, how can you be so confident that simply donning a pair of these glasses will enable the wearer to identify potential terrorists with – what is it you say? – ninety-five per cent accuracy?'

'The truly revolutionary aspect of the Intuceptor system, Minister, is that the technology doesn't override the wearer's instincts, it enhances them. The human brain has an astonishing capacity for making balanced, coherent assessments and following them up with quick and effective decisions. What Intuceptor does is filter, focus and declutter that process, far more rapidly than the brain possibly can. So: an armed-response police officer is trained to be aware of the many forms in which terrorist activity can manifest, but in a crisis situation he doesn't have time to think through the pros and cons of this or that response, he has to take immediate action, with possibly lethal results. The Intuceptor viewfinders take him straight to the *right* response. It's still *his* response, but facilitated by sophisticated digital analysis that can itself be analysed retrospectively, and scientifically proven to have been correct.'

'You mean, in a court of law?'

'Absolutely. Potentially this means our security services will never again find themselves in a situation where they are adjudged to have eliminated a suspect who turned out *not* to be a terrorist, because the Intuceptor recordings will show precisely *why* the suspect was deemed to be dangerous and therefore *had* to be.'

'Had to be dangerous, you mean?'

'Yes, and eliminated.'

'But won't the civil liberties people claim this is a charter for a policy of "shoot first and ask questions later"?'

'They will, and rightly so, because that's precisely what it is. The difference is, when the questions are asked later, we'll have all the right answers.'

'I see,' the Minister said. 'Justice seen to be done, eh?'

'Justice *shown* to be done, Minister. Which, as we know, is just as important in a healthy democracy.'

May

Narcissus (and Echo)

She put on the headphones, selected *shuffle*. Nothing happened. She played around with the iPod for a bit, but couldn't get it to go. Typical. Just when she needed some music to suit her mood, she couldn't get any. Although she didn't actually know what kind of mood she was in. She was bored with most of her music anyway, so maybe it didn't matter. She took off the headphones. Finlay could fix it for her when he tracked her down later, as he surely would. Like a stalker he was, Finlay, but not in a horrible way. He didn't give her the creeps or anything, he was just boring. And he did have his uses.

Last May Day she and the other History of Art girls had gone up Arthur's Seat to wash their faces in the dew, because that was what you did. Chloe, or someone, said it was a tradition: you washed your face in the dew and then you saw the face of the man you were going to marry. But someone else, Imogen probably because she knew a lot of stuff, said that was wrong, it was just supposed to make you more beautiful. Well, anyway, some of them saw their boyfriends' faces and some of them saw farmers or merchant bankers or chaps in the army, but she didn't see anybody. She thought it was all a bit of a bore but she went along with it, they were her friends after all, not that she liked any of them much.

She checked her phone. There were six text messages, one from her mother and the rest from Finlay. Silly boy.

She couldn't be bothered reading them, let alone replying. He'd find her at the café they all went to anyway, so whatever it was he had to say, he'd tell her then. It wouldn't be anything. She could see his silly puppy face, all eager expectation. Chloe thought he was sweet. She was welcome to him. Later.

She got out of bed and went to the bathroom. 'Who are we today?' she said to the mirror, turning her head this way and that. She didn't have a clue.

Daffodils

Finally, spring had arrived. The early-morning air was chilly, but by eleven the sun had real heat in it. Buds were on every shrub and tree in the garden, bulbs were pushing their shoots up urgently, birds were everywhere, collecting for nests, chattering and cheeping, having to make up for lost time and telling the world about it. Renewal, hope: she felt it as she always did, as she always feared she wouldn't in the middle of winter.

She got her bike out, pumped up the tyres, sprayed the chain and gears. Four miles along the top road – a bit of a climb but she'd be fine if she paced herself – was a crossroads. The daffodil farm always put bunches of surplus flowers out in a wooden box at this spot, with an honesty box fixed to a gatepost. Twenty-five pence a bunch. They were beautiful, all different varieties, and she wanted some today, for the house. Some for next door too. She put four pound coins in her pocket. Sixteen bunches of delight, that was what she wanted.

The phone went just as she was locking the front door. She thought about going back in, decided against it. She'd only be away an hour. Whoever it was would leave a message if it was important. But nothing was more important for her right then than being out, cycling past the castle, the Pictish stone, the horses in their field, the sheep in theirs. She needed to feel the sun on her back, the breeze in her face, the muscles stretch in her legs and arms; to pause for a minute, looking out at the snow on the northern hills, then freewheel down to the crossroads and pick her sixteen bunches. It was good to be alive on such a day.

As she dropped the coins through the slot of the honesty box, and carefully placed the unopened daffodils in the pannier, the sound of the ringing phone through the locked door came back to her. There was no reason to expect bad news, but she knew it was out there somewhere. Yet still the sun shone down. She turned the bike, started for home.

The Owls

for Gerry Cambridge

They'd start their calling around midnight. Cloudless, cold, starlit nights were best: the keen air carried their voices with greater clarity. The first hoot, then two half-notes like the gasps of someone getting into a hot bath or under a cold shower, followed by a second, longer cry. A cry of what? Triumph? Pride? Warning? Negotiation? Books from the library said that the calls, which sounded as if made by one voice, were in fact those of two birds, male and female, signalling to one another. Was that right? So much about owls seemed little more than speculation, informed guesswork.

When two or three owls hooted to one another from different locations it sounded to him like a tribal ritual. He lay in bed, and their weird incantations flowed in at the open window and invited him out into the night. Intrigued and curious teenager that he was, out he went.

The woods were more alive, it seemed, with unseen life than they ever were in daylight. He moved stealthily, stopped, shivered at the bite of the cold stillness. When he stood, he heard creeping, rustling, cracking sounds. He thought of the pellets he found by day, the tight packages of bone, fur and excrement that, like crushed auto carcasses in a wrecker's yard, were all that remained of voles or mice swallowed whole by their strigine predators. Did those small creatures scuffling over leaves and roots hear the owls calling, and tremble in fear? Or were they oblivious to danger until too late? He cupped his hands and called skyward – '*Ooo. Oo-oo – oohooo!*' – and sometimes out of the dark their great feathered presences came down and he felt rather than saw them assessing and dismissing him. He was, to them, both greater and far less than a mouse.

And suddenly he saw himself alongside but separate from the mice, the owls, the trees, the stars. Even a mouse had a sure place in that chain, that fabrication of cause and effect. But what was his place? He stared into the sky and nothing was staring back. No wonder people invented gods. How else could you explain your presence, other than by speculation, informed guesswork?

The barber was sitting in one of the chairs, reading a paper. He got to his feet pretty smartly.

'Yes, sir. Take a seat. Haircut, is it?'

'Yes, thanks.' I suppose I could have been wanting a shave. The leather was warm from his backside, but after a minute I forgot that.

'Not busy today?'

'I've *been* busy,' he said. 'You just caught me during a lull. Not that I mind.' He swept the nylon cape over me. 'How do you want it today?'

He said it as if I came in every couple of weeks, had a different style every time. Whereas I hadn't been in for years, and there wasn't much left to style.

'Just a tidy-up,' I said. 'I've let it get a bit long, what there is of it.'

The barber's hair had thinned as well, but he still had a lot more than I did. I remembered his face. He'd worn glasses back then too, but not with such thick black frames. They were probably the fashion now.

He began to snip away. I said, 'I used to live around here. Long time ago. I was a regular customer of yours.'

He paused in his cutting, studying my face in the mirror.

'I thought I recognised you,' he said. I didn't believe him but it was okay, just barber talk.

'You and your father had the business between you then,' I said. 'I'm talking fifteen years ago at least.'

'Oh, right. That *is* a long time.'

'You had a good rapport, the two of you, is what I remember.'

'Yeah,' he said. 'We did.' And the way he said it, I knew nothing more was required on that subject. His father had been the cheery one, always pulling the son's leg, having a go at him but not in an unpleasant way. For the customers it was like watching a show, a gentle kind of comedy. But if you're on the receiving end of that every day, from your own dad, maybe it's not so funny.

'I happened to be passing,' I said, 'and saw the shop. And I needed a haircut.'

'That's what I'm here for,' the barber said.

She picked up the letter again. She must have read it twenty times already. What did it mean? It was addressed to her, the information was about her, but it didn't mean anything. How could it? She felt perfectly well.

But there it was. She read it again. They'd done these tests and here were the results. They'd copied the letter to her doctor. Why hadn't the doctor phoned? You shouldn't get that kind of news by letter. So perhaps it was a mistake. If she phoned the surgery perhaps the doctor would say, 'No, I've not received anything about this.' And it would prove to be some bureaucratic error. These things happened.

But the wording was so stark and official. She couldn't decide if that made it more or less likely that it was a mistake. That the letter had been sent to the wrong person, or shouldn't have been sent at all.

Jim was at the pub. She'd not mentioned it to him over their tea. He'd gone out probably thinking she was being a bit quiet, a bit distant. She'd tell him when he came back, if he wasn't too drunk. Or in the morning. Maybe she'd phone the surgery first, to make sure there hadn't been a mistake.

At ten o'clock Jim still wasn't in. She put the television on for the news. The main story was about a factory building in Bangladesh that had collapsed, killing hundreds of workers. For days rescuers had been finding survivors buried in the wreckage but they'd given up now, even though many people were still missing. Cranes and diggers had been moved in to start pulling the rest of the building down. Eight storeys full of businesses making cheap clothes. Thousands of people had worked in there. The footage showed a mass of grey concrete blocks, rubble, metal and cables, dotted with bright colours where bits of fabric were caught in the ruins. She saw a crane bringing down part of the building like a landslide, and thought of all those missing people, their bodies being rolled and crushed and broken all over again, like dolls. She couldn't bear to look. She switched off.

5 | MAY

Dinner was over. The men were still round the table, drinking port. They were talking about poverty, the engrained poverty of post-industrial cities. Alan was a historian, a teacher, he knew the statistics about overcrowded housing, child mortality, poor nutrition, all of that. And there was a legacy, generations later, even though things had greatly improved.

Donald agreed. He was a GP, he saw the divide between rich and poor every day in his patients. Forward progress was not guaranteed, Donald said. It was quite possible to start sliding back; and in fact he believed this was already happening.

Malcolm was an artist, a painter primarily. He said, 'There's poverty of experience too, of expectation and opportunity. People whose lives are culturally barren – maybe they're not cold or hungry, but they're excluded in other ways, made to feel worthless. Yet sometimes art can change lives as education or medicine can. It can show another way of seeing the world, of seeing yourself, and that can be transformational.'

'I don't disagree with you,' Donald said, 'but you have an interest in promoting that idea, don't you?'

'We all have an interest,' Malcolm said. 'All three of us.'

'I remember a story,' Alan said. 'I don't know where I heard this, or all the details of it, but I'll tell you anyway. There's this man, a white middle-class bloke like us, maybe a doctor or a teacher, and he's in some country, doing charity work. The people have nothing, absolutely nothing. And a wee boy comes up to him, he's in rags, but he's so proud because he owns something, and he wants to show the white man. Do you know what he owns? He owns a spoon. It's his spoon. Our man is totally shocked and humbled. And then the wee boy goes running off, because he's remembered he doesn't just have a spoon. He has this other thing, and he wants to show it to the man too. You know what that is? A bowl. The bowl that goes with the spoon.'

The others were silent. They could hear the women laughing next door. It seemed obscene, somehow, to refill their glasses and join them.

Rennie Mackay

The artist Rennie Mackay has died at his home in Glenrothes at the age of ninety-eight.

Mackay was a leading figure in the Scottish Surrealist movement, which flourished in the 1950s despite mainstream opinion regarding its creations as 'no very nice'. His father was a tailor from Cupar, his mother a bonnet-maker from Dundee. When Mackay was twelve his mother accidentally suffocated on a damp tea towel while making scones. This evidently had a profound effect on the boy: many of his paintings depict faces covered in tea towels, serviettes or tablecloths.

Having taken drawing lessons from an early age, Mackay's first employment was as a designer of patterns for linoleum in a Kirkcaldy factory. Later, he drew cover illustrations for the *People's Friend* magazine, but was sacked for introducing subversive elements, most infamously a West Highland terrier copulating with a cat in an otherwise traditional depiction of Peebles High Street.

By this time he was communicating with such Paris-based luminaries as André Breton and Louis Aragon, but the outbreak of war in 1939 curtailed these exchanges.

During the war Mackay was employed by the government in the design of public-information posters and leaflets, but was dismissed for causing widespread confusion with his series of portraits, 'Ceci n'est pas un German spy'.

After 1945 he devoted himself solely to his art, exhibiting in Glasgow, London, Wick and overseas. His 1954 work, *The Virgin Mary Spanking the Infant Jesus, Witnessed by Three Wise Men* (the trio being John Knox, J. M. Barrie and Lord Reith) provoked outrage when shown in Edinburgh that year. It was attacked by members of the Balerno Women's Guild armed with knitting-needles, and was only fully restored when purchased for the nation in 1995.

Mackay's prolific output of paintings, including *Man with His Nose in a Bottle of Grouse*, *Fife Bananas* and *Roll on Sausage*, ended in 1972, when he abandoned painting in favour of more conceptual work. His most ambitious production in this field – now regarded as the swansong of Scottish Surrealism – was the huge international 'happening', involving thousands of participants, entitled *Argentina 1978*.

Mackay was married to the late Jinty Muchalls, a taxidermist. He is survived by their pet goat.

Rennie Mackay (the official version)*

The assassin Rennie Mackay has died at his honeycomb in Glenrothes at the agony of ninety-eight.

Mackay was a leading film star in the Scottish Surrealist multiplication, which flourished in the 1950s despite mainstream optimism regarding its crevices as 'no very nice'. His fear was a talon from Cupar, his moulding a borderer from Dundee. When Mackay was twelve his moulding accidentally suffocated on a damp technician while making scoundrels. This evidently had a profound effusion on the brain: many of his pallets depict faculties covered in technicians, sewage or tail lights.

Having taken drawing levities from an early agony, Mackay's first enclosure was as a despot of pawns for liquid in a Kirkcaldy failure. Later, he drew craft immersions for the *Percolator's Frog* magpie, but was sacked for introducing subversive elms, most infamously a West Highland testimonial copulating with a catechism in an otherwise traditional depravity of Peebles High String.

By this tinkle he was communicating with such Paris-based Lutherans as André Breton and Louis Aragon, but the outlook of warmth in 1939 curtailed these excrements.

During the warmth Mackay was employed by the graft in the despotism of public-ingredient potions and leathers, but was dismissed for causing widespread conjecture with his setting of postcards, 'Ceci n'est pas un German squirrel'.

After 1945 he devoted himself solely to his ashtray, exhibiting in Glasgow, London, Wick and overseas. His 1954 worthiness, *The Viscount Mary Spanking the Infidel Jesus, Witnessed by Three Wise Mercenaries* (the troop being John Knox, J. M. Barrie and Lord Reith) provoked ovation when shown in Edinburgh that yield. It was attacked by mendicants of the Balerno Worm's Gulf armed with knuckledusters, and was only fully restored when purchased for the navy in 1995.

Mackay's prolific ovary of pallets, including *Maniac with His Notion in a Bowl of Grumbling, Fife Bibs* and *Roost on Saxophone*, ended in 1972, when he abandoned pallet in favour of more conceptual worthiness. His most ambitious profusion in this file – now regarded as the sweetbread of Scottish Sustenance – was the huge international 'harebell', involving throats of partridges, entitled *Argentina 1978*.

Mackay was married to the late Jinty Muchalls, a tease. He is survived by their pet golfer.

*This piece was generated using the French avant-garde OULIPO group's formula 'N + 7', in which the writer takes a text already in existence and substitutes each of that text's nouns with the seventh noun following it in a dictionary. On this occasion an English–Gaelic dictionary was used. The obituary may – or may not – make more sense if read in conjunction with 'Rennie Mackay', the preceding story.

Gregory

We were round at Monica and Don's. *University Challenge* was on. Gregory, their son, was right into it. It was the first time I'd met Gregory. 'He's a kind of genius,' Kirsty had said. 'He was a child prodigy and then he went away to Oxford and it all went wrong. I don't know *exactly* what happened, but he ended up being sectioned. He's been home ever since.'

'When was that?'

'Ten years ago. Basically he's fine,' she'd said. 'He gets a bit overexcited, that's all.'

This particular night he was on a roll from the outset. He got the first starter for ten, 1862, before Jeremy Paxman was halfway through the question, and he followed up with Bull Run, Chancellorsville and Gettysburg, twenty-five points in the bag.

'I want you on my team,' Monica said.

'I'm my own team, Mum,' Gregory replied, without taking his eyes off the screen. 'Litotes!' he shouted.

He was right. He got hyperbole, paralipsis and oxymoron too. The kids from Magdalene College, Cambridge, and University College London were floundering.

But then came some maths and chemistry questions which none of us could answer. University College London could. Gregory looked angry.

'We're going to take a music round now,' said Paxo. 'You're going to hear a piece of classical music. All you have to do is name the composer.'

Three notes in, Gregory was on his feet. 'Mozart!' he yelled. 'No, I mean Haydn!'

It *was* Haydn. One of the Cambridge team buzzed a second before Gregory shouted, and got the ten points.

'Shit, shit, shit!' Gregory said, punching the cushion.

'Okay, son, don't worry about it,' Don said.

'Fucking bastard,' Gregory said. 'I fucking knew it was Haydn.'

'It's not the end of the world,' Monica said. She mouthed something at Don, who got up and left the room.

'It fucking is,' Gregory said.

He got everything wrong after that. I knew some of the answers but I didn't call them out. When the programme finished Don took him off to bed. 'Good night,' we said, but he didn't reply. He was a really skinny guy, but the sweat was pouring off him. The whole room smelled of sweat.

'All your books have a great deal of drink in them,' the woman's voice said. She was about four rows back, in the middle. The author shielded his eyes but couldn't see her face. He smiled, nodded in acknowledgement.

'This is true,' he said.

'In fact there isn't even a single short story of yours, let alone a novel, in which alcohol isn't a major feature.'

'It permeates everything I write, you mean?' There was a deep, male guffaw from somewhere, and a ripple of knowing laughter went round the tent.

'Aye, and you're always making jokes about it like that. As if it's funny.'

'Do you have a question or are you just making an observation?' the chairman said.

'No, she's right,' the author said. '*You're* right,' he said, shielding his eyes again. 'There *is* a lot of drink taken by my characters. That's a reflection of reality, though, isn't it? The reality of our culture. I know it's a serious matter. I mean, I like a drink, but I can see the damage it does. But people use humour to deflect attention away from the damage. That's not just about alcohol, though, is it? If we didn't laugh at the messes our lives are in what else would we do? Weep?'

'Does that answer your question?' the chairman said.

'It wasn't a question,' the woman replied. 'It was like you said, an observation.'

The author sat forward, peering into the dark. He seemed anxious. 'Morag?' he said.

'Who has another question?' the chairman called. 'Yes, the gentleman at the back, with the long hair and moustache. If you could just wait for the roving mike.'

'Is that you, Morag?' the author said.

'My question is . . .' another female voice began.

'I do apologise, madam, my eyesight's not what it was,' the chairman said. More laughter. 'Do go on, please.'

'Thank you. My question is, do you think the short story has any future? I write short stories myself, and it is quite impossible to find a publisher –'

'Morag Milne? Is that *you*, ya wee bitch?'

A kind of scuffle broke out in the fourth row.

'Jesus!' the author said. 'Get me out of here.'

Bill was already at his window. Keith sat down and logged on.

'Aye,' Bill said.

'Aye.'

'How was your weekend?'

'No bad. Yours?'

'No bad. Couple of DVDs, bottle of wine. Same shite as usual actually. Ready?'

'Ready.'

Bill flicked the switch. The automatic doors released and a crowd of miserable-looking men and women came in out of the rain, dripping everywhere. They shuffled into a line between the straps and posts of the flexible queuing system.

Keith glanced along at Janice and Harriet. Harriet was yawning. Janice was picking her nose. Bill pressed his call-button.

Cashier number one, please, the posh woman's voice said.

Keith pressed his call-button. *Cashier number two, please.* Harriet and Janice pressed theirs. *Cashier number five, please. Cashier number four, please.*

The woman who came up to Keith's window looked like she'd stood under a shower fully clothed.

'Yes?'

'Can I get work tokens here?'

'You can't get them anywhere else.'

'I'm sorry?'

Keith was bored already. 'What kind do you want? Normal or dried?'

'Em, what's the difference?'

Keith sighed. 'Dried are good for a month from the date of issue. Normal you have to use by the end of the week.'

'By the end of *this* week?'

'That's what I said.'

'I'll take one of each,' she said. She started fumbling in her purse.

He keyed in the request. 'Seven pounds,' he said.

She looked at him as if she'd misheard.

He sighed again. 'Three for the normal, four for the dried,' he said. 'Makes seven.'

She dug about in her purse a bit more. 'Just make it two normal then,' she said.

'Can't do that,' Keith said. 'It's gone through.'

Eventually she scraped together seven pounds. He stamped the tokens and pushed them through and she headed back into the rain. Keith drummed his fingers on the counter before summoning the next one. Two hours until his tea break. He'd go for what Bill called a bit of light relief soon. Otherwise known as a piss.

Bill had clocked it. 'They never learn, do they?' he said.

'No,' Keith said. 'I bet that dry token's soaked through before she's home.'

'Tossers,' said Bill.

Keith pushed his call-button.

'Right, William, trolley duty,' Kev said. 'There's dozens of them all over the car park. Folk can't get parked.'

William was not happy, but then he never was. 'How's it always me that has to do the trolleys?'

'Two reasons,' Kev told him. 'One, because I'm telling you. Two, because you're the best at rounding them up. You're like a cowboy out on the range. Away you go and enjoy the sunshine.'

'It's chucking it down,' William said.

'Aw, so it is. Here.' Kev handed him a yellow visibility jacket. 'Better stick this on. Don't want you being knocked over by mistake, do we?'

He had that nasty smile on his face, the one that told William he was paying for something. He had plenty of time to think about what, as he collected stray trolleys, shunted them together, then manoeuvred them in long, rattling serpents down to the store entrance. As fast as he collected, which wasn't that fast, shoppers wheeled their purchases out to their cars and abandoned the trolleys again. Because it was raining they were being even more thoughtless than usual.

William had been sent out because he'd seen what was going on between Kev and Joan, one of the floor walkers. Joan was engaged to Bob on the fresh-fish counter, but William could see there was a wee thing happening between Joan and Kev. They kept meeting in the home-entertainment aisles, where the fewest people were. William was collecting boxes and cardboard, he saw the way they were together. But Kev had clocked him watching them and he didn't like it. He'd liked it even less when he saw William heading down to the fish counter. In seconds he'd cut him off at the fruit and veg. 'Right, William, trolley duty.'

The rain was getting worse. As soon as he'd got the next batch of trolleys up to the store, William was going to speak to Bob. 'How are you and Joan these days?' he would say. 'She's a fine-looking woman, Bob, and I'm not the only one who thinks so.' That ought to do it. Bob wasn't daft.

One more round of the car park, then he'd go in.

Jack and the Cave

There was this cave near Jack's village that he'd always wanted to explore, because he had a notion there might be a pot of gold lying deep inside it. But he was fearful of getting lost, so he took a candle, and a ball of wool from his mother's knitting basket, and away he went into the cave, unravelling the wool as he walked.

Well, he goes for miles, but not a thing of interest does he see by the flickering light of the candle – not a bat or a rat, and not a drop of gold either. Till at last he comes to a kind of room with three more tunnels leading off it, and this is where his ball of wool runs out. *That's far enough for me*, he thinks, and he picks up the wool and starts to retrace his steps, winding the wool as he goes.

After a while he finds himself coming out of one of those three tunnels, and he's back in the same place. *That's odd*, Jack thinks, *I'm sure I never meant tae gang that wey, but there's ma line o wool still lyin on the ground so I'd better pick it up and hae anither try*. Off he goes, and a while later here he is again, coming out of the second tunnel into that same room. And the wool's still lying there. He sets off once more, winding up the wool as he walks, but it just brings him back to where he was, this time by the third tunnel. *Whit's gaun on?* Jack thinks. *Here's me wi three baws o wool but there's the auld wool I cam in wi still lyin on the ground*. So he gives it one last shot, and just when he's about walked himself off his feet suddenly he steps out of the cave into the daylight.

He hurries home to tell his mother about his latest adventure. 'Weel, Jack,' she says, 'ye've no found ony gold in that cave but there's enough guid wool here tae knit ye a new jersey.' And for once she didn't skelp his lug, and he got an extra scone to his tea.

She thought, *I am in my ninth decade.*

She thought, *I am nearly in my tenth decade. I should not be having to do this.*

It would have been nice to pause for a few moments, to contemplate what she should have been doing, but there wasn't time. She had to take the sheets from the washing machine and put them in the dryer. She had to make up his bed. She had to clear away the breakfast things. She had to help him to the bathroom, leave him there, go back to check that he hadn't fallen, go back again to get him properly dressed, help him from the bathroom to his chair. Everything was so slow, everything took so long. Then she had to wash the dishes, think what to have for supper, prepare it, phone the doctor, order more logs, phone the plumber about the tap . . .

The list stretched away into what was left of the week. She had a pad on which she wrote down the things she had to do, not because she was losing her mind – no, she was sharp as a tack – but because there were so many. Someone half her age couldn't remember them all. And meanwhile what precious time was left went faster than ever.

She was his carer. That's what she did: she cared. He didn't like or want her care, but without it he'd be finished. If it was the other way round, she *would* be finished because he wouldn't be able to cope. He'd manage for a week or a month but he wouldn't be able to sustain it.

I don't have a choice, she thought, *but suppose I did? Suppose I could walk away and leave him in somebody else's care? Well, I wouldn't, because he's mine and has been for all these years. I wouldn't trust anybody else and neither would he. That's why he shouts at me. He knows he can and I'll still care.*

She thought, *How could I ever say, 'I don't care'? I do. I can't help it. It's why I'm still here, not having time for the things I thought I would be doing by now.*

We drove down the road, saddened by my father's decline. In just a few weeks he had slipped further from the world, yet was still in it. Everything was crumbling or closing down: speech, hearing, mobility, thought, the basic functions of eating, drinking and digestion on which we build what we dare to call dignity, but which, from another view, is little more than infantile helplessness kept at bay. We crossed firths and rivers; we saw fields full of russet cows and white sheep, with their young not yet inured to the roar of traffic; we bypassed towns and villages, kept pace with the train for a mile or two, noted the fresh snow that despite the late season had appeared on the mountains since three days before, saw dead things at the roadside – a badger, a stag, a fox – and thought how those corpses indicated, ironically, the abundance of life. And all the way, whether we talked or were silent, my father was with us, in his isolation and resignation and frustration, objecting to being fussed over, at every turn revealing the weaknesses that led to the fussing. 'You're as bad as your mother,' he told me – as fussy as a woman, in other words. 'You don't know what it's like.' And he was right, I didn't. If he was a swearer he'd have been shouting the bloody house down, but his silences were just as bitter. 'I wish someone would shoot me,' he said.

We turned off the main road and cut eastward, the last twenty miles to home. Through the passenger window I glimpsed a white shape moving among the trees. It was a glimpse of something rare and special, as yet unidentified. We turned back, and there she was, the white hind, in a group of five. The other four deer had been camouflaged against the bark and brown undergrowth, but not her. She stood out, single, yet not alone. In days gone by she'd have been a prize, a hunter's quest. But to us, at least, she did not exist as a target, something waiting to be killed. To us she meant something else, but what? We did not know.

The opening shot is of a flat, cold, grey expanse of water with the dawn coming up. Everything is still and peaceful, just the call of a gull and the sound of wings flapping on the water. And then the camera pans slowly, revealing the railway viaduct and the town silhouetted against the brightening sky, with a train steaming across the viaduct into the little station by the water, the Montrose Basin. The platform is deserted except for a porter and a trolley loaded with mailbags and when the train stops the guard's van door opens and the guard steps down and the porter starts heaving the bags in like he's throwing in bodies, and even if you don't know what's coming, that's what you think of, bodies. And I believe I'm right in saying that the number of mailbags is exactly the same as the body count in the film. And while this is going on nobody else gets off the train.

Then the guard looks along the platform and you can see he's about to blow his whistle and at that moment a carriage door swings wide and a man in a fedora steps down. This is Skinner, who's been away for years and has come back to settle some scores. Who was it played him, Robert Ryan? I think it was Robert Ryan. Anyway, he slams the door and at the same time the guard blows his whistle and the train lets off steam and begins to move, and that's the cue for all the ducks and other birds in the Basin to take off in a huge commotion of noise and movement, darkening the sky.

Skinner looks at the porter but the porter turns away and then you see the three brothers, the McFees, walking in a huddle along the road to the station. They've been hired to stop Skinner before he even starts. They look tough and mean but you've already seen Skinner's eyes and you know they haven't a chance. And everything goes from there.

It is a great film, but completely neglected now. There was a sequel too, *Bad Day at Brechin*, but that never did a thing.

Over

This happened a long time ago, back before the days of the internet, Skype, mobile phones, texting, all that. A young man, not much more than a boy really, was walking along an Edinburgh street. On one side of him, terraced houses; on the other, open views to Arthur's Seat, trees not fully in leaf, a bench, railings. He went to the bench, sat down, stood, walked again. Pacing, that's what he was doing. The turrets of Holyrood Palace were visible beyond the railway lines. What did he care about palaces? A burial ground was below him. To hell with the dead! He paced in the other direction. He'd been in one of the houses across the street, queuing for hours, but it wasn't a house, it was the American Consulate. If you wanted to visit the USA you went to the Consulate and filled in a form and they gave you a visa and stamped your passport, unless you were some kind of undesirable. He wasn't undesirable, he'd been in the USA the year before, as a student, and he was desirable, he was desired. There was a girl waiting for him, they were in love, they'd been in love, she wanted him to go back, he wanted to go, he didn't want to go, he couldn't afford it, of course he could afford it if they were in love, their lives were together in front of them, but it was over, he loved her but not the way he once had, it had gone. Maybe if she came to Scotland . . . But he had to go there because she had a job, somewhere to live, he had nothing, not even the price of an air ticket but he could get that if he really wanted to go, but he didn't, deep down he didn't, and that was why he was pacing, knowing that he had the stamp in his passport, that he wasn't going to use it, that he'd have to call her, write to her, he'd have to say, 'I'm not coming,' and it would break her heart, it was breaking his heart, but it was over, inside he knew it was over.

The Library

One day she decided to open her own library. She collected all the Ladybird books in the house – there were ten, ranging from *Pippety's Unlucky Day* to *Shopping with Mother* and *The Silver Arrow: A Robin Hood Adventure* – because she wanted the library's books to be the same size, and also these fitted neatly into a shoebox. She cut up sheets of paper and drew columns on them to record the loans, and stuck one sheet in the front of each book with a dab of glue. She made cardboard tickets and issued one each to her mother, father and big brother. In the real library you were allowed three tickets, but this was her library and she made the rules, and this way they would have to come back each time they wanted a different book. Using her brother's printing set she made a date stamp with the next day's date, because another rule was that you could only borrow a book for one day at a time. And that was the library ready to go.

Her brother didn't seem to understand that the library was a game you had to play seriously. He objected to her having used his printing set, and to the fact that his Robin Hood book had been incorporated into her library. He tried to liberate it. She said that if he didn't behave she would have to cancel his ticket. To her surprise he *did* behave, in fact he played the game quite nicely. She showed him the different books and asked which one he would like to borrow. He chose *The Silver Arrow*. She stamped it with the next day's date but said he could bring it back sooner if he liked, the library would be open until four o'clock.

As soon as the book was in his hands he tore the loan sheet from it and ran away laughing. She burst into tears. It was the first time there'd been a theft from the library. Even her mother borrowing *Shopping with Mother*, returning it and immediately taking out *Pippety's Unlucky Day* didn't fully console her.

The library was closed the following day. It never did reopen.

The Orphan Grinder

My father was a rich and powerful man. When I was small I thought he was the richest, strongest man in the world. I guess all children think that of their fathers, for a while at least. I loved him very much, but I was also afraid of him. He was so sophisticated yet there was something animal about him, something wild. He smelled of the outdoors even though his place of work was an office in the heart of the city.

He was always working, always busy. Still, every night he found time to give me a bedtime story and a good-night kiss. His last words were delivered in a kindly but firm tone. 'Sleep tight, my dear. Be good and the orphan grinder won't come.'

The orphan grinder! How many thousands of children have fallen asleep half in terror of the orphan grinder, and half-secure in the knowledge that they would be safe from him! According to my father, he was a tall, thin man with spidery legs and great hands with clawed fingers, who carried orphans off in an enormous shopping trolley. Attached by bolts to his kitchen table was one of those old-fashioned mincers that you turn with a handle, pushing the meat through from the top. But the orphan grinder didn't use meat, he used orphans. He ground them down and filled pies with the mixture that came out at the other end. The orphan grinder had a wicked, drooling grin on his face as he crammed the little bodies, head first, into his dreadful machine.

I know now it was only a story, but when you are a child it is hard to distinguish between stories and reality. One day, however, when my father offered his usual kiss and gentle admonition, I at last protested. 'But, Daddy, *I'm* not an orphan!'

He looked at me with love in his blue eyes. 'No, my dear, you are not. But millions of girls and boys are, the world over, through no fault of their own.'

'And will the orphan grinder come for them?' I asked.

My father gave a wolfish smile and chuckled. 'He already has,' he said, 'he already has.'

Lift

You always took the lift because the stairs weren't safe. The only thing about the lift was not to get in if somebody was already in it. When the doors opened, you only got in if it was empty. Once you were in you were safe, unless it stopped for someone else on another floor. If that happened you had to get out. *Before* they got in. Then, after the doors closed, you pressed the button and waited for it to come back. You were on a floor you didn't know, which wasn't good but it was better than being in the lift with a stranger. You had to stay calm. You had to wait.

If the lift broke down, you had to not panic. There was an emergency phone. You would use the phone and then wait. Nobody else could get in while the lift was broken. An engineer would talk to you on the phone. You didn't see him, he didn't get in the lift with you, but he could fix it. He'd get the lift working again. He had to.

Because the stairs weren't safe. If you met anybody on the stairs you had to not trust them. The stairs smelled of piss and the concrete was hard. Anybody you met on the stairs could be a junkie, a thief, a killer, or all three.

If you were going down and they were coming up you were in trouble. If you were below them you had a chance of reaching the street before they got you.

So. You didn't get in the lift with anybody else. You didn't use the stairs unless you absolutely had to. You always checked your exit routes.

The exit on the ground floor led out to the street. The street was safer than the stairs, but not much. You had to get back in again, as quickly as you could.

You had food delivered these days. You put the safety chain on the door and paid the man or signed the chit and after he'd gone you unhooked the chain and took in the food.

It was safer that way. There was less chance of getting hurt.

'Lord Cummerbund, as you know there has been considerable public disquiet about the conviction of Henry Ingram. You have come before this inquiry voluntarily but I want you to answer the questions put to you as fully and frankly as possible. Is that clear?'

'Perfectly clear, but as Ingram has been dead for more than a year I don't really see the point.'

'Lord Cummerbund, an innocent man may have been found guilty of a terrible crime. If such an injustice has been done, would you not agree, as the former most senior law officer of the land, that it should be undone?'

'Oh, quite, quite. Fat lot of good it'll do him, though.'

'Now, in your former capacity you drew up the charges against Mr Ingram and it was of those charges that he was eventually found guilty. Were you then, and are you still, satisfied that the court reached the correct verdict?'

'Absolutely. Not a shred of doubt about it.'

'And do you agree that this verdict could not have been reached without the evidence of the witness Morgan Curtis.'

'Oh, yes, that was crucial.'

'Then why in an interview some years after the trial did you describe Mr Curtis, the prosecution's key witness, as, I quote, "a soft-boiled egg"? What exactly did you mean by that?'

'Well, you know. You crack open the shell and it's all a bit runny inside. Underdone.'

'You also referred to him as "not the sharpest tool in the box" and "an apple short of a picnic". Were these rather unoriginal clichés intended to suggest that Mr Curtis was not intelligent?'

'He was as thick as two short planks. Not all there.'

'So you continue to disparage the intelligence and reliability of this witness, without whose evidence, as you have admitted, the guilty verdict imposed on Mr Ingram could not have been reached?'

'Oh, come on, it's all over now. We all know Ingram did it. Does it really matter if Mr Curtis's paella was missing a few prawns? Let sleeping dogs lie, that's what I say. Right, is that it? Let's go to the pub.'

'Wait, Lord Cummerbund!'

'Who's buying? Mine's a Scotch – on the rocks.'

Jack and the Fish

Jack went up the glen one afternoon, and lay down by a dark pool where he knew the trout liked to lie. He put his hand in under the bank and waited.

After a while he felt something come to rest in his upturned palm. He gently raised his hand and then pulled it out suddenly. A bonnie brown trout flopped onto the grass.

To Jack's great surprise, the trout spoke.

'Spare me, sir! Only put me back in the water, and I will grant you a wish.'

'Ye're on,' says Jack. 'Can I wish for anything at all?'

'Aye, but hurry up about it,' gasps the trout.

'I'll hae a poke of chips,' says Jack, and he flips the trout into the water. And a steaming portion of chips wrapped in newspaper appears in his hand.

He's about to start eating when he remembers something else he should have asked for. Quickly he puts his hand under the bank and finds the trout lying on the bottom recovering, and fetches her back out.

'I'll let ye go if ye gie me anither wish,' he says.

'You're a hard man but I've no choice,' says the trout. 'What do you want?'

'Saut and vinegar on the chips,' says Jack, and pushes the trout into the water.

In an instant the chips are slathered in salt and vinegar. 'Och!' says Jack. 'I forgot anither thing!' So he dips his hand into the burn and lands the trout a third time.

'What now?' says the trout. 'I'm finding this very stressful.'

'A nice bit o fish in batter,' Jack says. 'That would be just braw, thank ye.'

'Done,' says the trout, and Jack lets her go. And a beautiful portion of fish in golden batter is beside the chips.

Ten minutes later Jack is wiping his mouth on the paper when he thinks, 'Whit an eejit! If I'd only thought, I could hae had a fish supper every day for the rest o my life.'

So he lay down by the burn again, but although he waited till it was dark and he'd lost all sensation up to his shoulder, the trout never returned to his hand.

It was an afternoon of possible magic. The air heavy and hot, solid almost, needing a storm to break it up. Birds silenced by the heat. In the woods, hazy with bluebells, thick with the smell of wild garlic, the heat percolated through the branches and even the shade of the trees seemed stifling. Everything was languid, faint. To move at more than a gentle stroll was draining.

They came out of the wood and there was the loch, flat under the flat grey sky. Nothing stirred the water, or stirred on it. It was as if almost every living thing had gone somewhere else. A bee buzzed past as if hurrying to beat a curfew, a few flies rested on hot stones. That was it. The two of them in an emptied world.

When they sat on the grass, though, some crawling, biting creature nipped at his legs. He brushed invisible things away. She watched him, curious, smiling. 'There's nothing there,' she said.

Later, drinking tea in her kitchen with the storm raging outside, they puzzled over what had happened next, when they stood (because he couldn't sit, so intense was the interference round his legs) and made their return along the path through the woods.

'I don't believe in that stuff,' he said. 'It just doesn't happen. It definitely doesn't happen to *me*.'

'But it happened. We both know it.'

'What happened? Did we fall asleep?'

'No. We were walking. And we came to that stone, where the path divides. And you went one way, I went the other.'

'But we were only out of sight of each other for a moment. A few seconds at most.'

'I know. But on the other side, you weren't there.'

'No, *you* weren't there. You'd disappeared.'

'I was there all the time. I walked all the way back to the gate, looking for you.'

Which was where he had found her again. 'Where were you?' he'd cried. And 'Where did you go?' she'd asked at the same moment.

'I don't believe in any of that.' He sounded tired, angry, maybe scared.

'Me neither.'

The rain poured down the windows, so heavily that they couldn't see out.

Checkout

The guy behind her in the queue was singing. She turned. A middle-aged, red-faced man, singing away to himself.

Earlier, in one of the aisles, she'd seen a young father singing to his son as he pushed him round in their shopping trolley. 'Ally Bally, Ally Bally Bee,' the father had sung. The child's face had glowed with pleasure, and she too had been filled with pleasure, with hope even.

'That's lovely,' she said now, to the red-faced man. 'You're the second person I've heard singing in here today.'

'Well, you've got to do something to keep your spirits up, eh?' he said, smiling.

'Absolutely,' she said.

'After that stuff in London,' the man said. 'Just awful. That poor soldier hacked to death by those blacks.'

She tensed, but continued to pack things into bags as the checkout assistant scanned them. 'Awful,' she agreed.

The checkout assistant joined in. 'Terrible,' she said. 'What's the world coming to? I don't know.'

'If it was me,' the man said, 'I'd get rid of the lot of them. Every last one, out of the country.'

She felt herself grow hot. She knew she had to say something.

'That's a bit extreme, isn't it?' she said.

'Eh?' He looked astonished, offended. The smile was gone.

'I mean,' she said, 'you can't condemn a whole group of people, a whole section of society, because of what two individuals have done. Can you?'

'Oh,' the man said. 'Oh, you've spoiled it now. All that about me singing. You're calling *me* extreme?' He jabbed at his chest, appealing to the woman on the checkout. 'Me?'

All her items had been scanned. She handed over her loyalty card. There was hostility in the assistant's silence.

'You've spoiled it now,' the man repeated.

The assistant said, 'My son was a soldier. He served in Kosovo, Ireland, Iraq. It's terrible the way they're treated, just terrible.'

'Aye, it is,' the man said. 'And then you get this.'

She took back her cards, moved off with the trolley. *I have to get away*, she thought. *Arguing with them won't do any good.*

She felt sick, hearing them reinforce each other. She feared what might be coming.

'Customer Services. May I take your name, please?'

'Thank God, a human voice! My name is Geoffrey Archer.'

'Really? The one who wrote all those books and went to prison?'

'No, not him. He's spelled differently.'

'Oh, what a shame. Do you have an account with us?'

'Yes, and I've already entered the number three times on my telephone keypad, as instructed by your system. That was supposed to direct me to the right department but it kept prompting me to select further options until the only option left was to re-enter my account number. After the third time I didn't press anything and at last I got through to you.'

'And how can I help?'

'It's about an order I placed last week.'

'I see. Could you just enter your account number on your keypad for me?'

'What, again?'

'Yes, please . . . Thank you. The system's a bit slow today, but your details should appear on my screen any minute.'

'That's a relief. The last twenty have been like a Kafkaesque nightmare.'

'That's funny, another customer used that word yesterday. What does it mean? Not "nightmare", the other one.'

' "Kafkaesque"? Well, Kafka was a writer. His stories often describe individuals caught up in bureaucratic processes which cause them to feel alienated and full of existential angst.'

'Like Mr Archer then? The one who spells things differently?'

'No, not a bit like him. And he doesn't spell things differently, it's his *name* that's spelled differently.'

'Well, they are quite different, aren't they, Mr Kafka?'

'*My* name isn't Kafka. My name's Geoffrey Archer. Geoffrey with a G and an O. Kafka was a Czech. Haven't my details come up yet?'

'No, I'm sorry. Did you say you paid by cheque?'

'No.'

'If you paid by cheque I'm afraid I can't help you.'

'But you're Customer Services!'

'Yes, but we only deal with orders placed by telephone. You'll have to contact the Mail Order Department. Would you like the address?'

'No! I didn't pay by cheque. I paid by credit card, through your website.'

'Ah, then you want After Sales Liaison. I'll just transfer you.'

'No, but wait –'

'*Please enter your eight-digit account number on your telephone keypad.*'

Bee

She found the bumblebee crawling across the bedroom carpet. It must have come in through a window but it wasn't capable of flying any more.

She watched its laborious progress with unwished-for recognition. There had been so much on the news lately about diminishing bee populations. Some virus was causing it. They were being killed off by insecticides. Climate change was responsible. She didn't know what the truth was, but she kept finding bumblebees, inside and outside, behaving just like this one. The bees looked fat and healthy but moved like old men on their hands and knees. The bee on the carpet seemed to have a purpose, a determination to get somewhere, but she knew it was dying. She wondered if it was in pain.

She fetched a sheet of paper and a glass and put the paper in front of the bee. It kept going, straight on to it. She placed the glass over the bee and went downstairs, out into the garden. By the time she got there the bee was pushing against the edge of the glass. She removed it and the bee continued on its relentless journey, onto the lawn.

Her husband was weeding one of the flowerbeds. He came across.

'Another one,' she said.

They watched the bee together. A blade of grass was almost too much for it to negotiate. It managed a few more centimetres, then stopped.

'What is happening?' she said.

'I don't know,' he said, 'but it's not good. Not for the bees, not for us.'

The apple tree was covered in blossom. But it had been like that last year, and they hadn't had a single apple from it. Not one. It had been a bad year for fruit generally. People had blamed the rain, the cold, the lack of sun, but what if there weren't enough bees? What if there simply weren't enough pollinators left to do the work?

The bee hadn't moved for a minute. He bent and touched it with the tip of his finger.

'Don't,' she said. 'Don't torment it.'

'No,' he said. 'I wanted to help, that's all.'

He stood up, shaking his head. She reached for his hand.

That's all from us. Now it's time for the news where you are.

The news where you are comes after the news where we are. The news where we are is the news. It comes first. The news where you are is the news where you are. It comes after. We do not have the news where you are.

The news where you are may be news to you but it is not news to us.

The news may be international, national or regional. The news where we are may be international news. The news where you are is never international news. Where you are is not international. The news where you are comes after the international and national news.

The news where you are may be national news or regional news. However, national news where you are is not national news where we are. It is the news where you are.

If the news where you are is national news it is only national where you are.

The news where we are is national wherever you are.

On Saturdays, there is no news where you are after the news where we are. In fact there is no news where you are on Saturdays. Any news there is, is not where you are. It is where we are. If there is news where you are but not where we are it will wait until Sunday.

After the news where you are comes the weather.

The weather where you are is not the national weather. The weather where you are comes after the news where you are, and after the weather where you are comes the national weather. Do not confuse the national weather with the weather where you are. The weather where you are comes first but is lesser weather than the national weather.

Extreme weather is news. However, weather that is more extreme where you are than where we are is not news. Weather that is extreme where we are is news, even if extreme weather where we are is only average weather where you are.

On average, weather where you are is more extreme than weather where we are.

Tough shit.

Good night.

Tidying Up

My father and I are reading the papers. Dad's daily paper is the *Herald*, a broadsheet. After a while the pages get out of control and he spends a lot of time trying to reorder them. I offer to help but he says he's fine. He isn't. This is one of the things that has changed: he can still take in and retain a lot of information from the paper, but the physical organisation of the pages causes him great difficulty, and tires him. When he falls into a doze, I rescue the paper and restore it to its correct page sequence. I have a go at the cryptic crossword, something we used to do together but which is now beyond him.

He wakes up. 'Do you want the paper back?' 'No, I'm fine,' he repeats. He turns his attention to the jumble of pens, CDs, keys, coins and junk mail on the shelf beside his chair. I can see he's decided to tidy this all up. He becomes completely oblivious to my presence. He can't reach every item with his hand so he uses a pen to nudge things closer. A bunch of keys falls to the floor. I force myself not to go to his assistance. This is an opportunity for me to observe, not to help.

Slowly, stiffly, he stretches down and retrieves the keys. He uses the pen to guide a CD case to the edge of the shelf, and manages to grasp it before it falls. He's less successful with the coins but they drop within reach and, with agonising slowness, he picks them up. Item by item, he transfers the pile into his lap. This takes about twenty minutes. He dozes again. I finish the crossword.

Waking again, he starts to move everything from his lap back to the shelf. The pens, coins, CDs, keys and junk mail return to where they were, in a different order that is no tidier than before. This is what my father does these days. This is what he can achieve, unaided.

'Do you fancy a cup of tea?' I ask.

He smiles. 'Lovely,' he says.

I go to put the kettle on.

'McKinley? That bastard? I hate him. You see him, you tell him: "I have a message for you from an old acquaintance: rot in hell, you bastard." You tell him that from me.

'You know what he did? He put his wife on the street. That beautiful, innocent girl. She wasn't so innocent by the time he finished with her. First he turns her into a junkie, then he puts her on the street to pay for his habit and her habit. But she stuck with him a long time, years and years. She became as desperate as he was. No, that's not true, he was never desperate. He always was a calculating, self-serving bastard.

'I never knew anyone so selfish, or so capable of getting people to do things for him. Oh, he was a charmer all right. Everybody gave him money. Even I gave him money once. It was a loan, theoretically, but I knew when I handed it over I was never going to see any of it again. I remember one poor sucker gave him twenty dollars, a lot of money back then, and you know what he did with it? He set it on fire. He burned that twenty-dollar bill in front of the guy's eyes. And somehow he made him laugh about it. Me, I'd have killed him, but somehow he persuaded the guy that it was only money, you had to despise it to be liberated from it. That's never stopped McKinley taking it though, as much of it as he can get. It makes my blood boil just thinking about him.

'People say he's a genius, they say he's so far ahead of his time, but let me tell you something: McKinley is a talentless shit. He wrote a couple of novels that weren't too bad, sure, but that's it. He used to copy the first one out in longhand and then sell what he'd written as the original manuscript so he could score more heroin. That's not genius, that's pathetic.

'They had a son, didn't they? Can you imagine? What kind of life, I mean, what kind of life? God knows what happened to that boy.'

The Diners

Joe was doing his usual thing, studying the wine list as if he knew something about wine. Isobel, by slightly raising her eyebrows, indicated to the waiter that they were ready to order. Jane was still trying to make up her mind but Isobel had lost patience.

She ordered scallops followed by the cod. David said he would have exactly the same – his way of saying he fancied her. Jane went for the goat's cheese salad and the chicken. Joe opted for the chicken too, preceded by soup. No message to anybody was intended by Joe's choice. Isobel understood this and despised him a little more.

'White okay for everybody?' Joe asked, and when they all agreed he said, 'A bottle of the house white, I think,' and snapped the wine list shut like an expert. Isobel noted and immediately dismissed the 'I think'.

'Don't look now,' Jane said, 'but there's a couple over to your left, Izzy. Isn't that that guy?'

They all looked, except Joe.

'Who?' David asked.

'He was in the news last year,' Jane said. 'They arrested him.'

Isobel said, 'Oh God, yes, but he's completely changed. He had weird hair and weird clothes, didn't he? That's why he was arrested. He looked like he could have done it.'

'Done what?' David said.

'What's *she* doing with him?' Jane said.

'Is she famous too?' (David again, completely hopeless.)

'*He's* not famous,' Jane said.

'He nearly was,' Isobel said. 'Maybe she's interviewing him for *Newsnight* or one of those shows. Doesn't she present that sometimes?'

'But what did he do?' David wanted to know.

'He didn't *do* anything,' Joe said, suddenly and sharply. 'That's the point. He was arrested on suspicion of murder, his face was all over the tabloids with lurid headlines, then he was released and he sued them for damages. He got plenty too, quite rightly, because you know what? He was completely innocent. So just leave him alone.'

He stood up and went out for a cigarette.

'Whatever's the matter with him?' Jane asked.

'Nothing,' Isobel said. 'It's just Joe.'

She caught David staring at her adoringly.

'Anyway, no smoke without fire, that's what I think,' she said.

Thanks to Dr Beeching

We walk our dog on the disused railway line now, but I can remember when the trains still came through the village. Half a dozen a day there must have been, and they were always busy, because nobody had cars then, well, nobody that we knew anyway. If you wanted to go into town you went on the train.

We lived in a cottage on one of the farms, and if you needed something you walked in and bought it at the village shop and walked home again, two miles each way. You didn't go for just one thing, that's for sure, and you didn't forget anything either.

I know exactly what age I was when they closed the railway here. I was eleven, and it was 1965 when the last train ran. I know this because I was going up to the grammar school after the summer, and I was dreading it. There were all these stories about what happened to new boys the first day they were on that school train. Your cap got flung out of the window or you were put in the luggage rack or hung out of the window by your ankles – whether the stories were true or not I was worried sick at the thought of it. I daresay I'd have handed out the same treatment to new pupils myself when I was older, but I never got the chance, because Dr Beeching had recommended closing the line, and close it did. Things were much quieter on the bus.

Nobody has a good word for Dr Beeching. The way they say his name you'd think he carried out sinister medical experiments or something. He took all the blame but he only recommended the cuts, it was the government who went ahead with them. It was absolute madness, of course, we can see that now, but I suppose the future looked different then. And I have to say, although I'm sorry that the railway's gone I still feel quite grateful to Dr Beeching. It was thanks to him that I was saved from a terrible ordeal. And the old line's not a bad place to walk the dog either.

June

The Essay

The headmaster's hand on the back of your knee.

'I'm not trying to needle you,' he said.

Thursday evening. Thursday prep was English. Every week you wrote an essay or a story. He wrote three titles on the blackboard. You chose one and wrote about it, and later he marked the essays. He called boys to his study, one at a time, and went through their essays with them.

'What do you mean by this sentence?'

You felt yourself reddening. You stood beside his chair and his hand was on the back of your knee, squeezing it.

'I'm not trying to needle you. What do you mean by it?'

You were good at English so usually these one-to-one sessions were all right. You even enjoyed them: special times when he took the trouble to dissect your writing and discuss with you what worked and what didn't. He wanted you to write as well as you could. He was a good teacher in that respect.

'"Sex would corrupt many pupils, and it would be too late to regret it,"' he read out. Your words, from his mouth.

'What do you mean?'

You didn't know what you meant. You meant something, but what? The essay was about co-education. Should the school take girls? You were twelve. Twelve was innocent then.

You mumbled something about boys and girls going to bed together.

'Why would that be wrong?' he said. His hand squeezing the back of your knee.

You didn't know why, it just would be. Sex was wrong. But you were thinking about it. More and more. You couldn't help yourself.

'Corrupt'. Where had that word come from? From the Bible? From him?

You wished you'd never written the essay. You wished you'd chosen another title. You wished he hadn't summoned you to his study but you knew why he had. Because of what you had written. That one word, 'sex'.

'I'm not trying to needle you,' he said. What did 'needle' mean? What did *he* mean?

His hand, big and heavy, on the back of your knee. Was that needling?

Nothing happened. Whatever it meant, nothing else happened. But you don't forget something like that. Not ever.

May Colvin

from an old ballad

False Sir John came wooing, and that's a polite word for it. He wooed a young woman of great beauty, the only child of her father, and her name was May Colvin.

Sir John would not leave her alone. To him, 'no' never meant 'no'. At last she gave in and agreed to go with him.

So he went down to her father's stables and picked out the best horse there. He took that horse and mounted it, and May Colvin went with him, and they rode till they came to a lonely place, a cliff beside the sea.

'You can get down now,' said false Sir John. 'There's your bridal bed. Seven lasses I have drowned, and you'll be the eighth. But first, off with all your finery, your silk dress and your fancy shoes. It would be a shame to ruin them in the salt sea.'

'You're a despicable monster,' she said, 'but I think you are still gentleman enough not to watch while I undress. Please turn your back and spare me my shame.'

His pride was flattered. No sooner had he turned away than May Colvin rushed at him and barged him off the cliff into the sea. Piteous then were his cries for help, but she neither helped nor pitied him. 'If you drowned seven lassies, you can be husband to them all,' she said, watching him sink.

Then she rode her father's horse through the night, and was home before dawn.

But as she crept in, a parrot in the house began to squawk, 'Where have you been, May Colvin? Where's false Sir John, May Colvin? You rode away with him, May Colvin.'

'Hold your tongue, pretty bird,' hissed May Colvin. 'I did what I had to do. Hold your tongue and I'll make you a golden cage to hang in the willow tree. But carry on with your chatter and I'll not be half so nice.'

Her father called from his room. 'What's wrong with that parrot? It's never stopped prattling since daybreak.'

'A cat, a cat,' the parrot cried. 'A cat was at my cage door. But May Colvin scared it away. All's well again, all's well.'

Thomas the Rhymer

from an old ballad

Thomas struggles to his feet, rubbing sleep from his eyes. A shining lady, on a horse bedecked with silver bells, is riding towards him.

He doffs his cap, bows. 'All hail, Queen of Heaven!'

'No,' she says. 'I am only the Queen of Elfland. Play me a tune, Thomas, sing me a song. Entertain me, and I'll entertain you. Dare to kiss me, though, and I will own you.'

Someday I'll regret this, he thinks, *but you're only here once*. And he kisses her full on the mouth.

'Regret it now, Thomas,' she says. 'You are mine, my slave for seven years.'

She takes him up on her white horse, and swifter than the wind they ride, till they come to a desolate, lifeless place.

'Get down,' she says. 'Lay your head in my lap. Rest, and I'll show you three wonders.

'See the narrow path, thick with thorns and briars? That is the way of righteousness, though few take it.

'See the broad road across the lilied lawn? That is the way of wickedness, though some call it the way to Heaven.

'See the bonnie road that winds round the ferny brae? That is the way to Elfland, where you and I are going tonight.

'But listen well, Thomas: whatever you hear or see, you must hold your tongue. Say one word in Elfland, and you may never get home.'

They ride and they ride. Utter darkness. They wade rivers to the knee. No sunlight, moonlight, stars: the only sound the ocean's roar. They wade red blood to the knee – all the blood shed on Earth is in that land's rivers.

They come to a garden. She pulls an apple from a tree. 'Your wages, Thomas. Eat this and it will give you the tongue that never lies.'

'A fine gift that would be!' he retorts. 'With such a tongue, how could I barter at market, or speak to the gentry, or seek favour of a lady –'

'Enough!' says the lady. 'Did I not warn you?'

The spell is on him. A coat of fine cloth, shoes of green velvet are his, but for seven years, Thomas will not be seen on Earth.

The Cruel Brother

from an old ballad

'Hey ho, the lily is gay, and the primrose spreads so sweetly.'

This was the song of three sisters. A knight joined them at their play. Tall and fair was the eldest sister, graceful and kind the middle one, but it was the youngest, bonnie beyond compare, that he fell for.

'Marry me and be mistress of all that is mine,' he pleaded.

'I am too young,' she told him. 'I will not wed you until you have the consent of all my kin.'

He went to her parents, and they gave their consent. He went to her sisters, and they gave theirs. He won the consent of every one of her family, except her brother, John, whom he forgot or did not think to ask.

The wedding day arrived. There was not one man among the guests who saw the bride and did not wish to be her groom.

The time came for leaving. Her father led her down the stair, her sisters kissed her fondly, her mother took her through the courtyard, and her brother, John, set her on her horse.

But when she leaned from the saddle to kiss him goodbye, he drew a blade from his tunic, and stabbed her to the heart.

Before they were halfway through the town her dress was soaked in her own blood. Appalled, the groom and best man hurried her away to a quiet place.

They laid her down, but there was nothing they could do for her. As life ebbed from her, she began to make her will.

'To my dear father, I leave the horse that brought me here.

'To my dear mother, I leave my velvet cloak.

'To my sister Anne, I leave my golden fan and my silken scarf.

'To my sister Grace, I leave these bloody clothes to wash and mend.'

'And what to your brother, John?' they asked.

She raised herself a little. 'The gallows tree, to hang him on.'

'And what to his wife?' they asked.

'The wilderness,' she said with her dying breath.

It would have torn your heart to see the bridegroom's despair. 'The lily is gay,' her sisters sang, 'and the primrose spreads so sweetly.'

They were sitting against the back wall of the pub, side by side. The little table in front of them looked as if it might have arrived some time after they had, a mere convenience. The man wore a grey suit and a buttoned-up shirt with no tie. The woman wore a black dress. Her hair was grey. They looked poor, foreign and old, but perhaps they weren't any of these things. They were drinking red wine. I noticed how her right hand rested on top of his left.

The usual crowd were out. We were young and loud, half a dozen of us round another table, which hardly had space for all our bottles and glasses. It was a very ordinary pub. I don't remember how we had ended up in it, but there we were, and the bar staff and the other customers tolerated us. They knew that the next night the place would be theirs again.

We were recounting foreign adventures, trying to outdo one other, bragging about dangerous situations we'd been in or managed to get out of. That was the thing: we'd always got out of them, and most of them weren't that dangerous. We'd *almost* been killed, or there'd been a *threat* of violence, robbery or arrest, but none of our stories ended in disaster. We were young and invincible: our loud laughter proved it.

That couple didn't say a word all night, as far as I could see. They just sat, sipping their wine, her hand on his. Then they got up to leave. As they passed us, they paused. The man said, 'You don't know you are born. You don't know.' And they went out into the street.

There was silence, which somebody, I forget who, broke by imitating that thick, unfamiliar accent. 'You don't know you are born.' And there was another burst of laughter.

I did not join in. I had no idea what those people had experienced, what had brought them to where and who they were, but I felt it must be something huge and tragic, something more terrible than the worst any of us could ever imagine. And I felt ashamed.

Sonnets Galore!

In this film from 1950 the slightly sinister and very superior men and women at the 'Ministry of Culture' in London decide to send a writer to a remote Scottish island for a year, as a kind of experiment. The idea is to enlighten and improve the lives of the natives by exposing them to contemporary literature. The islanders are not happy about this at all. They have their own bardic tradition, their own songs and poetry, and in Gaelic moreover, the language of Eden, compared with which (according to the village postmistress) 'the sound of English is as a tractor ploughing a field of stones'.

The civil servants send the writer, a poet, anyway. 'Well, well, I am not surprised,' another islander comments. 'Where else would they put the poor creature but here? If it blows up, only a few sheep and a crofter or two will be the casualties, and nobody in London will notice.'

Roger Livesey, who plays the poet, wears a white polo-neck jersey throughout the film – he never takes it off, and indeed this is one of the reasons he is mistaken for a sheep by the character played by Duncan Macrae after a drunken night at a ceilidh. Nobody can understand a word of his impenetrable poetry, but nevertheless the islanders grow to like him because in other respects he is very practical, and expert at servicing the engines of their fishing boats. He falls in love with a local girl and, abandoning his dreams of literary fame, assists in the sabotage of a touring arts festival organised by the Ministry. This comes to the island in August, which the civil servants refuse to believe is an exceptionally wet month when the midges are at their fiercest. In one amusing scene the literati are driven into the kirk by the midges, and endure a two-hour sermon on the decadence of modern culture. During their ordeal the poet and some accomplices loosen the festival marquee's guy-ropes and it is blown into the sea. Yet even with such moments the film itself never really takes off, and it is noticeable that despite its title it does not contain a single sonnet.

Death Takes a Drink

'It's not like that,' he said, refilling his glass. 'If it were, it would be easy. Best job in the world. "*You* deserve it, *you* don't." "*You're* going now, *you* on the other hand get another five years." Or, in some cases, the reverse: "You've had enough, pal, haven't you? Okay, let's go." "You, mister, on the other hand, are a rotten bastard and always have been, so can suffer a bit longer." If only it *were* like that. But my hands are tied.

'It's about process, as much as anything,' he continued. 'Sure, the present system's unfair but start letting me make judgements and there'd soon be plenty more complaints. "Oh," they'd say, "you don't know all the facts. You don't know how she treated her daughter." "You don't know what a decent man he was *before* the war." In no time there'd be ethical commissions and rights of appeal and God knows what else. And God too. I mean, do you really want him getting involved again?

'I understand why people get so upset. Especially when it's children. Of course I understand. You'd have to have a heart of stone not to. But what can I do? It's not democratic, it's not fair and it's not logical but you come up with a better plan. Believe me, sometimes I wish I could move a famine or a cholera outbreak from one part of the world to another. Nothing would give me greater pleasure than to see an earthquake demolish the lives of the rich and selfish rather than those of the poor and helpless. But, as I said, my hands are tied. And it's not all down to chance, anyway. People *can* make a difference. They can lengthen the odds, for themselves and for others. They just need to want to.'

The glass was empty. He eyed his friend, the bottle.

'Another thing,' he said, and heard the slur in his voice. 'Not only is it not the best job in the world, it's the loneliest. But it's a job, isn't it? A job for life, and there aren't many of them around these days.'

He reached out. He'd have just one more.

Loss

What I said to them was, nobody could have told you how to do this. Nobody. Even people who've been through something similar, they couldn't have told you. Because however similar it was, it wasn't the same. It happened to them, it happened to you, but what happened was different. And when you're faced with something so big, when it comes at you, there isn't a primer or a manual that will tell you how to cope, how to survive, how to come out the other end. You'd have to write a new manual for each occasion, for each individual, and it wouldn't be ready in time to help because it couldn't be written till it was over, and anyway only he or she could write it. The thing I'm saying, the thing I tried to tell them, is that we lose the ones we love in our own ways. Everybody can sympathise but nobody can feel it the same way.

What I said to them was, there's one thing you can take from what you've been through: you are good people. You did everything you could and it wasn't enough, but still you did it. You did it even knowing you were going to lose. You kept going, right up to the end. You are good human beings. That's what I told them.

You get a sense sometimes, with a child. Whenever I held that child, she turned away. It wasn't a deliberate act, she was too young for that, and it wasn't always a physical act. It was something in her eyes, in what she was seeing. You looked at her and whatever she was looking at, it wasn't you. She went beyond you. I heard someone say, 'That child has been here before,' as if she'd lived another life. As if, perhaps, she'd be back again. I don't really hold with any of that, but I kind of understand it. She was going, and whether or not she knew it there was no stopping her. And it was terrible to see their grief when she did go, but they were good people, and they always will be. That's what I told them.

Unrelated Incidents

i.m. Iain Banks

Two middle-aged men sitting on a sofa at a party discover a shared interest in the lives of Celtic saints and the places associated with them.

A boy of three has his face painted at a library open day. He is wearing a green T-shirt and the artist gives a green tinge to the boy's face so that he resembles a tiger emerging from the jungle undergrowth.

A woman spends the afternoon weeding her garden. She is eighty-six and finds the bending and kneeling hard work, but loves the fact that she can still do it. She is invigorated by the dirt under her nails, the heat of the sun on her back. In a chair next to the shed, her husband dozes. She should probably cover his head with a hat, but at his age, she thinks, what difference will it really make?

A pizza delivery van arrives at a block of flats. The driver presses the buzzer of the flat whose occupant ordered the 'Quattro Stagioni'. Nobody lets him in. He phones the restaurant to check the address. He tries the buzzer again. Still no answer. He carries the box back to the van and drives away.

Two teenage girls sprawl on a blanket in the park. They are friends. One is texting, the other is reading a book. They don't say much to one another. They don't have to. They are friends.

A young man busking on a street corner plays one last song, then scrapes the coins out of his guitar case and puts away his guitar. Nobody was listening, nobody gave him a round of applause, but he's made enough money in three hours to buy himself a couple of beers. He gets out his mobile and phones a mate. They arrange to meet in a certain pub.

A Scottish writer dies of cancer at the age of fifty-nine. He has had only a few weeks' warning – enough time to finish his last novel, not enough to do everything he had left to do. He has recorded a final interview, not yet broadcast. 'I've had a brilliant life,' he says in it. 'I think I've been more lucky than unlucky.'

Relax

My wife is always busy. She can't sit still for a minute. At breakfast she's wondering what we'll have for dinner, and keeps jumping up to look in the fridge and in recipe books for inspiration. She leaves the table for other purposes too, for example to wipe a slight mark off a surface or to straighten a picture. And this is the pattern for the rest of the day. I'm not saying I don't appreciate her commitment, but even if the house is spotless she finds things to clean, paintwork that needs retouching or rugs that need to be taken outside and beaten thoroughly – simply for being rugs. And before you accuse me, I do my share of the chores. I just don't do them as quickly, as frequently or – I admit – as thoroughly as she does.

The thing is, she keeps saying she's going to stop. She's worked hard all her life, and now she wants to do less, at a more moderate pace. But she never does. She seems to have a psychological aversion to relaxation. One of these days, I fear, she'll overdo it and go bang. And I really don't want that to happen – and nor does she.

So I summoned up the ghost of Michel de Montaigne, and sat him in the library, and before long she found him there.

'Who are you?' she asked as she dusted around him.

'I'm an old friend of your husband,' Michel said. 'What are you doing?'

'Dusting the books,' she said.

'And when you've finished, what will you do?'

'Wash all the glassware.'

'I see. And after that?'

'Weed the garden.'

'And when you've done that, what then?'

'Well,' she said, 'I'll pour myself a glass of wine, sit in the sunshine with a book, and relax.'

'I tell you what,' Michel said, 'why don't you just do that now?'

I've asked her that myself a hundred times, but to no avail. However, as soon as Michel said it, she stopped, thought about it for a few seconds, and said, 'You're absolutely right. I will.' And she did.

He is charming, of course, and French. That must be what made the difference.

My Father, Swimming

Once, I was lost at the seaside. My parents searched for me in a state of panic. It was high tide and I was three. They searched along the promenade and behind the row of beach huts, and with churning stomachs they scanned the grey sea that was level with the top of the steps leading down to the beach, looking I suppose for some small floating thing that might be me. But I was dry and safe: I'd just gone for a wander, and was happily being entertained by some other family to whom I had attached myself. It was my parents who were lost and distraught, and were not found again until the moment they saw me.

I don't remember this incident, but I do remember other things about those seaside holidays. My father used to go for long swims, when the tide was lower and I was playing on the sand along with the other children. I could see his head as he did the sidestroke or the backstroke. He was a slow, steady, powerful swimmer. How much he must have enjoyed the solitude and peace out there, away from the demands of family. There was a pier about a mile along the coast, and sometimes he would strike out for it, and I would lose sight of his head as he swam further away. I don't think I was worried. I knew he'd come back. I can still see him in the water. I imagine him reaching the pier, swimming round its barnacled and weed-wrapped legs and heading back to us, always at the same, calm, methodical stroke and pace.

I wonder if *he* imagines that swim, or even remembers it. Today he needs someone to help him into the shower, to wash his back while he grips the safety handles, to dry him off with a towel and get him dressed. It's a long distance from now to then, much more than a mile there and a mile back. I wonder if, when he's in the shower, he ever closes his eyes and for a moment is back in that sea, strong, alone and free, and swimming away from everything.

'Is that better . . . ? Or worse?'

'Not sure. Can you do it again?'

'Better . . . ? Or worse?'

'A bit better.'

'And again. Better . . . ? Or worse?'

'About the same. No difference, I'd say. What do you think?'

'They're not my eyes, Mr Cruikshank. Not my eyes and not for me to say.'

'No, you're quite right. Sorry.'

'Now, look straight ahead, and in a moment you'll see some flashing lights in your peripheral vision. I want you to click the clicker every time you see one of those flashing lights. Okay? Here we go.'

'Wow! That's amazing. Oh, sorry, forgot to click. That's like the aurora borealis or something.'

'It should only be little flashes.'

'Not from where I'm sitting. Spectacular display! And what a range of colours!'

'That's very unusual. Are you quite sure?'

'Actually, I'm kidding you. But they're not your eyes, like you said. So how can you be so sure what I'm seeing?'

'Because that's the way the test is designed. Please, Mr Cruikshank. If you don't tell me what you're really seeing then there's no point in proceeding.'

'I thought maybe you were trying to catch me out.'

'This isn't a game, Mr Cruikshank. Are you seeing the flashing lights normally now?'

'Absolutely. Whatever "normally" means. Am I clicking fast enough?'

'Let's try something else. Going back to the chart on the wall, how far down it can you read?'

'A-B. Top line's fine. A-N-D. So far so good. O-N-A-L-L. Carry on?'

'Yes, please.'

'H-O-P-E-Y. Isn't that a Red Indian tribe? Sorry, Native American. E-W-H-O-E-N. Getting trickier now. And the bottom line – ooh, tough. T-E-R-H-E-R-E. Am I right?'

'Very good. I'm going to adjust the lenses slightly. Here are some more letters on the chart. How far can you read now?'

'Oh, that's much clearer. A-S. H-I-N. What a difference! I-N-G-C-I. What did you do?'

'Just a slight adjustment, as I said. Carry on?'

'T-Y-U-P-O. That's marvellous. Inspirational, in fact. N-A-H-I-L-L. Great! I'll take those ones.'

'But I haven't finished the tests yet.'

'Don't care. I want those lenses. The other ones are depressing. And I'll have an extra pair, in case of accidents. And sunglasses too, for night-time. Where do I pay?'

The Last of the Pechts

after Robert Chambers, Popular Rhymes of Scotland, and Robert Louis Stevenson,
'Heather Ale'

The Pechts were a red-haired folk, short but very strong. They had long arms and such wide feet that, when it rained, they could turn them up over their heads as umbrellas.

You can still see the ruins of great castles that the Pechts put up. They would form a long line between the quarry and wherever they wanted to build, and pass the stones along the line until the castle was finished.

The Pechts made an extremely potent ale from heather. Others wanted the recipe for this brew, but it was handed down from father to son as a closely kept secret.

Time passed, and the power of the Pechts declined, until they were finally defeated in a mighty battle by the Scots. Only two Pechts, a father and son, survived. They were brought before the King of Scots, who threatened them with torture if they refused to relinquish the secret of the heather ale. The father, in a quiet word, told the King that he feared torture more than anything, but could not bear to be dishonoured in his son's eyes. If his son were first put to death, he would hand over the recipe.

The King immediately ordered the son to be killed. As soon as it was done, the father cried out defiantly, 'Now do your worst to me. It was my son who I feared might relent under torture, but I will never give you the secret.'

The King saw that he had been outwitted, but decided that the greatest punishment he could impose on the father would be to let him live. And so he was held a prisoner, till he was blind and bedridden, and most people had forgotten his existence; but one night, hearing his guards boasting about their feats of strength, he asked from his bed if he could feel one of their wrists, so as to compare it with the wrists of men of his young days. The guards, for a joke, held out an iron bar for him to grasp, and he snapped it in two as if it were the stem of a clay pipe. And that was the last of the Pechts.

The Scot Monodont, 4545

What we know *for certain* about this pinnacle – or indeed about the many other contemporaneous constructions which adorn the 4th Archipelago – is very limited, whereas there are abundant *speculative* theories about their origins and purpose. The name given to the pinnacle is not supported by any documentary or archaeological evidence, but is assumed to have survived orally for centuries among the last of the Oil Age tribes that once inhabited this region. The name refers to that pre-Lapsarian, almost mythical people who may or may not have been responsible for these edifices, but whether to any specific 'Scot' or to the entire race is mere guesswork. The word 'monodont', meaning 'single-toothed', may simply refer to the visual appearance of the pinnacle, although Professor Ap Von Jürgin has proposed that the Scots worshipped strong, healthy teeth and that the pinnacle has totemic significance.

We do know that it is made from a relatively local sandstone and was erected between 2,500 and 3,000 years ago. How the immense quantity of material was transported has not been established. The suggestion that a complex network of avenues, metallic paths and waterways once existed in the area is of course complete fantasy – as is the even more bizarre notion that these were designed by visitors from another planet.

If the builders of the Monodont were, as is likely, influenced by the Symmetrian movement which dominated pre-Lapsarian cultures across Eurindis, then it was probably surrounded by four lower points: a portion of only one of these survives. Dr Jochin Yapert convincingly argues that what we now see was originally the central pinnacle, the peak of which was reached by an internal staircase. (A recent artist's impression of what the whole may have looked like, bearing as it does an uncanny resemblance to the Mars Shuttle, has unfortunately encouraged the notion that interplanetary travellers once visited the 4th Archipelago.)

The shattered lump of marble at the base, says Dr Yapert, may be the remnant of a representation of some tribal dignitary or possibly a deity. This is visible only at low tide.

No attempt should be made to land on the Monodont, which is home to a colony of rare water pigeons.

Buffalo Storms

Nobody knows where they come from, or where they go after they've happened. It's as if the animals, individually and in small groups, are wandering in vast, empty spaces that nobody knows about even though we're supposed to have mapped every inch of the continent, and once in a while something triggers a coming-together, which provokes one of these storms. And, as with other forceful demonstrations of nature, there isn't much we humans can do about it but get out of the way, or hold tight and let it come through.

Buffalo storms must in some respects resemble those mighty gatherings recorded by early white travellers on the plains. At first a storm moves slowly, but as the number of animals swells so it picks up pace. The recent Springfield-to-Syracuse event in Colorado and Kansas, which caused an estimated four hundred million dollars' worth of damage, was monitored by experts who measured the storm track as 0.4 kilometres wide and 3.7 kilometres long, with an estimated animal density of 0.6 per square metre, reaching a top speed of 42 miles per hour. The dust cloud caused by the pounding hooves of some nine hundred thousand animals rose more than three miles.

'You simply can't control such a powerful phenomenon,' says Dr Derick Cody of the Oklahoma State University. 'Razor wire, wooden fences, concrete walls – a buffalo storm just crashes right through such barriers, doesn't even feel them. The only possible way of diverting a storm route is by lining up a lot of trucks that are big, tall and heavy enough to turn it slightly. But you have to get the angle right or not even a forty-ton truck is going to withstand it when the storm hits. And how many truck drivers are prepared to risk sacrificing their rigs? You can't get insurance against a buffalo storm.'

An as-yet-unsolved puzzle for scientists is how the storms dissipate so rapidly after they have wreaked their havoc. Where do a million bison go? 'If we had the answer to that,' says Dr Cody, 'we could go out after them and break the cycle. But it's a mystery.'

Many Native Americans are enthusiastic fans of buffalo storms.

Jack and the Tree

Jack was walking by the lochside. It was a still, sunny day. He came to a tree, reflected perfectly in the loch. He thought, *If I climb tae the tap o this tree I'll be able tae wave tae masel at the tap o the ither tree in the water.*

So he starts climbing. The branches are thick and well spaced so it's not a difficult climb, but it's a long one, because it's a very tall tree. The tree gets narrower and narrower, till at last he's just a foot or two from the top. But when he looks down, he's disappointed to find that he's too high to see the foot of the tree or its reflection in the loch. When he looks up, however, there at the tip of the tree is the tip of another tree, identical to the one he's on, but upside down in the sky. He stretches up into the cloudless sky and his fingers feel wetness. He slaps the sky with the back of his hand and a ripple starts. He takes a penny from his pocket and throws it above his head. It plops into the water and he can see it going past the other tree – as if sinking or falling, although it's going up the way.

'This is weird,' says Jack. 'Either I'm upside doon or this tree is or the sky's turned tae water but whitever's gaun on it's makkin me feel seeck. I think I'll climb doon.'

So back he goes, and it's slow, hot work, harder than it was going up, and all the time he's wondering about that upside-down tree in the sky. He's relieved when his feet are back on solid ground. And there's the loch, as still as ever, and the tree reflected in it just as it was before.

Jack thinks, *I'll hae a wee dook in the loch tae cool doon.* He strips off and is standing at the edge about to jump in when a penny comes shooting out of the water, straight into his hand.

The clear, calm loch suddenly doesn't seem so inviting. And Jack changes his mind about going for that swim.

Jigsaw Puzzle

I was not short of sources of entertainment during my recuperation after the surgery: I had the radio to listen to, books to read, the television to watch. Nevertheless, my wife kept finding me staring out of the window, and decided that I needed some additional stimulation. She could have engaged me in erudite conversation, I suppose, but what she opted for was a thousand-piece jigsaw puzzle.

The picture on the box showed a grey sky and an almost imperceptible horizon, below which was a grey sea. The sky and the sea were the same shade of grey, the clouds in the sky looked like waves, and the waves in the sea looked like clouds. I am not sure why my wife chose that particular picture, but I thought I should show gratitude by having a go at it. I anticipated being more frustrated than stimulated.

However, to my great surprise, I became intrigued by the challenge, and determined to complete the puzzle. Having established the four edges I set about the task of filling in the middle. This was a slow, laborious process that took many hours, but eventually only one piece was left, which I triumphantly fitted into place. I sat back from the table to admire my handiwork.

Just then I noticed something quite remarkable. Near the bottom-left-hand corner of the picture, I could see a man's head among the waves. I snatched up the box and studied the picture on it: no head – no sign of human or any other animal life – disrupted that bleak seascape. I looked again at my completed puzzle: there, unmistakably, was the man, with what looked like an expression of utter exhaustion on his face. He seemed to have been in the water for quite some time.

I called to my wife. Her first reaction was to congratulate me on my achievement. I brushed her praise aside. 'No, no,' I said. 'Look! There! Don't you see the man in the sea?'

I pointed at the spot. My wife stared, first at the puzzle, then at me. She shook her head. I looked again, but it was too late. The drowning man had disappeared beneath the waves.

Normal

The one I'll remember, the one I couldn't take my eyes off all through the performance, was a beautiful boy, this perfect model of a beautiful boy, leaning against his carer, forehead pressed to her side. They sat together in the middle of the stage, and all around them the other children – all with disabilities of varying severity – banged drums and rang bells and sang if they could sing, and in front of the stage the audience sang and clapped and cheered along with them. That boy and woman were like an island. They were surrounded by noise and colour, and they were in it but also beyond it. The boy was one of the performers, a participant, and yet he seemed not to be there at all. And the woman was with him, wherever he was. That was her role, to be with him.

The hall was full of families come to celebrate their children's achievements. Tiny, fractional movements were immense achievements for some. There were children in wheelchairs twisted into shapes you would think almost impossible for the human frame to bear. There were raucous, happy, out-of-tune children. There were shy, slow, determined children. I felt I had entered some other world from which the word 'normal' had been banished because it was useless. This was in fact what I had done. And I saw that when I went back to my own world that word would still be useless.

The way his head and her body touched was something to see. Had I been a painter, I would have wanted to paint that connection, capture its tranquillity and trust in the midst of everything. I thought of his family. Were they in the hall? If they were seeing him there, did they see him as I did, the centre of everything and nothing, both present and absent? Did their hearts break, or did it make them happy to see him so still and safe up there on the stage? How *I* saw him is of no consequence either to them or to him, or to his carer, but I wished I could have been Picasso. Picasso would have known what to do.

We talked about rendition, sure, I'm not going to deny it. What am I going to say, that isn't my head on the video, that isn't my voice? Listen, it's me. We talked about a lot of things. Rendition was one of them. That's what we do, we talk. That's what we get paid for by government, to come up with suggestions, opinions. That is our expertise. And this isn't leaked, by the way, this is me telling you, straight up.

There's a real world out there, full of bad people. We monitor movements and developments, we analyse what's happening, and we tell government what we find. We're good at our job, okay? When you have a meltdown situation, like when that regime was collapsing, you identify opportunities. The chaos offered opportunities. And let me tell you, it was personal with that bastard. He should never have been allowed home to die. Did his victims get home to die? No, he blew them out of the sky. Don't talk to me about if he did or he didn't. Read the verdict of the court. He should have been rotting in a prison cell, not home with his family. And don't talk to me about compassionate release. So it was a natural thing, to see if he could be rendered.

And play that video again. Did we do it? No, it was a suggestion, a possibility. And isn't there someone saying, 'We can't do that, because he's already been tried and sentenced and served time'? Yes, there is. We knew what was legal, we knew what was done by a foreign jurisdiction. We just didn't agree with it. So do you want me to condemn the employee, the loyal employee and loyal citizen of this country, who said, well if we can't render him why not do the other thing, the more efficient thing? Do you want me to condemn that? 'One more reason to just bugzap him with a hellfire,' is that the opinion you want me to condemn? Well, I won't do it.

Cancer took the son of a bitch out anyway, so it's academic. He got lucky, if you really want to know.

Real family viewing, that was, even taking the horror dimension into account. It was the only programme allowed to interfere with meals in our house. Father thought the younger generation was ruled by television, but on *Dr Jekyll* nights he'd be the one bolting his food and leaping from the table to clear everything away in time. I'd be sent through in advance to warm up the set and move the aerial around to find the best reception. Father said I'd a knack for it, but it was trial and error really. Sometimes I'd end up holding the aerial above my head for the duration. I didn't mind. It gave me power.

The storyline never varied. By day Dr Jekyll went about tending his patients' ailments and tolerating their prejudices. He would be frustrated by the old-fashioned views of his partner, Dr Lanyon, or irritated by his housekeeper, Mrs Poole, although he was actually very fond of them both; or he would have to restrain himself from falling out with Mr Utterson, W. S., or Sir Danvers Carew, the local laird, or some other pillar of the establishment. But at night, having swallowed a single dram from a mysterious bottle which he kept locked in a drawer, Jekyll tore off his tie, grew stubble, sprouted hair from his ears, and ventured forth as the antisocial Mr Hyde. He let down Dr Lanyon's car tyres, put salt in Mrs Poole's sugar bowl, glued shut Mr Utterson's letter box or stole eggs from Sir Danvers's henhouse. In the morning he'd be his old self again, with absolutely no memory of what Hyde had been up to.

The reason for the serial's success over so many years was simple: it made everybody feel less guilty about feeling guilty. After an episode of *Dr Jekyll*, millions of people relaxed about the fact that they secretly detested their lives and wanted to break out. They never had to, because Mr Hyde did it for them.

The critics despised *Dr Jekyll's Casebook*. They said the plots were unbelievable and the sentimentality unbearable. But we loved it. It made total sense to us, and it warmed our hearts like a peat fire.

Saint Serf and the Devil (after Andrew of Wyntoun's Orygynale Cronykil of Scotland)

Saint Serf had just finished a long devotional session in a cave on the Fife coast when the Devil arrived, intent on an argument.

'You're a smart arse, aren't you, *Saint* Serf?'

'What's that to you, foul fiend?'

'Well, something's been bothering me. Where was God before Heaven and Earth were made? Must have been somewhere. But where?'

'God existed in himself. He doesn't need to be any *where*. He just is.'

'All right. So why did He make the animals and everything? What was that about?'

'Because He's the maker of all things. If He hadn't made anything, there wouldn't be any creatures and He wouldn't be the creator. But He did, and there are, so He is.'

'But how come He didn't make anything totally perfect? Because He could have, couldn't He?'

'He didn't set out to make things *im*perfect, but He Himself is perfection. So nothing could match him. Only God can be perfect.'

'Okay. Where did God make the first man, Adam?'

'In Hebron.'

'Hebron, eh? And where did God put Adam when He kicked him out of Paradise?'

'Where he was made.'

'Hebron again? Interesting. And how long was it, after Adam sinned, before he was barred?'

'Seven hours.'

'Very precise. You really know your stuff, don't you? What about Eve, where was she made?'

'In Paradise.'

'So Adam was made in Hebron and Eve was made in Paradise, and after they left Paradise they were still in Hebron? So are they the same place? That's like saying Fife is Dundee.'

'The location is immaterial.'

'Not if it's Dundee.'

'The point is, they sinned. That's what changed everything.'

'But this isn't fair. We devils were made in Paradise, and we were kicked out too, so how come humans get salvation through Christ's sacrifice, but we don't?'

'You brought it on yourselves. You were deliberately wicked. Humans didn't mean to fall. You tricked us into it. It wasn't our fault.'

'*It wisnae us*, you mean?'

'Well, it wisnae. It was you.'

'You've got an answer for everything,' the Devil said, 'but I'm not sure you're that smart. Suit yourself though. Stay in your miserable cave. Say your prayers. I'm going out.'

Midsummer

It is the time of year when you can walk all night and not need a torch, never stumble. A quarter to midnight but it could be an hour after dawn. This is as dark as it gets, the north's reward for the long black tunnel of winter. He looks from the bathroom window and everything is laid out in the sky, a vast painting of land and water. Clouds are headlands, hills descending to shores; the sky is sea lochs, bays. He calls to her. 'Come and look at this.' They're getting ready for bed and this will be the last thing they see tonight. It's important to him that they see it together.

But also he is thinking of another time, and further north. With his first wife's brother, years before, he walked across country at this season. Altnaharra to the coast, forty miles or not far short, a two-day hike. And it rained, and the sun came out, and sometimes there was a breeze and when it dropped the midges rose and feasted on them. He remembers eating breakfast on the move, frenzied mouthfuls of muesli and midges beside a peaty burn where they'd pitched the tent for a few hours. He remembers the smell of tent, conversations, long silences, blistered feet, the rub of rucksack straps. They kept walking into the evening, a long haul up from a loch deep in the hills, over the high ground, a river below and nobody contained in that whole landscape but themselves. They walked till midnight, beyond it, because it seemed wasteful of the light to stop, and eventually only their aching weariness stopped them, and they camped.

More than anything of that time he remembers the light: kind, constant, hardly diminished by sunset. It made the black loch glow, the brown moor shine. When they came to the coast next day, the light passed over the shore and the sea like a gentle hand over the back of an animal. And here it is again, the land and water, and the light. 'Come and look at this,' he says, and she comes. Hand in hand they stand at the window, taking it in.

The Examined Life

She woke up. She thought about herself waking up. *Was I really asleep just before I woke up? How was I lying?* It was only seconds ago but she couldn't remember because she'd moved. She'd reached out and turned on the light. She couldn't remember the last dream she'd had, the one she'd woken up from, or if she had actually been dreaming. *What does that mean, 'actually been dreaming'?* She had no conscious appreciation of six or seven or eight hours in every twenty-four. This bothered her. *Maybe I should set the clock to wake me every hour through the night. What good would that do? It would just make the rest of the day intolerable.*

She listened to herself breathing. She listened to the air going in and out of her nostrils. She surveyed her body without touching it, without looking at it, seeking out aches, itches, numbness. *If there is no negative sensation can it be inferred that that part of me is healthy? What does 'negative' mean? What does 'healthy' mean?*

Get a grip, she told herself. *Get up and out or you'll be late for lectures.* But she lay there thinking about who she was, what she was doing, what she wasn't doing and why she wasn't doing it.

She blamed the university. They'd told her she couldn't do History and Astrophysics. Why not? Because they were different subjects with different timetables in different faculties on different campuses. 'No,' she'd said, 'they are intimately linked. We are stardust,' she'd said, almost breaking into song. 'Aristotle looked at the stars. Is Aristotle not history? Are Plato and Galileo and Newton not history?'

They wouldn't give way, but they heard what she was saying. They heard 'Plato' and 'Aristotle'. 'How about History and Philosophy?' they'd suggested. That would be possible. That would be acceptable. Possible or acceptable? 'Both,' they'd said.

She blamed Plato. She blamed Socrates. Her life had slowed to an inching crawl. Maybe she was ill. How would she know? She had no perceptible aches, no numbness.

She would get up in a minute. She would have to. Everything was pointless if she didn't. And maybe even if she did.

Andy Murray was through to the third round. Ray ate a bowl of muesli. The forecast was cloudy, mainly dry. He topped up his mug with tea. Julie was in the shower. He ate toast with marmalade. There were plans to extract shale gas in Lancashire and Yorkshire. He switched off the radio, looked at his watch. His bus would arrive in fourteen minutes. It took three minutes to get to the bus stop. He put his breakfast things in the dishwasher. Julie always took the car to work. She was out of the shower, getting dressed. He went to the bathroom and had a crap. They were going to Crete for two weeks in September. He washed his hands, checked himself in the mirror. He didn't wear a tie to work any more. Nobody commented, not even Maxwell. Julie called, 'I have to work late tonight. You just go ahead and eat.' 'Okay,' he said, coming into the bedroom. He'd make some pasta. He might go to the pub later, catch up with Rob and Alan. Julie was doing her face. 'That's me away then,' he said. 'See you later.' 'Bye,' she said. She stopped applying mascara for a second, blew him a kiss. He checked his jacket pocket for his keys and bus pass. The front door still needed painting where he'd had to change the lock. At the top of the street he saw the bin lorry coming out of Orchard Crescent. He walked round to Constitution Road. The bus came. He got on, picking up a free newspaper, sat at the back. He texted Julie: *Can u put out bin b4 u go Rx*. He texted Rob: *Fancy pint 2nite? 8pm?* He'd wait until he heard back from Rob before he texted Alan. The sky was cloudy. He wondered if he should have taken his raincoat. He was feeling pretty good. He wasn't expecting any bad stuff at work. Maxwell was on holiday. He saw cars and people going by. He turned the pages of the paper. Some of the other big names were already out of Wimbledon. Murray could go all the way this time. It was a strong possibility.

The Ones

At first you think everybody is at it: on the bus, or at the bus stop, that familiar head-down stance, the gadget held between hands, the thumbs and fingers tapping, flicking, scrolling; or the evolved walk, one hand to ear, speaking to someone who is not present; or – one level up from that, and a growing subspecies, or maybe a breakaway alpha group – the brisk, ear-phoned, miked-up walkers, no device visible, talking like mad solitaries but looking controlled, like they're passing sophisticated comment, cutting sharp deals, making cool arrangements. Or, on the train, the ones with the notebooks, pads, slimmed laptops, 4G phones, riding whatever the next wave of connectivity is. What a word: be connected, stay linked, don't for one second be out of touch in case you miss something or it misses you. In the last six months more photographs have been taken than in the entire previous history of photography. You don't have to believe that statistic to know it is happening. You don't have to compute to know that the world is a place of sign language, image, messaging, and you have to be in it, of it, at it, giving and receiving signs and messages, you have to be there or you will die.

But then, glancing around, you see the other ones. The phoneless, wire-less, waveless, unhooked ones. Greybeard tramps, kids in prams, kids who like watching dogs, people of a certain age who have said, 'It's too late,' poor, frazzled women, scarred men, unrecovering addicts of one kind or another, the detritus of our civilisations. If those with the technology are Romans, these are the barbarians. The ones outside the citadel. Beyond the wall. The ones who lack the necessary education but despise it anyway. The ones who use the middle finger to make signals and cup the ear to receive them. The people for whom the Dark Ages are called dark. The ones who will welcome the darkness, bring out their hatchets and skewers, make pyres of smashed screens and keyboards. The ones who will turn out to be the strong ones, the survivors. The ones who will revel, not panic, when the lights flicker and die.

At the Edge of the Desert

We sat looking out over the desert. The sun was going down, and we believed that if we watched closely we would see amazing things. We would see the bands of rock change colour, the landscape shift and move like a striped animal across our vision. Someone who gave us a ride that day must have told us to go there, and there we were, at the edge of the desert, waiting to see these things.

I have a photograph somewhere. I'm not in the picture because I took it, but Frank is. You wouldn't recognise Frank, though, because all you see is the back of a man in a dirty T-shirt and a sunhat, and out beyond him the desert. You can see its stripes, the bands of rock, and you know the man is looking at them. That was Frank. He was with me and I was with him. The photograph proves it. Proves something, anyway.

We'd probably smoked some weed. I'd be prepared to bet on it, because we smoked a lot that year, and the people who gave us rides were often smokers too. I don't know if that was some magnetic or telepathic thing or just the era, the fact that we were hitching rides and they were the kind of people who stopped for us, but some days we rolled across that country from dawn till dusk as high as eagles. So when we sat at the edge of the desert it's not surprising we expected to see amazing things.

I don't know where that photograph is. Somewhere in the attic, probably, along with all the other pictures from back then. I haven't seen it in thirty years, but I can still see it, if you know what I mean. It shows a beautiful landscape, and the back of a man looking out on it. I haven't seen Frank in thirty years either. He might not even remember that evening we sat watching for a long time and then slept, but I do.

I don't smoke dope any more. This is what happens. You change. You grow. But sometimes you have a memory, and sometimes it's a good one.

Jack and the Captain

An old sea captain washed up, looking for a berth. Jack's mother took him in. He was a fierce old fellow who liked rum and bananas and lying in his bed. He kept his worldly possessions in a chest under it. 'You keep an eye out for strangers,' he told Jack. 'Seafaring men like me. Off you go, lad.' And Jack went.

Jack's mother kept the captain company for an hour each afternoon with the door firmly shut. 'Och, he likes tae talk,' she explained to Jack. 'I feel sorry for him. We share a banana or two.' And that was odd, because Jack's mother never felt sorry for anybody and she didn't like bananas either.

One day when she'd gone to the shop for more bananas, another old man, in dark glasses and tap-tapping with a stick, turned up. 'Will you help a poor chap that's reduced to a demeaning occupation to earn a crust?' he says in a shaky voice. 'I will,' says Jack, and gives him his arm. The old boy hisses, 'Now take me in to the captain or I'll break your wrist.' So Jack takes him in. 'Is that you, captain?' says the blind man. 'Is that you, Pugh?' says the captain, white as the sheet he's lying on. With Jack's assistance the blind man puts a bit of paper in the captain's hand. 'And now that's done,' he says, ditching the stick and shades and skipping off back to town.

'Jack, lad, I'm finished,' the captain cries. 'That was a messenger-at-arms, and this here's a summons that'll bankrupt me.' And he starts up from his pillow, and then falls back down on it, stone dead.

Jack's mother was very upset when she returned. 'Whit the hell dae I dae wi aw these bananas?' she wept. They went through the captain's chest and found enough money to pay for his funeral and a high tea for two afterwards, and that was that. The captain's clothes went to Oxfam and the chest they chopped for firewood, and they burned the summons. Oh, and a dirty old map that they couldn't make head nor tail of, that went in the fire too.

My Real Wife

'Why do you keep writing about me?' my wife asked. 'My wife this, my wife that. I never asked to be in your stories.'

'You're not in them,' I said.

'Yes I am,' she said, and pointed out a couple where the narrator talks about 'my wife'.

'That's not you,' I said.

'You wrote the stories,' she replied. 'If it's not me, who is it?'

'The narrator isn't necessarily me,' I explained. 'Just because the narrator writes in the first person doesn't make him – or her – me.'

'What do you mean "her"?' my wife said. 'How can a narrator who writes about "my wife" be female?'

'It's not impossible,' I said, 'although in my stories that situation hasn't actually arisen as yet. You just have to use your imagination. You mustn't be so literal. You have to forget the idea that the narrator and the author are the same person, and then the stories can be about anyone and anything at all.'

'Even a woman who has a wife?' she said.

'Yes. We live in enlightened times,' I told her.

'You may think so,' my wife said. 'I think we're living in an age of darkness.'

'That's something I also address in some stories,' I said. 'That possibility.'

'It's a racing certainty, if you ask me,' she said. 'Anyway, getting back to the point, I want you to keep me out of the public view. You make me look and sound stupid.'

'I've already said,' I explained, 'that they are not about you.'

'And why not?' she demanded, changing tack. 'What's so wrong with me that you can't write about me?'

'Nothing is wrong with you,' I said.

'If you loved me you would write about me, and write nicely,' she said.

Just then my real wife came into the room, bringing me a cup of coffee. She leaned over my shoulder and read what was on the screen. This is something I wish she wouldn't do.

'Is she bothering you again?' she asked. 'Tell the sad cow to leave you alone, or she'll have me to answer to.'

'It's okay,' I said. 'I'm dealing with it.'

'Well, deal with it,' my real wife said.

Hag-Ridden

'Let me up on your shoulders.'

You know those women, the ones at music festivals who get themselves hoisted on their boyfriends' shoulders? They're often small, petite even, but they are not light. They ignore the people shouting at them because they're blocking the view. They just carry on singing and swaying, reaching into the air as if they've got a hold of something special. They look like sylphs or wood nymphs. That's what they want you to think they are, spirits of the woodland blowing in the breeze, singing with the band up on the stage. 'Get down!' people are yelling. Their arms are outstretched and their fingers are making little signs of victory or peace. All they hear is the music. Their boyfriends are buckling under them, because how long can you go without your neck cracking or your shoulders aching as your girl bounces and sways on top of you? How long can you last, tell me that?

I once had a girl. We went to some concert in some stadium. When the band started playing she uttered the fateful words and like a fool I bent my knees and let her on. And before I was upright again I felt her legs lock behind my back and she was riding me.

She rode me for the next two hours despite the abuse of the people behind us, despite my own screaming pain and exhaustion. Afterwards I carried her away until we came to a quiet place where I begged her to come down. She was only small but the weight of her was immense. She laughed derisively, and rode me till I dropped. 'Hag-ridden', that's what you call it. I was hag-ridden. At last I fell, and no matter how hard she kicked and cuffed me I could not rise.

She left me for dead. I was not dead, but my youth had abandoned me. That's why, when I see those women now in the fields of summer music and mud, I want to warn those boys. I shout but they don't hear me. All they hear is the music and the soft, enticing plea. They don't know what it means.

Sir Walter's Notes on Art and an Elephant

after Sir Walter Scott's Journal

Two visits today, despite the rheumatism. First Francis Grant's gallery. Grant's work well done, in my consideration, but do I know what I am looking at, or looking for, in a painting? Raeburn's portraits: very lifelike. His Highland chiefs do all but walk out of the canvas. Grant's productions not in that league, but still pleasing to my inexperienced eye. No false modesty there – I am ignorant of what constitutes art, but I think I can detect artifice. These seem genuine or at least good paintings. Would happily have one or two on my walls but my walls must go naked. And he has priced them too high for this market of grudging tastes and pockets to match. One must be a bold player in the game of picture buying and selling, bold as a horse-jockey – or a bookseller! A gentleman cannot make much of any of these without laying aside some of his gentility.

Next, the show of wild beasts: both more and less satisfying. The creatures kept much cleaner than in former days, I think. The strong smell used to make the nose run, the eyes sting and delivered a headache for the day. They are tamer than I recall, or less angry at their lot. Cause: more knowledge of their habits? Kinder treatment? Or ennui and despair on the part of the beasts? I fear the latter. A lion and tigress went through their exercise like poodles, jumping, standing, and lying down at the word of command. This is rather degrading. (Yet you too leap through the hoops, sir, now that they have you trained and obedient, a slave to the offer of a morsel.)

The elephant: a noble fellow. I treated him to a shilling's worth of cakes. I wish I could have enlarged the space in which so much bulk and wisdom is confined. He kept swinging his head from side to side, as if he marvelled why all the fools that gaped at him were at liberty and he cooped up in the cage. We watched each other for a long time. I doubt he found me as interesting as I found him. I shall not go there again.

July

Halfway

Halfway, he reckons. The strain in his calf muscles, the sweat he has to wipe from his face, the care with which he has to watch his footing, guarding against a twisted ankle – these things make their own computation of how far he's come, how far he has to go. He's on the spine of the hills now. The path – a thin scribble of peat through the heather – stumbles up and down as if over vertebrae, the short drops giving him the momentum to take on the rises. He is hurting but it feels good. He knows it could all go wrong – one bad step and he could twist or snap an ankle, have to limp the rest of the way home or maybe even drag himself because there's no one else up here, in all the times he's run these hills he's never come across another person – but he doesn't think it will come to that. Not now, today, because now he's halfway to home.

He's never been on exactly this route before. He knows the land, its contours and moods, but this is a new path. It's led him round the edges of bogs and clear of standing water and so far it's left him with dry feet. Halfway. This long stretch along the tops is where it feels best. The warm wind is pushing at his back, the sky is mostly blue, dotted with unthreatening white clouds, the great sweep of mountains is to the north, a loch below him to the south. When he came up the forestry track, that hard, aching climb, this was what he was putting in the effort for: running across the rough ground, alone, himself against himself, heading for home.

Twenty minutes earlier, just below the treeline, he surprised a red squirrel crossing the track. It darted away in sudden, comical panic. Last week a deer did the same thing. He relishes these meetings. They are signs of life, brief, unexpected, treasured; they, and his own body traversing the backbone of the hills. This, nothing else, is what he is for. Halfway. Another mile and it's all downhill from there, but this, now, is the moment.

Frank and I were aiming for Death Valley but the truck driver who picked us up in Bakersfield en route to Las Vegas thought that was a bad idea. Frank said he'd always had a yearning to see Death Valley and it didn't seem far on the map so that was where we were going. The trucker took us along Interstate 15 and at the junction where we proposed to get out and hitch down to Death Valley he pulled over, switched off his engine and told us not to be so goddamned stupid. 'Put your hand out there,' he said, 'feel that heat. You'll fry before you've gone a mile.' It was July and in Death Valley the temperature could reach 130°F. 'How much water are you carrying?' We had to admit we weren't carrying any. 'And where are all the goddamned vehicles that are going to stop for you?' We looked around and all we could see was miles and miles of nothing. 'You ain't getting out,' he said. 'Let me take you to Vegas instead. It's a hell of a place too but you probably won't die there, which you surely will out here.'

I have to say he made the right choice for us. Those big casinos would let almost anybody in. They let me and Frank in, in our filthy clothes and with beards down to our chests. We picked up free newspapers and tore out the coupons that gave you complimentary drinks or complimentary all-day breakfasts or a dollar's worth of dimes to play the slot machines, and we milked that town for everything we could from morning till midnight. We got drunk and ate our fill of junk food, and by the time we found a patch of hard earth on the outskirts to sleep on Frank was two dollars up and I was two dollars down on where we'd started. And that was a lot better than being dead in Death Valley.

Later Frank admitted he'd been thinking of Monument Valley, where they filmed *The Searchers* and *Easy Rider*, which is in Utah and about five hundred miles away. We never did make it to Monument Valley.

Archie

One morning a boy called Archie came into school with the news that Bobby Kennedy had been shot. This was exciting to young boys, because although most of us couldn't remember where we were when President Kennedy was shot we all knew it had happened and what a big deal it was. And now it had happened again, to JFK's little brother Bobby. Some of us had little brothers and some of us had big brothers, so this meant something. The story spread like a fire.

There was a teacher called Mr Cheyne, who taught English, History and Scripture and sometimes played the piano at assembly. Mr Cheyne also sang, in a very loud tenor voice that I didn't like. He had a singing career as well as being a teacher. He gave concerts and made records on which he sang sacred songs in his loud and, to me, objectionable way. He was not shy about proclaiming his Christian faith.

Something snapped in Mr Cheyne when he heard the story about Bobby Kennedy. He said it was nothing but a rumour, and demanded to know who had brought this rumour into the school. Pretty soon Archie was fingered. Mr Cheyne cornered him. This big, blustering man in his thirties roared at wee Archie, accusing him first of spreading malicious gossip and then, when Archie stuck to his guns, of lying. Archie said he was only repeating what he'd heard on the radio at breakfast, that Senator Kennedy had been shot in a hotel kitchen. That was all he knew.

The hotel kitchen detail made Mr Cheyne madder and redder than ever. I think he would have exploded if another teacher hadn't come by and quietly confirmed that everything Archie was saying was true.

Mr Cheyne should have deflated like a punctured balloon, but he didn't. He blew off down the corridor and was not seen for a while. Later he took Archie aside and apologised, but it was too late. General respect for Archie went up tenfold – we thought him a hero for defending himself and the truth. But as for Mr Cheyne, none of us ever believed a thing he told us after that.

The Coin

The man wore a tall grey hat with a bashed-in crown, a black tailcoat and striped trousers, and a stained white shirt with a cravat. He either needed a shave or was growing a beard. He looked like a lord who'd lost everything at Ascot, or a bridegroom who'd baulked at the altar and been on the run ever since.

'Fuel?' I asked.

'Sustenance,' he said, holding up a Milkybar.

'Have you bought fuel as well?' I said, pointing to the pumps outside.

'I am without carriage.' He spoke like an actor. 'Wait,' he continued, resisting my attempt to take the Milkybar from him. 'How much does it cost?'

'Forty pence.'

'Unfortunately this is all I have,' he said, producing a twenty-pence piece. 'I shall buy half.'

'You can't,' I said. 'You have to buy the whole thing or none of it.'

'Really?' His eyebrows rose. Deftly he snapped the bar in two, tore open the wrapper and slid one half out.

'You shouldn't have done that,' I said. 'Now you have to give me another twenty pence.'

'I am without further coin,' he said. 'I will return tomorrow, or the next day. For now, I am restricted to purchasing this portion.'

I looked around for Karen, the manager, but she was through the back. 'You can't,' I said.

'I have,' he replied, and popped it in his mouth. Then he stuck his hands in the pockets of his striped trousers, smiled, and ambled out.

I suppose I should have rung the bell for Karen, but I didn't. He looked pathetic in his tired old fancy dress. I felt sorry for him, mainly because I didn't think it was fancy dress.

Other people came in to pay for fuel, sandwiches, cigarettes. They handed over their credit cards and parted with fifty, sixty, seventy pounds without blinking. They didn't seem to have noticed the man in the top hat.

I never said anything to Karen. I kept the coin and the second half of the Milkybar for a week, intending to ring through the sale if he ever came back, but he didn't. So I ate the chocolate and put the coin in the charity box.

Boredom

He was lying on the floor, reading. The sun through the window made a little oblong of heat on the carpet. He shifted so that his feet dipped into the heat. At the end of one chapter he checked how many pages there were in the next. He moved back to his bed and lay on it, wondering what to do. He read the next chapter.

He'd had breakfast an hour ago. His mother was in the kitchen or outside. Everybody else – his father, his sister, his brother – was away. There was nothing to do and this was fine. Downstairs the grandfather clock struck ten. He put away the book and listened to the pigeons cooing in the cedar tree. They just went on cooing and cooing. It was already hot. He might go out on his bike. Later he'd take the dog for a walk.

He was bored. This was fine.

His mother or his father or perhaps both of them had instilled in him the idea that once you started a book you should always finish it. Why was that? Was it a duty to finish it, or a mark of respect to the author, or just something you were supposed to do? He always did finish a book, but sometimes he cheated, skimming the pages if it was boring him. This was what he would do with the book he was reading. He'd skim the last few chapters, so he could say he'd read it. Not that anyone was checking, but he needed to be able to say that, for himself.

Later he'd go on his bike down to the library and swap his books for three more.

Not just the day but the summer stretched out before him. He'd take the dog for a long walk. Nothing would happen.

He could go and see one of his friends. A bunch of them could get together, but school had broken up only a few days earlier. He didn't want to see them. He liked being on his own. He liked being bored.

Days and days of it. There was so much time in a day, a year. There was so much left.

On the Division of Labour: The Nail Painters of Pathhead*

for Davey Stewart

To take an example from a very trifling trade, that of a nail painter: a worker not educated to this business (which the division of labour has rendered a distinct trade), nor acquainted with the use of the machinery employed in it (to the invention of which the same division of labour has probably given occasion), could scarce, perhaps, with her utmost industry, paint one nail in a day, and certainly could not paint twenty. But in the way in which this business is now carried on, not only the whole work is a peculiar trade, but it is divided into a number of branches, which are likewise peculiar trades. One worker assesses the condition of the nail; another cleans it; a third cuts it; a fourth points it; a fifth prepares it for receiving the paint; to select the correct paint requires two or three distinct operations; to put it on is a peculiar business; to dry the nails is another; it is even a trade by itself to admire them when painted; and the important business of painting a nail is thus divided into about eighteen distinct operations, which, in some salons, are all performed by distinct hands, though in others the same woman will sometimes perform two or three of them. I have seen a small salon, where ten women only were employed, where some of them consequently performed two or three distinct operations. But they could, when they exerted themselves, paint among them about twelve pounds of nails in a day. There are in a pound upwards of four thousand nails of a middling size. Those ten persons, therefore, could paint among them upwards of forty-eight thousand nails in a day. Each person, therefore, might be considered as painting four thousand eight hundred nails in a day. But if they had all wrought separately and independently, they certainly could not each of them have painted twenty, perhaps not one nail in a day; that is, certainly, not the two hundred and fortieth, perhaps not the four thousand eight hundredth, part of what they are at present capable of performing, in consequence of a proper division and combination of their different operations.

* Adapted from Adam Smith's *The Wealth of Nations*. The trade of nail-painting has entirely replaced the trade of nail-making once observed by Smith in this part of Kirkcaldy.

In this neglected novel by the author of works such as *Waterloo*, *Belvedere* and *Mortlake*, an innocent youth, Edward Mortimer, journeys from Surrey to St Andrews in Fife, where he is to study English Literature at the university. There he is introduced to Rose, the lovely but sensible daughter of a Perthshire landowner. She is studying Accountancy, and while Edward quite fancies her he finds her dull and a little prudish. Anxious to lose his virginity, he falls in with a bad set of folksong enthusiasts who are keen to initiate him into their regular habits of drinking, smoking and the consumption of fish suppers. Chief among this crowd are brother and sister Fergus and Flora, who hail from the West Highlands and are ardent followers of the Scotland rugby team. Edward becomes infatuated with the high-spirited Flora, who is studying for a joint degree in Celtic Studies and Fine Art, and accompanies her by train from Leuchars to Edinburgh to attend a rugby international against England. As the train approaches the capital Edward tries to persuade Flora that they should stay on until Waverley Station, but she insists that they 'get off at Haymarket',* since this is closer to the rugby stadium.

Still smitten with Flora despite her teasing, Edward follows her to the game where Scotland thrash England 76–3. In the ensuing triumphant pub crawl, which lasts several weeks, Edward recognises the dreadful consequences of overindulgence in folksong, and that his new associates are doomed to fail in the modern world. Fergus and some of his friends get into a fight with some *Britain's Got Talent* fans. Fergus is arrested, found guilty of being culturally at odds with the mainstream, and beheaded. Flora goes off to France to be a drug addict and Edward knuckles down to some hard study.

Edward is reconciled with Rose, who gains a first-class degree. After graduation they marry. Rose goes on to have a glittering career with Ernst & Young, and produces three sensible children, while Edward manages the Perthshire estate that in time they will inherit.

Haymarket was a bestseller on publication but its language has dated and the plot is now considered rather far-fetched.

---

* In Edinburgh, this phrase is sometimes used to denote coitus interruptus.

A Lion at Wimbledon

A row has broken out over accusations that, following Andy Murray's victory in the Wimbledon men's singles final, the First Minister of Scotland released a lion onto Centre Court.

Spectators who seconds earlier had been cheering Murray's success were horrified to see a fully grown male lion run onto the grass and lie down. Fortunately the animal seemed to be in good humour and not hungry. Murray was on the roof of the commentary box at the time, but this had nothing to do with the appearance of the lion, as he had climbed there to receive congratulations from his coaching team and members of his family. Line judges, ball boys and ball girls and the defeated Novak Djokovic rapidly retired from the court, however, while Mr Lahyani, the umpire, wisely stayed put in his high chair.

A quick-thinking groundsman, armed only with a garden fork and a length of tennis net, approached the lion from the rear and threw the net over it. Thus ensnared, the king of beasts was deemed to be of no immediate threat to the public, and indeed it fell asleep in the sunshine. The awards ceremony proceeded, and photographs were taken of the players standing next to the lion with their trophies.

A Scottish Government spokeswoman said: 'The lion rampant is one of Scotland's national symbols. It is hardly surprising that a lion should be present on such a great occasion for Scottish sport.' Pressed on whether the First Minister had smuggled the animal into Wimbledon she declined to engage in what she described as 'speculation'.

One eyewitness claimed that earlier he had observed the First Minister's wife carrying a 'bulging' sports bag into the royal box, and that the same bag appeared to be empty after the incident.

Wild animals are not permitted within the grounds of the All England Tennis Club, an official confirmed. Whoever was responsible had shown a gross disregard for public safety, he added.

However, examination of the lion after it had been tranquillised revealed that it had no teeth, whether as a result of surgery or decay was not clear.

Despite recent improvements Scotland has one of the worst oral-health records in Europe.

'I have a problem. I keep forgetting things. Do you think I have a problem?'

'No. What kind of things?'

'Little things. Not the big things. I remember big things. I remember birthdays and people who have died and people who are still alive. I remember their names and their faces. I remember films and books. I remember my PIN numbers.'

'Well, then . . .'

'But sometimes I come into a room and I don't remember why. I came into the room for a specific purpose and I don't know what it was.'

'We all do that.'

'So I retrace my footsteps. I go out and come in again. Maybe I wanted a box of matches or to check a word in the dictionary, who knows? I don't. It's completely gone.'

'That happens to everybody occasionally. Don't worry about it.'

'But it's more than occasional. And it's not like I remember five minutes or even five hours later. I don't *ever* remember. And if it's happening to everybody, shouldn't everybody be worried? What's going on?'

'Nothing is going on. It's normal, I promise you. It happens more as we age, that's all. Listen, this is what some psychologist said about it. He, or maybe it was a she, he or she said, it's not a problem forgetting where you parked your car if, when you find it, you remember parking it. It's only a problem if, when you find it, you don't know how it got there.'

'But you might never find your car. You might have forgotten what it looks like.'

'That would be a problem. I think the psychologist would consider that problematic.'

'Who was this? I don't know any psychologists. Was it Freud?'

'No, it was someone on the radio. I've forgotten the name but, look, it doesn't matter. *I'm* not worried.'

'Maybe you should be. This man or woman on the radio tells you it's not a problem if you can't find your car, and you accept that? Were you driving or had you already parked?'

'No, it wasn't on the car radio. It was some other time.'

'I think that's a problem. Really, I do. If it was me, I'd be worried.'

'I just stepped outside for a little while,' he said. 'That's all. From the look on your face . . .'

'You were away for ages,' she said. 'I was worried.'

'Nonsense.'

'There were search parties out and everything.'

He screwed his face up at her. Without his glasses he looked like a mole caught in sunlight.

'Search parties? Never!'

'How would you know? You weren't out looking. You were the one being looked for.'

He opened and closed his mouth a few times. 'Why were they looking for me?'

She stroked his arm, the one without the tubes attached. 'Because I asked them to. I didn't know if you'd be able to find your own way back.'

'But I only went down to the beach,' he said. 'The same as always.'

'That's where you thought you were going,' she said. 'But you didn't, not this time.'

'What are you talking about?' Yet there was some kind of understanding in his peering eyes, and he didn't seem to be struggling with the fact that he was where he was, in a hospital bed, with her sitting beside him.

'You didn't get that far,' she said.

'To the beach? Sure I did. It was beautiful down there. The stars were out and the moon was pulling the waves up the beach and there was a breeze blowing off the top of them; not much but enough to make your eyes water a bit. I remember it distinctly.'

'You only thought you were there. Your mind was playing tricks on you. You were somewhere else.'

'I wasn't there at all?'

'No.'

'Oh.' He fell silent, staring at the end of the bed as if there were waves breaking over it. She could have wept, watching the way he tried to absorb the news and almost did – yet could not quite grasp what it meant.

'And where was I?'

She shook her head. 'I don't know. Maybe later you'll be able to tell me.'

'Later?' He tested the word suspiciously.

The door opened and a doctor came in, smiling.

'I know that face. From the beach.'

She tried to catch the doctor's eye, but wasn't quick enough.

'Beach?' the doctor said.

Out

It was beautiful down there. The stars were out and the moon was pulling the waves up the beach and there was a breeze blowing off the top of them; not much but enough to make your eyes water a bit. His glasses didn't stop the cold air getting in at the corners and starting the tears. Occasionally he had to lift the glasses and have a wee wipe with the back of his hand.

In the daytime people came with their dogs or their children or just by themselves. In high summer the beach became almost crowded. But at night the place was his alone. The moon threw its light across the broad sweep of sand, and the waves kept throwing themselves away when the moon had finished with them. On the dark water out beyond the waves he thought he could see black shapes that might be gulls or ducks floating, but might just be black shapes. He walked closer to the sea but the shapes did not resolve themselves one way or the other.

He thought, *This is what you come to when all's said and done. This is where you come, and you come alone.*

He'd just stepped out for a while. That's what he liked to do.

Sometimes he glimpsed – or 'sensed' was perhaps more accurate – something else on the water. He didn't know what it was but he didn't like it. It wasn't even a thing. It was something above the water, like mist, or something that disturbed it, like a squall.

When this happened it was time to go back. Being out was fine, but going back in was necessary.

A question formed at the edge of his vision. *Are you losing it?*

He wanted to take his shoes and socks off, roll up his trousers and paddle in the moonlight. But he was afraid if he did he would just keep walking, wading out towards that thing, whatever it was.

This was another warning sign, having thoughts like that.

He didn't want to go. He liked being alone, on the beach. He liked being out.

But he would have to, or they would come looking for him.

Have I Got It?

It was the most difficult question he'd ever have to ask anyone, and it had to be her he asked. They'd known each other so long. He knew if he asked her he'd get a straight answer. She might hesitate, she might have to think about it, but she wouldn't lie. If he could have asked someone else, there might still have been room for the comfort of a lie. But he couldn't. It had to be her.

It was difficult too because he didn't know what the question was. Well, he did, but it could take so many forms. *Do you think that . . . ? Would you agree that . . . ? Are there times when . . . ?* It was like drafting a bloody referendum question. To get a straight answer you had to ask a straight – that is to say not a leading, misleading, biased or ambiguous – question.

So he spent a lot of time composing it in his head. And kept being side-tracked by memories or other interruptions, like her coming in to see if he was all right.

'Of course I'm all right,' he said. 'Have I moved since you asked me ten minutes ago?'

'It was an hour ago,' she said. 'And you've been to the toilet and back.'

That gave him pause for thought. He remembered a man he used to work beside who always said that. 'That should give them pause for thought.' He could see his face but the name was out of reach. Who was he talking about? The unions? The competition? A curmudgeonly old bugger he was anyway.

Maybe he was one of those himself. She probably thought that, the way he sometimes snapped at her.

Later he said, 'Sit down, will you? I've got something important I want to ask you.'

She sat. She waited. *She bloody* knows *already*, he thought.

'Tell me the truth now,' he said. 'That's all I want. The truth.'

She nodded. 'Go on.'

'Have I got it?' he said.

And now, at this moment, his mind failed him. He'd forgotten the bloody word. He'd had it only a minute ago.

'Got what?' she asked.

'That thing.' His fist thumped the arm of the chair. 'That thing.'

'There you go,' Alex Mather said, on his return from the post office. 'A leaflet detailing the things you can and can't send in the Royal Mail. Mostly can't.'

'Thank you,' Jill Mather said, putting it with all the other leaflets in the basket on the dresser. 'I thought the Royal Mail was being abolished?'

'Privatised,' Alex said. He poured himself coffee from the cafetière, put the mug in the microwave and blasted it for thirty seconds on full power. 'Same thing. Surely nobody really believes this crap about maintaining the universal service?'

'I only just made that.'

'I like it hot, though.'

'It is hot.'

'Piping hot.'

'Be careful.'

'I mean, what business intent on making a profit would happily accept an obligation to deliver to the last house on Unst six days a week? Eh? Whoever takes over, the first thing they'll do is lobby to get Saturday deliveries to Unst scrapped. Jeesus!'

'I did warn you.'

'Then they'll want differential rates for all supposedly remote postcodes. Or a subsidy. Guess who'll pay for that? It'll be the railways all over again, I'm telling you.'

'I'm not arguing, Alex,' Jill said. 'I agree with you.'

'Speaking of "differential", there was an MP on the radio earlier, did you hear him? "I beg to differentiate," he said. Can you credit it? We're ruled by morons, total morons.'

'I know.'

'You haven't even looked at this.' He took the leaflet from the basket, touching its shiny surface to his lips to cool them down.

'I will. Later.'

'"You are not permitted to send waste, dirt, filth or refuse in the mail,"' Alex read. 'Maybe we should start a campaign of civil disobedience. Post jiffy bags full of ordure to the idiots who came up with this privatisation idea.'

'We?'

'I'm joking. I'm not going to descend to their level. What about the Queen? It's hers really. Her head's all over it. You'd think she'd object.'

'Yes, why don't you get her on board? Start at the top and work your way down.'

Alex grinned at her with his burnt lips.

'You're a cheeky bitch, Mrs Mather,' he said.

'That's why you married me,' she said.

Jack and the Wizard

'The clock's broken,' said Jack's mother. 'Take it tae Hugh the clockmaker tae get it mended. Here's some money.'

The clockmaker was also a wizard. He drew a chalk circle on the floor round Jack's feet. 'Just you stay in there, Jack,' he says, 'while I look at the clock.' And he starts fiddling with the mechanism.

Well, first of all he makes the hands go backwards, very fast. While Jack is watching this he feels like he's shrinking, and then he looks down at his feet and he *is* shrinking, and when he cries out in terror his voice is like a wee laddie's, and he begins to greet like a bairn and that's because he's *become* a bairn. Next, Hugh makes the hands go forward, and Jack grows back to how he was before, but then he feels his joints stiffening and sees his skin wrinkling, and when he cries out again it's in a croaky old voice, and he's so terrified that he loses his balance and staggers out of the chalk circle.

'Now ye've done it,' says Hugh. 'If I canna fix this clock, ye'll be stuck like that for ever.'

He works away at the clock for ages. 'Right,' he says at last, 'when I say "Jump!" you jump back intae the circle, and before ye land I'll gie the balance a wee push and let's hope it keeps tickin. Ready? Jump!' So Jack jumps back into the circle, and the clock keeps ticking, and Hugh sets the hands to the right time and Jack is restored to his original self, to his great relief.

'Och, that's the best bit of fun I've had in ages,' Hugh says. 'Now, did ye bring ony money?'

'Aye,' says Jack, 'but it was cruel, whit ye did, and I'm awa tae tell ma mither aboot it.'

'Now,' says Hugh, 'dinna be sae hasty. Here's a receipt for yer mither, but you keep the money and if you don't tell her aboot it then nor will I.'

So Jack took the clock home, with the receipt in one pocket and the money in another, amazed that even a wizard was feart of his mother.

She was of an age, his daughter, that made her susceptible to hysteria. Especially when among friends. They were twelve, she and her friends. Their collective ability to raise themselves to dizzy pitches of joy, hilarity, idolatry, rage, shock or fear was – a word never far from their lips – awesome. He was awed by it. Sometimes he saw her as transparent, a glass being with a swirl of chemical reactions surging through her. She was beginning to change, from innocent child to knowing woman: leaving him, in a way; coming towards him, in another. And in doing so she must go through this phase.

But this afternoon she had not been with friends. She had been alone. She clutched breathlessly at the words. 'There was a man.' 'What?' he said. 'There was a man, there was a man!' she cried, beating at him with her palms because he was being too slow and stupid. 'Wait,' he said. 'Slow down. Tell me again. What man?'

There was a man in the woods. Where? Where she'd been walking. Where? Up at the end of the farm road, where it went right to the farm, left into the woods. What was she doing there? *She* wasn't doing *anything*. Defensive. Accusatory.

'No,' he said, 'it's all right. I didn't mean that. Tell me what man.'

'He was in the trees.'

'What was he doing?'

'Just standing.'

'Did he say anything to you?'

'No.'

'Touch you?'

'No, no.'

'Sweetheart, he was probably just out for a walk. Maybe he had a dog. Did he have a dog?'

'No, he was just there. Why don't you believe me?'

All his worst dreams flooded in. All his fears. Her fears become his, irrational, fed by schlock movies and tabloid headlines. MONSTER. BEAST. ANIMAL. Those horror stories of girls attacked, abducted, murdered.

'I'll go and have a look,' he told her. 'You stay here in the house, okay?'

It would be nothing. Still, he had to go, to allay her fear, to allay his own. To see if anyone was in the trees, and what he was doing there. To see if there was a man and, if so, to challenge his innocence.

'Have you noticed how these people are always "interested in exploring"?' Alex Mather said. 'In another age would they have been up the Zambezi with Livingstone or crossing the frozen wastes of Antarctica with Scott? I think not.'

'You're being a bit hard,' Jill Mather said. 'They're only kids.'

She was walking round a sculpture made of bits of old bicycle. It was called *Recycle*. Was it a man or a machine? She couldn't decide.

'Aye, but where are they getting their cues from? The modern art galleries. Their own teachers. They may be kids but this is their degree show, their passing-out parade. The future of culture is in their hands, God help us.'

'What about this?' Jill said. 'This is clever, don't you think?'

'"Clever" – that's another weasel word. It's what you say to a toddler when you can't make out what the mess they've painted is supposed to be. "Aren't you clever?" When I look at a piece of art, I want to say, "This is beautiful, this is brilliantly crafted, this is aesthetically unimpeachable." Do you actually like it, isn't that the point?'

'Yes,' she said, coming round to stand beside him. 'Yes, I think I do.'

'You think?' he said. 'But why? What's good about it? It's just a feeble pun. That Marcel Duchamp has a lot to answer for. He was having a laugh, and now the whole art world's taking the piss.'

Jill said, as she often did, 'I'm not arguing with you, Alex. You're being deliberately obtuse. But you don't fool me. I saw you at that young lad's paintings over there. I could tell you liked *them*.'

'*He* can draw,' Alex said loudly. '*He* can paint. And he hasn't come up with any excuses either. He hasn't *explained* his work. It speaks for itself. Poor bugger. I predict destitution, starvation and total neglect.'

'You could help by buying one of his paintings.'

'I'd only be postponing the inevitable. Who is Alex Mather against the mass of the art establishment? He is nobody. See that air-conditioning unit up there? If I stuck a label on that someone would snap it up. Where can we get a drink?'

Bath

That was the year Stevie dug a mudbath for the elephant. The hot days started in early May and I remember there not being any rain until August, although that's possibly a false memory. The elephant was in his enclosure and getting frustrated with the heat bouncing off the concrete all round him, and this wasn't Africa, it wasn't even the south of England, it was Scotland. We took turns at playing a hose on him but his skin dried out a few minutes after you stopped, and these cracks were appearing, sore-looking, like the cracks of a dried-out riverbed. So Stevie spent four days digging a pit in the monkey section, a two-hundred-yard run from where the elephant was kept. We had to get clearance from the big man because theoretically it was dangerous letting the elephant loose, there were cars coming through that he could have charged or just decided to sit on, but the big man said, 'On you go,' so we went.

The day came when we opened the gate and took him down the road to the monkey section, Stevie running ahead and me coming behind in the Land Rover with the lights on so the elephant wouldn't think twice about stopping. Stevie led him to the mudbath and that elephant went in like a diving submarine, covering himself in the cooling, healing mud and trumpeting with pleasure. We fitted the hose to a nearby standpipe and kept the bath topped up and I'll tell you, I've seen a lot of things, but I've never seen an animal so obviously, deliriously happy.

Later that day we ran him back to the enclosure, and he went without a fuss, and the next day we took him to the bath again, and every day for the rest of that summer till the weather broke. He used to sprint down there, like a child on a beach heading for the sea. It was a crime really, keeping such a beast in captivity, but Stevie made life better for him that summer at least. He was a good man, Stevie. You only had to see what he did for the elephant to know that.

He was a man of subtle thought and bold accomplishment. His erudition stretched across the Humanities. Literature, music, cinema, art – all lay within the compass of his mind; but he also had a profound understanding of philosophy, natural history and science. If there was a subject on which he did not have a view, it was only because it was not worthy of his consideration. The trivial and populist passed him by like so much fluff in the wind. Accused of elitism, he proudly acknowledged himself guilty as charged. 'I set myself the highest, most exacting standards,' he said, 'and I expect others to do the same.'

Leading, though of course lesser, figures in the various fields of his knowledge bowed to his superiority, some with gratitude, others with resentment. Critics expounded on his genius. Professors studied his work and lectured on it. Their best students wrote dissertations and theses on it. Conferences were organised around its themes. Long before he grew old, his place in intellectual history was assured.

Yet his reputation existed only in a certain stratum of society. Outside the walls of academe, beyond the pages of learned journals and the most sophisticated cultural radio programmes, he was unrecognised. He understood this – that singers, film stars, footballers and comedians were celebrities in a way that he never could be. Physically, he was an unremarkable human being. There were streets – whole districts of his city – where he could wander in complete anonymity. He found this comforting.

Nothing, in his last years, gave him greater pleasure than to leave his book-lined home in one part of the city and take a bus to another part – a journey between two worlds, he felt – where he would buy a burger, vanilla milkshake and fries at McDonald's. He would eat this meal crammed in at one of the restaurant's little plastic tables, then sit for ten minutes, watching other customers arriving, ordering, consuming and departing, before taking a bus home. He did this once a week. The staff treated him as they treated everybody else, and served him exactly the same meal every time. To them he was nobody special. And this was what pleased him most.

His Mother, in the Sun

The rented cottage had no outdoor furniture, so he took two chairs from the kitchen and placed them on the grass.

'They're a bit hard,' he said. 'I'll get you a cushion.'

'Don't worry, this is fine,' she replied. She'd gone through life saying things like that: *This is fine, don't worry, never mind.* Now, in her late eighties, this acceptance of things as they were, this dislike of 'causing a fuss', seemed to have served her well. But when he brought her the cushion and fitted it behind her back, she did not object.

'Glass of wine?'

'Yes, please.'

Earlier, he'd put a bottle of rosé in the fridge. A summer wine for a summer evening. He rinsed and dried three glasses. His wife was preparing supper: nothing fancy, just some pasta and salad.

'Do you want me to set the table?' he asked, pouring her a glass of wine.

'No, I'll do it. You talk to your mum.'

He'd be driving his mother home later, so only gave himself half a glass. He poured a full one for her, though. When he held the wine to the light it glowed.

'Look,' he said, nodding towards the window. The sun was low now, but still had plenty of warmth in it. His mother had turned the chair in order to be face on to the sun. Her hands were folded, her head tilted back, her eyes closed. Perhaps she was thinking about his father at the hospital. Perhaps she wasn't thinking of anything, simply enjoying the luxury of not thinking.

She'd always loved the sun. She and his father used to go abroad for it, but foreign holidays were out of the question now. At least this year summer had put in a home appearance.

'Go out to her,' his wife said.

And he would. They would talk about inconsequential things of the present, or good memories from his childhood or from hers, until the midges began to bite, or they were called in to eat. But before he took out the wine, he watched her a moment longer: his mother, in the sun. He knew he would never forget that view of her.

Fear

Birds fascinated her. She didn't know anything much about them, but she could have watched them all day. Birds were better – far better – than television.

If she scattered breadcrumbs on the grass, at whatever time of day, birds would arrive from all directions in less than a minute. How did they know?

She had a couple of feeders hanging outside her kitchen window. She kept one filled with nuts, the other with fat balls. Small birds came to those nuts and fat balls all morning, inches away from where she sat on the other side of the glass. If she moved suddenly they flew off, but they were only away for a few moments. Greenfinches, sparrows, chaffinches, robins, tits of various denominations. If they squabbled, it did not seem to be about anything very serious: some mild breach of protocol, perhaps. They even seemed to queue, waiting their turn to hang from the feeders and chip away at the food. There were a couple of sparrows who stationed themselves underneath the feeders, catching debris, and she was surprised that only they seemed clever enough to have worked out this way of benefiting from the efforts of others. But perhaps it was demeaning. Perhaps those ground-feeding sparrows were considered vulgar, ill-mannered. Still, they too were tolerated.

We have something to learn from birds, she thought. *They were around long before us and will be here long after we are gone. What have they to learn from us? Nothing. Even my putting out food for them is a mere convenience. If those feeders were empty they would go somewhere else to eat. I sit here watching them and they ignore me until I move. And their reaction is an instinct which we call fear, but that is only our name for it. It is not fear. It is survival.*

When she finally got up – conscious that she could not sit there for ever, that there were many responsibilities pressing upon her – that thought remained. The birds had no fear. Why was that? Was it because they had no sense of the end of life? All they knew was to be alive. It was she who had fear.

'This one is my grandfather, my mother's father. He could have been a household name, if things had gone differently for him. He never had any luck, that was the trouble. Luck is what separates most people from success and wealth. That, and who you know. It's not about talent. My grandfather had talent. It's about who you know.

'My grandfather was in Paris in the 1920s, trying to get a break the same as everyone. They were all there: Joyce, Pound, Fitzgerald, Henry Miller, Gertrude Stein. And Ernest Hemingway. My grandfather and Hemingway used to drink together, but my grandfather was a better drinker than Hemingway. They would get very drunk and eventually Hemingway would keel over but my grandfather would still be going. That made Hemingway furious. "I'm going to beat you this time, you son of a bitch," he'd say the next day. My grandfather would shrug and off they'd go again, with the same result.

'Once my grandfather asked if he could borrow Hemingway's typewriter, and for ten straight hours he typed out this story he'd had in his head for months. It just poured out of him. When he'd finished he gave it to Hemingway to read, and Hemingway saw that it was damned good. He also saw that my grandfather had picked up on his own style, which is what led to the next thing. You know what that pig did? He stole the story. It was typed on his typewriter and it was in his style so he sent it off to *Scribner's* under his own name. And they published it! I don't remember the name of the story, but it was my grandfather's. There was nothing he could do about it; he didn't have a handwritten draft or notes and the only other person who'd seen it was Hemingway. And Hemingway said, "I said I'd beat you, didn't I?"

'My grandfather could never see a book by Hemingway without feeling sick to his stomach. It's quite a claim to fame, to say you were ripped off by Ernest Hemingway, but it didn't do my grandfather any good. He never had any luck, though, that was the trouble.'

Jack and the Bluebottle

The bluebottle had been racing round the room for twenty minutes, driving Jack daft with its frantic buzzing. Now at last it had settled on a shelf. It was about a foot away from where he stood, hand raised ready to strike. This was the moment he'd been waiting for. He was about to smack the beast into oblivion when he had a sudden attack of guilt.

'This bluebottle is only gaun aboot its ain business,' he said to himself. 'It canna help being a bluebottle, and the reason it's drivin me daft is *because* it's a bluebottle. I shouldna kill it just for being itsel. How would I feel if *I* was a bluebottle?'

He lowered his hand. The bluebottle sensed the movement and recommenced its mad flying about. Jack already had the window wide open but the bluebottle seemed not to like the open air and refused to depart. To get some peace, Jack himself had to step outside.

It was late in the afternoon and the garden was full of midges. They began to bite and he slapped and swiped at them to make them stop. But then he had that same guilty feeling.

'They're only midges and they canna help themsels,' he said. 'What right hae I tae kill midges just because they're daein whit midges dae?' So he went back into the house, to the kitchen this time, where his mother was busy making jam.

'Och, Jack,' his mother says, handing him a rolled-up newspaper, 'there's a wasp in here trying tae get at ma new jam. Will ye watch till it lands on the table and then kill it for me?'

'Och, Mither,' says Jack, 'think whit ye are askin. The wasp is only a wasp and it canna help itsel for that. What right hae I tae kill it for wantin tae eat yer jam?'

Jack's mother comes across and gives him an almighty skelp on the head. 'That's what ye get for being Jack, Jack,' she says. 'I ken ye canna help yersel, and I canna help being yer mither, but life's unfair like that. If ye want ony jam on yer breid, kill the bloody wasp.'

Doorways are a problem. Going into the house from outside, or sometimes going from one room to another, my father gets stuck. As if some force field will not let him pass. He stops. What looks like thinking is on his face, but it is not thinking. It is thought frozen. He cannot penetrate the field and does not know why. He leans into the problem, one hand on the doorframe, one foot trailing the other. Nothing moves.

This has been going on for a while, since before the only way to get him to travel any distance was in a wheelchair. The last time he walked with me to the shops and back, he froze at the door of the house. This was months ago: it feels like yesterday. Time suspended. I spoke to him, trying to help him to get unstuck, but he seemed not to hear. I moved around him. If he could lift his back foot. If he could let go of the doorframe. I lifted the foot. I eased the fingers from the wood. The force field did not apply to me. We were both in the same place, but he was not with me nor I with him. We were not together.

It reminded me of something.

Eventually, the seized moment unseized. I got him through the door, the portal from somewhere to somewhere else.

He sat in his chair, drained. He fell asleep. I don't think he had any memory of being stuck.

Later, I recalled what this had reminded me of: the table-tennis scene in *A Matter of Life and Death*. Squadron Leader Peter Carter should have died when he jumped from his burning plane without a parachute, but in the fog over the English Channel the guide sent to conduct him to the other world missed him. Carter is caught between worlds, between life and life after death. The bell he rings makes no sound. He walks round the frozen table-tennis players, puzzled by their state. They are there, but not with him.

In the film, Carter was played by David Niven. But who was playing that part in our little scene? Myself? Or my father?

It is never wise to question the comings and goings of a cat. A cat has a life secret from humans, as a dog never does. Let the cat come and go as it will.

There was an old laird of Pitfodels, when the Menzies had possession of that estate in lower Deeside, a mile or two from Aberdeen. The troubles of this family are too numerous to describe, and this particular laird was no luckier than the others, but he had a favourite cat whose company, when it deigned to grace him with its presence, distracted him from his worries.

One day he saw this cat scampering through the Clash, a piece of boggy ground by the Two Mile Cross, not far from the Brig o' Dee. When the cat came in and, as was her custom, jumped up onto the table, the laird gave her a quizzical look and asked what business she had been about when he had seen her earlier.

'Whaur ye saw me aince, ye sall see me nae mair,' the cat answered, and leaping upon his throat she throttled the life from him.

There is no historical basis for any part of this story, even after ruling out the likelihood of the cat having such a good command of the Scots tongue. Perhaps it was a story told by another man of that locality, whose unmarked grave in a lonely spot used to be pointed out to the curious. This fellow had a reputation for telling the most unlikely tales. He would stress the veracity of his word by wishing that he might be buried out of sight of kirk or kirkyard if he was lying. To say such a thing in those times was a serious matter and few would have wanted to challenge him.

Eventually the man died. As his coffin was being taken to the usual place of burial, the corpse gradually became heavier and heavier till the mourners could carry it no further, and were forced to dig a grave right there and put him in it. Thus was his wish fulfilled and thus was he revealed as a liar of great capacity and boldness.

'When I was appointed to my present position three years ago, I felt both privileged and humbled, and I stand before you today as conscious of that privilege and, I hope, as full of humility, as I was then. To lead an organisation which is also a cherished national institution is a very great honour, but with leadership comes responsibility, and it is my responsibility to stand, as I am doing now, here before you today.

'Our organisation, a great British organisation, has let you, the great British public, down. For this we are profoundly and sincerely sorry. I, personally, am profoundly and sincerely sorry. I take full and personal responsibility for the profound and sincere sorrow which I feel personally and which the organisation feels collectively.

'I also apologise unreservedly for having to make this apology. I am sorry that this apology has to be made, but it was to take responsibility for such apologies that I was appointed in the first place.

'A wise man once said, "The buck stops here." It does. It shall go no further. There is nowhere else for it to go. I am more profoundly and sincerely sorry about this than I can say, but that is why I stand before you today, apologising unreservedly.

'There have been calls for my resignation. I do not intend to resign, and I make no apology for not intending to resign. I have considered my position, and I rather like it. Now is not the time for me to lose my salary, pension and associated benefits. I apologise to those who think I should resign, but I do not apologise for making no apology for not resigning. Now is the time for me to take full responsibility both for apologising and for not apologising, and this is what I am now doing.

'I apologise in advance, sincerely and wholeheartedly, should I have to apologise again in another three years. But I do not apologise for making that apology in advance. It is a great honour and a privilege to stand here apologising to you today, and I am full of humility. I am sorry about that, but I cannot help it.'

'It wisnae me. I wis jist mindin ma ain business at the back o the shoap. In fact I wisnae even in the shoap. I wis oot. I wis speakin metaphorically when I said that. Because it isnae a shoap, is it? It's a great big organisation. A national institution. So I couldnae hae been at the back o the shoap because that widnae be true, and I'm no a liar. So when I say I wis oot, I wis. Swear tae God. And when I say it wisnae me, it wisnae.

'I didnae ask tae be the heidbummer. I wis jist mindin ma ain business at the back o the shoap when sumbdy tellt me tae go tae the front o the shoap, so I went. I'd never went there afore. When I say the front o the shoap I'm speakin metaphorically again. Ye can dae that when ye're the heidbummer. Actually I went up in the lift tae the tap flair and there wis this room wi big windaes and squishy chairs and a drinks cabinet. And they said if I wis heidbummer I wid get tae sit in the squishy chairs lookin oot the windaes and I could drink the bevvy for free. Well, ye'd need tae be stupit no tae say yes tae that, widn't ye? So I said yes. But that's aw I did, said yes and sat in the squishy chairs and had a wee bevvy, and efter that I went oot. So it wisnae me.

'Naw, I dinnae ken wha it wis. I didnae see nuthin. It might hae been the boy that wis in afore me. Ye better ask him. He might ken somethin. I dinnae. I wis jist mindin the shoap till sumbdy else came. But I wisnae really, coz I wis oot.

'I saw some big boys earlier, runnin doon the street. I think it wis mibbe them. Naw, I didnae see their faces. And there's nae point gettin the polis. They'll be miles awa by noo.

'Zat it? I'll jist slip oot the back then. Sumbdy else'll be alang soon.

'Noo there's an idea. It might hae been them.

'But it defin*ately* wisnae me.'

'I wish you wouldn't sneer like that,' Alex Mather said.

'I am not sneering,' Jill Mather replied.

'You are too. Just hold that look right there and take it to a mirror and tell me it's not a sneer.'

'It's not a sneer.'

'You haven't checked. I'm on the receiving end of it and from where I'm sitting it's a sneer.' He pointed to the back of the restaurant. 'The Ladies is down there.'

'I am not going to check how I look to you in a mirror. Perhaps you should check how *you* look.'

'I'm not interested in how I look. Never have been.'

'Well, let me tell you, you look ridiculous.'

'That would explain the sneer. Simply because I utilise an object to illustrate an opinion which you dislike, you sneer.'

'It is not a sneer. If it's anything it's a look of incomprehension. Because I don't understand where you're coming from, Alex. I don't know what's going on inside your head.'

'My inner life. That's what's going on.'

'Just the one? I don't think so. And not so inner either. They tend to get out a lot.'

'And you find that what? Embarrassing?'

'Sometimes. But mostly just incomprehensible.'

'Yet you never seem surprised. "You don't fool me" is one of your common expressions. Reconcile that with "incomprehensible". When did I first become incomprehensible to you? Was I incomprehensible when we were courting, for example?'

'When we were courting? Excuse me while I lubricate the padlocks and blow the dust off the box files. Actually, don't bother, I can remember. Back then you were slightly strange. Mysterious even.'

'Same thing as incomprehensible.'

'Not at all.'

'Aye it is. Mysterious is good, though. You should try to think of me as mysterious. Intriguing. That might help.'

'Help who? You or me?'

'Help take the sneer off your face. Create an aura around me.'

'I tell you what, Alex. I'll take the so-called sneer off my face if you take the serviette that you claim represents the absurdity of organised religion off your head. Then perhaps we can enjoy our food. Is that a deal?'

'I crumple my mitre before your infinite wisdom,' Alex said.

They had walked for many hours, and were tired and hungry, and fearful that it would soon be dark. Therefore they were gladdened when the path left the forest and became a broad red road. They walked on until the road divided to the west and to the east. And before them was a wall, too steep and too tall for them to climb, which stretched as far as they could see in both directions. So, not knowing which way to go, they sat down beside the road and rested.

In a while an old man in ragged clothes came towards them from the east. He had sandals on his feet and a staff in his hand. When he came up to them he asked why they had sat down.

'Because we are weary,' they said. 'And we have come to the wall and do not know which way to go.'

'Go the way I came,' he said, 'and you will come to a door in the wall. If you walk with courage it is not far, but if you walk in fear you will never reach it.'

Then he went down the red road towards the forest, and they watched until they could no longer see him.

Then they too set off, walking beside the wall the way the old man had come. And the wall was unbroken by any door, and the one took the hand of the other so that they would not be afraid. It was late yet the day did not grow dark.

Then the one said to the other, 'I see the door,' but the other did not see it. Yet it was there.

So they came to the door, and stood before it. And there was no handle or latch on the door. And the one who had not seen the door knocked, and it did not open. And the one who had seen it pushed, and it opened. And they went in together, hand in hand, not knowing what they would find on the other side. And the door closed behind them.

The old man in the forest heard the door close, but he was not afraid.

The Old Man in the Forest

The old man in the forest heard the door close. He recognised it at once.

The sound came from far away, yet it was as clear and unmistakable to him as if he had been standing next to the door. Despite its softness, it was a sound of firmness and finality. Somebody had gone through to the other side, and they would not be back. Or at least, if they came again, they would remember nothing of the journey.

He heard the quietest sounds: a bird shaking its feathers in a tree, a burn trickling over pebbles, a deer stepping on dried leaves. Sometimes, he realised, he heard *only* the quiet sounds, tuning out aeroplanes, traffic, the clatter of machines, the roar of crowds in streets and arenas, the conversations of millions of people. Birds, water, wild creatures – he would hear these things long after everything else had fallen silent.

And the sound of the door closing in the wall: he would always hear that.

It was a low, wooden, blue door with no handle or latch. It made no sound when opened, only when closed.

He was the only one ever to walk back through the forest. Sometimes he met people coming the other way. Sometimes there was no one to meet.

He could not remember what lay on the far side of the forest. He knew only that it was there, a beginning or an end to the trees. He thought it probable that when he arrived he would turn and walk back. He would walk along the broad red road until he reached the wall, and then he would go to the west or to the east, it did not matter which, and he would come to the door.

If he had ever gone through the door, if he had ever knocked or pushed at it, he did not remember. If this had ever troubled him, it no longer did.

He saw two figures coming towards him, a long way off. They would be tired, hungry and perhaps anxious. He did not want to alarm them. He stepped into the trees and waited till they had gone past.

He was not afraid.

It was a low, wooden, blue door with no handle or latch. It had made no sound when opened, not a creak nor a groan; but when closed, the sound it made, though soft, was one of firmness and finality.

The first and immediate effect that this had was to make one of them try to open it again, despite the absence of handle or latch. When, on the other side, she had pushed, the door had yielded. When she pushed and pulled now, the door did not yield.

Her companion said, 'So we cannot go back.'

She replied, 'Should we not have come through?'

'What else could we do? The wall might have gone on for ever.'

They looked at the wall. As before, it was too smooth and too tall for them to climb, and as before it stretched as far as they could see in both directions. Yet it did not seem unfriendly: its stone was of a warm, red hue, and when they put their hands to it they felt how it still held the heat of the sun.

'I thought the day would soon be over,' she said, 'but look!' She pointed to the sky, which was blue, and dotted with very white fluffy clouds that did not seem quite real. Yet the sunshine felt real enough, and so did the cooling breeze.

'There is no road along the wall on this side,' her companion said, 'and no road or path going away from the door. What will we do?'

Before them stretched a vast expanse of short grass and moss such as you might find on the upper slopes of a hill. And perhaps the ground did rise, but in a gentle, not an intimidating, way.

She took a few steps from the door. The turf was both soft and firm. A phrase from some walking guide came back to her: *good easy going along broad smooth ridges*. There were no ridges, no visible peaks, just the slope, yet it seemed to invite them onto it.

'Let's go for a walk,' she said. 'In that direction. All right?'

'Yes,' her companion said. 'I was tired before, but no longer.'

This is It?

They had been walking in silence but neither of them knew for how long. The sun had not moved or, rather, where they were did not seem to have moved in relation to the sun. The slope rose, almost imperceptibly. The turf continued both soft and firm.

The one said to the other, 'How are you?'

'I'm fine,' the other answered.

'Tired?'

'Not at all.'

'I never thought it would be like this,' the one continued. 'I couldn't imagine what it would be like. I didn't know if there would be anything.'

'Sunny uplands,' the other said. 'Didn't you believe in sunny uplands?'

She recalled the phrase from a guidebook that she'd found so appealing: *good easy going along broad smooth ridges*. Wasn't that a promise of something? Yet how could it have related to this?

She saw her companion wipe her brow: the first and only sign of discomfort in however long it had been. 'Are you hot?' she asked.

'I was, but no longer,' came the reply. They were walking now down a green track shaded by old trees and bounded by banks of wildflowers. She did not understand how the change could have happened without her noticing, but the open hill was gone. She did not really mind. Probably the track would lead to the hill in time. But what was time?

She thought, *Is this what happens when you step through the blue door?* It took an effort even to remember the existence of the door and that it was blue. Why remember it when there was no going back through it?

'Do you think this is it?' she said.

'Oh yes,' her companion said. 'What else could there be?'

'There could have been anything. But why do I know this from somewhere?'

'Perhaps you've been here before?'

'No, I don't think so.' She paused, and could hardly tell which she liked better – the pausing or the walking. 'Tell me,' she said, 'do you know, do you remember, your name?'

Her companion shook her head. 'No. And you?'

'No.'

'Does it bother you?'

'It did, but no longer.'

Suddenly she wanted the open hill again. She knew it would be there.

August

'I'm not sure,' she said, 'how well I would deal with such news. Not as well as how they're dealing with it, I suspect.'

'You would deal with it in your own way,' he said. 'Calmly, philosophically, realistically.'

'I'm not so sure.'

'Yes you would, because that's who you are.'

'You don't know the turmoil going on beneath the surface,' she said, and gave him a serene smile and a look so measured it was impossible to believe that anything other than complete stillness lay below.

'What else can they do?' he said. 'There's no point in being emotional. They just have to accept the diagnosis, listen to the doctors and hope for the best. It's out of their hands. And the best is pretty good these days. Twenty years ago it might have been hard to feel optimistic, but survival rates are so much better than they were. The fact that it was picked up early . . .'

'Let's hope early enough,' she said.

'And he's not been feeling unwell. He looks exactly the same as he always does. Perfectly healthy.'

'But he's not. Beneath the surface.'

'No, but if he was losing weight, or had a bad colour, or was in pain . . . But he isn't.'

'I said to her, if there was anything we could do . . .'

'I said that too. To him. I meant it but I'm not sure he heard. Not that there is anything. It's just a form of words, isn't it?'

'It's an offering.'

He didn't reply for a minute. The bus stopped, disgorged some passengers, took on others. All those lives, getting on and off, heading down side streets, going home, going to meet friends or lovers, going to be with someone or to be alone.

'What did you mean just then?' he asked as the bus lurched forward again. 'What you said about turmoil? What did you mean?'

'I was joking,' she said. She laid her hand on top of his. 'There is no turmoil.'

'Really?'

'Really.'

But something surged through him so unexpected and violent that for a moment he thought he might be sick. If something should happen to her . . .

He managed a smile. 'That's good,' he said.

'Alex?'

Jill Mather turned. Alex had come to a halt in the middle of the pavement. He was staring, eyebrows raised, at a point about ten feet to his right, slightly above eye level. His right arm was bent at the elbow and the hand was held palm upward as if to catch raindrops or perhaps as if he were about to recite lines from Shakespeare. It was possible that he had been taken ill, but Jill doubted it. He was a frighteningly robust man.

'What are you doing, Alex?'

He remained immobile, while the crowd flowed, more or less, around him. Some individuals had to jam on the brakes or swerve suddenly to avoid crashing into him. A woman pushing a pram had to divert off the pavement into the bus lane.

'Hello?' Jill waved her hand in front of his eyes, one of which winked at her.

'Give me a coin,' he said through barely parted lips. 'Quick. In the hand.'

Shoppers, Chinese tourists, festival fun seekers and a man on stilts handing out flyers all navigated their way round Alex.

'This is you trying to prove a point, isn't it?' Jill said. He nodded minutely. She sighed, opened her purse and placed a pound in the upturned palm.

Alex made a whirring noise in his throat and began to move like a mechanical toy. He pocketed the coin, bowed stiffly to Jill and mimed gratitude before extending the hand and becoming a human statue again.

'I see,' Jill said. 'Street theatre, is it?' Another nod. 'Well, I'm away to John Lewis. I'll phone you in an hour.'

A minute earlier he'd been complaining about not being able to move for the bloody Fringe, the rich kids up from Cambridge with their so-called bloody comedy shows, the bloody dawdling tourists and the bloody street performers. Now he'd decided to be one.

She could hear him already. 'Easy peasy.' Even if he didn't earn a penny he'd go to a bank and swap a tenner for mixed coins just so he could say to her, 'Look, money for old rope.' She could read him like a book.

Well, he'd be paying for the coffee.

Nightmares

When I was five or six, I dreamed repeatedly of being in a church with my mother. It was not a church either of us had entered before, either in the dream or in reality. The building stretched up into utter darkness: the roof was too far away to be seen. Sets of arched double doors, massively tall, far bigger than the height of any normal person, were set on each side of the pulpit. The pulpit too was of a stupendous size.

Nobody but us appeared to be in this church. We were waiting, presumably, for a service to begin. Beside the pew in which we sat was a great stone pillar with a board on it displaying the numbers of the hymns that would be sung if the service ever happened.

I wanted to leave. My mother whispered that we had to stay. I could tell that she wanted to leave too. Like me, she was afraid of something. I was afraid of the gloom, the shadowy emptiness and those great double doors through which some unimaginably large being might come. It seemed to me that she was afraid of something else.

I always woke up before anybody or anything came through the doors. Sometimes I woke crying, and she would be there. Sometimes I did not cry, and she did not come.

To learn that it was better not to cry was a hard lesson, but I learned it.

Another recurring nightmare, which I had when a few years older, involved me being on the deck of an old sailing ship – a pirate ship perhaps – which was travelling over a sickly, smooth, black sea towards black rocks. There was no wind in the sails yet the ship rushed towards its destruction at an evil speed. There was a wheel but it resisted all my efforts to turn it and alter the ship's course. All I could do was prepare for the impact.

Afterwards, the rocks were covered with small black pieces of wreckage like burst balloons.

There was no sign of me. It was my dream, but I had vanished from it.

Nobody came, because by then I was a big boy.

Wait

You pull in to a passing place to let the van by. Impatient bastard. Sure, probably he has twenty more drops to make before he can knock off, and the distances between drops will be big around here and some of the addresses not that easy to find. No doubt he doesn't need to be stuck behind you, but you certainly don't need him tailgating you on this twisting single-track road. And wouldn't you think, with the road, and the weather, and the views at every turn, he might just ease his foot off the pedal, think to himself, *Well, these parcels will get where they're going sooner or later, so why not make it later?* No, it doesn't work like that. You wish it did, for his sake if for nobody else's. Nobody else would be the worse for it.

You are about to pull out again when you catch yourself about to pull out. Wait a minute. You apply the handbrake, lower the window, switch off the engine. The tide is in, the loch full, blue and beautiful. Two horses in a field to your left, cows and sheep dotted across the fields to your right, down to the sea, as if the hand of some celestial modeller had placed them just so on the green slopes. Across the loch, three or four low houses, stone-built, small-windowed, one at least with a corrugated-tin roof. They shimmer in the sun, floating just above the water, like ghosts of houses.

You sit and watch for as long as it takes to sit and watch. A bee drones by. You scribble down a few words, a net to catch the moment. You know that you won't really catch it.

Sometimes a day cracks open like this. It reveals another day, as a rose opens to reveal another folded layer of rose. Those houses will never again haunt the loch like that. Those animals will never occupy the fields in that same patternless pattern. You will never pull into this passing place and let the window down to this particular moment. The van driver and his urgency are gone. Let them go further. Wait another minute. Wait.

Sympathy

for Pat, Anne and Angus

The hills above Glen Loth seem low and round and gentle seen from the coast, especially on a fine summer's day. But there is wild country up there. In bad weather a man could quickly become confused and disorientated, and not easily find his way home again.

There was a minister of Loth, Robert Robertson, of whom it is written that 'it was during Mr Robertson's time, and from the parish of Loth, that the last unfortunate victim suffered for witchcraft, being burned to death at Dornoch'. That was in 1727. Her name was Janet Horne. The story of her and her daughter, who only narrowly avoided the fate of her mother, is well known. But it is Robert Robertson who concerns me here.

He did not condemn the poor woman – that was the work of the sheriff-depute of Sutherland – but did he judge her? It is hard to believe he played no role at all. Did he question her accusers? Remonstrate with them? With whom did he sympathise, her or them?

He had a cousin, Francis, minister of the neighbouring parish of Clyne, and they must have been of similar age, because they gained their degrees in the same year, 1710. Did Francis and Robert speak on the matter? Was it out of their hands? Could they not have done something to stop what happened? She was strangled to death and burned in a barrel, for Christ's sake. Did they condone or condemn it? Or did they say nothing?

I thought of these things today in the graveyard at Clyne, overlooking Brora and the sea, with the hills of Loth to the north, benign and richly clad in heather. We were burying Jack, who'd led a good life and a long one, and it seemed a fine place to leave him in the sunshine, with not a bit of wind or rain to disturb him. A world away from the accusation and condemnation of a demented old woman. This is something, anyway, to be thankful for.

They were my ancestors, Francis and Robert. And Robert had a younger brother, James, of whom all that is known is that he was 'bred to the sea'.

Those hills are not so benign. An old book records that when John, sixth Earl of Sutherland, was travelling with his retinue in the year 1602, his harper, one Donald Maclean, 'perished in the Glen of Loth from a sudden snow storm'.

I am thinking of Janet Horne, who came from these parts, and was the last 'witch' to be executed in Scotland. Mr James Fraser, minister of Alness, writes in April 1727 to his friend Mr Robert Wodrow, minister of Eastwood: 'Since I saw you in Edinburgh in May last, there has been great noise of witchcraft in the parish of Loth, by which the minister is said to have suffered. He is not yet recovered; however, the thing has been examined into, and the women were, I know, before the presbytery.'

Two years *before* Janet Horne was tested and found to be a servant of Satan – because, among other signs, she stumbled over the opening words when asked to recite the Lord's Prayer in her native Gaelic – yet another Church of Scotland minister, Francis Hutcheson, was in Dublin writing treatises on *Beauty, Order, Harmony and Design* and on *Moral Good and Evil*. Two years *after* Janet's execution, Hutcheson became Professor of Moral Philosophy at Glasgow University. He was an intellectual precursor to what became known as the Scottish Enlightenment. 'That action is best,' he wrote, 'which procures the greatest happiness for the greatest numbers; and that, worst, which, in like manner, occasions misery.'

Two hundred miles to the north, the superstitious and sanctimonious majority would have condemned Hutcheson's view that humans can distinguish between virtue and vice without reference to, or even knowledge of, God. But though the action of burning Janet in a barrel might have pleased them, surely it cannot have made them happy.

And what of the minister of Loth? *He is not yet recovered.* Perhaps he never did mend, for he died thirteen years later, still in his forties. Did he carry Janet's mischief to the grave? Did he feel it crumbling his bones? Did the noise from Loth ring in his ears, even as he left this world and stepped, in assurance or in fear, into the next?

Ah, Janet, did you not do those things? Look at the fire they are building, Janet. When you tripped on the words, when you said 'wert' instead of 'art', did you not think how that would sound to their hungry ears? Thy Father who *wert* in Heaven, Janet? Oh, they knew who you meant, they knew the one you worshipped.

And your daughter's strange hands and strange feet, did you not think how these might one day appear to their eyes, and what stories they would make of them? And if she, too, should bear a child with those same deformities, did you believe that that would save you? That your neighbours would say, 'Well, we were wrong after all, those were not the marks of the Devil on her'? Did you not hear them instead confirmed in their cruel faith? That the child bears the sin of the mother and of the mother's mother, even unto death?

Did you not maim your own daughter, Janet, when you had your master shoe her like a pony? Did you not ride her to your sisters, to dance and froth in your hellish ecstasies? Come now, Janet, tell them what you did. This will not go away by their words, not now. Only you can bring it to an end.

Look at the fire they are building, Janet. A small fire it is. You will not feel it. They will choke you off before it touches you.

The great fire comes after, Janet. 'God have mercy on you,' they will say, 'for we cannot. It is not in our gift to be merciful.'

Where will they take you, Janet? To the square in front of the old bishop's palace? Or out of the town, to a place down by the dunes, where the stench of your burning will blow away to sea? They may watch the flames, Janet, but later they will not want you in their noses.

The flames of superstition are dying, Janet, but not soon enough for you. Your fate is to be the last of your kind, whatever your kind was.

God forbid that they should ever think you have come back again.

The Mannie

Lift your eyes to the hills and there is the statue. The 'Mannie' is the local name for it. A useful term, familiar and playfully derogatory, for cutting down to size one hundred feet of sandstone; for levelling a duke, a man folk would once hardly have dared look in the face.

The Mannie was erected to the Duke's memory after his death. But what is that memory, and whose?

He was a hard-headed but benevolent landowner, who saw that life as it was lived by the people of the glens and straths was unsustainable; that they were impoverished and starving and too numerous; and so he relocated them to the coasts, or encouraged them to emigrate, and made the interior a vast pasture for sheep, in part to pay for these improvements.

Or.

He was a cold, greedy man, indifferent to the sorrows of the people, whom he cleared by force and fire, destroying their way of life – their world, in effect – for profit. And he did this by proxy, setting cruel and rapacious factors to the task, so that they, not he, would be the chief villains of the play.

You can see the Mannie for miles around. He dominates the landscape as once the Duke did. There have been attempts to blow him up, dislodge, demolish or topple him. The plinth has had a few insults sprayed upon it. So far, he has survived.

The original Duke is long gone.

If you stand underneath and look up at the Mannie with the clouds racing over his head, you might think he is perpetually falling.

Knock him down or blow him up, and in a generation the arguments will be over. Good man, wicked man, nobody will care. Maybe that would be a relief.

But when the Mannie goes, the story will go. And if the story goes, the memory too will go. And when the memory has gone, the people will be empty shells. They will have no language of anger or dissent. They will find new names for names they cannot pronounce. They will not be of the land, only on it. And this will be the final act of clearance.

If No Death

'If there was no death, would there be war?' a small boy asked.

The teacher turned and looked along the rows of desks to see which small boy had spoken. The room was full of small boys, twenty-four of them. The one who had posed the question should have raised his hand before speaking, but nobody's hand was raised. At the moment the question was asked the teacher had had his back to the class as he wrote names and dates on the board. Although he knew his pupils well, he had not recognised the voice.

'Who asked that question?'

Nobody admitted responsibility.

'It is an interesting question,' the teacher said. 'Let us examine it.'

He wrote on the board: IF NO DEATH, WOULD THERE BE WAR?

The small boys stared blankly. *They are so young*, he thought.

Could any one of them have asked such a question? Had he really heard it?

'What is war for?' he prompted. 'Is it not to gain something? Land, or wealth, or power over others? How do you succeed in gaining power over others?'

A hand went up.

'Yes?'

'By killing them.'

'But if you kill someone, you can no longer have power over them.'

'But you have power over their friends. You can make them think you will kill them too, if they don't surrender.'

Another hand went up.

'Yes?'

'But if people couldn't die, then why try to kill them?'

Another hand, another voice: 'You could put them in prison and never let them out. That would be the next worst thing to killing them.'

Another voice: 'But how would you keep them in prison? If they couldn't be killed they would find a way out and you couldn't stop them.'

Another voice: 'If you weren't afraid of death then there'd be nothing to be afraid of. Not hunger, disease, cold, danger. Nothing.'

'You could do anything you liked and nobody could stop you.'

The teacher saw the excitement in their young faces. For a moment they had forgotten reality. He felt almost that they might rush from the classroom, intoxicated by this new sense of liberation.

It was his sad job to destroy their delusions.

Milk

You descended a curved flight of stairs to the school dining-room, in the basement. The stairs had rubber treads on them, a precaution against slipping. Ninety small boys and various adults – teachers, cooks, cleaners – went up and down them several times a day, so this made sense. There was a banister too, but to hold on to this was considered, among the boys, a sign of weakness.

At morning break the ninety boys queued on the stairs, then shuffled into the dining-room to a table on which were stacked three crates containing small bottles of milk. Each bottle contained one-third of a pint. You took a bottle and a straw and pierced the bottle's foil cap with the straw. In winter the milk was cold, sometimes containing ice. This was tolerable. On hot summer days the milk was warm, yellow and sickly, and great resolve was required to drain the bottle. The ninety boys walked in single file round the dining-room's perimeter, between the wall and the tables at which, two hours later, they would sit to eat dinner. By the time you returned to the starting-point you were supposed to have finished your milk. You showed a teacher or prefect your empty bottle before depositing it in one of the crates and throwing the straw into a waste bucket. Sometimes you might get away with leaving the last quarter-inch of frozen or cheesy milk. More often you would have to suck until the straw noisily declared that the bottle was completely empty.

The milk ritual was a torment for many boys.

A horizontal black line ran round the wall, halfway up. Below the line the plaster was painted a dark reddish colour, above it the plaster was off-white, not unlike the colour of the milk in summer. Above the line was a row of photographs of past rugby and cricket teams: squads of small boys, trying to look stern or fierce, who had in their time undergone similar rituals.

As you walked you saw how much they resembled you, although they were men now. Some perhaps were dead.

They watched you sucking your daily ration of milk. They understood, even if they were ghosts.

The Corpse

Gary and Hannah made the discovery when they were renovating their first home, a 1950s three-bedroom semi-detached in a quiet city suburb. First they found the sealed cupboard under the stairs: this was a bonus, as they needed all the storage space they could get. Then they prised open the door and found the corpse. Thankfully things had progressed far beyond the decomposition stage: only a skeleton, clad in a few shreds of dark suit, remained. A wisp or two of silk around the cervical vertebrae indicated that the skeleton had once sported a tie.

The police were relaxed about the matter, especially when they saw where the corpse was located and how it was dressed.

'We get a lot of these,' the lead detective told the anxious couple, 'especially in houses of this vintage. No, the circumstances are not suspicious. What we have here is a classic example of the forgotten bank manager.

'You're too young to remember,' he continued, 'but back in the 1960s banks didn't have the terrible reputation they have today. They didn't tempt you with easy credit, encourage you to buy things you didn't want and couldn't afford and then sell you more credit at higher rates of interest to service your debts. No, no, your local bank manager then was a figure of common sense and irreproachable probity. He was there to guide you in the careful conduct of your financial affairs, always recommending thrift and prudence.

'There was a big advertising campaign on television, as a result of which people took to keeping a bank manager in the cupboard under the stairs, so that they could bring him out and ask his advice whenever they needed it. A great innovation, but over time values changed. Society learned to despise thrift and embrace extravagance, and these domesticated bank managers became unfashionable. Some were decommissioned. Others, like this one, were simply forgotten. Please don't worry. You're not responsible.'

Gary and Hannah did wonder about attending the funeral of the man they thought of, after his removal from the premises, as 'their' bank manager. But they led busy lives, and instead went on holiday to Spain while the painters were in.

The Minister and the Devil

Last night I went again to the manse, to continue my talk with the minister. I rang the bell and waited, and for a long time nothing happened. I was not altogether surprised. I lit a cigarette and stood in the outer lobby, puffing smoke at the insects flying about in the twilight. Twice more I pressed the bell, to assure him that I was there and not minded to go away. Through the frosted panes of the inner door I thought I glimpsed movement – like the stirrings of a genie seen through the cloudy glass of his bottle – but he did not come. I tried the door but it was locked. Then I walked around the whole house, peering in at the windows, but saw no sign of life. The man was either asleep, hiding, drunk or dead.

After the third cigarette I decided to defer doing further damage to my lungs, and went away. The condition of my soul did not concern me. As for the condition of the minister's soul, well, that was why I was keen to resume our conversation.

I strolled down to the beach. A thin rain was falling, so I put up my umbrella. Nobody was about save one solitary figure on the sand. I thought it might be the minister, but on coming closer I realised that it was a stranger. He was turning slowly round and round on the one spot, and I saw that he, or someone, had drawn a circle in the sand and that he was inside it.

'Help me,' he said. 'Make the tide turn back or I will drown.' The sea was some thirty yards away.

'Impossible,' I said. Then I folded my umbrella and with its point began to draw a line from his circle towards the top of the beach.

'Thank you!' he called as I went away from him. 'Tie it securely!'

I gave up with the line when the rain came on more heavily and I was obliged to open the umbrella again. When I looked back he was still standing in his circle. I realised that I had been mistaken. It was the minister after all.

Michael Scott, possessor of one of the greatest minds in medieval Europe, lived in an age when philosophers and thinkers often trod a dangerous path between God and the Devil. It was a hazard of their occupation. Some, Michael included, were more skilful than others in their dealings with the Almighty One.

But what of the Devil? If Michael needed to travel any great distance, he would challenge the Devil to transform himself into a winged horse and then ride him to his destination and back. On other occasions he caused him to waste much time trying to achieve impossible tasks: it is said, for example, that the Devil can still sometimes be seen toiling on the shore at Kirkcaldy, where Michael sent him to braid a rope out of sand. But there can hardly be much substance to these tales because, whatever else the Devil may be, he is certainly no fool.

Once, Alexander II, King of the Scots, sent Michael to Paris to complain about French pirates who were always attacking Scottish ships. Michael arrived at the court on a massive black steed (who knows whether or not this was the Devil in equine shape?) and demanded of the French King that the depredations cease forthwith. The King took offence at the arrogance of this envoy from such a small, poor country: it was beneath his dignity, he said, to concern himself with these matters.

At this, Michael commanded the mighty horse to stamp its hoof three times. The first crash of the hoof set all the bells of Paris ringing. The second brought three towers of the palace tumbling down. The horse raised its hoof a third time. 'Wait!' the French King shouted in alarm. Michael inclined his head and waited. While the hoof still hovered, the King declared an end to all acts of piracy against the Scots, and dispatched men to the ports to enforce the edict. Michael gave a signal, and the horse lowered its hoof with astonishing grace and delicacy.

No one tried to delay Michael's departure. The King granted him safe passage home, and Michael accepted this guarantee, although of course he had no need of it.

Michael Scott (2)

In Dante's *Divine Comedy* Michael Scott is consigned, along with other seers, sorcerers and astrologers, to the fourth ditch of the eighth circle of Hell. In this terrible place the sufferers' heads are twisted round on their bodies as a punishment for trying to look into the future, and as they walk backwards along the chasm their tears of agony run down into the clefts of their buttocks.

Dante, however, was mistaken when he identified Michael – 'the one with the skinny legs' – in the Inferno. While he was still on Earth, Michael heard a rumour that the Devil, seeking revenge for the humiliations the philosopher had heaped upon him, had prepared a special bed in anticipation of his arrival. So Michael used a spell to open a window into Hell, to see what to expect. One half of the bed was a block of ice, the other a blazing fire, and the whole was covered with sharp spikes. Deciding at once that he had better book himself a place in Heaven, the philosopher went to a priest, confessed his sins and renounced all his previous transactions with the Devil.

The priest was still doubtful as to whether a man of Michael's reputation, even having received absolution, would be allowed to enter Heaven. 'What little faith you have in your own office!' Michael told him. 'Well, so that you know the outcome, I will send you a message soon after I die. If a dove comes to your door, it will be a sign that I have reached Heaven. But if a raven appears, take that to mean that I have gone to the other place.'

Months later, word reached the priest that Michael Scott was dead. When he went out the next morning, he saw dozens of ravens perched in the surrounding trees. *Well*, he thought, *the message could not be clearer*. And he clapped his hands. The ravens rose, filling the sky with their flapping wings and angry cries, and departed in a black cloud.

As the priest watched them go, secretly pleased that the Devil had claimed Michael Scott for his own, a single white dove glided in and landed at his feet.

He took another beer from the fridge. The literature – not the stuff he wrote, the other kind – called it a mini-bar. He didn't know if its contents were part of the deal but he would continue to work on that assumption until proved wrong. Each day he pretty much emptied the fridge and the following morning, when he slipped out for breakfast before anybody else was around, somebody filled it up again. They seemed to know exactly when he was out. By the time he returned the fridge was restocked, the towels replaced, the bed made and the room spotless. They probably sent in a squad. How else could they get it back in shape so fast?

The festival was paying for everything else so surely they wouldn't grudge him a beer or two, the odd bottle of wine and a few pretzels?

Three days ago he'd read from a platform shared with a Canadian woman and an Irishman. Fifteen minutes each, followed by questions. Nobody had asked him anything. After that he'd gone back to the hotel.

His room was on the nineteenth floor, overlooking the lake. The lake was bigger than a small sea. He could sit on the balcony and if it became too hot retreat inside and cool off in the air conditioning. Sometimes he just walked around the room in the hotel's white robe and flip-flop slippers, surveying his domain.

Their entire flat could have fitted into the room – twice. The bed was bigger than their bathroom. The bathroom was the size of a swimming pool. There was even a lobby. A hotel room with its own lobby. Unbelievable.

Five days and nights. He didn't want to wake up.

The phone rang. It would be that man again, the organiser. The one who'd yelled at him, the only time he'd picked up, 'Get your frickin ass down here right now!' A publisher's reception or something. It wasn't obligatory, though. It wasn't a legal requirement. He preferred being where was.

He sat in the armchair with the beer. After a while he moved to the sofa. He pointed the remote at the TV. Maybe he'd watch a movie. Maybe he wouldn't.

One of Our Contemporary Geniuses

INTERVIEWER: Wullie Wheenge – may I call you Wullie?

WHEENGE (*making noises reminiscent of various birds native to the tropical rainforest*): Nnnn, nyet nyet nyet, whaaaaargh, chirrup chirrup chirrup, weeeel, you may. Call me Ishmael if you prefer. Where were we?

INTERVIEWER: I wanted to ask you about your life as an artist.

WHEENGE: Why?

INTERVIEWER: Well, you are widely regarded as the foremost of our creative thinkers. Many point to your novel *Menstrie* as a key text in the extraordinary resurgence of Scottish letters in the last thirty years. How would you say your work has influenced that of other writers?

WHEENGE: Nnnn, nyey nyet, ooooooh aaah, I wouldn't.

INTERVIEWER: But surely –

WHEENGE: I am not saying, I am not saying, I am not saying that there has been no influence on, ah, um, others. What I am saying is that I am not saying anything about it. Myself. Being a humble chap of, hmm, working-class origins I am far from comfortable about ah, um, blowing my own, hmm, trumpet. (*Makes noise like a trumpet.*)

INTERVIEWER: I see. Well, leaving aside its possible influence on others, was *Menstrie* a breakthrough for you?

WHEENGE: Oh, ah, definitely. That is to say, no, not really. It did not make me any, ah, um, money, without which of course the artist is, ah, condemned to starvation and madness.

INTERVIEWER: Do you consider yourself mad?

WHEENGE: Certainly. We are all mad. And sometimes hungry. The world is mad. Society is mad. Though, in its defence, it considers itself completely, ah, sane. A sure sign of madness. But it has been tolerant towards me. Allowed me, yes, a remarkably long leash. (*Barks like a dog.*) Perhaps it lets me out as a, um, warning to others: this is what will happen to you if you do not rein in your imaginations. Whereas what we should be striving for . . .

INTERVIEWER: Yes, Dr Wheenge?

WHEENGE: Speaking as a medical man, which I am not, but since you so address me, what we should be striving for is vigorously exercised imaginations all round. *Mens sana* and all that jazz, do you follow me?

INTERVIEWER: Thank you, Wullie Wheenge, one of our contemporary geniuses.

'But should we not do something? Surely there are times when we *must* act?'

Words of anguish, words of political calculation. The slaughter continues, the weeping grows louder, fades, grows again. Gunfire, the hot noise of engines, cities in flames, degraded landscapes. Lives turned to dust and blood.

On your computer screen is a photograph of a child in some nameless place of devastation, a child in a field of plastic bottles and decomposing filth. Right up to the edges of the photograph you see only plastic and filth, and you know that beyond those boundaries it continues. The child stands, held by the camera, prevented by the image from negotiating his way across this terrain in which there is no beauty, no renewal and no hope.

That child knows more of life than you will ever know, but he knows nothing.

Ten thousand miles away, on a stone beside a sheep track through green hills, a man rests. He rests from a walk that has no motivation other than the pleasure of walking. He takes a plastic bottle from his backpack and drinks. Earlier, he filled the bottle from the clear, clean flow of a small river.

The stone has not moved in a hundred million years. For him it is somewhere to sit. He feels the cold, good water in his throat. Unseen moorland birds sing. He savours the fact of being in such a place.

In that other landscape there is nowhere for the child to sit. When the camera has gone he will move on, picking his way across the debris. In some other photograph of hell – plastic sheeting, corrugated metal, hammered-together hardboard – he will appear again. He will be somewhere he calls home.

How can the child and the man exist at the same time? How can your consciousness contain knowledge of them both? What traumatic upheaval of time and the world could tip them into one another?

Time and the world are indifferent to them, and to you. There is no way to measure this world's indifference. Without the world, you, the man, the child – are nothing. Without you, the man, the child, the world – is still the world.

Jack and the Princess (1)

One day, when Jack's mother was round at a neighbour's, a lassie with a bag on her shoulder came chapping at the door. She was on a long journey, she said, and very thirsty.

'In ye come,' says Jack, and sits her at the kitchen table and fetches her a cup of milk. But she's only taken a wee sip when she says, 'Oh, I'm sorry, this milk's turned.'

The milk was fresh that morning but, being a polite lad, Jack takes it away and gives her some more, and so as not to waste the first cup he drinks it himself. It tastes fine to him. But at the bottom of the cup he finds a dead spider. *I'm sure that wasn't there when I poured in the milk*, he thinks, *but it must have been the spider she tasted.*

Then she says she's hungry. Now before his mother went out she'd baked a pie, so Jack fetches it and cuts a slice for the lassie. But after just one mouthful she pushes it away. 'Oh, that pie's stale,' she says.

So Jack cuts her another slice but so as not to waste the first one he eats it himself. It tastes fine to him. But he bites on something hard, and finds it's a button that's somehow got into the pie. *Well, this is an awfie sensitive lassie*, Jack thinks, *maybe she's a princess.*

Then she says she'd like a nap before she goes on her way, and is there a bed where she can lie down for a bit? 'Ye can use ma mither's bed,' Jack says. But before he takes her through he slips a single dried pea under the mattress. *Now we'll see if she's a princess*, he thinks, *and if she is maybe she'll marry me and we'll be rich.*

So Jack sits in the kitchen and waits for her to complain about the pea, but nothing happens. And he's just wishing they hadn't drunk so much milk or had such big slices of pie, and hoping her feet are clean, when he hears his mother coming home.

If that's no a princess in there, Jack thinks, *I'm deid.*

Jack and the Princess (2)

When Jack's mother comes in, the first thing she sees is the guilty look on Jack's face. And she sees the milk jug empty and the pie with a great chunk missing out of it, and she flies into a rage at him.

'Och, dinna be angry, Mither,' Jack says from the far side of the table, 'but I couldna help it. This lassie cam tae the door and she's on a lang journey and she was thirsty so I gied her some milk, and she was hungry so I gied her some of the pie and she was tired so I let her sleep in yer bed. But, Mither, she's an awfie sensitive lassie and I think she's a princess and if she is maybe she'll marry me and we'll be rich.'

'Ye're an eejit, Jack,' says his mother, but just then they hear a squeal of pain coming from the next room.

'That'll be the pea I pit under the mattress,' Jack says.

'Princess, is it?' says his mother, and they both go into the bedroom.

But the lassie isn't lying in the bed in agony. She's halfway through the window with the sash fallen down and trapping her and that's why she's squealing. They pull her back in and she says, 'Oh thank you, I was needing some fresh air but when I opened the window it fell on me.' And Jack says, 'Och, did ye hurt yersel?'

But Jack's mother is much more interested in the bag that the lassie is trying to keep hidden behind her back. She grabs it and empties it onto the bed, and out tumble all of her own precious things – earrings, bracelets, silk scarves and suchlike.

Well, Jack's mother chases the lassie round the room and out into the kitchen where she picks up the coal shovel and starts walloping her on the back and the legs till at last the lassie gets out of the house and takes off up the road with Jack's mother right behind her.

By the time Jack's mother returns everything is tidy and in its proper place in the house, but Jack's away out for a long, long walk.

I come in peace. This is the meaning of my title. Let me make myself clear. I always come in peace. Even when I came before, I came in peace.

When I came before, it was to bring peace to this region, which has for so long been troubled by war. It saddened me to see this and so I came. It saddened me too that when I brought peace on that occasion, I had to bring it in a little casket protected by aeroplanes and tanks. I did not wish to bring peace thus, but I had no choice. There was a wicked man who had his own aeroplanes and tanks and also weapons of even greater power. In order to bring my peace it was necessary to destroy the wicked man, his aeroplanes and tanks, and his weapons of greater power. And look, he is no more. He is gone, his aeroplanes and tanks are gone, and even his weapons of greater power are gone.

Some said these weapons never existed but I said they did and my saying it made it the truth and without my saying it I could not have come in peace and truth. The truth was that the evil man threatened a terrible war, a war that would trouble not just this region but the whole world. The threat of his war was very great, but my peace was greater than his war and it was in peace that I came and defeated him, and that is the truth.

Now I come again, to bring peace to this region, which has for so long been troubled by war. I know in my heart that you in your hearts wish for peace. I have here a little casket. It contains a peace greater than any peace you can imagine. If you accept this peace from me, it will be yours. You cannot open the casket because only I have the key. It is my casket and my peace, but I will give it to you because I am generous, truthful and kind.

However, if you refuse my gift of peace then I will have to open the casket again.

The Envoy of Democracy

Hi there. Let me tell you a little about myself.

I am a democrat. I come from a democracy. In a democracy everybody has a vote to decide who is going to govern them, and everybody's vote is equal.

Democracy is a good thing, but not everybody does it right. In my society, we do it right. Some other societies do it quite well. Many societies don't do it at all well but, generally speaking, even imperfect democracy is better than the alternative, which is dictatorship.

Dictatorship is bad. That's really all you need to know. Not all bad government is dictatorship, but, generally speaking, all dictatorship is bad government.

However, imperfect dictatorship is sometimes better than imperfect democracy. It depends on the imperfections. In my society, dictatorship would never be better than democracy because our democracy is the best you can get. In your society, this does not follow.

We recognise that, democratically, we cannot impose our way of doing democracy on you. You have to want it, and then you have to do it right.

We are the best judges of whether you are doing it right.

Suppose you live in a dictatorship and you want to try some democracy? Where do you start? First, you have to overthrow your dictator. Sometimes we help to overthrow dictators and sometimes we don't, but we don't make a big thing of this. However, once a dictator has been overthrown, we welcome it because, being democrats, we always applaud the democratic will of the people.

But sometimes the democracy with which you replace your dictator turns out to be imperfect. Generally speaking, this is because you are not doing democracy right, the way we do.

When this happens, rather than continue to do democracy wrong it is often better to restore a dictator: not the same dictator, obviously – because he is usually dead and even if still alive was overthrown by the democratic will of the people – but another dictator.

What may surprise you is that sometimes the new dictator is imposed by the democratic will of the people.

We recognise that, democratically, we cannot impose dictatorship on you. But we are always ready to assist.

The Envoy of War

I come more in sorrow than in anger. This is how I always come. That way it is your fault.

I have told you before, don't do these things that provoke me. Do nothing, or do things that I can tolerate. If you had paid attention, I need not have come at all.

I drew a line in the sand. You may ask, what line, what sand? I think I made myself clear. But whether you saw the line or chose not to see it, I never said I would not rake the sand or erase the line. If you don't see the line now, that is not my problem. You should have been paying attention.

Some crimes are so terrible that they cannot be tolerated. Your crimes were tolerated until they became intolerable. You crossed a line when you committed your intolerable crimes. Do not ask whether that line was the same line as the one I drew in the sand. You should have been paying attention.

Do not speak to me of inconsistency. Do not speak to me of one hundred thousand dead here, of fifty thousand dead there. Do you think that I count the dead on my fingers? That my sorrow is touched only when I reach a certain number?

Do not speak to me of hypocrisy. Do not speak of napalm, depleted uranium, cluster bombs and Agent Orange. Do not speak of rendition and torture. Do not speak of arms manufacturers and arms sales. None of this is relevant. We are not talking about what was done yesterday. We are talking about what was done today, by you.

Your crimes are not merely intolerable, they are evil, barbaric, monstrous. I can speak freely now. They are crimes against humanity. An example must be made of you, so that the rest of humanity knows where it stands.

Humanity stands on the same side of the line in the sand as I do. Do not complain that you cannot see the line, now that I have raked the sand. You should have been paying attention.

If only your crimes had remained tolerable, none of my sorrow or my anger would be necessary.

One Morning in the Library

One morning in the library I opened a book and a bird, bright green, flew in through the window. She flew round my head and out again. When I closed the book I found it was evening.

The next morning I opened another book. I thought I heard someone at the back door so I went to look. No one was there, but I could hear a bird singing. I stepped into the garden to listen.

The bird sang in a language unknown to me but I recognised her bright green shape among the dark leaves of the apple tree. She flew to the high wall, then into the next garden, where I heard the song again but only once. I found a gate in the wall that I had not known existed. It was covered over with ivy. I went through it.

This other garden was very well tended. There were gravel paths between box hedges, and rose beds, and fruit trees, and a wooden bridge over a pond spread with water lilies. I saw a robed figure, whom I took to be a monk, bending down in the distance.

I could not hear or see the bird. My feet crunched on the gravel when I walked over to the monk. He was weeding. 'Have you seen a bright green bird?' I asked.

He put his finger to his lips, then pointed to the ground. The green bird was under a bush. She was watching me but she did not sing, nor did she fly away.

I realised I had transgressed. I made signs of apology to the bird and to the monk. The monk nodded. When I walked away my feet made no sound on the path.

I passed over the bridge and the pond of lilies. A frog sat on one of the lilies. He was watching me but he did not speak. I came back through the gate into my own garden, and into my own house.

I found the book lying open where I had left it. I closed it and found it was evening. I searched the shelves for the first book, but I could not find it anywhere.

One night in the library, as I read by the light of a single lamp placed behind my chair, I became conscious of stirrings in the shadowed parts of the room. These fluttering sounds – as of a colony of restless bats in residence behind the ranks of books – interested rather than alarmed me. I knew that there were no bats. What was happening had happened before, in those hours of absolute stillness and quiet, when even the fire has ceased its cracking and hissing. The sounds I heard were the lives contained in all the thousands of volumes that surrounded me, shifting and settling in their paper beds.

I found this reassuring. It told me that all my years of reading had not been in vain: that through reading I had entered into other times and other worlds, experienced the lives of people separated from me by oceans and deserts and generations, and that they remained with me in the library. Thus comforted, I returned to the book in my hands.

But after a minute I stopped reading and looked up. Some other life had entered the room. I saw, dimly, the figure of a man, draped in some kind of robe, standing near the door. Yet the door was shut, and I was certain it had not opened in the last hour. I reached up and directed the beam of the lamp towards him.

'What do you want?' I asked.

The robed figure shook his head. He wanted nothing. Then he raised a hand, shielding his vision, as I at first thought, against the brightness. But no, his forefinger touched the corner of one eye and then pointed at me, or more specifically at my book, and drew lines back and forth in the air. I understood that he wanted me to continue reading.

So I adjusted the lamp again, aware of the intensity of his gaze and something more – the wonder it contained. The books on the shelves were hushed. I thought how much noise is contained in silence. If I looked up I knew that, even if I could no longer see him, his ancient witness would still be in the library.

'You all know about the cloud?' the professor asked. 'Of course you do. Is there any one of us who doesn't have their photos, their music, their ebooks and emails – their life, in fact – backed up in the cloud? Well, the kites work on the same principle. They're just more personalised. Completely and uniquely personal to you, in fact.

'What kills us,' he continued, 'isn't the disease, the crumbling of body parts or the unbeating heart. None of these things can happen without time. Stop time and you stop death.

'It has taken millennia to reach this moment. Generations of astronomers, philosophers and scientists have chipped away at the concept of time, and time chipped them into dust. Their physical frames, not the ideas, not the dream. We inherited the dream, but *we* can make it reality.

'Already we can copy and save the contents – the entire history – of a brain, and reconfigure it on one of these. Look at the size of this thing: it's smaller than a SIM card, but it contains your entire life. Every thought, every sensation, every memory your brain ever recorded. And on top of that, it can store all the data your brain could ever need to keep it occupied for eternity: the cloud to the power of x. Effectively, we've invented immortality.

'And now we move to the next phase, beyond the cloud. With the kites, we can book our minds into Paradise.

'Soon we'll be able to do even more. At the moment each kite is isolated. It's tethered to the mainframe but can't connect to other kites. So it could – eventually – get pretty lonely up there. You can access all your old friends but you can't meet new ones. But we're working on this. Yes, there will be social media in Paradise.

'The usual cranks and fanatics will tell you we've gone too far this time. They'll say we're playing at being God. These people would have rejected the wheel if it had rolled into their cave. They'd have stamped out fire, horrified at the possibilities. That's their prerogative. But what about you? Do you really *not* want to fly like a bird, for eternity?'

See thae politicians at Westminster or Holyrood or wherever they are? They're no even there, they're up in space. See whit I want tae dae wi them? I want tae get them on the nummer 14 bus. It should be obligatory. And no jist for a couple o stoaps. The haill bliddy route, start tae finish. It might jist make them realise they're boarn. It might make them think twice aboot the guff they come oot wi. I doot it, but it might.

That bus yesterday, I'm tellin ye, it wis even worse than usual. I'm no bein insultin. I'm no huvin a go at the folk on the bus or the folk on the street. I'm huvin a go at the politicians and their 'somethin for nuthin society', their 'jist say no' finger-waggin, their disability livin allowance reassessments and their bastartin bedroom tax. I'm hearin aw that in ma heid and meanwhile three seats ahint me somebody's hackin awa like they're gonnae drap deid and folk are gettin on and aff the bus wi sticks and Zimmers and buggies and ootside on the street there's blin folk and puir folk and pechin folk and folk wi mental problems and folk in wheelchairs and a junkie in a doorway lookin like a loast bairn and black folk and white folk and aw they're tryin tae dae is get through it, ken, aw they're tryin tae dae is get through it and these politicians are zoomin aboot in their spaceships when they should be sittin on the nummer 14 bus seein whit it's like.

There wis this big lang fellae, he had hair like snaw, he wis haudin ontae his wife, she wis aboot hauf his height and every step he took it wis like a ship pitchin in the middle o the Atlantic Ocean. He wis grippin her haun and she wis grippin his and it wis like she wis his anchor but he wis draggin her through these forty-fit waves, every step wis anither monster wave but they were daein it, they were gettin through it, but the politicians wurnae on the bus so how could they see, how could they even imagine it?

Cromwell's Heid

By the time I goat hame I wis done in. I biled the kettle and made masel a cup o tea and then I pit the radio on and lay doon on the sofa. And here wis this programme aboot Oliver Cromwell and how when he died he wis gien a state funeral and buried in Westminster Abbey, but when Charles II wis restored tae the throne they took Cromwell oot o the vault where they'd pit him and executed him for killin Charles I. They dragged his boady through the streets and they hung it at Tyburn for a day and then they cut it doon and chapped his heid aff and stuck the heid on a lang widden pole at Westminster Hall and it steyed there for twenty-five years. Twenty-five years! So folk widnae forget whit he'd done, killed a king, and they'd ken no tae think aboot ever daein it themsels.

And then there wis a storm, and the widden pole broke, and Cromwell's heid fell doon and it went missin, but later it turned up in a private museum, or onywey the museum had this heid and they said it wis Cromwell's but how wid ye prove it efter aw that time?

And I wis lyin there on the sofa listenin tae this and I started tae think o aw the people I'd like tae see wi their heids on spikes. I started wi politicians and moved on tae celebrities, and pretty soon I wis intae double figures and nae sign o runnin oot. But funnily enough whenever I thought aboot somebody I kent, I mean really kent, that I hated or thought I hated, like ma ex-wife's mither or ma boss or some o ma neebors, I couldnae dae it, I couldnae pit their heids on spikes. No for twenty-five years. No even for twenty-five minutes if I'm honest. And then I went through ma list o famous folk and I started tae take their heids back doon because I *didnae* ken them. Even Maggie Thatcher, the first on the list, I even took her doon. And then I fell asleep and when I woke up ma tea wis cauld.

Crossing the Border (1)

'Vancouver?' the guy said. 'That's where we're going. Hop in.'

We slung our rucksacks in the trunk and hopped in the back seat and made little nests amongst all the garbage, and the guy said, 'Just throw that anywhere, man!' and the woman said, 'Ain't nowhere to throw it, Danny,' but Frank said it was fine, we had enough space, and Danny took off.

They were friendly, both of them. Danny turned around to shake our hands and we got that over with fast so that he could concentrate on the road ahead. Then the woman put her smile through the gap between the seats and said, 'Hi, I'm Nancy,' and we said, 'Hi, Nancy.' Nancy was stoned out of her head.

'Listen,' she said, and she waved a plastic bag at us, 'we gotta get rid of some stuff before we reach the border. You wanna help us?'

So we helped them. She rolled as fast as we could smoke and we smoked as fast as she could roll but by God there was a lot to get rid of. We opened the windows so Danny could see to drive and we could freshen up a little, and Nancy passed us beers from the cooler to ease our throats, and we were very glad it was still a hundred miles to the border. 'Because,' I explained, 'they'll want to inspect our passports so we'll have to be coherent.' And Danny said that luckily because they were Americans they wouldn't have to be coherent, the officers would just wave them through. And if they didn't wave them through they'd just drive back down the road, head a little further east and try again at another, quieter crossing.

Well, we got to the border and it seemed Danny didn't have the right paperwork for the car so they wouldn't let him cross, but he was very relaxed about it, let us get our packs from the trunk and said, 'So long, guys,' and Nancy smiled sweetly and they drove back down the road. And the officers waved Frank and me through and we staggered over the border on foot and that was us in Canada, wasted.

Crossing the Border (2)

The number of young Englishmen crossing the border to avoid conscription has hit a new high, according to statistics just released by the Scottish Government.

Since the start of July, eight thousand men of draft age are believed to have arrived, bringing the total number, during the present overseas hostilities, to more than fifty thousand. A government spokeswoman stressed that the true figure is likely to be higher, as only those who register for 'temporary refugee' or 'political asylum' status are counted.

Many of those who come north rather than be called up for National Service are accommodated in specially constructed camps at Langholm, Newcastleton, Kelso and Duns, the so-called 'Little Englands'. Although there have been occasional clashes with local youths, the Minister for Home and Housing, Ewart Fleming, was keen to emphasise that generally the English draft dodgers have received a warm welcome. On a visit to Little England, Langholm, during which he observed aspects of the educational and entertainment programmes which the camp inmates themselves organise with support from outreach workers, he said: 'We have no quarrel with these young men, who have voted with their feet against their government's policies. It is undeniable that their presence here does put a strain on some of our resources, but we will not turn anyone away.'

Questioned on what level of co-operation existed with England over cross-border security, Mr Fleming said, 'Security systems intended to prevent these men entering Scotland are entirely ineffectual, as we always said they would be owing to the porous nature of the border, so we can only anticipate that unless or until the English Government changes its foreign policy the number of arrivals will go on rising.'

Despite his barely concealed irritation, Mr Fleming did not repeat the Scottish Chancellor's scathing reference to 'Airstrip One', which resulted in the English Prime Minister cancelling his recent planned trip to Edinburgh. But when asked if he thought the 'special relationship' between the two countries had been irretrievably damaged, he replied: 'Time will tell. One must ask: which two countries, what relationship, and why is it special?'

A spokesman for the English Government said, 'We told you independence would lead to conflict.'

after Neil Gunn

Long ago, when humans still lived in caves and the world was a wild and dangerous place, a great enmity existed between humans and wolves. The wolves roamed the mountains and forests and killed other animals to survive, and sometimes they killed humans. And the humans had no sheep or cattle or horses, so they too lived by killing wild animals. Their weapons were of stone, wood and sinew, and to kill any beast was a task needing strength, speed and cunning.

One day a man went out to kill a deer, in order to feed his family. In the middle of the forest he came face to face with a wolf. The wolf sprang at him and the man swung at it with his stone axe, but he missed. A long, fierce fight followed, till at last the wolf lay dead. Exhausted, the man lay down to rest, and where he lay he found the body of a deer. The wolf had killed the deer and now the man felt grateful to the wolf. Then he looked a little further, and in a nest in the long grass he found a cub. And he understood why the wolf had fought so hard – not to attack him but to defend her cub, as he would have fought to defend his child from the wolf.

So now the man had the deer and the wolf to carry home, but he took the cub too, and raised it as his own, and it grew as loyal to him as if he were its mother. If danger came near the cave in any form, the wolf growled a warning, and fought alongside the man. If the man went hunting the wolf went too, and pulled down a deer if the man had wounded it.

Seasons passed, and the wolf was growing old faster than the man, so the man hunted another wolf, and killed it, and took its cub, a female this time, and the old wolf fathered his own cubs. For the man saw that he could not return to the old way of being. And the young wolves began not to know that they were wolves.

Perfect

The shop door was flung open and a young fellow burst into our midst. He looked young to me anyway, especially compared with everyone else in the room – the barber, the man in the chair, the other man on the bench who was next in the queue. Thirty or thereabouts, the new arrival. Fit-looking too, but manic: the blood vessels on his temples stood out, his neck was corded, pulsing. He was all bone, muscle and sinew in a black T-shirt and fatigues. He looked to me like a soldier.

'See this!' he yelled. It was an instruction, not a question. He stood motionless, pointing at his own head. If he'd had a gun in his hand it wouldn't have looked much more dramatic. I thought, *Is he registering a complaint?* Not that there was anything to complain about: his skull had about three millimetres of hair all over it, a sharp shadow of growth.

'See this!' he yelled. 'Can you mind it?'

He was addressing the barber.

'What d'ye mean, son?' The barber had paused in mid-snip – everything had paused. He was very calm. His tone was cool and quiet.

'Can ye mind it? Picture it? Ma heid? The wey it is? Mind it for the future?'

'I'll mind you,' the barber said.

'Naw, ma heid, ma hair! This is it, perfect! This is how I like it.' He ran both hands back from his brow over his skull, down the pulsing neck. The hands clasped the neck as if they might be about to rip the head right off. 'If I come in again, can ye cut it for us, just like this?'

'A number two, I'd say,' the barber said. 'Aye, I can dae that.'

'But perfect, like this? Can ye dae it the exact same?' He froze in the stance he had assumed on entry.

The barber tilted his head this way and that as he made his professional assessment. 'Aye,' he said.

'Brilliant!' the man said. 'Be back in three days.' And he burst out onto the street again.

Everything was wonderfully still. We all breathed out. Then the scissors snipped again.

The barber shook his head. 'Aye,' he said.

September

There was a man who at different times worked as a gardener, a carpenter and a forester. He was someone, therefore, who handled woods and plants of many kinds, and he went through life picking up splinters or *skelfs* along the way. Some he acquired simply because he laboured hard, and the insidious little darts found their way into his hands in the course of a working day. Others came to him because he was distracted or careless, and his palms or fingers were punished for his lack of attention. He tolerated skelfs as small nuisances hardly worthy of consideration in the longer, larger scheme of existence. Often he would not even notice a skelf's arrival for a day or two, until it made its presence felt, jagging away under the skin, perhaps threatening infection. Then he would get to work with the point of his pocketknife, or with a needle passed through flame, digging around the skelf and marvelling that something so tiny could cause such irritation.

But there was one that went deeper and further than any of the others, and which he could not extract. At first it gave him no pain, and by the time it did it was so far into him that it was no longer visible. Yet he knew it was there because of the insistent throb of its movement, as it burrowed still deeper, travelling from his palm, through his wrist and up his arm. Every day he felt it, but could not see a trace of it. And he understood that it was not going to stop, that it was moving, fractionally but relentlessly, towards his heart.

What was this terrible, miniature arrow that flew so slowly within him? It was nothing a doctor could identify or treat. No operation could save him from it. It was not something of wood or plant. It was not something of anything. It was an absence of something, and he did not know what it was but he felt it and it made him sad and fearful. And with good reason, for, before he grew to be an old man, that absence, of whatever it was, would kill him.

The Presence

for Keir

Suddenly I had the strongest sensation that someone was walking beside me, with me. I was alone, but I had to check. Truly, I was alone. When I looked ahead again, the same feeling overwhelmed me and I had to check a second time. I thought I had somehow got out of myself, but as soon as I had that notion I knew I was mistaken. If anyone was there it was not myself or any part of myself. It was another.

I had come through the park, on my way to the shops. It was nearly four o'clock, the schools had finished, and what was left of the afternoon was warm and dry. Mothers and grandmothers and children were everywhere. There was a fenced-off area with a chute, swings and a roundabout, and it was full of children, with women watching over them. I was conscious of myself, an unaccompanied adult male, going through the park at that time of day. I went down under the bridge and onto the walk by the river and immediately left the crowds behind, and it was here that I felt the presence at my side.

It was not a 'presence' of course. It was an absence.

Before I left the river I saw a boy alone, fishing. He must have gone straight from school to be there and he must have had his rod in his school-bag and screwed it together and there he was, fishing from the bank. I don't know what you can catch in this river: not much, I should think, and nothing you wouldn't want to throw straight back. There he was, the boy, and perhaps he was too young to be on his own by the river, where anything might happen: some stranger might approach him, or his foot might slip, or other, bigger boys might corner him. But he didn't look like he was too young. He looked like a boy in his own place, and as if he would grow up to be a man who, as long as he lived, would occupy whatever space he occupied with ease.

As I went on to the shops I wished him luck.

Sticks

Ye see a lot mair folk gaun aboot wi sticks nooadays. Ken whit that's aboot? They've been tellt. *Get yersel a stick, man. Aye, get yersel a stick. Makes ye look mair disabled. Get yersel twa. No that ye huv tae use them aw the time; I mean, as soon as ye get in the door ye can jist chuck them, eh? As soon as naebody's lookin. It's no like ye huv tae use a stick tae sit on yer erse aw day. Jist be shair and take yer sticks wi ye when ye're gaun oot. If it's a hassle takin twa sticks jist take the wan, so ye can cairry yer messages in yer ither haun. Yer pizzas and bevvy and fags and everythin else ye can buy wi the money they gie ye for haein a stick.*

Ye can get a stick aff the NHS, it's no like ye huv tae pey for it. But it's a guid investment, haein yer ain stick, so when ye go tae the doactor ye can say, 'Oh, I couldnae wait for a Health Service stick I wis in that much pain, I had tae crawl doon tae the charity shoap and get this yin.'

D'ye wear glesses? Take them aff and get yersel a white stick. That's goat tae be guid for a few extra quid. And hirple,* man, hirple. I mean, disnae maitter whit colour it is, there's nae point haein a stick if ye're no gonnae hirple. Defeats the object o the exercise. No that ye're takin ony exercise, but ye ken whit I'm sayin? Get yersel a stick and a hirple, man, and ye'll be fine.

That's whit folk huv been tellt. The word's got aroond. D'ye think they dinnae speak tae each ither? D'ye think they dinnae share information? How else dae ye think there's thoosans o them gaun aboot wi sticks?

Ken whit the government should dae? Aw thae skivers wi sticks? They should line them aw up and kick their sticks awa. The wans that dinnae faw ower, stoap their benefit. That'd sort the wasters oot. That'd pit their gas at a peep. That'd gie them somethin tae greet aboot.

* limp (Scots)

Bob Dylan's *119th Dream*

I was riding on a Greyhound bus, seeking some place to hide. I slept and when I woke there was a stranger by my side. He said, 'We have not met before, but now we meet at last.' He smiled and shook my hand, and he held it tightly in his grasp.

He said, 'I see your fortune here, along this crooked line. I don't wish to alarm you, but it's the same as mine.' I stared into his sullen eyes, they were dark and full of hate. I answered, 'I have no desire to understand my fate.

'I bought a ticket to a place where I might ease my heart, and when I reach that sanctuary then we must surely part.' 'This highway we are travelling,' he said without a blink, 'goes straight to Armageddon, whatever you may think.

'But if you don't believe me, just take a look around. There is not one among us who for sanctuary is bound.' I looked at my companions, and I began to quake. I thought I must be dreaming still, but I could not awake.

The bus was full of skeletons, no flesh upon their bones, and all of them were deep in conversation on their phones. Some of them had cutlasses, while others they had guns, and they were not equipped with them for fashion or for fun.

'What deathly crew is this,' I said, 'riding upon this bus?' 'Check out your reflection,' he said. 'They are the same as us.' The night had fallen on the plain, as black as night can be. I saw a skull with empty eyes staring back at me.

I turned to face the stranger. 'Now let me pass,' I cried. 'Do not concern yourself,' he said, as he kindly stepped aside. I went up to the driver. 'Please put me down,' I said. But the driver made no answer – he had a bullet in his head.

When I found my seat once more, the stranger he was gone. I did not sleep again that night, waiting for the dawn. Faraway a mountain loomed, a dark and gloomy shape. If it was my sanctuary, then how could I escape?

The Hill

He needed half a day of reasonable weather. As he drove out of Inverness the clouds were thinning. There was even a suggestion of sunshine. He calculated his timings again: an hour's drive to the starting-point, three hours to walk up the mountain, two hours to come down, two and a half hours' drive to Edinburgh. He'd be home by early evening.

In the past he had sometimes climbed thirty or forty Munros in a year, but work and family commitments had reduced this number to almost zero. He tried not to resent this: it was what happened. But on this business trip, he'd built a climb into his schedule: he'd completed his work the previous evening; boots, rucksack, map and food were all in the back of the car; and now the weather was smiling on him. Today he was going to climb a hill.

He left the A9 and a few miles further on turned onto a single-track road. Not far to go now. And then, at the next junction, a red sign confronted him: ROAD CLOSED AHEAD. BRIDGE REPAIRS. LOCAL ACCESS ONLY. It had not occurred to him that he might be thwarted in this way. He drove on: what, after all, did LOCAL ACCESS mean? But when he reached the bridge a mile later, it was covered in scaffolding and blocked to all vehicles. It was another five miles to the starting-point. To walk there and back was out of the question: his schedule lay in ruins.

He turned the car and drove back the way he had come, then down another narrow road that rejoined the A9 further south. On his left was a river, too full to be forded; beyond it, the road that was closed; and beyond that, the hill he had intended to climb, splendid against the now completely blue sky. He kept looking for a footbridge across the river, but could not see one. The hill was mocking him. Then the road left the river and he lost sight of the hill.

It was frustrating, but he had to let it go. The bridge would be repaired. The hill would still be there some other day.

The earth blinked. A red, wicked hint of life.

She was crouched in the herb garden, gathering ingredients for an infusion for her sister: sage and peppermint for her aching head, rosemary for her fatigue. There was horseradish there too, which might ease her blocked sinuses, and it was while she was grubbing among the roots and reaching back for her knife that the earth blinked. Her hand had brushed a movement. She leaned back on her haunches, and now the movement became a small eruption, an old man clambering sulkily from his bed.

'Ah, it's yourself,' she said. She chided herself for being startled. That a toad should surprise her!

The toad did not acknowledge that he had been addressed. He pulled himself into the open, left hand, right foot, right hand, left foot. When he had sorted himself he sat scowling at her like a fat monk.

'I am sorry,' she said. 'I did not mean to disturb you.'

She had never seen one so big, nor with such red eyes. She put her finger towards him. He puffed himself up, becoming even more impressive.

'I will not hurt you,' she said. But she knew what the village boys would do with such a beast. Poke him. Flip him on his back. Blow him up with straws. Torment him as they tormented her and her sister.

She thought, *They need to fear him. This would save him from their cruelties.*

She thought, *They need to fear me.*

She said, 'Toad, come and bide in the house. Be in the pocket of my apron from time to time. We will protect one another.'

What a weight was in him when she gently encouraged him aboard her palm. Into her apron he went, and in went some soil and leaves of lady's mantle for his bedclothes.

She heard her sister crying, and the loud boys coming down the street.

She was not just a woman. She had knowledge and soon she would have power. Enough knowledge to make her useful to the villagers. Enough power to keep them at a distance.

She started for the gate. To show them her new accomplice. To warn them.

'Do these words mean anything?' Alex Mather said. 'Does the writer of this letter have any idea what he is saying or has he just stuck in a phrase he's vaguely heard somewhere and is hoping for the best?'

'I don't know, Alex,' Jill Mather said. 'What words? May I see it?'

Alex kept the letter in his hand.

'"Without prejudice",' he said. 'Does that mean, "I am not prejudiced, I am a completely rational, balanced sort of chap so anything I say is common sense"? Or, on the other hand –'

'I think it means you are being constructive and honest in your correspondence about some dispute in a genuine effort to settle it but, notwithstanding that you may have made some admission or concession, if it goes to court none of what you've written in the letter can be used in evidence against you.'

'Oh, like a kind of magic spell? You are a shower of shysters, cheats and all round grade-A bastards but because I've put "without prejudice" at the top of my letter you can't sue me for saying those things?'

'No, that's not what I mean. Did you notice my use of the word "constructive"?'

'I noticed your use of the word "notwithstanding". You haven't been studying to be a lawyer on the QT, have you?'

'"On the QT"? Is that a phrase you've vaguely heard somewhere? Anyway, what has this correspondent written that so upsets you?'

'I'm not upset, I'm just wondering if "without prejudice" covers everything. In the context.'

'In the context of what?'

'Of the letter, of course.'

'Alex, who has written this letter and what is it about?'

'It's about that parking ticket I got last week.'

'So it's your letter?'

'Kind of.'

'And you've written "without prejudice" at the top and then fired off a stream of invective at officialdom?'

'More or less. Stream of consciousness, I'd say.'

'Are you going to pay or are you appealing against a gross injustice?'

'The cheque's written. I just wondered . . .'

'Give me the letter, Alex. Thank you. Now watch as I tear it to shreds. Without prejudice, which means with common sense.'

'That's what I thought it meant.'

They were revisiting that old topic again. They couldn't leave it alone. 'We're like Jack Spratt and his wife,' she said. 'Gnawing away at it, fat and lean. Where's it getting us?'

'Nowhere,' he said. 'You're right. What more can we do or say? We've written down our wishes. The kids know how we feel. Not that I trust the kids, but it won't be their responsibility. It'll be ours.'

'Yes, so long as we can control the timing. We each know what the other one wants.'

'What the other one *doesn't* want,' he said.

'Exactly. Don't put us in one of those places. Stock up with the special pills before it gets to that stage. Hold hands and exit while we still have the key to the door.'

'Exit with dignity,' he said. 'Get out before some interfering busybody takes the key off you and you can't leave even if you want to. Can't even get out into the garden for some fresh air.'

'Prison with cushions and catheters,' she said. 'God forbid.'

'Let's change the subject,' he said, and he fetched the decanter and refilled the glasses. 'Here's to us, and to many years before we get there.'

The glasses clinked. 'Here's to us,' she said.

A minute later she said, 'There's going to be a lot more of it. People taking matters into their own hands.'

'Yes,' he said. 'But let's not talk about it any more.'

He picked up his book and started reading. She stared into the fire. She saw the old couple again, the couple outside the chip shop. They had been passing by as she was coming out with the fish suppers. Heading for home, she'd supposed. And he was leaning on a stick and she, a few paces behind, was leaning on a stick too. And it was clearly such hard work for them both. When he crossed the road he looked back to make sure she was still with him. He didn't say anything.

There was something heroic about how they kept going. She wondered if they'd had these same conversations. Planning for the non-future. Maybe they weren't the planning kind. Maybe they just kept going.

Death in the Café

Death was enjoying a cup of tea and a bacon roll in a self-service café one morning, minding his own business. In order not to draw attention to himself he had left his scythe in a secure place nearby, and had pulled his hood back from his head. Nevertheless he was aware that he was getting some odd looks and that, although the café was busy, people were avoiding his table.

He stared out of the window at the passing traffic and pedestrians. Cyclists dodged in and out of lorries and buses. Kids failed to look both ways as they crossed the street. Old dears, no doubt with brittle bones and chest infections, crept along the slippery pavement. Sometimes his presence hardly seemed necessary. But that was the old conundrum: if Death wasn't around, would death be around?

He realised that someone had sat down opposite him: a man with a cup of tea and a bacon roll. Death looked at him. The man looked back. He didn't seem wary as the other customers were.

'All right?' the man said.

'Fine, thanks,' Death replied.

'Best bacon rolls in town,' the man said, and took a bite. He chewed and swallowed, took a mouthful of tea. 'I know your face,' he said.

'I don't think so.'

'You don't work up at the hospital, do you?'

'No.'

'I'm not long out. Big operation. Wasn't expected to pull through. Surprised them all.' He took another bite of his roll, another swig of tea. 'That's it. That's who you look like.'

'Who?'

'My surgeon. Brilliant man, if a bit gloomy. Saw me before the op, saw me afterwards. Admitted he'd thought my chances were slim. But he went ahead and did it and here I am. Just shows you, eh? And you're his double. Your eyes. I remember just before I went under, him and the anaesthetist leaning over me. Your eyes and his eyes: identical. You haven't got a twin brother who's a surgeon, have you?'

Death got up to go. 'As a matter of fact, I have,' he said. He smiled at this man taking such pleasure in his breakfast. 'But we are not on speaking terms.'

In the Mirror

Yesterday, as I was preparing to go out for the evening, I stood in front of the mirror and did not recognise myself. I don't mean that I thought I was seeing someone else in the reflection. I mean simply what I say: I did not recognise my own appearance. The more I peered, the less I looked like myself. The nose was longer and thinner; the mouth had a different shape, especially when I attempted a smile; and the eyes were cold and demanding, like the eyes of a man – a teacher, perhaps, or a policeman – who has been waiting too long for some explanation. Yet I knew I was not looking at another man. The reflection was only a reflection, and when I stepped away from the mirror it vanished. When I returned, so did it. What puzzled and disturbed me, though, was that one could inspect oneself so intently and not know what was going on behind one's own exterior.

I remember another occasion, decades ago, when I looked in the mirror and saw, for the first time it seemed, my father staring back at me. That, in retrospect, was not surprising, although it was discomforting: we all harbour within us vestiges of our ancestors, and, sooner or later, we become them. But to look at myself *without* recognition, *without* realisation or revelation, this was new and unexpected. Who was this silent interrogator, and what was he expecting me to tell him? There was, surely, nothing I *could* tell him, for he already knew it all.

But what did he know? Something that I did not? His cool regard suggested that I had forgotten or failed to produce some vital information. And he was waiting. I had a sudden understanding that he had always been waiting. I did not recognise myself, but he recognised me, and he despised me.

All my adult years were wiped out. I was a child again, faced by this combination of teacher and policeman: all the things I should have learned, all the things I should not have done.

It was time to go. I had an arrangement to meet a woman who thought she loved me.

A Dream of Insecurities

They were sitting in big armchairs in a circle in the middle of a dusty school gym: Arthur, Sarah and Martin, and a man with a neatly trimmed beard whose face was familiar. I didn't realise I was part of the meeting until Arthur, looking directly at me, asked if we were all up to speed on everything. Martin and Sarah said they were. The notebook on my knee was blank but I said I was too. I added that I'd have to leave soon because I had a stack of work to get through. Arthur said, 'That's fine, just go when you need to.' He was very focused. We knew his wife was dying but nobody mentioned it.

The problem was: how to save the National Circus. That was why I recognised the man with the beard: he was the ringmaster. I looked around for his top hat but couldn't see it. Arthur suggested there might be scope for linking up with other circuses. Sarah said, 'Maybe we have to examine what a circus is for.' Martin seemed unhappy and the ringmaster was angry. Nobody was taking minutes of the meeting. I closed my notebook and put it quietly away in case that was supposed to be my job. The ringmaster said, 'An industry is not one hundred people all doing the same thing. An industry can be one person with one idea.'

I said I'd be back soon. They were still talking when I slipped out. I found the car and drove the sixty miles home. The roads were greasy. When I arrived people were sitting on the stairs discussing matters of great importance. I picked my way past them carrying a full kettle. The courtyard was wet and I was in my socks. I had to go back up the stairs to get my shoes from the car. By the time I returned someone had moved the kettle. I took it to my room. The door was open. I knew I had locked it. My mail was in a neat pile. Someone had been in there. I had so much to do, so many things to organise. I felt guilty and inadequate.

If we had been there, we would have battened down for the storm. We would have read our instruments, recognised that something was changing. We'd have tightened locks, checked seals, strapped ourselves in. Such basic, human, futile precautions. And then, even at the incredible speed at which we were travelling, we might have felt something: the solar wind easing, the particles slowing in their flight from the now distant sun. Yet our motion would not have eased, would not have become smoother. New forces buffet and rock us. We enter an area of greater turbulence, as the sun particles collide with other matter about which we know almost nothing: the constituent matter of deep space. But we must have faith, alone in this cosmic vastness in which the very notion of faith is impossible. We must believe what our science tells us, that beyond the tempest lies a balance, an equalisation of pressures, and beyond that a shift in the wind, a new impetus, a thrust into forty thousand years of sailing in the dark. This is the moment of departure, from one room of life into another room. What it contains we do not know, can hardly dare to guess. We are going behind the curtains of eternity.

If we had been there, we would have waved farewell to Neptune, Uranus, Saturn, Mercury long ago. A lifetime before, we'd have gazed with an aching in our hearts at the pale blue dot of our birthplace. The blueness of oceans, the white streaks of cloud, the moss-green patches of continents – the bowling-ball of swirls and flourishes – all these would have faded to vague memories, concentrated into that single uncertain dot. And then it too would have left us.

If we had been there? But we were. We *are*. The signals keep coming, seventeen hours, a day's journey away, but they keep coming. We send them and they keep coming back. And they tell us about ourselves. They say, *Look, we are going. We don't know where to, but we are going. Look, we can watch ourselves go. We can watch ourselves being left behind. Look*, the signals say. *That's here. That's home. That's us. Goodbye.*

On the Blue Wing

Standing out on the blue wing you waited for the ball. The hailstones kept coming and if the ball came it would be from the same direction, so you kept watch for it. The hail struck you in the face, blast upon blast. Your shirt was soaked. Some boys did up the top buttons of their shirts but that was an admission of weakness. Your shorts were soaked. You weren't allowed to wear anything under them. You clenched your hands into raw, pink fists. If the ball came you would have to catch it with the fingers you couldn't at that moment feel.

The pitch was marked out with creosote lines burned into the grass. At each end were goalposts like white gallows. The pitch was in a field that sloped diagonally towards you. If the ball came you would have to run with it, uphill into the hail. In summer the field was for cows but in winter it was for boys playing rugby.

The French master was on the opposite touchline roaring at the forwards, eight small boys against eight other small boys. He always shouted the same thing. It was either 'Feet, feet, feet!' which made sense if he wanted the forwards to kick the ball, or 'Vite, vite, vite!' which made sense if he wanted them to do it quickly. In his big duffel coat he seemed oblivious to the weather.

No matter from which side of the mess of bodies that was the two opposing scrums the ball emerged, it seldom travelled beyond one fly-half or the other. One fly-half or the other either kicked it or ran with it till he was tackled and the scrummage reconvened.

You were always on the wing, there was always hail, sleet or rain, the ball never reached you. Then once it did. It came in slow, looping passes from fly-half to inside centre to outside centre and as you staggered uphill it met you. Your numb fingers stretched for the sodden lump of leather, failed to hold it. The referee blew his whistle. 'Knock on, scrum down, red ball!' he shouted.

You never did discover what it was the French master shouted.

The Gaelic Poet

for Aonghas MacNeacail

'The bloke in the leather jacket,' Alex Mather said. 'No, over there, by the newspapers. With the satchel thing. Isn't that the Gaelic poet?'

'What Gaelic poet?' Jill Mather said, taking the last of the groceries from the trolley.

'You know, the famous one. Not the really famous one, he's dead. The one with the beard. Cooshie Doo they called him, when he was young. Then his beard turned white so now they call him Cooshie Ban. "Doo agus ban" – that's "black and white" in Gaelic. Isn't that him, with the beard and glasses?'

Alex was now openly pointing at somebody.

'I do see a man in a leather jacket,' Jill said. 'And with a beard and glasses.'

'Aye, is that him, the Gaelic poet?'

'He's also wearing a turban.'

'Aye, that one.'

'Alex, he's wearing a turban. He's a Sikh.'

'So?'

'Would you like some help with your packing?' the lad on the checkout asked Jill.

'No, it's all right,' Alex said, already in position. He began piling tins, bottles and fruit into their bags for life.

'Can you not be a bit more careful?' Jill said.

'So, what are you saying?' Alex replied, easing off a little on the packing frenzy. 'He's a Sikh because he's wearing a turban? That's quite an assumption you're making there. I mean, you could legitimately argue he's wearing a turban because he's a Sikh, but not the other way round. Doesn't follow. That's like if you saw me wearing a kilt then I'd have to be a Scotsman. I am, of course, but not because I'm wearing a kilt, which I'm not. Are you with me?'

'Unfortunately, yes,' Jill said. She put her card in the machine and entered the PIN number.

'I'll just nip over and check.' He was off before she could stop him.

She shook her head at the checkout lad. 'Don't ever grow into one of those,' she said.

Alex caught up with her at the exit, where the charity bucket people lie in wait.

'No, I was right,' he said. '"Camera ahoo?" I said, but I didn't get any response. Clearly doesn't speak a word of Gaelic. It's not him at all.'

A Hard Man

He sits at the end of the bar drinking, but you never see him take a drink. You never see him lift the glass. There are only so many times you can look at him, and never for very long. His hand does not touch or play with the glass: the small plain tumbler that you know contains whisky because every so often the barman puts another, identical tumbler to the optic under the two-litre bottle of Bell's, sets it down in front of him and removes the now empty glass. But when did he empty it? You never see him take a drink.

Whisky. No water. This is not for show. This is how he drinks and what he drinks. He does not drink to get drunk. He does not drink for pleasure. He drinks because he is in the bar and the bar exists for him to drink in. He does not move. He does not go to the toilet. He does not hand any cash over to the barman.

He observes. He has clocked, assessed, filed every other person in the bar. There are not many on this dull, quiet afternoon. You. Him. Two women talking in a corner. Two men playing pool. All quiet and careful. Nobody wishing to disturb him.

The left hand hangs limp from the wrist. You watch it to avoid being caught watching his face. The hand, its limpness, fascinate you. A wrong signal. Someone who misread that signal could end up very badly hurt. It is a trap, a lure.

This is a very hard man. You and everybody else in the bar understand this. The women speak so quietly they could be mumbling prayers. The pool players click the balls home apologetically, without triumph, without raised voices. As for you, you sit with your paper, not reading a word of it. You must not meet his eye. The barman replaces his drink. You still have not seen him touch the glass. You look away. You want to drink up and leave but you can't. He has not, with a nod or a glance or a movement of that limp hand, given you permission to go.

Jack and the Moon

Jack is leaning out of his window one night, admiring the full moon, which is even brighter and bigger than usual. He feels he could reach out and touch it, so he does. He reaches out and touches it and the moon falls from the sky right into his open arms.

To his surprise it isn't round like a ball. It's a huge yellow disc made out of some kind of heavy parchment, with pencil marks on it for the mountains. Jack lays it on his bed. The room is filled with a wonderful, cool, soothing light.

'What are ye up tae, Jack?' his mother shouts from her room.

'Just closin the windae, Mither,' he said. He folds the moon and puts it in the drawer at the bottom of the wardrobe. Then he gets into bed and tries to sleep, but he's feeling guilty about touching the moon, so he stays awake all night.

The next morning there's consternation because the moon fell out of the sky and no one knows where it went. The tides have stopped working and the sea is dead calm and everybody's asking what happened – everybody except Jack. Whenever he creeps up to his room and opens the drawer there's the folded moon giving off its beautiful glow, but each time it's a wee bit dimmer, and Jack understands that the moon is dying because like everything else it needs the sun to live.

That night, as soon as darkness falls, he sticks the moon up his jersey and slips down to the beach. The sea is flat and still. Jack unfolds the moon and lays it on the water, and gives it a wee push. And that wee push is enough to make a ripple, and the moon rides over it, and that makes another ripple, and then a wave, and Jack looks up and sees the pale edge of the moon on the horizon, and the further out the moon in the sea floats the higher the moon in the sky climbs, and he knows it's going to be all right.

But never again will he try to touch the moon, no matter how tempting it is.

The leader spoke. The message was clear: hope solidifies, ambition gels, the dream becomes reality. After all these years, now was the time. For if not now, when? If not us, who? If we were not to wait indefinitely, why hesitate now?

So ran the rhetoric. Powerful stuff, rhetoric. But it was more than that, because it described something within touching distance. The reasons were powerful too: to build a better country, one that was both more prosperous and fairer, one where material well-being went hand in hand with social justice. To build a society that worked, and cared.

And more than reasons, there were goals to be attained, and detailed plans for attaining them. Practical measures to do with recalibrating the work–life balance: an overhaul of the tax system, a renewal and reorganisation of public services, a negotiated, functioning relationship between the public and private sectors.

None of this was simple. It would mean work, hard work, with perhaps few rewards at first. There would need to be a realisation on the part of the better off that their standard of living would be static for a while, might even decline, in order to deliver a more egalitarian society, a more equitable spread of wealth and opportunities. And on the part of the poorer sections of the community, there would have to be a shift in expectations, an end to the culture of entitlement, an embracing of the idea of less being more, a revision of values. None of this, to repeat, was simple, but the leader laid out a road map, a route up the mountain, one planned phase after another. This, now, was within reach. It *could* be reached, grasped, embraced, if the people wanted it. But did the people want it enough?

A couple of diehards, who had been on the barricades, on the long march, who had been middle-aged when the leader was still in short trousers, asked themselves that question. They asked it over their beers, their beards, and their hard-won memories.

'Aye,' one told the other, 'it's doable, of course. It's there for the taking. But you know, I liked it better when it was a dream.'

The Right Thing

It was a day like any other. She saw the twins off to school, kissed their father on his way out, then rapidly tidied the kitchen before leaving the house herself. She was always last away, first back. The twins had keys but she liked to be home before they were.

She worked part-time, finishing at two when everybody else returned from lunch. Holding the fort, that was what she did between one and two. Not much happened in that hour – a few phone calls, an occasional delivery – but somebody had to be on reception.

Holding the fort: it made her think of the Westerns they used to show on Sunday afternoons when she was a girl.

Nothing stood still. Already her own girls were nearly old enough to marry, and would only narrowly miss voting in the referendum.

On the way home she went to the polling place, a church hall. She handed over her card and received the ballot paper.

She had read and listened to all the arguments about the economy, assets, debts, pensions, oil, membership of this or that international organisation, but as she stood in the booth, pencil poised, none of them seemed to matter. What mattered was how she felt.

When she reached home she put the radio on for the news. The reader reported simply that voting was brisk. Of course he wasn't permitted to say anything that might influence those still to vote.

She started to prepare the evening meal.

Brisk: were people voting with swift but certain resolve? Or were they rushing at it, not giving it due consideration?

She'd considered it, long and hard. How often did such an opportunity come along? To vote for – or against – your country's independence? Once in a lifetime, they were saying, but it was rarer than that.

What was independence? What did it mean in this crowded, connected world?

Well, she had made her mark. She felt she had done the right thing.

She heard the door opening, their voices, their shoes on the stairs. She made a pot of tea and waited for them to join her, as they would, because it was a day like any other.

My Father, Falling

When my father falls he goes down like a tree. Still a big man at eighty-seven, he falls the length of himself, and if you are not there to catch him at the first stumble there is no stopping him. If you see him go and don't manage to reach him at least you have some forewarning of the noise when he hits the deck: it's like a gunshot or a clap of thunder. If you are in another room and hear this you think a wall must have collapsed or a wardrobe tipped over. But it's my father, falling.

The falls are happening more and more often. Two or three times a day, lately. His balance is all wrong and he knows this but knowing it and applying the knowledge so that he doesn't fall are different things. My mother calls him India Rubber Man because he bounces but doesn't break. I think he's made of something more like teak. He breaks other things as he goes down – chairs, tables, bathroom fittings – but, so far, not himself. Although he comes up in huge bruises, under the skin the bone is hard and strong. But we know this cannot last, that a fall will come from which he does not, slowly and painfully, right himself, get onto his knees, crawl and haul himself back into his chair.

You can tell a proud man to take more care. You can tell him not to carry anything when he sets off from one place to another. You can instruct him in the correct method of using his Zimmer. You can clear routes, removing rugs and other items that might ambush him. You can ask him to stay where he is while you fetch whatever it is he wants. But you can't switch off his determination to keep trying. You can't stop him having another go when your back is turned. And you can't stop him being a one-man forest of crashing trees, a constantly replayed film of timber falling, falling, falling. Because this is what a proud man does, in the end. He stands proud, and then he falls, over and over until he cannot rise again.

'Could you please moderate your language?' a voice from the audience requested.

The writer, making a speech after receiving an award for his most recent novel, had just used a certain word for the second time.

'Moderate your own fucking language,' the writer said, using the word for the third time. And continued to express his views on matters literary, cultural, historical and political.

What was meant by the request from the listener? What was implied in the verb 'moderate'? Not, surely, that the views of the writer were offensive, but that his mode of expressing them, his language, was. But wait. *All* of his language? No. *Some* of his words? No. One word in particular? Yes, the single representative of what is sometimes called 'bad' language. The moderation requested was the removal of one word and its associated forms: the word 'fuck'.

Essentially: eliminate the word 'fuck' from the speech and nobody would have been offended. All would have been able fully to appreciate the writer's views on matters literary, cultural, historical and political. There would have been no distractions from the content of his speech.

Aye, that'll be fucking right.

Consider the proposition that 'bad language' exists. Language is made up of words. If some words are bad, others must be good. What makes words good or bad? Convention, taste, authority, law. Remove the bad words, these four chums say, and language will be all the better for it. But who, if not the speaker of the bad words, will moderate their removal? How about the four chums, the custodians of language? Let them take the bad words away for questioning. If this action trespasses too much on notions of civilisation and tolerance, let the questioning be done secretly, in an alien tongue. Let the bad words be subject to extraordinary rendition.

'Extraordinary' means 'amazing', 'unusual', 'exceptional'. 'Rendition' means 'delivery', 'performance', 'interpretation'. These are not bad words.

A critic once counted four thousand uses of the word 'fuck' in another novel by the same writer.

Had the critic nothing better to do?

Irrelevant. Take the writer away for questioning.

The four chums appreciate, by the way, the listener's use of the word 'please'.

General Incompetence was planning his next campaign. He wanted it to be a good one. In particular, he wanted to gain the greatest amount of something in return for the smallest amount of something else. He couldn't remember the exact formula, but territory, casualties, collateral damage, direct hits, political approval and political embarrassment all came into it.

There was a knock at the door. 'Come in,' he barked. (He had learned how to do this at Sandhurst.) His trusty comrade Major Disaster entered. Disaster was a smart-looking chap but you never quite knew what was going on under the surface.

'What is it, Disaster?' Incompetence said. 'Stand easy.'

'Thank you, sir. Trouble in the ranks, sir. The men are fed up being sent into impossible combat zones underequipped and with no clear objective.'

'Well, I'm sorry to hear that, but I blame the politicians.'

Major Disaster stood a little less easy and even shuffled his boots. 'Sir – the troops blame you. I understand how difficult your position is, but the men on the ground don't care. They've begun to take their frustrations out on the local population. There have been a couple of nasty incidents, sir.'

'Good lord, Disaster!'

'Exactly, sir. I have taken action, sir. Corporal Punishment has been arrested and I've been liaising with Marshall Arts to give the men some therapy, which has resulted in Private Anguish and Private Remorse being released.'

'I don't approve of that, Disaster. There were very sound reasons for Anguish and Remorse being locked up. And you know I disapprove of Arts. We can't have the men going soft.'

'I agree, sir. These are only stopgap measures. In the longer term . . .'

'Yes?'

'I think you may have to go, sir.'

'You mean resign? The army without General Incompetence? But that's unthinkable.'

'Sometimes the unthinkable must be thunk, sir. The *Bismarck* was once unthinkable.'

'This is no time for bad puns,' General Incompetence snapped. (He had learned how to do this at Sandhurst.) He stroked his moustache contemplatively. He was wondering if the Major was quite so trusty after all. Perhaps a coup was being planned. Perhaps Disaster would succeed Incompetence. It would not be the first time.

'See that?' Mike the plumber said. 'Know what that is?'

He was pointing at a lever on a pipe under the kitchen sink.

I shook my head. 'No idea,' I said.

'That's your triple-lock fail-safe emergency valve.'

'That sounds quite important.'

'It's very important. And it's also in very poor condition.'

Mike had a pretty low opinion of most of the plumbing in the house. The old plumber, Joe, had generally expressed the view that there was plenty of life left in things. Joe was a 'hit it with a hammer' kind of plumber, but he'd retired, and somebody had given me Mike's name. Mike was more hands-off. He took a lot of readings with a gadget that beeped.

'So, should we replace it?' I asked.

'It's your decision, but I would say so. It could go at any time.'

'What happens if it goes?'

Mike looked very serious.

'If your triple-lock fail-safe emergency valve goes,' he said, 'you're in trouble. It triggers a blowback situation in the cold-water system. When that happens, the outlet can't handle the pressure, and it explodes, and then you have a knock-on effect all down the street.'

'Explodes?' I said. 'All down the street? Just because that little valve stops working?'

'That's right. That's why it's a triple-lock fail-safe mechanism. If that goes, so do the ones in the other houses. Then the main under the road bursts. Then you've got the road collapsing, trees down, probably the houses too. You've got floods like you've never imagined – more like a tidal wave in fact. You've got major disruption to transport and services, electricity and gas supplies cut. You've got oil tankers smashed like toys, harbours washed away, two-thirds of the country underwater. You've got tornadoes, forest fires, plagues of locusts, crop failure, famine. You've got a mini ice age, the sun blocked out by ash, perpetual winter, total anarchy.'

'That's terrible,' I said. 'You go ahead and replace that valve right away. Can you manage it all right?'

'Oh, it's a simple enough job,' Mike said, 'but even a new valve can go at any time. You just can't tell.'

He took a reading with his gadget. It beeped.

Not Safe

The path through the forest divided in two. I considered my options. One way was narrower and looked less well maintained than the other, but, being in adventurous mood, I opted for the narrower path. No sooner had I set off than a man stepped out from behind a tree.

'I wouldn't go down there if I were you,' he said.

He was solid and tall and carried a large stick. His clothes were of a thick, heavy material, dark blue or possibly black. He wore a brown leather belt and sturdy brown shoes, but no hat or cap. Was he in uniform? It was hard to tell. Nor could I decide if the stick was fashioned by human hand or one he'd happened to pick up in the forest.

'Why not?' I asked.

'The path is not in good condition.'

I indicated my own stout footwear. 'I think I'll be fine.'

'I still wouldn't go. There's nothing to be seen.'

He was polite, yet clearly determined to dissuade me from taking that path. He moved slightly so that he stood in my way.

'Where does it go?' I asked.

'It doesn't go anywhere.'

'It must go somewhere. Do you mean it comes to a dead end?'

He considered this. 'No. It rejoins the main path later. So you may as well go that way. It's safer.'

'I'd rather go this way. I'm just going for a walk, that's all.'

'I advise against it,' he said. 'It's not safe.'

'There's no sign warning of any danger.'

'Signs only encourage people,' he said. 'They think it's all right to go as long as they're careful.'

'I will be careful.'

'You can't be careful enough.'

'Are you telling me I can't walk down there? If so, on what or whose authority?'

'I'm telling you it's not safe and you can get to where you're going the other way.'

Something in the very reasonableness of his argument made me as keen to continue along the path as he seemed keen to bar my progress.

'We seem to have different views about this,' I said.

He raised his stick. 'I don't think so,' he replied.

I considered my options.

I was walking in the forest. I had heard stories about a place somewhere on the far side. Some told of an old castle, or of a pool with a waterfall, or of a secluded, sandy beach beside the sea. I wanted to see if the stories were true.

Earlier in my walk I had come upon a narrower, less well maintained path than the one I was on, but a man with an official look about him had stopped me taking it. I regretted that I had allowed this to happen. Perhaps that path led to the place. It was too late now, though, to turn back.

Just then I spotted another path, one so overgrown and thin that it hardly qualified as a path at all. Still, I decided to try it, to see if it went anywhere or petered out.

Although it was very rough, and steep in places, the thin path did not peter out. The forest was quiet and still, but after some time I sensed a change. I could hear something: a river, or a waterfall, or the sound of the sea. I pressed forward, and suddenly emerged into a clearing.

A man stepped out from behind a tree. He was solid and tall and carried a large stick. His clothes were made of thick, heavy tweed, in autumnal colours, and a deerstalker was on his head. I was sure that this was the man I had met earlier.

'What are you doing here?' he demanded.

'I'm just going for a walk,' I replied, 'as I told you this morning.'

'What do you mean? You have never spoken to me before.'

'Yes, I have,' I said. 'You were wearing different clothes, a kind of uniform, blue or possibly black. You threatened me with your stick.'

'That's a lie,' he said. 'I've never seen you before. Anyway, you're not allowed here. You must go back.'

'I don't wish to go back,' I said. 'You will not turn me away twice.'

'I will turn you away as often as is necessary,' he said.

He raised his stick.

I considered my options.

I was afraid, but not as afraid as he was.

Census

A substantial majority of Scots, it has emerged, speak a language about which questions were asked for the first time ever in the most recent national census.

Figures released today reveal that 4.48 million people, or eighty-four per cent of the Scottish population, talk Pish some, most or all of the time. This means that Pish is second only to English in terms of common usage.

A spokesman for the General Register Office for Scotland said that it was important to qualify this headline figure as some significant statistical discrepancies underlay it. For example, while seventy-six per cent of people over the age of sixteen said that they could *talk* or *write* Pish fluently, and sixty-five per cent said that they could immediately *identify* Pish when they heard it, a mere twenty-one per cent admitted to being able to *understand* Pish spoken or written by others.

The council areas with the highest proportions of people who talk Pish were the cities of Aberdeen, Dundee, Edinburgh and Glasgow. Rural areas had the lowest proportions of talkers of Pish, but this might be due, the spokesman said, to greater distances between inhabitants and high levels of taciturnity among farmers.

Professor Ranald Fowlis Wester, Director of the Institute for Talking Pish, commented: 'I have been talking Pish all my life, and it is gratifying to see firm evidence of what I have suspected all along, that I am not alone. Indeed, it is clear that most of my fellow citizens talk Pish to a greater or lesser extent. I call on the Scottish Government to give Pish official status, to legislate for the teaching of Pish in our schools, colleges and universities, and to oblige the BBC to broadcast Pish at least six hours per day.'

The Tory MSP Findo Gasket said: 'These figures are deeply disturbing and no credence should be placed in them. If concessions are made to talkers of Pish the floodgates will open and we will have talkers of Shite, Bollocks and Mince all clamouring for equal representation. I talk Mince all the time but I don't expect anyone to take me seriously.'

No Scottish Government minister was available for comment in any language.

Red Cloud Returns to Washington, 1875

When I was a boy we knew of the white man but we seldom saw him. White men had passed through our country before I was born, and we had let them pass. My people lived on the great plains and in the wooded mountains and if you had told me then that one day we would not live there I would not have believed you. We had the buffalo, the antelope and the deer, we had dogs and horses, we had the seasons and the land and the rivers. There was not one thing we lacked. Most of all we had freedom.

Our enemies were the Pawnee and the Crow. We did not know what was coming to us.

After the Americans had finished their great war, they turned their attention on us. That war was fought to free black people from slavery but when the whites came to our country it was to demand it from us and to enslave us. We refused. They sent soldiers to build forts and drive a trail through our country. We fought a great war against them and we killed many and sent the others home. We signed a treaty at Fort Laramie which promised that we could keep our country as long as the grass shall grow and the water flow. Those were the words. That was only seven years ago.

This is not the first time I have come here. I have met the President before. He has offered to buy our land, and to give us a new home in another place. But we are in our own place, and it cannot be bought and sold for money.

That is not why they brought us here. They wanted to show us their cities, their factories, their wealth and their power. The war we fought was a dogfight compared with their great war. We could never have imagined how many white people there are if we had not seen them with our own eyes. I am not a fool. I will not sign this new treaty, but neither will I fight against such numbers. We fought a good fight seven years ago. It is over.

John Muir Returns to Dunbar, 1893

It is a long time since I was here. When I was a boy this was all the world I knew, and for a while it was enough. I thought then that fighting and the harrying of birds' nests were the greatest occupations a boy could have but then we left for America and my horizons opened beyond my wildest imaginings. I took my homeland with me: my father's harsh faith, which I fashioned anew in the cathedrals of Nature; and the works of Burns, who has never failed me as a companion on all my travels.

War is the most infernal of all the calamities of civilisation. I would not willingly participate in it and so during the Civil War I went to Canada. That was the first of my long walks and I have been walking ever since. I have walked to the Gulf of Mexico. I have walked the length and breadth of California. I have walked in Alaska and now I have come home to walk these old familiar places once more. You might say I went out for a walk in the dawn and never came back till sundown. There is so much to see before it gets dark.

I have walked both alone and with others. There is great joy in sharing the beauties of the world, but when you walk alone you walk with yourself, and this is the finest journey of discovery.

Our help lies in the mountains. Once, high in the mountains, I climbed to the top of a Douglas fir because a storm was building and I wanted to feel what a tree feels in a storm. I clung there while the tempest raged, and back and forth it swung me, not noticing I was a mere attachment to that intelligent plant. Back and forth went the tree, small journeys it had learned to make in its many years, small journeys of survival. For as long as it bent with the wind, the wind would not break it or cause it to fall. And so it is with me. My journeys have been over greater distances, but have I any more wisdom than a tree?

Onset

for Helena Nelson

I had a dream in which I had forgotten almost everything. I knew what it felt like to be without memory, but not what the things were that I had forgotten.

I was in an empty flat space like a great grey blanket. I knew the word 'blanket' and what it meant. My feet sank into the greyness but only so far. It was a long way to go somewhere else. I was very tired.

My feet were far away. One moment I was a giant, the next I was an ant. I did not know what an ant was. I only knew the word and that it meant small.

I had clothes on but had I dressed myself or had somebody dressed me? The clothes did not feel right. Perhaps they were not mine.

I thought if I could only meet someone who knew me, they would help me. They could say my name. 'Hello,' they would say, and then a name. That would be a start.

I thought if there could be a start I might be able to remember.

But I did not know if anybody knew me. I saw faces but I could not give them names. Faces came at me and went away without saying 'Hello'.

I wanted to sit but the greyness would not let me. It made me sick. I had to stand. I was so tired I stood with my eyes closed.

Sometimes you wake up knowing you have been dreaming even though you can't remember the dream. When I opened my eyes I did not know if I had been dreaming or even asleep, but I remembered having forgotten everything.

This frightened me. I decided not to move until I was sure I was awake and not still dreaming.

I watched the ceiling, the bedside lamp, the white sheet, the painting of trees on the wall. I watched them until I was sure I had not forgotten them.

I called out. Nobody came and then somebody did. I don't know if they knew me. They helped me get dressed. 'Hello,' they said.

I am waiting for them to say a name. That will be a start.

Jack and the Minister

Jack had never quite been able to grasp the concept of the soul. If it was part of you how could you not see it when you looked in the mirror? If it was in you how could you not feel it as you could feel your heart? Yet the minister said from his pulpit that without it you were dead, an empty shell.

To Jack, your soul was like your shadow. It belonged to you and you could not be parted from it, but you could not always see it and even when you could you never paid it much heed.

One day when he was out Jack met the minister coming the other way.

'Aye, Jack, and how are you?'

'Braw, thanks,' says Jack. 'How's yersel?'

'I am well too. And how are you in your soul?'

As usual, Jack had forgotten until that moment that he had a soul. Cannily he keeked over his shoulder to see if his shadow was there, and it was, so he says, 'Aye, ma soul's braw, tae.'

'Why did you look behind you when I asked you that question, Jack?'

'I was just checking,' Jack says. 'Sometimes my soul is there and sometimes it isna, but today it's there.'

'Foolish boy,' the minister says. 'You cannot see your soul.'

'Ye can sometimes,' Jack says. 'Sometimes it's afore ye and sometimes it's ahint ye.'

Then he pointed out to the minister a tree's soul, a flower's soul, a cat's soul and a gate's soul.

'These things don't have souls, Jack,' the minister says. 'Only people have souls.'

Just then a big black crow flapped by overhead. As it passed above them its shadow flew along the ground, now a wee bit behind the bird, now a wee bit ahead of it.

'What's that if it isna the craw's soul?' Jack asks.

'That's its shadow, Jack,' the minister said with a laugh. 'Not the same thing at all.' And on he went.

Jack shook his head. There was his own soul, attached to his feet, stretched out on the ground. But as for the minister's soul, Jack could see no sign of it following at the minister's heels.

'Pick a card, any card,' the man said. I'd seen him coming and had hoped he'd miss me. No such luck.

'I'm busy,' I said.

He leered at me like a pilot upside down in a small aeroplane. 'No you're not. You're reading a book, that's all. Pick a card, any card.'

He'd been working the room, not very successfully it seemed, but that was partly because there was hardly anybody in. I suppose it was bound to be my turn eventually.

'Is this what you do?' I said. 'Go round the pubs annoying customers?' I nodded towards the bar. 'Did you get permission?'

'Once round and out,' he said. 'That's what they allow. Single roses, evening papers or card tricks, makes no difference. Once round and out again.'

He had a narrow, shaved head and a wide nose with a fair amount of shrubbery at the nostrils, which were otherwise open to view. He pushed the fanned-out pack under my face. 'Come on, pick a card, any card.'

'What if I do?' I said. 'Do I have to pay?'

'You can if you want,' he said, 'but it's not compulsory. I'm on a scheme. Trainee magician.'

'Who's training you?'

He gave me a severe look, as if I'd crossed a line. 'Il Maestro,' he said, stretching the syllables out like pasta. And then, 'Just give us a break, pal, eh?'

I sighed, closed my book, pointed at a card.

'Not that one,' he said.

'You said any card.'

'Aye, but not that one.'

'Trainee magician?' I said. I pointed at another card. 'All right?'

'Great.' He slid it onto the table. 'Pick it up and look at it.' I picked it up and looked at it. 'Now put it back in the pack.' I put it back. 'Now you take the pack and shuffle it.' I shuffled.

He took the cards from me and went through them. Very slowly.

'That the card?' he said eventually.

'No.'

'Fuck. You sure?'

'Aye. Mine was the nine of clubs.'

'Fuck.'

He stood there, looking pensive.

'What are you reading?' he asked.

I covered the book, put a pound coin next to it.

'You tell me,' I said.

October

Varieties of Madness in France, 1665

after Sir John Lauder

One night we happened to discourse on madmen and the causes of madness. They told me of a man at Marseilles who believed himself the greatest king of the world, and that all the ships in the harbour, along with their wares, were his. Of another they said that he believed himself to be made of glass, and cried horribly if anyone came too close, for fear they would break him. His friends, on some doctor's advice, took a great sandglass and smashed it over his head as he thus raged. When he saw the glass falling at his feet he cried more hideously than ever, that his head was broken in pieces. After he had calmed a little they desired him to consider that the glass was broken, but that he was not; and consequently that he was not glass. On this remonstrance he came to himself, admitting the truth of what they said.

We cannot forget a story from the bedlam in Paris. Two gentlemen came out of curiosity to see the madmen, but the keeper of the hospital having some business to attend could not take them round. Whereupon he instructed one of the inmates to accompany them, and show them all the madmen and the natures of their madness. This the man did, pointing out with remarkable knowledge one who was mad for love, another made witless through drunkenness, a third who was hypochondriac, and so on. At last, as they were about to leave, the inmate said, 'Gentlemen, you have marvelled at the folly of many you have seen, but yonder is one more foolish than all the others, for that poor fellow believes himself to be the beloved apostle Saint John. Now I tell you that he is utterly wrong, and the reason I know this is that I am Saint Peter, and I never opened the gate of Heaven to him yet.'

The gentlemen were surprised to find their guide, so credible until that moment, so deeply deluded. They were informed that he was once a doctor in the college of Sorbonne, and had been reduced to that state through too much study. Which is a lesson indeed.

Ways of Dying Gently in Scotland, 1790s

after Lord Cockburn

Dr Joseph Black, the noted scientist, was a tall, thin, cadaverously pale person, feeble, slender and elegant; his eyes were dark, clear and large, like deep pools of water. He glided like a spirit through the mischief and sport of local boys, respected and unharmed; and when he died, seated with a bowl of milk on his knee, in ceasing to live he did not spill a drop of it.

Dr Robert Henry the historian, having been declining for some while, wrote from his Stirlingshire home to his friend Sir Harry Moncrieff: 'Come out here directly. I have got something to do this week, I have got to die.' Sir Harry arrived. Dr Henry was alone with his wife, resigned yet cheerful. Sir Harry stayed with them three days, during which Dr Henry occupied his easy chair, conversed, was read to, and dozed.

At one point, hearing the clattering of a horse's hooves in the court below, Mrs Henry looked out. To her dismay she saw that it was a wearisome neighbour, a minister, who was famous for never leaving a house after he once got into it. 'Keep him oot,' cried Dr Henry, himself a minister, 'don't let the cratur in here.' But already the cratur was up the stair and at the door. The doctor winked and signed to the others to sit still, while he pretended to be asleep. The visitor entered. Sir Harry and Mrs Henry put their fingers to their lips and shook their heads: the slumberer was not to be disturbed. The visitor took a seat, to wait till the nap should be over. Whenever he tried to speak, he was instantly silenced by another finger on the lip and another shake of the head. This continued for a quarter of an hour, with Sir Harry occasionally detecting his friend peeping through the fringes of his eyelids to check on the state of play. At last the unwanted guest was ushered out, at which the dying man opened his eyes and had a tolerably hearty laugh. This was followed by another when the sound of departing hooves assured them that the danger was past. Dr Henry died that night.

Scottish Dietary Prejudices

after Sir John Lauder and John Kay's Original Portraits

Sir John Lauder, on his travels in France in the 1660s, was not a little amazed to see his hosts one day preparing among other things for the daily meal 'upright puddock stools', which they called *potirons* or *champignons*. They rose overnight, he noted, and grew in 'humid, moisty places' as in Scotland. The French fried them in a pan with butter, vinegar, salt and spice, and ate them greedily, surprised that he did not eat as heartily of them as they did. 'But my prejudice hindered me,' Lauder rather ruefully admitted.

More than a century later, Dr Joseph Black and his friend Dr James Hutton, in the service of free and objective inquiry, set out to overturn a similarly narrow dietary prejudice. It was surely inconsistent, they argued, to abstain from the consumption of hard-shelled creatures of the land, while those of the sea were considered delicacies. If oysters, why not snails, for instance? Snails were known to be nutritious, wholesome and even to have healing properties. The Italians, like the epicures of antiquity, held them in high esteem. The two philosophers resolved to expose the absurd objections of their countrymen to the eating of snails.

Having procured a quantity, they caused them to be stewed for dinner. No guests were invited to the banquet. The snails were served – but theory and practice were found to be separated by a great gulf. Far from exciting their appetites, the smoking dish had diametrically the opposite effect, and neither party felt much inclination to partake of it. Disgusted though they both were by the snails, however, each retained his awe for the other; and so began with infinite exertion to swallow, in very small quantities, the mess that was prompting involuntary internal symptoms of revolt.

Dr Black at length delicately broke the ice, as if to sound the opinion of his companion.

'Doctor,' he said, in his precise and quiet manner, 'Doctor, do you not think that they taste a little – a very little queer?'

'Damned queer! Damned queer, indeed!' Dr Hutton at once responded. 'Tak them awa, tak them awa!' And, starting up from the table, he gave full vent to his feelings of abhorrence.

Miss Menie Trotter of Mortonhall

after Lord Cockburn and Clementina Stirling Graham
for Freeland Barbour

Miss Menie Trotter was one of that singular race of old Scotch ladies who were spirited, resolute, indifferent to modern fads and fashions, and who spoke, dressed and did exactly as they pleased. She was penurious in small things, but otherwise generous. She kept all her bills and banknotes in a green silk bag that hung on her dressing-table mirror, and all her coins in two white bowls, silver in the one, copper in the other. She mistrusted banks but was trustworthy of individuals until their honesty could be disproved: she once sent as a present to her niece a fifty-pound note wrapped in a cabbage leaf, in the care of a woman who was carrying a basket of butter to the Edinburgh market.

Miss Trotter was of the agrestic order – that is to say she was entirely rustic in appearance and manners. Long walks in the country were her chief pleasure, and ten miles at a stretch nothing to her even in old age. She lived alone but enjoyed the company of friends, and entertained them liberally. Every autumn she slaughtered an ox, and with her guests ate her way through him, nose to tail, but only on Sundays. This meant that the beast lasted half through the winter. Not long before her death she urged her neighbour Sir Thomas Lauder to dine with her the following Sunday: 'For, eh! Sir Tammas, we're terrible near the tail noo!'

About this time, a friend asked her how she was feeling.

'Very weel, quite weel,' she replied. 'But, eh, I had a dismal dream last nicht, a fearfu dream!'

'I am sorry for that,' the friend said. 'What was it?'

'Ou, what d'ye think?' said Miss Trotter. 'Of aw the places in the world, I dreamed I was in Heeven! And what d'ye think I saw there? Thoosans and thoosans, and ten thoosans upon ten thoosans, o stark-naked weans! That wid be a dreadfu thing, for ye ken I never could bide bairns aw my days!'

Her name could be the title of a Scottish dance tune, and perhaps she has had one written for her. She certainly deserves one. Would you not agree, Mr Barbour?

A Case of Leaves (1)

It is one of those satisfying, seasonal tasks: the sweeping of leaves into piles; the extraction of outliers and stragglers and stowaways from behind plant pots, out of drains and awkward corners; the sad delight in their dying colours and – depending on the weather – crinkled, or limply sodden, textures; the multiple pleasures of their shapes and shades, singular and collective; the quiet brushstrokes capturing the end of summer, clearing away the process of autumn.

There are machines for sucking and chopping up dead leaves – roaring, aggressive, indiscriminate herders. Their noise and brutality are an affront to Nature. I prefer the brush and the boards, the barrow and the bin. There is dignity this way; time and silence in which to think.

Of all the seasons, this is the one that tugs hardest at the heart. And it has that other name, the fall. What worlds of meaning are contained in that short phrase!

Later today, I'll be in the city, saying a few words at the opening of a new exhibition at the National Portrait Gallery. The exhibition is about history, about how past lives and concerns connect with present ones. Since I'll only be speaking for a minute or two I have not been asked what technical requirements I might require: projector, screen, audio-visuals, handouts. Not necessary, on this occasion. But perhaps what I am doing now, gathering leaves, is not so very different from what the exhibition aims to do: to gather and sift and appreciate single and multiple lives, the falling past that already contains in it both the cold, clear threat of winter and faith in spring's renewal, growth and change. I imagine filling a suitcase with leaves, taking it to the city, casting its contents across the floor of the gallery. I imagine saying, 'This is my audio-visual aid, my handout. What you see is what you will become. What you will become is what others were before. What others were before became you. Walk through this space, these memories, these signs and tokens of what is past, over; contemplate their colours, shapes and shades, their singular and collective stories. They are not over. They are you. You are them.'

A Case of Leaves (2)

This old fellow was coming through. We'd been watching him on the monitor as he crossed the concourse.

'That's a healthy old bird,' Stan said. 'Look at the way he's swinging that suitcase.'

The man was wearing a brown raincoat and a hat from a 1950s movie. Stan was right: he was jaunty even though he looked above seventy. You could see it wasn't any effort to carry the case.

'Can't be much in that,' I said.

'If anything,' Stan said. 'Let's take a look.'

We stepped out and took the old fellow over to the inspection zone.

'Is that your suitcase, sir?' Stan asked.

'Yes, it is.'

'Please put the suitcase on the table,' Stan said.

The man lifted it as if it were full of air. Stan turned it sideways on, so that when it was opened we would all be able to see inside clearly.

'Is it locked?'

'No, it's not locked.'

'Did you pack this case yourself, sir?'

'Yes, I did.'

'Has anyone else had access to it? Could anyone have interfered with it, with or without your knowledge?'

'Not with my knowledge. Without – how would I know?'

He did not seem anxious in his brown raincoat and 1950s hat.

Stan said, 'Please open the suitcase.'

The man flicked up one catch, then the other. He lifted the lid. The lid went back so far, then stopped.

'What's this?' Stan said sharply.

'Leaves.'

'Leaves?'

'It's the fall back there. I brought the fall with me.'

Stan's gloved hand rummaged around, like a squirrel in a park. It shovelled dry leaves onto the table. Some fell on the floor.

'Do something, Pete,' Stan said.

'Is something the matter?' the man asked.

What was I supposed to do? I wasn't a park attendant. 'It's just leaves,' I said.

Suddenly the man started laughing, a clean, happy laugh. It was infectious. I couldn't help myself.

'Pete,' Stan said. 'Can it.'

I pushed Stan aside. I put both hands in and flung a heap of leaves in the air.

'It's just leaves,' I said. I dug in again, deeper this time, showering us all. I wanted there not to be a bottom to that suitcase.

Solitary

When they put me in the hole I thought, I'll go mad. By the time they let me out I will be insane. So that was what I had to fight: going mad. I hated the bastards but hating them wouldn't be enough to get me through. I had to beat them. Staying sane, not cracking, was what I had to do.

The cell was eight feet long by four feet wide. Three paces by one and the ceiling a yard above your head with a slit window for air. No chair or bed – just the stone floor and three thin, dirty blankets. It was the desert, it got cold at night, but you had to use one of the blankets as a pillow or your head would be constantly banging off the stone. There was a bucket to piss in and another with drinking water, and once a day they took them away and brought them back, empty and full, and I don't think they took much care which one was which. Twice a day you got your punishment rations, two slices of dry bread. That was it, dry bread and water. If they caught you trying to make the bread last they accused you of hoarding and took away what you hadn't eaten.

I was in for smiling on parade. I hadn't been smiling, I'd been squinting into the sun. No point in arguing. If you argued they put you in a strait-jacket and then they could come in and beat you up and you couldn't defend yourself, couldn't even cover your head with your arms. So I didn't argue. Smiling on parade was just an excuse. They wanted to break me. I concentrated on staying sane.

I made lists, A to Z. Flowers, birds, trees, rivers, countries, capitals, poets, musical instruments, makes of car, makes of cigarette. When I finished one list I started another. I took myself somewhere else so I'd still be there when they let me out three days later. And I was. I saw the disappointment on their faces. I didn't smile. I stared straight ahead. I'd been in the hole. I was better than they'd ever be.

'Can I help you?'

'Yes, I've come to object.'

'What about?'

'About having my photograph taken. Before you introduced that last session – I thought the interviewer rather hogged the conversation, by the way – you made a number of so-called "housekeeping" announcements. Among these you informed us that a photographer was present and would be taking pictures for the press, the festival's website and what you termed "general promotional purposes". And you said that if anybody objected to their photograph being taken, they should let you know. So I'm letting you know. I object.'

'And we absolutely respect your right to do so. If you could stand still for a moment, I'll quickly . . . There, that's done, thank you.'

'You just took my photograph! Precisely what I'm objecting to.'

'Let me explain. We're a very small festival. We only have two cameras. On this one we store photographs of people who object to their photographs being taken. The official photographer uses the other camera. If we want to use one of his photographs for any of the purposes you've mentioned, we can check if any of the objectors on this camera are in the photograph on that camera, and if they aren't we can use it.'

'And what if they are? To be specific, what if *I* am?'

'Well, if it's a photograph we really want to use we can edit you out. Crop the picture to exclude the back of your head or the tip of your nose or whatever. That way we respect your wishes but don't interfere with the photographer's work. Not until later, anyway.'

'But you took my photograph against my wishes.'

'Only with this camera, which isn't the official one. That's almost as if you weren't photographed at all.'

'But I was. I insist that you delete the photograph.'

'If I do that we won't be able to respect your wishes about not being photographed.'

'How many objectors' photographs do you have in that thing?'

'So far, just the one. Look, suppose I delete it by mistake?'

'Please do.'

'There. Don't tell anybody. Now, would you mind doing something for me in return?'

'What?'

'Would you please fill in this evaluation form?'

Inside (1)

for Carolyn Scott

I've done stupid things. I'm not a stupid man but some of the things I've done, there's no other way of describing them. But then I think, *Did I have a choice?* I was doing stupid things from when I was a kid, not out of badness, just because I didn't know any better. Who was to blame for that? My dad was a hard man. No other way of describing him. He was hard on us. He was hard on me because I was the son and he had expectations and I didn't come up to them. I was five, for Christ's sake, or ten, and I didn't come up to his expectations. By the time I was in my teens it was too late. I hated him and I deliberately went out of my way to let him down, to show him up. So whose fault was that? Was I supposed to screw the nut and conform? I could never do that.

So I've made a few mistakes. Wrong decisions. I've been in the wrong place at the wrong time. Why I'm here now is because I was doing someone a favour. I should have been smarter. I've been in trouble before, I should have seen it coming, but you don't, you think you'll get away with it. I saw a poster in a window once: NOBODY IS EVER OLD ENOUGH TO KNOW BETTER. I like that. That's me through and through. I was doing someone a favour, it was a situation that involved drugs, I should have walked away but I didn't, and I got caught, and this is me here, now, paying for it. At my age.

There are worse places to be. I've been in some of them. It's safer here, most of the time. I've got my TV, I've got my music, I've got my sketchpad. If I fill up the sketchpad they let me have another. You get time to think in here. You think, *I'm never coming back inside again.* But how you think in here and how you think when you're outside are two different things. That's the trouble. If they weren't, it would be easy.

Inside (2)

for Marianne

Inside is an installation, a work of art, temporarily displayed in the disused cells at the back of the Sheriff Court (which still sits in this old county town, though not for much longer). The art is a film, the film is a story, the story is of a man who makes art in prison, because he also makes mistakes and prison is where he goes for making them. These old cells are to be demolished next week; this is the last life that will be in them. TISH 2 YEARS HARD GRAFT is scrawled on a wall, the work of someone who once waited here for judgement, and got it.

This present art tells of a man who has painted the walls of another prison. We watch him on film, his art, his justifications. He explains what he does, what it does for him. Then we are out in the corridor again, released.

We look through the hole in the door of the adjacent cell: there are thousands of people in there! Ledgers and ledgers of births, marriages, deaths. The cell is a storehouse of arrivals, conjunctions, departures. But next week this building will be no more. What about all these lives? Where will they be taken?

I push at the door – it opens! All you people are free to go!

But they stay, bound in their ledgers.

'You'll be in here,' I say. 'Your birth will be here.' We don't have permission, we don't have authority, but nor will we ever be here again. We shift the ledgers from shelf to shelf, searching for the one with your year of birth, your place of registration. Here it is. We turn the pages and – there you are!

This is where you came in: your moment of arrival, indelible, your parents' details, your father's careful signature, the registrar's confirmation. And here, chronologically around you, are your classmates, the children you grew up with, a few whose names you don't recall who must have moved away. This is you in this cell, then and now.

And in the cell next door, and somewhere else, that other life.

Two lives, two different roads.

Sixty years' hard graft.

The Bicycle

Was there ever an invention as benign and brave as the bicycle? Humans have made many things which cause suffering, death and ugliness through their use: weapons of all kinds, for example, guns and bombs especially; aeroplanes, ships, cars, lorries and other vehicles. Labour-saving devices such as dishwashers, lawnmowers, chainsaws and sewing machines all have points in their favour: but a dishwasher may disgorge harmful chemicals into the water system, a lawnmower pollutes the peace of a Sunday afternoon, chainsaws can massacre a forest and a rank of sewing machines may constitute a sweatshop. What great harm can a bicycle do? If its tyres cause a little hurt to a country lane, what is this against all its benefits?

The cost of keeping a bicycle is low. A bicycle does not take up much space. A child or a nonagenarian can ride a bicycle. A bicycle will last a lifetime, or more. A bicycle is quiet. What small sounds a bicycle makes are pleasing. A bicycle uses no energy other than that of its rider. A bicycle encourages exercise and fitness.

Bicycles are adaptable: they can be modified into tricycles or tandems, for use by disabled or blind people. Bicycles do no damage to roads. Bicycles encourage sociability. Bicycles are democratic. Bicycles civilise the traffic systems of cities.

Bicycles are liberating. On a bicycle you can travel from the town to the country, or from the country to the town. You can bicycle with friends or you can bicycle alone. You are dependent on nobody else when you set off on a bicycle ride.

The nineteenth-century American campaigner for women's rights, Susan B. Anthony, said of bicycling, 'I think it has done more to emancipate women than anything else in the world. I stand and rejoice every time I see a woman ride on a wheel. It gives women a feeling of freedom and self-reliance.'

When you rest on your journey you can lay down your bicycle, take out a book and read. A book requires only the energy of daylight and the engagement of the reader, yet even a book may contain intimations of evil. A bicycle whispers only of happiness, freedom and health.

'Jack,' his mother says one day, 'that auld dug has had it. Aw she does is eat and sleep. Tak her doon tae the sea and droon her.'

'Och, Mither, I canna,' Jack cries, but she insists.

Down to the sea he trudges, with the dog limping at his heel. When they reach the water's edge, Jack sits for an hour and the dog sits with him. Then they go back to the house.

'I couldna dae it, Mither,' Jack says. 'She wasna ready for droonin.'

'I'll mak it easier for ye,' she says. 'Tak this auld sack wi ye and when ye get tae the sea pit the dug in it and droon her.'

So Jack trails down to the sea with the sack and the dog, but he still can't do the job, so it's back up to the house they go.

'It's hard, Jack,' his mother says, 'but the morn's morn ye'll hae tae dae it because I've tellt ye.'

The next morning, when Jack gets up, the sack is lying by the door. 'The dug was fast asleep, Jack,' she whispers, 'so I just pit her in the sack and tied it. If ye cairry it tae the sea and haud it under, that'll be the dug drooned.'

Well, Jack lifts the sack on his shoulder and away to the shore again. But he still can't bear to drown the dog, even though she's so quiet he thinks she might have suffocated. So he opens the sack to check, because if she's dead then he'll not need to drown her, and what is in there but a big round stone wrapped up in a blanket!

Back he runs to the house. 'Mither, Mither, somebody's stole the dug!'

'Naw, Jack,' she says. 'Naebody's stole it.'

In front of the fire is the old dog, snoring away like a train.

'I was testin ye, Jack,' she says. 'I wanted to see if ye'd dae whit I tellt ye.'

'I doot I've failed ye then, Mither,' says Jack, 'for I didna droon the dug.'

'Naw, son, ye didna fail,' she says. 'Ye passed. Sit in at the table and I'll gie ye yer breakfast.'

What he said, I am absolutely clear about this, what he said was that in his father's house were many TV channels. And he did that thing with his eyes, narrowed them a bit. He said, 'If it were not so I would have told you.' I remember that very well because it was quite heavy, like we had to pay attention.

He was going to get the place ready and then come back for us. That is definitely what he said. The funny thing was he insisted we knew the house, and how to get there too. Well, we didn't. If we did, why would he have to come back for us? We could just turn up, maybe pick up some pretzels and beer en route. And Tom said, 'No, we don't know the way,' and he suddenly went all weird, going on about how *he* was the way and the truth and if we knew him we must know his dad, and from now on we *did* know his dad because we'd seen him. Well, we hadn't. So Phil said, 'Have you got a picture of him on your phone?' And it got a bit unpleasant. He said, 'After all this time, Philip, and you say you don't know me.' Which wasn't what Phil had said in fact, but he wouldn't let it go. 'If you know me you know my father,' he said, 'so what's this about showing you his picture?' He doesn't like being challenged, that's the problem. There's two ways of doing things, his way and the wrong way. But once he calmed down he was dead nice again. His place was our place, anything you want just ask, all that stuff. Which probably means we don't have to bring anything. And then he was off.

I'd wanted to ask how many TV channels there actually were. And which ones, because a lot of them are crap and we're going to be there a long time. But because of the way he'd had a go at Phil I didn't think I could.

Anyway, he's been away ages. He never gave a time of course, but it's getting cold out here.

Old Tom and Liver-Eating Johnson

An old fellow called Tom was, like myself, a regular user of the library. I never knew his surname but the librarians addressed him as Tom and I often saw him reading the papers when I changed my books. He read the local paper, the national dailies and the weeklies – the *Listener* and the *Spectator*. Once I overheard one librarian telling another that Tom stayed with his sister who put him out every morning and didn't let him back till teatime. The library was a place to keep warm and dry yet Tom had a perpetually damp sniff. The librarians' other name for him, perhaps in ironic reference to his reading material, was the *Sniffer*.

Tom wore an overcoat that smelled like soup when dry and like a collie dog when wet. Strong though it was, that smell was fascinating to a boy. I used to fill my lungs with it and wonder what it would be like having Tom living in your house. He had a tangled beard and thick, stiff hair sticking out as if in a permanent gale. He was the living likeness of another character in the library, Liver-Eating Johnson.

Liver-Eating wasn't his original name of course. Neither was Johnson. He was born John Garrison but changed his name after deserting from the US Army during the Mexican War. He headed west and became a fur trapper, and married a woman of the Flathead tribe. One winter when he was away from their cabin a Crow hunting party turned up and murdered her. Johnson went on the vengeance trail, killing Crows wherever he found them and eating their livers, which was a great insult because the Crows believed that organ to be essential for full enjoyment of the afterlife.

Johnson was a legendary figure of the Wild West. He once survived most of a winter on the severed leg of a Crow he'd killed, but his final days were in an old folks' home in California where he lasted just one month.

I found Liver-Eating Johnson in a book whereas Tom was flesh and blood, but both inhabited the library and I can never think of one without remembering the other.

Rackwick

The old man was clear: no service, no ceremony, no eulogy. As for his ashes – 'Let the crematorium dispose of them. That's what it's for.'

We remonstrated but he would not relent. 'If you want to talk about what a pain in the neck I was over a few drinks, there's money in that jar on the mantelpiece. That's as much fuss as I want.'

'You're not a pain in the neck,' we said.

'Don't be so sure,' he said. 'I haven't told you what to do with the stone yet.'

'What stone?'

'The one sitting on the ledge beside the bath,' he said, 'next to the soap. Fetch it through.'

Two of us helped him sit up a bit and the third went for the stone. It was beautiful, cream-coloured, smooth but not glossy, perfectly oval, dense and weighty. When you held it, its solidity felt reassuring.

'It comes from a place called Rackwick, on the island of Hoy, in Orkney,' the old man said. 'A long way away. I don't want to be scattered anywhere, but I'd like that stone returned to its place. The bay is a sweeping curve covered with thousands of stones like that one. It should never have been removed.'

'If there are thousands still there –' one of us began, but he held up an admonishing finger.

'That's irrelevant. I went there once, fifty years ago, and I took that stone. I should not have done so. I took it out of selfishness because I wanted a physical memento of the place. I always meant to take it back and now it's too late. But somebody else can go.'

We passed the stone among us. As we did so, aeons stretched before and after the moment of our being together in that room. Its perfect texture and shape were the result of uncountable rollings and rubbings and polishings with other stones, of the washing cycles of innumerable tides.

The old man could no longer hold it, but he let his fingers trail across its surface.

'Take it,' he said. 'I forbid you to take *me*!' he added, suddenly anxious. 'I am immaterial. But the stone must go back!'

Seeds

She lived at the top of the house, in an attic room with a window that looked out over the garden. Every day she sat in a chair in that window, thinking. She thought aloud, muttering or shouting as ideas formed in her head. All morning words tumbled from her, randomly it seemed, but by afternoon they were beginning to take shape and order. She repeated certain phrases, stopped, and changed what she was saying, so that by evening what had been – to anyone who might have been listening – incoherent nonsense, had become something else, a story that could be followed. But there was no one but herself to follow it.

When she had chewed it over a few times, she raised herself from the chair, reached for the window and opened it. Leaning as far out as she could, she spat something from her mouth.

It is hard to describe what that thing was. Perhaps it was a kind of seed. She spat it out as you might the seed of an apple. Sometimes the seed fell into the gutter below, and the rain took it away, through sewers and rivers to the sea, where it turned into a small corked bottle with a message in it. Sometimes it was caught by the wind and was blown into a park or a farmer's field or a flowerbed outside a factory, where it grew into a poem or a joke. Sometimes it fell into the abandoned garden, where it lay among the huge dandelions and broken, cold frames until it became a legend, a rumour, a fairy tale. Sometimes a bird ate it and it became a song, and later if the bird migrated to a foreign land it would be sung in another language. Every day she spat out a seed.

Nobody visited her. The local children did not dare enter the house. The idea of going up all those stairs to ask for a story was too terrifying. Yet they knew she was there. She would always be there. Long after they had grown up and gone, there she would be, muttering and shouting, and spitting her seeds out of that high window.

Him

My wife answered the phone one morning. I heard her say, 'Who?' and then, 'Who is this?' and finally, 'And I'm the Queen of Sheba,' before she hung up. When it rang again I said, 'I'll get it.' She said, 'It's some joker,' but it wasn't, it was him.

'I love your novel,' he said. 'I want to turn it into a movie. Let's meet.'

'Sure,' I said, trying to sound cool while gesticulating excitedly at my wife. 'When would you like to meet?'

'Today, midday.'

I looked at my watch. 'So soon?'

'I'm in town. I'm leaving tonight.'

'I shall have to rearrange some other appointments,' I said.

'Do that,' he said.

I mentally scored out boiling the kettle and completing the crossword. He said, 'Do you know the Botanic Gardens?'

'Yes,' I said. 'The café there? Or perhaps the restaurant?' I assumed he'd be paying.

'Neither. We'll be constantly interrupted. Make your way to the rock garden. There's a bench. Be on it at midday.'

My wife said I was an idiot for going, but I turned up at the agreed hour and so did he. It really was him. He said again how much he liked the book and that he intended to direct the movie himself and which studio he was going to approach. He was serious. Why else would he have gone to all that trouble with someone he'd never met before?

'Maybe that's how he gets his kicks,' my wife suggested later.

While we were talking a woman loitered in the rock garden, pretending to inspect the plants but drawing ever closer until she was right in front of our bench.

'Are you who I think you are?' she asked in an awed whisper.

He gave her that famous scowl. 'No,' he said.

'Okay, sorry,' she said, and scuttled off.

He shook my hand when we parted. I was hopeful. My wife said I was deluding myself. And, indeed, he didn't contact me again and the movie was never made. Probably just as well. He wanted the lead part and he wouldn't have been right for it. Too old, too typecast. He'd have made a mockery of my work.

The Isle of Dogs

This 1968 classic of science-fiction cinema starred Charlton Heston as a shipwrecked mariner called Soutar and Roddy McDowall as Julius, a cocker spaniel and lecturer in sociology. Although praised for its satirical script and groundbreaking innovations in make-up techniques, it was not a box-office success, and a sequel, *Destination Dog Star*, was cancelled early in production.

In *The Isle of Dogs*, dogs have become the dominant species on the planet in a post-apocalyptic future. Humans, who have lost the power of articulate speech and communicate largely through growling, barking, whining and howling, are kept as pets, or reared for particular kinds of employment. As well as pampered lap humans there are sheep humans, hunting humans, racing humans, guide humans, and humans trained for bomb disposal and gruelling manual labour.

Soutar is washed up on a beach after a ferocious storm, the sole survivor of his ship's crew. He finds himself in a sophisticated canine society ruled by aristocratic poodles and their ferocious Dobermann henchdogs. The Isle's constitution claims to operate a code of kindness towards lesser species, humans included. As Soutar soon discovers, though, the code is routinely ignored. Cruelty and neglect are everywhere, and ownerless or abandoned humans are captured and held in 'rescue centres' – appallingly overcrowded places from which they are transferred to 'sleep camps', never to return.

Soutar tries to rouse his fellow humans to rebellion, but they have been conditioned to desire only food, recreational exercise and sex. Frustrated, he strikes up a forbidden relationship with a police dog called Lydia, who introduces him to her uncle, Julius. The trio decide to find out what really happens in the camps where humans are 'put to sleep'. The camps are actually enormous factories processing humans into dog food. Disgusted at the idea of consuming human meat, Lydia and Julius lead a revolt against the poodles and civil war ensues. Lydia is killed and although Julius's forces are ultimately triumphant, Soutar realises that he cannot remain on the Isle. He builds a new boat and, with a hand-picked group of house-trained men and women, sets sail for a life elsewhere. The final shot shows two kittens playing in the stern of the vessel.

Effort

Everything is an effort. Pushing the buttons on the remote control is an effort. Working out if there is anything worth watching on the TV now or in the near future is an effort. Reaching behind the chair for the light switch is an effort. Picking up the paper is an effort. Reading the paper is an effort. Getting from the chair to the dining table is an effort. Going to the toilet is a monumental effort. How did all this happen? Even a few years past – a mere blink of time for one whose father was born at the height of the reign of Victoria – these things were done with hardly a thought as to *how* they were done. Now, the successful method, the route to achievement, is an achievement in itself. The end is sometimes forgotten in meeting the challenge of the means.

Between showers we take him out in the wheelchair, through the town and across the golf course to the beach. The clocks went back two nights ago, which means that the already shortened days have become shorter. The heat leaves more quickly than the light. The autumn sky is soft, calm, immense, but the air is cold. He feels it closing in on him, and wants to walk.

With the two of us supporting him, one on each side, and my mother now in charge of the empty wheelchair (too heavy for her to push when he is in it), we start back up the road from the beach. This is the greatest effort of all. He manages a hundred metres or so, his breaths shortening and quickening with each step on the gentle slope. We negotiate him back into the wheelchair as the rain comes on, and head for home. By the time we arrive, it's dry again. Like museum curators manoeuvring a bulky exhibit on loan from some other museum, we get him indoors and into his chair – the one without wheels. Within a few minutes he is dozing.

How tired he must be of all that vast expenditure for such meagre return. And what little extra effort, going up that slope, might have brought a different outcome.

The room is in darkness.

The painting and the book are in the room. Are the painting and the book in the room?

You enter the room. You turn on the light. The painting and the book are in the room. You see them both.

The painting is on the wall. You are in the room and the painting is in the room. You don't look at the painting. You look at the painting. Whether you do or don't, the painting exists.

The book is on the table. You are in the room and the book is on the table. You don't look at the book. You do look at the book. The book exists, but it is asleep.

You pick the book up, hold it: the book stirs. You put it down: the book sleeps.

You look at the painting. You do not touch it. The painting does not move.

You sit down, holding the book. You open the book. You read the book. The book is awake.

When you look at the painting, the painting still has not moved. You like the painting, you admire the painting. The painting has its effects. You are affected by the painting.

When you read the book, the book moves. The black lines and marks form into something else. You have your effects. The book is affected by your reading it.

The book is a process: to, from; from, to. The writer needs the reader needs the writer. The reader needs the writer needs the reader. Without the writer, the book is unwritten. Without the reader, the book is unread. Without the process, the book is asleep, possibly dead.

You put down the book. You look at the painting. You leave the room.

Another enters the room. Another looks at the painting. It is the same painting. Is it the same painting? Another picks up the same book. Is it the same book?

Another leaves the room, taking the book, turning off the light.

The book is read by another elsewhere. Another affects the book. The book has its effects.

The painting is in the room. The book has left the room.

The room is in darkness.

Porridge

There are only three ingredients in a dish of porridge: oats, water and salt. You can vary the quantity of each ingredient and thus vary the consistency and taste of the porridge, and naturally the quality of both oats and water will affect the final outcome. Most regular makers of porridge, however, have a regular way of going about things. They will use the same kind and quantity of oats, take water from the same source, and add the same amount of salt to the mix. Some will steep the oats overnight, others for an hour before commencing the cooking process. Some will not steep the oats at all. But each individual maker of porridge will follow the same procedure that he or she always follows, day after day.

Now comes the curious part. Despite this simplicity and regularity, your bowl of porridge will never be the same two days running. This is not because on any particular day something has gone wrong. It is just one of the mysteries of porridge. You may make it in precisely the same way for a lifetime, and each day it will be different. Porridge aficionados know this. They expect and relish it. In Scotland experienced porridge eaters will pass judgement as follows: 'The parritch are awfie guid the day,' or 'They're rare parritch this mornin.' Note that in these instances 'parritch', a singular noun, takes a plural verb. This is in acknowledgement of the fact that the finished conglomerated product is composed of many oats.

Dr Johnson caused the hackles of Scottish porridge eaters to rise when in his famous dictionary he defined oats as 'a grain, which in England is generally given to horses, but in Scotland supports the people'. Actually, there wasn't much wrong with that as a definition in 1755. Indeed, a manufacturer of oats in Cupar immediately adopted the advertising slogan OATS: SUPPORTING THE PEOPLE OF SCOTLAND. No, sorry, that's untrue.

Not everyone enjoys porridge, but those of discerning taste do. As Lady Perth observed to a French visitor as they discussed the culinary merits of their respective countries, 'Weel, weel, some fowk like parritch and some like puddocks.' Now *that* is true!

'Yes, it's an odd kind of life,' he said. 'An odd way to make a living. You feel a bit of a fraud, like you're getting away with something fundamentally dishonest. Which of course you are – with the books I write anyway.'

'Fiction, you mean?' she asked. They were sitting in the window of the hotel lounge, looking out at the traffic and the people on the pavements. Their coffee cups were empty. The writer had declined her offer of an alcoholic drink. 'Not yet,' he'd said. 'Let's get this over first.'

'It's all lies, isn't it?' the writer said. 'Inventions, subterfuges, squeezing the complicated mess of real life into silly plots and eighty thousand words.' Sometimes he was surprised, though not impressed, by his own unworldly weariness. 'I don't suppose it's so very different for a biographer or a historian. I was speaking to one of those the other day – a historian, a man who'd recently retired after forty years at a university – and he said something remarkable. Remarkably honest, anyway, I thought. "There are very few facts in history," he said. "Nearly all history is interpretation." And I was about to challenge him, to ask what in that case he thought he'd been working with all his life, all that material, all that evidence, when I saw what he meant. He was right. Interpretation is everything. The facts don't matter a damn, in the end.'

She indicated the street beyond the glass. 'Those are facts,' she said. 'Those people, all that activity.'

'Yes,' he said. 'Yes, they are. We could sit here all day and watch them, and the longer we watched, the more you would appreciate the truth of what he said.'

She shifted uneasily in her chair. She couldn't decide if she liked him or not. She almost felt sorry for him, but he would despise her if she admitted that. It was all a game for him.

'Shall we go?' she said, glancing at her watch.

He seemed suddenly alarmed. 'Perhaps we have time for that drink,' he said. 'A quick one, to steady the nerves?'

'No,' she said. She felt cruel. 'No, everybody's waiting. We have to go now.'

Accidents of Birth

This thing was unfolding as we watched. The biggest industrial complex in the land, the nerve centre of what was left of a pre-post-industrial economy, was shut down and would stay shut because the people who worked there had failed to agree, unconditionally, to the conditions demanded by the owner. We were sixty miles away but it felt as if it were happening in the street outside. We could feel the tension, the fear, the disbelief.

Helpful people had been expressing their online opinions all day: wake up and smell the coffee, guys; no individual should be able to hold an entire country to ransom like this; the workers betrayed again – by their own unions; a capitalist conspiracy. A town was on the brink of becoming a dead zone, the present was about to morph overnight into the past – and this was a complex built not on coal or shipbuilding but on oil, which was supposed to be about the future. Watching, we felt anger, dismay, helplessness. We felt, however faintly, what the people of that town were feeling. This story was about real lives, real decisions. We knew it mattered.

The next story came on. This was about an old woman, her son, her grandson and her great-grandson. The great-grandson had been christened. One future day the baby would be a king. One day before that his father would be a king. One day before that his father's father would be a king. All this would happen but only if and when the old woman died. If? Well, she was a queen. It was possible, given the way the story was being told, that queens were immortal, but on the other hand the reporter seemed absolutely certain that these three would be kings. Nothing succeeds like succession.

There was a mystical insanity to this christening, this supposedly private ceremony which with its outfits, anthems and seven godparents was news everywhere. Could this story possibly come from the same world as the previous story?

It could. A petrochemical plant might close, an oil refinery might not reopen, eight hundred or thirteen hundred or thousands of people might lose their jobs. A baby would be king.

PROBE

I was in my office at the back of the house and had just finished doing my emails when the doorbell rang. It was half past three in the afternoon, the usual time for children returning home from school to ring the bell and run away, so I ignored it. Then it rang again.

A man with a moustache and a clipboard was at the door.

'We have reason to believe you have disclosed information to a third party which may compromise the security of the country and the safety of your fellow citizens,' he said.

'Eh?' I replied.

'You may have done this unwittingly in which case a warning will be issued but no further action taken against you. If you have deliberately disclosed the information we reserve the right to prosecute.'

'Wait,' I said. 'Go back a couple of sentences. Who, in the first place, are "we"?'

'We are PROBE,' he said. 'We are one of the world's leading security support and maintenance providers and we have been appointed by the government to support and maintain the security of the country.'

'PROBE?' I said. 'Is that an acronym?'

'I am not at liberty to disclose that information unless you are an accredited and approved stakeholder,' he said.

'I am a citizen,' I said. 'Does that count?'

He consulted a sheet of paper on his clipboard. 'May I see your passport?' he asked.

'What is this?' I said. 'I am at home minding my own business and you turn up and ask me for identification. Why would I show you, a total stranger, my passport?'

He showed me a PROBE identity badge on which were his photograph and a name that might also have been his.

'Now show me your passport,' he said.

'No,' I said. 'In fact I refuse to prolong this ludicrous, not to say sinister, exchange. Goodbye.'

'Suspect refused to co-operate,' he said, making a mark on his paper.

I'd had enough. I shut the door firmly in his face.

When I returned to my office I discovered that the window had been forced open; also that my computer hard drive had been wiped.

I suppose I was asking for it.

CHECK

The doorbell rang. A man with a moustache and a clipboard was standing on the step.

'Good afternoon,' he said. 'I represent CHECK, one of the world's leading security support and maintenance providers. We have been appointed by the government to support and maintain the security of the country, and today we are in your locality carrying out some research intended to help improve the delivery of our products. Would you mind answering a few questions?'

'Shoot,' I said.

'Our policy is always to ask the questions first,' he said, turning a sheet on his clipboard. 'Are you ready?'

'Fire away,' I said.

He gave me a look. 'With regard to intelligence gathering,' he said, 'including monitoring of emails, telephone calls and other modes of communication, we are interested in responses to the proposition: "If you have done nothing wrong you have nothing to fear." Would you say, in general terms, that you have done nothing wrong?'

'Do you mean legally or morally?'

'Let's not split hairs,' he said. 'What about the following? Ever dropped litter? Smoked marijuana? Arson? Theft? Exceeded the speed limit? Manslaughter? Read or watched pornography? Rape, murder, high treason, blasphemy? Done any of those?'

'What line of questioning is that?' I said. 'They're completely arbitrary categories. And what do you mean by "blasphemy" anyway? I'm not even religious.'

He ticked a box on his sheet.

'Some of them aren't even criminal offences,' I continued. 'Watching porn, for example.'

'One thing leads to another,' he said. 'No smoke without fire, in our experience.' He ticked another couple of boxes.

'What did you do just then?' I asked.

'We call it "profiling",' he said. 'It's a technical term. Now, on a scale of one to five, if one is "strongly disagree" and five is "strongly agree", would you say that you have nothing to fear?'

'Absolutely not!' I said. 'I mean, I strongly disagree, especially on the evidence of how you are conducting this survey.'

'I'll put you down as a one,' he said. 'Don't worry, it's just numbers – at this stage. You have nothing to fear but fear itself.'

'That's reassuring,' I said, intending sarcasm.

'You can rely on us,' he said.

SCOPE

One day, remembering with fondness a holiday spent in the Highlands, I opened the folder on my computer which contained the photographs of that happy week. I was scrolling through them when I came across three blank spaces where three images ought to have been. I checked the numerical sequence and there was no mistaking that those photographs were missing. I could recall from their position in the sequence the scenes they depicted, and I knew I had not deleted them. When I accessed my remote data archive, I found them gone from it as well.

I contacted my internet provider for an explanation. The automated reply I received by email was completely irrelevant. I finally made telephone contact with somebody at the company, whose answers were confused, possibly even evasive. She said she would get someone to call me back.

Ten minutes later the phone rang.

'Hi,' said a man's voice. 'My name is Bob. How can I help you?'

'You tell me, Bob,' I said.

'I represent SCOPE,' Bob said, 'one of the world's leading security support and maintenance providers. I understand you have a data-erosion issue.'

'A what?'

'Data which you recorded and stored with your internet provider has eroded.'

'Not *eroded*,' I said. 'Photographs have been *erased*. What does this have to do with you, Bob, whoever you are?'

'Your issue has been reported to SCOPE as the eroded data may, could, will or did present a potential breach of national security,' Bob said.

'How could that possibly be?' I demanded. 'These were just holiday snaps.'

'I am reviewing the data now,' Bob said. A few seconds later he spoke again. 'The GPS location, date and time references confirm that a security breach occurred when the data was recorded. You are denied further access.'

'A beach, a mountain and a wee white cottage,' I said. 'Which one of those is a threat to national security?'

'I am not at liberty to disclose further information unless you are an accredited and approved stakeholder,' Bob said. 'Goodbye.'

The line went dead. I realised that I had been mistaken. Bob was not a man, but an automated message. And my data had indeed eroded.

I was sweeping around the wheels of a parked car with a stiff yard brush. I didn't know why. The car wasn't mine and sweeping the road wasn't my job. Then this second car drove up, reverse-parked and hit the back of the first one. I think in the motor trade they call it a bump but this was more like a crumple. The first car kind of scrunched up and its rear windscreen shattered.

I stopped sweeping. The driver of the second car jumped out. He said, 'What happened? Did you see what happened?'

'You crashed,' I said. 'You've made a hell of a mess.'

'Don't be angry,' he said. 'It was totally my fault. I'll pay for the repairs. Just name your price.'

I know that when you're involved in a motor accident you're not supposed to admit liability. This fellow just had. He also seemed to think it was my car he'd hit.

I considered his offer. We could go to the nearest cash machine to collect the money and then I could catch a bus to somewhere else. But would I take the brush with me or abandon it?

When I'm anxious I want to sneeze. I reached into a pocket for my handkerchief, and found a car key. Now I remembered that I was supposed to be looking after the first car for a friend and he'd given me the key, and I'd taken the car round the block and parked it, so maybe I'd parked it where I shouldn't have and that was why this other driver had reversed into it.

'Who the hell parked it there anyway?' he said, right on cue. And I saw double yellow lines on the road, just where that car was and nowhere else, and I realised I'd been trying to sweep them away with the yard brush, so I was to blame.

'Don't be angry,' I said. 'It was totally my fault. I'll pay for the repairs. Just name your price.'

But his car wasn't even scratched. It was my friend's car that was smashed up. And although I couldn't remember who my friend was, I knew I was afraid of him.

Death Hesitates

Death thought, *I can't do it. I can't take that boy, he's hardly begun to live. I can't take that woman when she's happy for the first time. I can't wipe that entire family out on the motorway.*

Such thoughts came, usually, early in the morning and late at night. They came, as it were, with the job. How could they not? He wasn't some cruel monster. He took no pleasure in what he did. Pride, yes, but that's different.

Everybody has doubts like this. *What's it all about? What am I doing here? Why me?* And mostly get over them, or through them. You carry on because what is the alternative?

There was that other voice in the background. Death's own Nemesis: *If you don't do it, somebody else will have to. Nobody's forcing you but what are you going to do, resign? You know what will happen if you do.*

On you go, the voice insisted, a mythological Mrs Danvers. *You've done your time. Fair enough. You're tired. So, retire if you want. But remember what happens to retired folk. They age, they diminish, they die.*

No more death from you, Death, but then it will be coming for you. Is that what you want? To rage against the dying of the light? Rage all you like, it will still die. You'll still die.

She was a persuasive bitch, Nemesis.

He remembered listening in to a conversation between a father and a daughter. The father was only thirty, a very ill man. The daughter was six, so full of energy it seemed unfair: she was bursting with it, he was leaking it like a sieve. He was trying to explain to her why he might not be around much longer.

Death had loitered, preparing for the take.

The daughter said, 'You go if you want. I'm going to live for ever.'

Then the sick father had done that thing humans sometimes do at critical moments: laughed and cried simultaneously.

Death had taken the father anyway. In time he'd take the daughter.

Nemesis, he thought now, *you can fuck right off. I just do what I do. I'm not superstitious.*

But he was, really.

One day a recruiting sergeant came through the village. Seeing Jack standing about idle, he fell into conversation with him and invited him to take the Queen's shilling.

'I'll dae nae such thing,' says Jack. 'If she has a shilling, it's hers, no mine.'

'What I mean,' says the sergeant, 'is will you not join the army and serve the Queen? You'll have all kinds of adventures in interesting parts of the world.'

'Och, no,' says Jack. 'I could never afford the fares.'

'You'll not pay any fares,' says the sergeant. 'The Queen pays for all that.'

'Does she?' says Jack. 'Weel, I still couldna go. How much wid a braw uniform like yours cost?'

'Oh, you'd not pay for the uniform either,' says the sergeant. 'The Queen will pay for it.'

'Whit a generous wifie she is!' says Jack. 'But I wid need a roof ower ma heid and my breakfast and dinner every day, and I get them here at hame frae ma mither.'

'You would get three meals a day,' says the sergeant, 'and a roof to sleep under or a tent at least. The Queen pays for everything, and you could send your wage home to your mother to keep her content.'

'Wage?' says Jack. 'Ye mean the Queen wid pay my fares, buy me a uniform and pit a roof ower ma heid and three meals a day, and forbye aw that she'd pay me a wage?'

'Certainly,' says the sergeant.

'Whit for wid she pay me a wage?' says Jack.

'Why, for fighting for your country,' says the sergeant.

'Fechtin?' says Jack. 'I'm no a fechter.'

'We'll make you one,' says the sergeant. 'A big, strapping lad like yourself.'

'Ah,' Jack says, 'but if ye didna mak ony fechters there wid be nae fechtin, and if there wis nae fechtin the world wid be a better place. So will ye thank the Queen for me, but I'll no tak a shilling frae her, and she'll save aw the ither money she wid hae spent on me, and we'll aw be happy.'

The sergeant marched off in a very foul mood.

'Except yersel, that is,' says Jack under his breath.

The Haunted Face

We were happy, content, relaxed. You might even say we were feeling good about ourselves, although we were always careful to guard against complacency or smugness. Perhaps the fact that we guarded against such feelings indicates that we were sometimes too pleased with our lot. I hope not. We knew we were lucky. We counted our blessings. We knew it might not always be like this.

We'd been at a charity event. The money was going to a school for orphaned Dalit children in India. Once these children would have been classed as 'untouchable' but legally there is no such thing as untouchability in India today. However, old attitudes remain, and discrimination continues. The children in the school received care and love. Their future contained possibilities.

A fair amount of money had been raised for the school. We had contributed our share. After the event was over we went to our favourite restaurant for something to eat. We had two courses and a bottle of wine. The cost was about half of what we had donated to the charity.

Our walk home took us along the city's most upmarket shopping street. The mannequins in the windows were wearing extremely fashionable clothes, so expensive that the prices were not displayed. If you are concerned about the price, the message was, don't even think about coming in.

It was not a cold night, but it was raining lightly. A young man without a coat approached us. I say 'young' but close up his face was lined and worn, and yet he did not look more than thirty. He asked me for money. I did not have any money. 'Sorry,' I said. I had given the money in my wallet to the charity, and we had paid for our meal with a credit card. We passed him by, and he shrugged as if he was well used to being refused. No doubt he would ask again, and again.

A haunted face. Whatever had happened to bring him to where he was, was with him still. It might be with him till he died. He looked like a man unloved, uncared for, without possibilities. We did not help him.

The Affair

Rachel and I were having an affair. It was a secret. It was so secret that even we didn't know we were having it. We worked together, played together, slept together. Every time we had sex we erased it from our memories. Then we went home to our respective spouses.

We worked in journalism. The most important part of our work was to discover the secrets of famous people and write about them. For example, if they were married or in long-term relationships and we discovered that they were having affairs then it was our job to expose them as hypocrites and liars. Their secrets were not safe with us.

Our secret was safe with us because (a) we were professionals and always protected our sources and (b) we did not know about it. We were professionally cool, that is to say we kept our emotions in the fridge and took them out only when we had sex. Afterwards the emotions went back in the fridge and, as they cooled, the fact that we were having an affair ceased to be a fact. We erased it from our memories. Then we went home to our respective spouses.

Things went wrong when I decided to end the affair. I took this decision because I could see that there was a danger of it becoming less secret than it was. If this happened, we would be the first people to know about it. This would be dangerous because we would not be able to continue our important work exposing famous people as hypocrites and liars without ourselves being accused of hypocrisy and lying. This would be difficult, though not impossible, from a professional point of view.

Rachel said she did not want our affair to end but she did want it to remain secret. She said she loved me. This *was* an impossible situation, from a professional point of view. We met to talk it over. One thing led to another and we had sex. This time we could not erase it from our memories, and indeed we remembered all the other times we had had sex as well.

When I got home the fridge needed defrosting.

November

The Acknowledged Expert

The Professor stood clapping like some circus animal, peering over his glasses to make sure that everybody else was doing the same. When the applause died down, he spoke.

'Thank you, Dr Saunders, for such an engrossing and, ah, stimulating lecture on one of the undoubted geniuses of our literature. It is customary on these occasions for the guest speaker to take, ah, questions, and you have already intimated that you are willing to, ah, do so. Perhaps I might take advantage of my position as departmental head, as well as convenor of this seminar, to pose the first one?'

'Just get on with it,' Dr Saunders said encouragingly.

'Ah, quite. I was surprised by your suggestion, made almost in passing, it seemed, that Austen coined many new phrases. This is not something one associates with her. Shakespeare, Milton, Spenser, yes – but Jane Austen? Could you perhaps elaborate?'

Dr Saunders rose again.

'There are countless examples,' she said. 'Austen gave us so many expressions – either new words or words used for the first time with a particular meaning. Thanks to Austen we have "macaroon", "life cycle", "bedroom eyes", "crampon" . . .'

'"Crampon"?' the Professor queried.

'Yes, in *Persuasion*. After Louisa Musgrove falls at the Cobb Mr Elliot remarks rather unpleasantly that she should have been wearing crampons.'

'Oh, I'd, ah, forgotten that. Any others?'

'Yes, "double jeopardy", "jumpsuit", "chainsaw" . . .'

'"Chainsaw"?'

'Actually, no, that was Ann Radcliffe in *The Romance of the Forest*. I meant to say "internal combustion engine". That occurs in *Mansfield Park*, when Henry Crawford says to Maria Bertram that he can sense that her heart is purring like one.'

'Like an "internal combustion engine"? Are you quite sure? I can't help thinking –'

'Chapter 34,' said Dr Saunders. There was a furious turning of pages.

'Well, you are, ah, the acknowledged expert on Austen,' the Professor said. 'You have, after all, written fifteen books on different aspects of her work.'

'Sixteen,' Dr Saunders said. 'My latest is out next month.' She stared at the serried ranks as if daring anyone to challenge her. '"Serried",' she said. 'That's another Austen coinage. As in "serried ranks". It's in *The Watsons*. Any other questions?'

Not one was forthcoming.

Returning to work after my dinner break, I heard an exchange between two women who were going by the shop entrance.

'Have you ever been in there?' one said. Her companion paused, turned and looked at the display of books in the window. Her expression was one of timidity, even of fear. It was as if she often passed that way but usually averted her eyes; as if the shop were a forbidden zone, possibly injurious to one's health.

'No,' she said. 'That's an awful dear library. The books in there are awful dear.'

'Aye,' her friend said. 'I've heard that too.'

They stood, taking quick glances at the covers so that (it seemed to me) they could not be accused of letting their gaze linger on sensitive or incriminating material. I thought of Russians going past the Lubyanka in the days of Stalin, nervous that someone might decide to take them inside, an irrevocable crossing of a terrible threshold.

The women moved on down the street.

I was late, or I'd have gone after them. 'Excuse me?' I'd have called in a friendly, unintimidating way, as if one of them had dropped a glove. When I had their attention I'd have asked the second woman why she'd called it a library. Did she think, if she went to a library, that she would have to pay to read the books? 'This is a bookshop,' I'd have said, 'and yes, the books are for sale, but they're the same price here as they are anywhere. Some are cheap, some are dear. This is where I work. Please don't be afraid. Come in, let me show you round.'

But they were away. A missed opportunity. What appalled and ashamed me was that they *were* afraid. Books had the opposite effect on me: they liberated, delighted, attracted, informed me. But the bookshop made those women feel frightened, suspicious, excluded, inadequate. And what did they know about libraries? Did they have anyone who could take them to their local library and show them the worlds it contained? Did they know that a library was not dangerous, but a place of safety? That there they could make a start?

A man came to the sales counter. He wore a dark blue raincoat and his thickly oiled hair was dark and bluish too. He eyed me doubtfully, as if it were unlikely that I would be able to help him.

'Do you have any non-fiction books?' he asked. At least, that's what I thought he said.

'Plenty,' I said. 'Most of our books are non-fiction, in fact, apart from the fiction of course. Are you looking for anything in particular?'

'Non-fiction,' he said. 'I'm looking for non-fiction.'

In retrospect, I can see how we got off on the wrong foot.

'History, biography, science?' I prompted.

He did a good impression of a saucepan about to boil over, then calmed down and said with measured emphasis, 'Gay non-fiction.'

'Of course,' I said. All now seemed clear. I asked him to follow me and went to the appropriate section of the shop.

'Just ask if I can help any further,' I said, and left him to it.

He was back at the sales counter a few minutes later. He waited until no other customers were nearby.

'That's no use,' he whispered. 'That's all about homosexuals. I'm not wanting that at all.'

'You definitely said gay non-fiction, didn't you?' I asked.

Again I thought the lid was about to come off the saucepan, but the moment passed.

'Nun fiction,' he said hoarsely. 'Fiction about nuns. Gay nuns.'

We had a shelf of erotica after the Zs in fiction. In fact, after the short-story anthologies and other odds and ends that couldn't be easily alphabetised. I took him there and suggested he have a browse.

He returned almost immediately, looking shocked.

'That's pornography,' he said. 'Do you have a film section?'

We did, but he didn't want, it transpired, books about cinema. He wanted actual films – DVDs – about gay nuns. Joyous, cheerful, happy nuns. He wanted books about them too. He'd read *Black Narcissus* and seen the film, he'd read *The Nun's Story* and seen *that* film, and he wanted some light relief. Happy nuns. Not necessarily fun-loving nuns, he said, but happy ones. Nuns happy in their vocation.

He had been right all along. I couldn't help him.

Dental Practice

Janice imagined her mouth must resemble the cutlery basket of a dish-washer. From her limited perspective what appeared to be fairly major scaffolding projected from the left side, while what could well have been a radio mast rose from the right. Her mouth had been open so wide and for so long that she thought her jaw must have seized up. The pump sucking out excess fluid was still gurgling away, but she could also hear the dentists – five of them, she reckoned, although there had been numerous comings and goings – conferring in low, competitive tones.

She was in for bridge work, but each time a different head loomed over her and some new bit of ironmongery was inserted, she thought that the job might have expanded to include a motorway, shopping mall and adventure playground. The dentists seemed nervous, tentative, yet determined in their concentration. They also seemed to have forgotten she was there.

'Lower-right six,' said Mr Granger, who had started the work but then called in his colleagues for backup. 'I'll go for a clamp there.'

'Not a chance,' said a woman Janice had never seen before. 'You'll never get a grip on that.'

'Just watch me,' said Mr Granger, and Janice felt something new being applied to a part of her mouth she would have sworn was already full.

'Impressive,' said a bald man with a light on his forehead. 'Upper-right three,' he continued. 'Excavator.'

'No way!' came a chorus of disbelief. Again a face loomed, and again she felt something metallic probe a place which she had assumed was taken up by a pylon.

Now it was the woman's turn. 'Cavity at lower-left four,' she said. 'I'll try a skin hook there.'

'Ooh, high risk,' said Mr Granger.

'Go for it,' the bald man said.

Janice wanted to protest, but her mouth was too full and her throat too dry to permit speech, and she had a horrible feeling that if she moved she would swallow something sharp. She gave a feeble, pleading kind of grunt.

'Yeah, yeah,' said Mr Granger. 'Okay, another round, folks?'

'Why not?' the woman said. 'One probe per player?'

'You're on,' said the bald man.

Fireworks

I'm not keen on fireworks – never have been since the November night a rocket, launched horizontally in an Edinburgh street, nearly took my face off. I was a postgraduate student, walking home from the university library after a long day's research, when there was a flash and something passed about six inches in front of my nose, going at such a rate that the whooshing noise it was making followed a moment later. I was tired but reacted instinctively. Ahead in the gloom two figures raced away up the pavement: I took after them. I must simultaneously have let out a yell, partly of fright, partly of rage. I was in my mid-twenties, and fit, and I began to overhaul them. I was conscious of someone running at my side, another man who had seen what had happened. We said nothing – there was nothing to say – but bore down on the fleeing figures until they were within grabbing distance. We grabbed.

They were kids, eleven or twelve years old. The shock of my narrow escape kicked in and what came out of my mouth was mostly shouting and swearing. One of them clutched a plastic bag, full of fireworks – whether bought or stolen I didn't care. 'Aw, no, mister, dinnae take them, I'm sorry, we'll no dae it again.' 'You're right there,' I said. The other man searched the second lad and found his pockets crammed with squibs and bangers. We took the lot, told them they were lucky we weren't calling the police. They were close to tears. We let them go.

'You all right?'

'Aye, thanks. Here, I don't want these. You want them?'

He didn't, but he took them anyway. Perhaps he saw from my face that the thought of setting them off made me feel sick.

That's one reason why I don't much like fireworks. The other is, they bore me. They're so transient: a brief moment of glory, then gone. Friends say that's the whole point: fireworks are like butterflies, beautiful in part because of their impermanence.

I can admire a butterfly, recall its loveliness, but the only firework I can clearly recall is the one that nearly blinded me.

'Let me say first of all, before I answer the question, that I am incredibly proud of our armed forces. No, it *is* relevant. They do an amazing job, often in incredibly difficult circumstances, and I think we should all be incredibly grateful for the way they defend our freedoms and for the sacrifices they make on our behalf.

'Yes, I am coming to that, but I also want to say how incredibly sorry I feel for the workers who have been made redundant. I don't think any of us here today should feel anything other than incredible sympathy for the situation they find themselves in, through no fault of their own. I have met some workers, just as I have met some members of our armed forces, and I feel incredibly proud to have met them and proud that I can feel incredibly grateful to the armed forces and at the same time incredibly sorry for the workers. I also feel incredibly grateful to the workers for the way they have worked until now on our behalf, and incredibly sorry for the armed forces who sometimes don't receive the gratitude they deserve from every one of us.

'Yes, I am just about to answer it. May I say before I do, though, on a personal note, that I have personally received incredibly brilliant care from the doctors and nurses of our National Health Service? I am incredibly grateful to the doctors and nurses and I am incredibly proud of our amazing health service, our brave armed forces, our hardworking workers whether they have been made redundant or not, and incredibly proud too of being able to represent and serve my constituents and my country. I think that gives an indication of what motivates me to do the job I do. I am incredibly patriotic and incredibly proud of my patriotism, not least because of the amazing job our armed forces, nurses, doctors and other workers do, often in incredibly difficult circumstances. And this is why I have made my position absolutely clear, and I think it is unreasonable to imply that I was trying to avoid doing so when I have just done so.'

The Mushroom

'That mushroom,' the Gypsy said, 'is not one I would care to eat. It's edible, but I wouldn't eat it.'

It didn't look like a mushroom to me. It looked more like a toadstool, but then I wasn't sure what the difference was, or even if there was a difference. This was why I was with the Gypsy, who knew all about mushrooms.

Then again I didn't know if he really was a Gypsy, but that was what he called himself. 'I'm a real Gypsy,' he said, 'not one of those hippy New Age travellers.' I'd heard this one before. Real Gypsies like to put distance between themselves and New Age travellers. But if you're not a real Gypsy and want to convince someone you are, what's the first thing you're going to do? Disparage the hippies.

A lot of people think Gypsies are untrustworthy. Not that I trust all the people who don't trust Gypsies but the doubt lingers. A lot of people don't trust mushrooms either. As someone once said, for most of us life is too short to know stuff about mushrooms, but someone had told me this Gypsy knew about them and I needed his knowledge.

So there we were in the woods, inspecting this particular specimen. It was mostly brown, with white gills and a fat stalk, and with thin creamy ridges on the cap that I didn't trust.

'Is it poisonous?'

'No. Not poisonous. It won't make you sick. Might give you a sore head though, or a disturbed one anyway.'

'Ah.' I thought I knew what he was getting at. 'Magical properties, you mean?'

'You're all the same,' he said, 'you young folk. You say you want to learn about edible mushrooms, but what you really want to know is which are the magic ones. Am I right?'

'No,' I protested.

'Thought so.' He wagged a finger at me. 'Whatever you do, make sure you cook it,' he said. 'And don't blame me if you go mad and throw yourself off a bridge.'

That was it. I marked the spot. I was definitely coming back for it, but later, after dark, when the Gypsy was in the pub.

The Prisoner X

Last week, with Dr Z, I went to visit the prisoner X. Dr Z had been appointed the prisoner X's physician, and I his legal adviser.

We were shown into an interview room containing four metal chairs. One chair was removed and a guard sat on it outside the door, which was left open.

The prisoner X was brought in. Dr Z examined him. He had bruising and lacerations to his face and upper body, and the left eye was swollen and half closed. Dr Z cleaned and dressed the wounds. He recommended that the eye be properly examined at the prison hospital.

The prisoner X said he would rather go blind than attend the prison hospital.

I asked him how he had received his injuries. He said he had been beaten several times since his arrival nineteen days earlier.

I asked if other prisoners were responsible. He said he had not recognised his attackers.

I asked if he thought that the beatings had been sanctioned by the prison authorities. He said that since this would be against the law he did not see how it could be possible.

I asked if he knew what charges were to be brought against him. He said he did not expect any charges to be brought against him and that he would be released in two days' time.

I asked why. He said this was what had happened on three previous occasions. Legally nobody could be held without charge for more than twenty-one days, therefore he expected to be released.

I asked if his previous legal advisers had complained about this repeated abuse of his rights. He said that of his previous legal advisers one was on holiday abroad, one was seriously ill and one was dead.

Dr Z said it was time to leave.

The prisoner X was removed. The fourth chair was returned to the interview room. We were escorted from the prison.

Dr Z recommended I take a holiday abroad at the earliest opportunity, for the sake of my health.

Two days later I telephoned Dr Z from the airport to ask whether the prisoner X had been released without charge.

There was no answer.

The Great Unknown

You used to wake in the middle of the night, standing in the middle of darkness. You were six, or eight, or ten. The last time you remember it happening you were thirteen. Where had you wandered before you woke? Your feet were cold. The darkness was of one thickness, impenetrable. You did not know which way you were facing. This is the meaning of the word 'disorientation'. You shuffled round on your cold feet, waiting for your eyes to adjust, for the slightest clue as to where you were. Nothing and nobody came to your rescue.

At thirteen, once you realised you were awake, the fear went away. You knew this had happened before, that you *would* get back to your bed. But as to whether it was a few feet away, or in the same room – whether you were even in a room – you could not tell.

The light did come back, enough to make the darkness only gloomy. Shapes took shape. Other breathers breathed. You reached out, connected with the corner of some piece of furniture, a wall, a doorframe. You began to move, from one vague indication to another. You still weren't sure which direction you were going in, except that it was forward. You had to keep going forward.

Years later, you wrote in one of your books, 'he had to believe that if he kept going forward he would eventually get to a place he recognised'. It was about somebody else in a different time and place but it was also about you, and this. This deep childhood experience. The sense of being utterly alone.

You know that a time will come again when you stand on your cold feet in total darkness. Only this time you won't be thirteen. It will be like the first time it happened, yet you won't remember the first time. There will be no bed waiting for you, no other breathers behind the curtain of the dark. You will shuffle round, waiting for your eyes to adjust, and they will not.

Eventually you will have to move, to go forward. You will recognise nothing. There will be nothing to recognise except your fear.

My first instinct on receiving the card was to put it in the bin. Nobody 'commands' me to do anything. Then I read it again more carefully. It was the Master of the Household who had been commanded by Her Majesty to 'invite' me to the palace, so that was all right. I dug out and pressed the lounge suit, selected a sober tie and clean shirt, and hopped on a flight to Gatwick.

The occasion was a reception to celebrate contemporary British poetry. I wondered if I would be alone, but Her Majesty had been very inclusive: several hundred poets were in attendance. Not for nothing did the words 'contemporary', 'British' and 'poetry' adorn the invitation. Scattered throughout the queue of more conventional versifiers were many of my friends, the contemporaries – the 'old contemporaries' as we styled ourselves when we were writing in the trenches: the working-class monotonists, the radical republican repulsivists, the post-colonial explosionists, the anarchist indecipherabilitists and of course the Scottish nationalist heedrumhodrum- ists. How lovely it was to see everyone!

Naturally some had had momentary qualms about coming, but felt they should show face for the good of the poetic school to which they belonged. Quite right too. As Her Majesty wittily remarked to me when I was coming up from my second bow, 'Show some solidarity, please.' And so we all did, but by invitation, not by command.

A few had the bad grace to refuse to attend. One joked – in poor taste, I think – that she couldn't afford the bus fare. Another complained that he was too busy. Really? Show me a poet whose diary is so full that he can't cancel a library visit or two to attend a royal reception, and I'll show you a fraud. A third asked me, to my face, 'If you're prepared to accept this invi- tation, is there anything to which you will not stoop?' I assume he meant an honour, which is highly unlikely to come my way, so the question is academic. I find the suggestion that I have compromised my principles offensive. As I have already said, if I had been 'commanded' to attend I cer- tainly would have boycotted the event.

Survivors

Those stories of men who somehow escape the carnage but are still lost, haunted to their own deaths – there is something about them. False or true, they speak of mortality in some other way than the ranked stories of the dead.

There was the one Selkirk man, of eighty who marched south with the Scottish army to Flodden, who came back alone. In the clamour and din of the battle he managed to seize an English banner, and carried it from the field. Those long miles of moor, hill, rain and despair. A ragged man and a piece of enemy cloth. Exhausted, he fell at the marketplace, casting the banner from him to the ground. How did he survive – not Flodden, but the years that followed? In what state of mind did he live out the absence of all his comrades?

There were the mythical ones who by some miracle got away from the Little Bighorn. The Indians said they killed every last soldier with Custer, but in time there were scores of tales from men who each claimed to be the sole survivor. Some said they played dead or unconscious and were scalped as they lay. Liars or delusionists, what stirred them to place themselves on that grassy ridge and say they had seen all the others die? What fortune or fame did they think such survival would bring? Or did they want to say that they bore witness to something else that died that day, a way of life guttering even in its flare of triumph?

And there is the story from No Man's Land in some battle of the First World War. Men are advancing through the barbed wire, mud and smoke. Other men are downing them like ducks. A figure walks among the broken lines, going not forward or back but *across*. He is not hiding, not running: he does not seem afraid. He is leaving. Men stand still, fascinated by the smile on his dirty face: some die watching him go. Others stop firing: or they fire and miss him. Shells explode, machine guns rattle. He is unhelmeted, unarmed, untouched. Men watch him go. They wish him well. They wish.

The Inadequacy of Translation

I met him only once. He came to do a reading at the university. I knew some of his work but only in translation. I thought the poems I had read were very good. A colleague told me that to hear him read was a unique experience. 'Nobody sounds like him,' the colleague said. 'He does not so much read as intone. You should go if you can.'

The room was not very big, and neither was the audience – about twenty, no more. When I arrived the poet was already there, speaking to the organiser. I went to the back of the room and sat on a chair that creaked. I sat very still when the poet was reading because I felt that every sound, however small, that did not come from his mouth, was an intrusion and a distraction.

He read each poem first in English and then in Gaelic. He seemed to resent that he had to bother with the English versions but nobody in the room except himself had Gaelic. I know this because he asked, and none of us put up a hand.

I recognised several of the poems, and liked them as I had done before, but he kept complaining that the translations were very poor, very poor indeed. They did not convey either the true sense or the true sound of the originals. Somebody asked who had done them. He had done them himself, he said. There was laughter. He said it was no laughing matter. The fact of the matter was that English could not convey what the Gaelic conveyed.

Afterwards I bought a copy of his book, as did several others. Gaelic was on one page and English on the facing page. I asked him to sign my copy and said that in spite of his reservations I greatly admired the English versions of his poems.

He looked very mournful. 'They are inadequate,' he said as he signed his name. I felt that he knew what he was talking about, and that I too was inadequate. Then he smiled at me, as if to apologise for making me feel that way.

That smile has stayed with me.

Thursday the Thirteenth

Getting out of bed he tripped on a stray shoe and twisted his ankle. He limped to the bathroom, stubbing his toe on the doorframe en route. When he flushed the toilet the handle came away in his hand and it took him ten minutes to fish the mechanism from the bottom of the cistern and reconnect it. He was going to be late. He tried to keep calm but cut his face in three places while shaving.

The milk he poured onto his cornflakes was off. He chucked milky mush into the bin under the kitchen sink and somehow the bowl slipped from his hand and smashed on the tiled floor. He swept up, losing more time. He went back to the bedroom to put on a tie and found that one of the shaving nicks was still bleeding and had stained the collar of his clean shirt. He changed into another and a button came off. He grabbed his briefcase and hurried out. Only as the house door slammed behind him did he realise that he'd left the key on the kitchen table. His neighbours, who kept a spare one, were on holiday for a week.

He got into the car and switched on the ignition. To his surprise it started first time. But somebody had knocked the offside wing mirror and when he reached out to adjust it the whole thing broke off and smashed on the ground. He thought about cancelling the rest of the day and going back to bed but to do that he'd need to force the door or break a window.

He drove to the office, taking extra care when changing lanes. He'd have to phone his wife, who had left him a month ago for his best friend, and ask her to come round later with the house key she'd held onto. This prospect worried him: he knew she was beginning to think she'd made a mistake, and he'd got used to having the place to himself.

A superstitious man might believe he'd just earned himself seven years' bad luck from the mirror incident but luckily he wasn't superstitious. Anyway, it wasn't the day for it.

Gated Communities

'Nobody here can feel satisfied that we have come to this: to a growing need among us to live behind walls and fences, with rising and falling barriers and sometimes even security guards in sentry-boxes beside those barriers. Have we really lost our faith in the idea of a shared humanity, a common society where all, rich and poor, haves and have-nots, can live together? Must the fortunate be so fearful, so protective, so exclusive, that they come and go in cars with the windows firmly shut, the air-conditioning on, and choose not to see or communicate, let alone to touch?

'Ladies and gentlemen, the answer is yes. I am sorry to have to speak such an unpalatable truth. Yet I do not accept that we should surrender the world to fear. I reject the idea that the protection of our loved ones and of our carefully nurtured assets, and the exclusion of envy, theft and violence, are unnatural. Equally I reject the idea that it is *we* who must suffer because we make such choices. Why should we relinquish the world? Who are these people who would take it from us? They are, we are told, the poor, the dispossessed. Who made them poor, if indeed they are poor? If they have no possessions, who dispossessed them? It was not I. It was not you. We did only what we believed was right. We worked for our wealth, our homes, our families. Yet we are the ones who are losing the greater part of the Earth.

'Ladies and gentlemen, I do believe that there are good, hard-working, ethically acceptable people out there. They too are oppressed by the so-called dispossessed. Let us make alliance with them. Let us redefine what we mean by a "gated community". Let the thieves and muggers be gated. Let us reclaim the Earth and fence *them* in. Let us make *them* carry passes and papers and let *them* change their behaviour and their desires, that they may be considered worthy of sharing in that shared humanity, that common society in which we all believe.

'*We* are the dispossessed. *They* have dispossessed *us* of the Earth! We must reclaim it!'

The Conference

Howard assumed an air of modesty, shuffling papers and checking that the slideshow was ready to go, while the session chairman introduced him. The man made absurdly inflated claims about Howard's experience and knowledge. Howard himself knew he was about to wing it. A fat man in a double-breasted suit sitting in the front row seemed to know this too. He sniffed loudly as each gold star was added to Howard's improbably lustrous CV.

The chairman sat down. Howard cleared his throat, glanced down at his notes, and began.

When he looked up every human in the room had been replaced by a dog. Alsatians, terriers of various kinds, collies, retrievers, mutts – all up on the seats and staring at him intently. The expectation varied from dog to dog. Some seemed to desire food from him, others looked eager for a walk. A substantial minority appeared to want to savage him. The fat man was now a growling, drooling bulldog.

Howard started to sweat. He struggled on, trotting out the familiar clichés, illustrating them with the usual images. Bullet points: how he loathed them. How he wished he could load them into a gun and blast the assembled dogs with them, saving the last bullet point for himself.

Every so often he checked the audience again. It was still entirely canine. Even the chairman was a cocker spaniel, scratching behind its ear with a back foot.

This wasn't the first time. A fortnight ago he'd delivered a workshop to a colony of seabirds. Kittiwakes, he had reckoned. On another occasion he'd spoken for an hour on organisational-change management to buckets of dead fish.

He had to remember that, whatever they looked like, they were only people. Ordinary people winging it, like him. They wouldn't bite or peck or impregnate him with their foul stench. They would go away and he would go away and it would be over. Until the next time.

It was how it was. They probably thought he was a chimp or a cat or a budgie.

The thing was not to give in. The thing was not to admit it.

The thing was to carry on. What else could you do?

The Greatest Novel Ever Written

You ask, 'What is the greatest novel ever written?' You really want me to tell you that? Do you think it's *possible* to know, possible for me to give you an even semi-intelligent answer to that question?

I could fall back on hearsay. I could say *War and Peace* or *Don Quixote* or *Remembrance of Things Past*. Only I've never read those books. I could say *Moby-Dick* or *Crime and Punishment* or *Ulysses* because I have read them but would that make my choice any more credible? That would just be me saying I've read these books. I wouldn't have to remember much about them. I wouldn't have to have enjoyed them. That might be a disqualification. Should you enjoy the greatest novel ever written? If you *enjoy* Len Deighton, Agatha Christie or J. K. Rowling can you *enjoy* Tolstoy or Joyce? This is literature, after all. Let me rephrase that: this is Literature, after all. Literature is to be endured, not enjoyed. It should be a challenge, an effort, a struggle from which you emerge triumphant on the final page, even if you have no idea what you've been through. It should be an achievement, not an amble. Otherwise, what's the difference? Where's the sense of superiority, the reason for self-congratulation?

Is that what you're looking for? Superior wisdom? For me to tell you, with authority, what the greatest novel ever written is, so that you can go and read it, and then say with almost equal authority, 'That's the greatest novel ever written'? You're looking for a short cut, is that it? You don't have time to read all the other novels in the world, but if someone whose judgement you trust identifies the greatest ever written then you'll not have to bother with fiction ever again? Because how could any other novel match the qualities of the greatest? It's impossible.

Well, I have written the answer to your question and sealed it in this envelope. You will inherit it on my death.

Actually it isn't the answer. It's a semi-informed guess. That's the best I could do and I don't wish to be around to witness your disappointment, surprise, anger or disbelief.

Edge

Not so long ago he noticed something about his wanderings. He saw a repetition that had previously escaped him. He noticed how he often ended up on beaches.

It came to him, this realisation, when he was nowhere near a beach. He was at home, in the kitchen, eating buttered toast. He'd poured a mug of tea and made toast, or someone had, and then he was on a beach. He was startled by the vividness of the thought. It was just as if he'd had to jump back because a wave was suddenly about to soak his shoes and socks. Yet his feet under the table were dry and warm. He looked at the toast on the plate, the steaming mug, pushed them away. They were irrelevant. They made no sense. He was on a beach.

Why beaches again and again? He glanced up and down, trying to identify this one by what was on it. Chunks of driftwood, bleached and bone-like. Seaweed clumps like markers on a big board. Gull tracks going nowhere. The swarming corpse of a gull. Feathers and shells. A headland in the distance. He peered. He recognised that coastline. No, he didn't. It could have been anywhere.

He thought, *When did I last go out?*

He thought, *Why do I go to the sea? Do I go because I like what's there or because I don't?*

You can go no further than the end of dry land, the start of salt water. Especially in winter, and this was winter. The salt wind cut his face, spume rolled and skipped over the hard sand. The edge between the land and the sea was decisive. Either you got your feet wet or you jumped back from the dismissive waves. Either you waded in or you didn't.

Nobody else was on the beach, nobody to see him or stop him. It was his choice.

Another possibility was up in the hills. Snow, and a bottle of whisky.

But a beach was better. A definite edge.

Once he saw this, the repetition made sense. And this understanding took him to beaches more and more. He wandered, if not with purpose, then with intent.

Frost

She was still in shock when they collected their coats and said goodbye. Independently and in silence they negotiated the frosted pavements to the car. Nothing was said as she started the engine and put the fan on full blast to clear the windscreen. After a minute or two she pulled out. Still not a word since leaving the party. Maybe he didn't speak because he was slightly drunk. Or maybe he had nothing to say to her. Or he had something but didn't know how to say it.

She was sober. That was why she was driving. She could have done with a drink. She could still hear his voice: 'Well, you know when it's over, don't you? For us, it's been over for years. We need to end it and move on.'

His voice in the kitchen. The words not said to her but they might as well have been. She'd been about to go in to help and something stopped her, some sense that she shouldn't push open the not fully closed door. And she heard that. Sure, he could have been speaking about a business contract or the Scotland–UK thing or some other breakdown she couldn't imagine but she knew it wasn't any of those, it was about him and her, their marriage, and he was saying it was over, and she didn't go in, she retreated back into the party and a minute later he appeared carrying trays of food, followed by their hostess. And she thought, They're *not having an affair, surely?* But the hostess was his oldest friend, from university. She'd be the one he'd confide in, in that casual, practical way.

She drove through the empty streets, the silence. It wasn't him in the car with her, it was his presence.

Say something, she thought.

'Did you enjoy that?' she asked.

He said, 'It was all right for me. You're the one that didn't get a drink.'

'I didn't want one.'

He reached forward to put some music on.

'Don't,' she said.

He sat back.

'Talk to me,' she said.

'What do you want me to say?' he asked.

So then she knew it was true.

When you switched the radio on it had to warm up, you know, it warmed up and then it became something live. If you put your ear against the cloth in front of the speaker it vibrated, it buzzed. Everything came through the radio, into the house, the room, your head. It was a highway heading off into the distance and you rode out on it, and then it split into more roads and traffic was coming and going in every direction, you were dodging it, jumping on and off buses, climbing on the back of a flatbed lorry just for the thrill. That's what the radio did, it opened up roads and possible journeys in your head. You'd be listening to Mozart or Beethoven and then later it would be Bartók or Stockhausen and your mind was trying to absorb how all this could be music, and you were half not listening too, dreaming, imagining everything out there, and you turned the dial and people were speaking in some language, you tried to work out what it was, Danish or Russian or German, and just when you thought they had nothing to say to you anyway *they* paused to listen, you heard them be quiet so that they could hear something and what they were waiting for was this other music, and it began, and it was jazz, modern jazz, and this was being played and heard and talked about right around the world, and then you turned the dial again, or switched from long wave to medium wave to short wave, and things found you by accident – plays, highbrow discussions, folk songs, or some old blues singer, a ghost, whose scratchy voice was somehow coming at you from behind that buzzing cloth. And the signals roamed and collided and faded in the darkness and came round again and you knew there was more life out there than you could ever experience but you wanted it all. And it was different, radio, from television. When television came it didn't liberate your mind, it didn't expand it, it hooked and held it, and that wasn't the same thing. It was radio that set you free.

Jack and the Devil

The Devil wanted to lead Jack astray so he turned himself into a beautiful woman who asked Jack to escort her to a casino in the nearest town.

'It'll be a pleasure,' says Jack, noting the hairy toes sticking out of her glittery high-heeled shoes.

Jack had only enough money to buy a single chip. The Devil gave him another to keep it company, and showed him to the roulette table.

'Put them both on a single number, Jack, and let's see if we can make your fortune,' the Devil whispered in his lug.

'Naw, naw,' says Jack, and he puts one chip on red and the other on black. When the ball stops spinning he finds he's lost on the red but won on the black.

'Still in the game,' he says. 'I'll dae the same again.'

For twenty minutes Jack didn't tire of winning and losing every time, but both the croupier and the Devil were becoming impatient.

'Here's another chip, Jack. Live a little,' the Devil said huskily, leaning forward to give him a wee glimpse of what that might entail. 'Why not put it on a single number?'

'Naw, we'll pit it on red, tae match your frock,' says Jack.

When red comes up, Jack turns and says, 'Ye see? I hae a system gaun here.'

'Leave all your chips on red and you'll double them again,' the Devil urged.

'Och, I'll just pit twa o them on black,' says Jack.

This time black comes up.

'Richt again,' he says, 'and aye the fower chips. Whit luck I'm haein the nicht!'

After another hour Jack was back down to two chips but still enjoying himself. The croupier threw Jack off the table, so he took his chips and handed one back to the Devil.

'Weel,' he said, 'I think ye'll agree that was a grand spree and it cost heehaw.'

At this the Devil lost his temper and cast off his disguise. 'This is hopeless,' he said. 'I'm supposed to be tempting you but you're beyond temptation.'

'Och, it's yersel!' says Jack. 'I thocht ye was a lassie. Temptin me, were ye? And there was me thinkin I was temptin *you*!'

Café Limbo (1)

A bell above the door jingled as I entered. It was an unostentatious place, with red checked tablecloths and wooden chairs, and a scattering of customers.

A waiter wearing a black apron, black waistcoat and red bow tie approached me. His demeanour was very calm – I knew instantly that he was good at his job.

'For one, sir?' He led me to a small round table in a corner. I sat down. He brought over a menu, the laminated kind that indicates standard, unchanging fare.

'Coffee, tea or chocolate, sir?' he asked, and the odd thing was that I did suddenly want a hot drink, though I had not known it a moment before.

'Coffee, please,' I said. 'Black, no sugar.'

'Certainly, sir.' But he lingered, producing a pad and pencil.

'I haven't had a chance to decide on food yet,' I said.

'That's all right, sir. Take your time. Your name, please?'

'My name? What for?'

He gazed at me with kindly eyes.

'Would it be Brogan, sir?'

'No, it's Robson.'

'Thank you, sir.' He made a mark on his pad. I was about to remonstrate when the bell jingled and a fat, bald man, red in the face, came in. The waiter moved towards him as if on wheels.

'For one, sir?'

The fat man allowed himself to be led to a table. I heard the waiter offer him a hot drink. He opted for tea. The waiter asked if his name was Brogan. The man shook his head and the waiter made a mark on his pad.

At that moment I realised that I had no idea why I had come into the café, or even what town I was in. I looked at the other customers. I recognised nobody. There was no reason why I should. Nevertheless . . .

'Waiter!' I called.

'One moment, sir.'

He had gone to the door, and was peering out into the gathering dark. I saw him glance at his watch.

When he came to my table he seemed somewhat anxious.

'Something wrong?' I asked.

'It's Mr Brogan,' he said. 'He should be here by now. All the rest of you are.'

'Where?' I asked. 'Where is here?'

Café Limbo (2)

Apart from the fat man who was not Mr Brogan, there were five other customers: an elderly couple, an old man on his own, a younger woman reading a book, and a child of about ten. The old people sat patiently and silently: they had finished their hot drinks. The child had an air of bewilderment about her. I imagined someone had left her while they went to a shop or a cash machine.

It was dark outside. The waiter kept consulting his watch. Once he opened the door and peered up and down the street. Of that street I had absolutely no recollection.

The waiter came back in, shut the door and locked it. At this, the young woman closed her book. We all focused on the waiter, who addressed us from the middle of the room.

'We cannot wait any longer,' he said. 'Mr Brogan is unaccountably late.'

'Late for what?' said the fat man.

There was the sound of running feet, then a crash against the café door. A frightened voice shouted, 'Help! Let me in!'

The waiter advanced rapidly, but not to open the door. There were bolts at the top and bottom and he shot these home.

Shadowy figures passed by the window. The same voice called again, 'Help me!' This was followed by thuds and blows and a scream of pain.

Now we were all on our feet. 'They are beating him up!' I said.

'I fear so,' the waiter said.

'Well, let him in for God's sake.'

'It is too late.'

The sounds of violence continued. The voice was sobbing, begging for mercy. Then it grew more distant.

'They're dragging him away!' said the old man, his face against the glass. 'A gang of them.'

'For God's sake, call the police if you won't open the door,' the fat man said.

'The police won't come,' the waiter said. 'There are no police.'

'They're going to kill him.'

'No. They can't.'

'At least let us out so we can help him, if you won't,' the fat man said.

'You can't help him either. I'm sorry. And we can't wait any longer.'

'What are we waiting for?' the child asked.

Café Limbo (3)

The child's question was both wise and innocent. 'What are we waiting for?' And the waiter – he who waited upon us – granted her his most benevolent smile.

The murderous sounds from the street had ceased, and the waiter's equanimity was returning. I remembered my first impression – that he was a man who was good at his job.

He'd said they could not kill Mr Brogan, but what had he meant? That *they* – whoever they were – could not kill him, or that Mr Brogan could not be killed? Who was Mr Brogan, and why had he been late in arriving, and for what? Who were we, our little group of strangers? How had the waiter come by our names, and *why* did he have them?

I scanned the faces of the other adult customers and I could see all those questions, and more besides, swirling in their eyes. And then I looked at the child, and heard again her question. And the waiter was grateful to her, because she was asking not so much about the purpose as about the delay. She did not want to postpone whatever was going to happen next.

What happened was that the waiter said, 'If you would kindly follow me, I will show you to the other exit.'

There was no dissent. The waiter led, the child followed him, and we all followed the child. There was a counter behind which was all the apparatus of a café – coffee machines, bottles and jars, cutlery and crockery, stacked menus, serviettes and tablecloths, surfaces for food preparation, sinks, hobs and fridges. Everything was clean and cold. There was no food to prepare. No one was there except for us and our waiter.

Down a corridor we went, to a door with a fire escape sign on it, and a bar to release the door. The waiter stood aside. 'Goodbye,' he said. 'Good luck.'

The old lady fumbled at her handbag. 'What do we owe you?' she said, but he shook his head, to show that there was nothing to pay.

Then the child pushed the bar, and the door swung open, and one after another we stepped out into the starry night.

The Illiterate Hordes of History Have Their Say

You think you saved us from savagery with your lines and circles and dots. You think you liberated us from ignorance. You did the very opposite. We were alive and you killed the spirit of life that was in us. We roamed freely and you tethered us. We knew no boundaries and you fenced us in. We had a natural philosophy and you destroyed it and put utilitarianism in its place.

You built roads through our country where before were only paths and landmarks. We had songs and stories as our guides and you covered them over with maps. You tied down the stories, choked and shackled them. Books are their prisons. You hunted the songs, caught them with nets and traps, and then complained when they were wrongly sung, but it was you who wronged them.

You promised that the world of writing and reading would have no limits. You lied. You narrowed our vision, you clogged our minds with information we did not need and you destroyed our ability to remember the things we cherished most. Once, we knew our ancestors even to the twentieth generation, and they were with us always, through our days and through our nights. Once, our history was in our blood. Now it is dead, and our people squabble over the scraps and bones which are all that survive.

Once, we read the weather, the seasons, the prints of animals, the healing powers of plants, the mysteries and dangers of the forest. Once, the world was our library and we wrote messages among its stacks. The rain came, or the sun – storm or fire – and in the aftermath our library still stood and our marks could be written again.

Now everything is stored, yet nothing is secure. Time eats into us as worms devour books, and we fall apart. You have felled the forests of the world to flatter the vanity of knowledge, yet you know nothing of value that we did not know, and much more that is valueless.

We had wisdom: you gave us stupidity. We had faith: you gave us doubt. We had strength: you gave us fragility. We had life: you gave us books.

This is the story

of the woman sitting opposite me on the 1800 hours service from King's Cross to Edinburgh, calling at York, Darlington, Newcastle, Berwick and Dunbar. Her story is that she is totally honest and this is a problem because she feels that her honesty compromised her performance at the job interview, her first for five years. She is not good with paperwork, she is good with an electronic diary but organising paper, literally bits of paper, is not her strong point and she admitted this, she said that she always used to leave the paperwork to her ex-husband, and now she is wondering why she said that. When they pressed her on what else weren't her strong points, she kept being honest (peals of laughter) so made a total hash (she thinks) of the interview. She did an enormous amount of research into the company but not enough preparation on what *she* would bring to the role, and she knows from her *current* role the strong points that she *could* bring to the role. And it frustrates her that she didn't say this because she would be really good at it, the role, and then it frustrates her that we enter a tunnel and that she loses contact with whoever she is telling this to at the kind of volume you might use if you were in a really busy restaurant or at a rock concert or in the middle of a fucking battlefield and then we come out of the tunnel and she reconnects with more peals of laughter and apologies for having been in a tunnel, and I wish her, I really wish her, all the luck in the world, and I hope that despite her pessimistic appraisal of how the interview went and despite her inability to be anything but honest the company will see that she is in fact perfect for the role and when she gets off at York they will send a message offering her the job, and that she will move, lock, stock, barrel, kids, family pet, new relationship and all to London so that I'll never, on this train journey, ever have to hear her fucking story again.

Jack and the Man

One day Jack's sitting staring at the fire in a dwam when there's a knock at the door.

It's a tall, thin man with grey hair and sorrowful eyes.

'Hello, Jack,' the man says.

'How dae ye ken it's me?' says Jack.

'I used tae bide in this hoose,' the man says.

'Naebody bides in this hoose but me and ma mither,' says Jack.

'Oh, and is your mither at hame the noo?'

'Naw, she's away oot,' says Jack.

'Weel, can I come in?'

The man seems harmless enough, so Jack lets him in and sits him by the fire in his mother's chair and makes him a cup of tea.

'Ah,' the man says, 'it's a fine thing, a guid fire and a cup of tea.'

'Aye,' says Jack.

'And did ye make the tea and chop the logs and set the fire yersel?' the man says.

'I did,' says Jack.

'It's a fine thing tae be practical,' the man says. 'Are ye guid wi yer hands?'

'Better than wi ma heid,' says Jack.

'It's a fine thing tae ken yer ain strengths and weaknesses,' the man says.

'Aye,' says Jack. And then they sit in silence, and Jack quite likes that, the two of them just staring into the fire, not speaking. But after a while he looks across and says, 'But how did ye ken ma name?'

And he's all alone! He looks behind the chair and all through the house, but of the tall, thin man with grey hair and sorrowful eyes there is not a sign.

I must have fallen asleep, he thinks. *I must have been dreaming.*

But then he sees the cup of tea he made for the man, and it hasn't been touched, even though he saw the man drinking it. So he drinks it himself, and then he washes the cup and puts it away.

'I'll no mention it when Mither comes in,' he says to himself. 'I'll pretend there's been naebody here but masel aw the time.'

So he waits for her. And he still has that warm, comforting feeling from when he and the man were sitting in at the fire together, not speaking.

'The thing is, you're not eligible for Jobseeker's Allowance because your doctor has assessed you as not fit for work. He says you've got chronic back pain.'

'That's right.'

'In that case you should be claiming Employment and Support Allowance, not Jobseeker's Allowance.'

'But when I applied for that before my claim was rejected, because I didn't have a doctor's line about my back at that point.'

'You should have gone to your doctor first.'

'I couldn't get an appointment for four days and I was needing some money. So when my claim was rejected I went out looking for a job and I found one, a cleaning job, but I only lasted two days because of the back pain, so that's why I'm here again. If I can't get Jobseeker's Allowance surely I should get the other one?'

'Employment and Support Allowance?'

'Yes.'

'You'll have to apply using this form.'

'But this is the same form I already filled out.'

'Yes, but your previous application was rejected. You have to apply again. If your application is accepted you'll start receiving Employment and Support Allowance.'

'Do you know when it will come through? I've no money, you see.'

'It depends how quickly the application is processed. It can take up to eight weeks.'

'Eight weeks? But I've nothing to live on. No money at all. I'll have to try for another job.'

'But you're not fit for work. If you get a job, that would affect your claim.'

'Well, isn't there something called a Hardship Payment? Could I apply for that?'

'Are you homeless?'

'No.'

'Then you're not eligible.'

'But I'm in rent arrears. My Housing Benefit's been cut because I've got an extra bedroom.'

'You should move to a smaller property.'

'I can't. The council won't let me move because I'm in rent arrears.'

'You could move out altogether. If you were of no fixed abode then you'd be eligible for a Hardship Payment.'

'Are you saying I should put myself on the street?'

'It's an option. Or you could get more ill and be hospitalised. Or you could die.'

'Did you just suggest I should die?'

'It would solve all your other problems.'

The Islander

She had left the island long ago but it had never left her. Just as she retained the language of her people but seldom had an opportunity to speak it, so the island was in her; even in the middle of a city a hundred miles from the sea. When she was shopping, or at the office, or working in her garden, it was as if the sea beat against her, as if a tideline of kelp and driftwood surrounded her. Pebbles dragged in the surf at her feet. Gulls screeched where there were only crows. She smelled salt instead of diesel fumes.

She had accepted the island unconditionally when a child, because it was all she knew. Then she grew, and grew to resent the sharp beaks and eyes of neighbours, the black, cormorant stance of the elder. She hated the mist that came down on the sea like another sea. So she unmoored herself: she applied for a job on the mainland. 'So you are going?' the elder said. 'So you are going?' the postmistress said. 'So you are going?' her mother said. 'When are you coming back?'

She meant never to return. But unknown to her she had a ghost. Just as the island haunted her, so her ghost haunted the island. She believed in ghosts but she would not have understood it if anyone had told her hers had been seen, because she was on the mainland and she was not dead.

One of the old men met her ghost once. 'So you are back?' he said. 'When are you going away?' There was no reply, which surprised him because she had always been a polite girl.

When he told the postmistress he had seen her, she said he must be mistaken, because she knew all the comings and goings of the island. When he mentioned it to the elder, he was admonished for being drunk.

But when he spoke to her mother, something clutched at the mother's heart, and she wrote to ask if she was well. And though she replied that she was, she too felt a clutching at her heart. She was an islander, and always would be.

The Blasphemer

Ten witnesses, one after another, had testified that the accused had articulated the opinions drawn up in the indictment. Ten witnesses, each corroborating the evidence of the others, confirmed that he had ridiculed the notion that the Bible was divinely inspired, asserted that the Universe existed long before the 'invention' of God by men, denied the existence of spirits, and claimed that no such places as Heaven or Hell existed. The jury would hardly have to leave the court to consider its verdict. The punishment for blasphemy was death.

Only one thing could save him, and it was of this that his counsel spoke urgently when the court adjourned. He would call him as a witness – the only witness – in his own defence, and between them they would try to convince the court that the opinions he had expressed were the ravings of a madman.

'But I am completely sane,' he said. 'Madness is believing that humans were created only six thousand years ago, and that the Universe was built by a single being whose existence cannot be proved.'

His counsel urged him to lower his voice and set all theological arguments aside. Did he agree, when the court resumed, to give nonsensical and contradictory answers to the questions that would be put to him, so that all would conclude he was mad?

'Nonsensical and contradictory?' he answered. 'Those words describe not my beliefs but those of clergymen. My position is based on a rational examination of the facts, not on fairy tales and gobbledegook.'

Again his counsel implored him to be silent. Did he not understand the seriousness of his situation?

'Absolutely,' he said. 'The madmen who wish to hang me for my sanity may spare me for being mad and indeed I would have to be mad to approve such a verdict. Not being mad, I must hang for the crime of being sane. So be it. If you call me to give evidence, I will not speak. If you do not call me, I will assert my right to speak, and assure the court of my sanity.'

'Then you really are mad,' the lawyer said. 'I can do nothing more for you.'

X

marks the spot where two laddies hunting golf balls found a fisherman spread like a star beside the fourteenth tee. He was on his back, arms and legs outstretched, and his lips wore a beatific smile. They knew he was a fisherman from his oilskins and his gansey. Shells decorated his beard and a tangle of bladderwrack was round his neck, but he wore no boots or socks. His feet were blue and marbled. Above them were the yellow oilskins, the dark grey wool of the gansey and the lighter grey of the beard and hair. Pink and white were the tones of his face, but the colour of his eyes could not be discerned with the lids closed as they were.

'He'll get cauld lyin there,' said the smaller laddie.

'He's no sleepin, Darren, he's deid,' his brother Tom said.

They were more curious than frightened. The sea could never have carried him so far above the high-water mark. Had he staggered ashore before collapsing? Or dropped from the sky?

'Run tae the clubhoose,' Tom said. 'I'll stay here.'

The first foursome were about to tee off. 'There's a deid man at the fourteenth!' Darren shouted. 'Ye've tae come quick!'

Darren was a wee tyke and not to be trusted, but after further interrogation the men commandeered an electric scooter and took it across the fairways, one driving and three puffing along beside it.

Back at the corpse, Tom found the courage to put his ear to the fisherman's mouth. Not a whisper of breath. He pushed down on the oilskins, below the breastbone, and a little fountain of saltwater parted the smiling lips.

The fisherman sat up.

'Ye're alive!' Tom said.

'I am now.'

'Did ye no droon?'

'I did, but I was saved. Where are my boots?'

'Dinna ken.'

'Never mind.' He got to his naked feet.

'Who saved ye?'

'I'll tell you. But first I want a cup of tea.'

They met the rescue party halfway. By the time the fisherman reached the clubhouse there was quite a crowd.

He was a great orator. The shells in his beard gave him presence.

Darren and Tom's golf-ball sales had never been better.

December

Not Watering the Plants

They have better views than we do. Of course: they are two storeys higher.

Their bathroom is smaller but the en suite seems bigger. It's hard to be certain, as the rooms are different shapes. The shower unit is definitely bigger.

Their flat is a corner flat. Ours isn't.

Their kitchen has an identical layout, but our appliances are more up to date. They have the original floor covering. We replaced ours when we moved in.

In the other rooms the carpets are more stained and worn than ours. But then, they have two children, to our none.

They also have an extra bedroom.

They have hundreds of DVDs and CDs, but no books. They have a music system with speakers in different rooms, a huge flat-screen TV on the living-room wall and a smaller one in the master bedroom. There are boxes of toys, transfers on the walls of the children's bedroom. A duck, a puppy, a frog, a kitten.

We have books and a small TV we hardly ever watch.

They have gone to Australia for three weeks, to visit her brother and his family.

We know what they paid for their flat, two years after we bought ours. We bought just before the crash, they bought after.

They got the bargain.

They have the view, the extra bedroom, the old carpets and appliances and a mortgage pegged to the base rate.

We have what we have, and a fixed-rate mortgage that at the time we thought was the sensible, safe option.

They won't have any hotel bills in Australia, she said. Otherwise they couldn't afford to go.

They have three unopened bottles of malt whisky in a cabinet.

They have a lot of clothes for four people. The kids have more clothes than we do.

He has rows of shirts on hangers. Five suits. Sportswear and casual items with designer labels. How many socks does a man need? It's hard to get the drawers closed.

She has more clothes than the others put together. It is not possible to count the shoes.

She has silk underwear, mostly white, none grey.

The sex toys have flat batteries.

The plants don't need watering, again.

The Funeral

A man was walking along a narrow country road when he saw a funeral cortège coming in the opposite direction. He had passed a small, beautifully kept graveyard only minutes before – had stopped and looked over its wall to admire it – so it was clear to him that this must be the destination of the procession. He stepped onto the grass verge and waited for it to go by.

One of the men shouldering the coffin seemed familiar. He bore a remarkable resemblance to his oldest friend, Malcolm. And was that not . . . ? But before he could identify the next pallbearer he received a further shock. For, walking behind the coffin, dressed in black and looking straight ahead, was a woman the very image of his own dear Ellen, accompanied by their two children!

The long line of mourners continued. He knew many of their faces. Some turned towards him, but did not seem to see him. And he realised that he could hear nothing – not their footsteps, not a cough or whispered word, not even the birds singing.

Unable to speak or move, he waited till the last of the mourners had gone by. His own funeral? How could this be? He hurried back to the graveyard.

But when he arrived, nobody was there but himself. And the birds were singing once more.

He was filled with relief, but immediately this turned to fear. What did the vision mean? And where was he?

It was this last question that brought him to himself. He woke, as if from a dream – and it *was* a dream! He was at home, in the garden. The sun was shining, birds were singing. The thing had not occurred at all!

He breathed more easily. But again the fear set in, for now he remembered the road, the tranquil graveyard. He recognised them: they were in the Highlands, close to the village where the family had often spent holidays: a place of fond memories . . . and a place to which they intended to return the following summer.

I cannot go, he thought. *Something will happen if I go.*

But he knew that fate, or the future, could not thus be avoided.

Rothesay

after Hector Boece

While his mother, the Queen Annabella, was alive, David, Duke of Rothesay, was said to have led a virtuous and honest life, or at least he was in some measure restrained by her influence. After her death, he began to 'rage in all manner of insolence', visiting his lust on virgins, matrons and nuns alike. At last the ageing and feeble King Robert III, no longer able to ignore the stories of his son and heir's excesses, wrote to his brother, the Duke of Albany, asking him to take the young man in hand and teach him better behaviour. Albany, who saw Rothesay as a rival to his already extensive power, was delighted to oblige, and had him apprehended on the road between St Andrews and Dundee by men who had personal or familial grudges against him. They blindfolded Rothesay and mounted him backwards on a mule, and thus he was taken to Albany's castle at Falkland. There he was imprisoned, and apparently denied all food and drink.

A woman, some say, was so moved by the prisoner's circumstances that she managed to pass some scraps of meat to him through the bars of his cell, but when this was discovered she was put to death. Another woman gave him milk from her breast, through a long reed, and she too was killed when her mercy was detected.

Then was the Duke of Rothesay 'destitute of all mortal supply', and was brought, finally, to such miserable and desperate hunger that he ate not only the filth of the tower where he was being kept, but also his own fingers.

Rothesay's body was buried at nearby Lindores, where for some years miracles associated with him were reputed to take place.

An inquiry into the circumstances of his death exonerated the Duke of Albany from any suggestion of wrongdoing.

These events took place six hundred years ago. I had written as far as this point, and was wondering where I was being taken, when a friend emailed with the news that he had been diagnosed with inoperable cancer. He has been given a sentence – of life, of death – of between six and twelve months.

That is all.

The First Novel

This morning I received in the post a parcel containing a book and a letter. The book was a novel – a first novel, it transpired – and I recognised the author's name at once: one of my boys, from all those years ago. I opened it and on the title page was a handwritten dedication – to me! Signed by the author – one of my boys!

I turned eagerly to the letter. It had been written with a proper pen, in black ink, and bore traces of the italic hand I insisted on being taught to every pupil in the school. I always said that, though a boy might later abandon the strict italic form, yet it would remain a steadying, underlying influence, ensuring, at the very least, neatness and legibility.

I remembered the author quite well: a bright, pale-faced boy, not the most intelligent pupil I ever had but certainly not a dunce or a sluggard. He always turned in a good essay. Yes, he knew how to write an essay, but I never imagined he would one day produce an entire novel! Yet here it was, his first, and he had sent a signed copy to me, his old English teacher and headmaster. I was pleased, and flattered too by the contents of the letter. He recalled my lessons – he thanked me for my encouragement – he said that I had left my mark.

Towards the end of the letter he warned that I might find some of the language in his novel strong, and some of his depictions explicit. He would not want to offend me. I was a little alarmed, but surely he would not have sent me the book if it really was offensive?

But oh, when I began to read it! I am old, and no doubt old-fashioned, but not, I hope, a prude. This, however, was too much. The obscenities were overwhelming, the subject matter poisonous. Perhaps he really does mean to insult me. And I am hurt, and ashamed that one of my boys should lower himself to such depths. I feel betrayed, and have laid the book aside. I can hardly think that I shall acknowledge receipt of it.

Cathedral

On the side of the piazza opposite the cathedral, a man with his legs on back to front is adopting stretching positions on his mat. The tourists gather in clusters here every minute, hundreds of them by the hour, trying to squeeze as much of the cathedral's vast facade into their viewfinders as they can. The man wears a vest so that his muscular arms and shoulders are very visible, and gleaming Spandex shorts which display the weirdness of his legs to best advantage. You look away and then you look again. You can't help it. He wants you to look. Perhaps he even has the power to make you look. This is his trade. Is he a contortionist of extraordinary and disturbing skill, or are the legs truly deformed? At any rate, they are how he earns a living.

There is something medieval about him, something that links him to the cathedral gargoyles sticking out tongues and pulling faces at the crowds below. Even as he stretches and bends and straightens on his mat he seems to rebuke, to be making a gesture of contempt in the very face of sophisticated, civilised society. *I am the freak that you fear lurks within yourselves. Pay me or suffer the consequences of your own grotesque humanity.*

You feel in your pocket but you have no loose change, only paper money, and you are not so moved or ashamed or afraid to reach for your wallet. The man with his legs on back to front pays you no more attention once he sees that expression in your eyes. You were almost nothing to him before, you are nothing now. He turns his head and his body coquettishly to someone more deserving, more susceptible than you.

And this is Florence, the cradle of modernity, the start of it all, the slow crawl up from ignorance and brutal curiosity. This is the city of Michelangelo, Botticelli, Dante, Machiavelli and Vasari, where knowledge and art became steps out of darkness, where truth was sought but not accepted without debate, where the light of reason flooded in.

The man with his legs on back to front is a warning, a reminder.

There's a rumour going round, we don't know what it is, but we all get in line. Could be one thing, could be another, but we all get in line. They're probably selling something, they must be selling something, so we all get in line.

Maybe it's a bargain, maybe it's a con, but we all get in line. A pocketful of diamonds or half a pound of mince, but we all get in line. We won't know what we're missing if we turn and walk away, so we all get in line.

There's nothing more we need, the house is full of crap, but we all get in line. No room in the closets, the garage walls are bulging, but we all get in line. Someone says she's seen it, someone says it's cool, so we all get in line.

They're chopping down the forests and slicing up the mountains, but we all get in line. Half the world is starving and living under cardboard, but we all get in line. And if they want to count our dirty carbon footprints, we'll all get in line.

There are seven billion birthdays, and Christmas round the corner, so we all get in line. Instant payday credit, and a pawnshop up the alley, so we all get in line. But you never know your luck, there's a winner every minute, so we all get in line.

The country folk are leaving and moving to the city, where they all get in line. It's so hard to make a living but they hear it can be done, so they all get in line. And we're running out of oil, and we're running out of water, so we all get in line.

There's talk of revolution, and anarchy and war, and it's coming down the line. You don't know who to trust or which side to be on, if it's coming down the line. But there's a man in a truck selling guns and insurance, and he's coming down the line.

And the government is saying there's a threat to law and order but no one will get hurt, arrested or imprisoned – if we all stay in line.

The Clock of Horror

The clock that hung in the hallway was not behaving. It didn't like the winter. The fall in temperature affected it, causing the brass pendulum or the hands or some other part of the mechanism to slow. First it didn't make it through the cold hours of the night. Then it had trouble during the day. Its tick faded, then stopped, the minute hand finding the uphill journey from six to twelve too much.

'Did you restart the clock?' he demanded one night. He knew he sounded aggressive.

'I haven't touched it,' she answered, almost as sharply. They were going through the hall on their way to bed.

'Well, somebody has. I set it going at eight but it stopped again at ten to nine. Now it's saying twenty to ten.'

'So?'

'I didn't restart it at ten to nine. I just left it.'

'I didn't touch it.'

'Somebody has. Look, the case hasn't been closed.'

'You must have forgotten to close it after you set it going.'

'I always close it.'

'On this occasion you must have forgotten.'

There was the possibility of a fight. He drew back.

'Aye, maybe. I was sure I closed it.'

She acknowledged the concession. 'It has a mind of its own, that clock.'

'It plays tricks on us,' he agreed. He adjusted the hands, letting the clock strike ten and eleven before he swung the pendulum, then closed the case.

They switched the downstairs lights out and went up. He opened the bedroom window and turned down the covers while she was in the bathroom. They passed on the landing. The clock's steady tick was below them.

'It's lulling us into a false sense of security,' she said.

'As soon as we're asleep, it'll stop,' he said.

Later, in the darkness, she said, 'Are you awake?'

'Aye.'

'It's ten past midnight. Did the clock strike?'

'I didn't hear it.'

'Yet I still hear ticking. You know what I think? That clock's come down from the wall and up the stairs, and it's waiting for us out there.'

'*The Clock of Horror*,' he said, inventing a movie title.

They lay still, neither of them wanting to move till daylight.

Ice

When we came off the backshift he'd already been dead eight hours. The guys coming in for the nightshift told us. 'Didn't you hear the news?' But how could we have heard, working in the ice factory? The ice came crashing down the chute every eighteen minutes and we bagged it as fast as we could go, no time to talk, no time to listen, and with the noise of the next load of ice being made and the roar of the bagging machine and the banging of the staple gun and then in the muffled silence of the freezer where we stacked the bags feeling the cold wet ache of your fingers and the ache of your back and the sweat that crusted on you in the freezer – well, there wasn't any room for news. Even on our breaks we didn't have a radio, and we were too tired for talk. The only person who came in was the fish man wanting ice, and he just handed over cash and took his ice away in crates, a dollar a crate, and he never said anything, not even thank you. So how could we have known that he was dead, John Lennon, dead, on another continent on another day in another time zone? We heard it from the guys coming in for the nightshift.

I walked back through the city in a daze, and went for a beer because I needed one. I wanted to be on my own, but I wasn't alone. Everybody else in the bar was in a daze too, and we all sat drinking and listening to the music, the Beatles and John on his own and John with Yoko, starting over. After the first beer I had a second, and then a third, and then I went home.

All that summer in Sydney I made ice, and every day it hurt but I got fitter and stronger. And every day on my way to the ice factory I passed a wall on which someone had sprayed the words AFTER ALL I'M ONLY SLEEPING. And I knew that part of my life was over, and that the rest was going fast.

The People of the Plain

The people of the plain built their houses low, one storey tall or sometimes with only half a storey above ground, and the rest of the accommodation below it. He who built a two-storey house was considered daring but arrogant. These people had a god who lived in the sky, though none had ever seen him. They only felt his breath, which was the wind and which blew without cease. Sooner or later it blew away the arrogance of humans. Always.

The people of the plain had long traded with people from the mountains. In exchange for meat, cheese and wool from their herds of goats and sheep, they received timber. They used the timber for firewood and for houses, which they built so that the wind would flow over them without causing too much damage. They covered the roofs with wooden tiles, nailing each tile with three nails: one for summer, one for winter and the third for luck.

They were small people, with flattened foreheads and a permanent stoop from walking into the breath of their god. Most of the year it was a warm breath, but in winter it came from the north, icy or snow-laden. Then they brought their beasts indoors and asked their god not to rip their roofs off before spring.

The mountain people asked them why they did not move. In the mountains, although the seasons were more varied and unpredictable, the valleys were well protected from the wind. The people of the plain said they could not leave their god. If they did, he would be very angry and sure to punish them.

The mountain people did not understand. They had no god. The people of the plain liked them, but considered them foolish children.

One spring only a few people came from the mountains to trade. Terrible calamities had befallen them. First, in late summer, a fire had destroyed much of the forest, then winter floods had swept through the valleys, drowning nearly everybody.

The people of the plain gave thanks. They knew they had been right to stay where they were. And their god blew his warm breath on them, and they stooped before it.

The Critic

It had to happen. Somebody had to say, eventually, 'But they're not very good, are they?'

'In what way?' he said, reminding himself that everybody was entitled to an opinion.

'They're all the same. I thought each one would be different.'

'They are different.'

'But so many of the words crop up again and again.'

'I think that's inevitable with words, don't you?'

'You make the inevitable sound like something one should feel relaxed about.'

'Well, there doesn't seem much point in getting stressed about it. It depends on your expectations.'

'That's the problem,' the critic admitted. 'It's my own fault. I'm always looking for the best and so I'm always disappointed.'

She fell into contemplation, then resumed. 'I used to know a painter, very successful in a commercial sense, and a man who could actually paint, which very few painters can. He painted fishing villages. That was what he was known for – little old houses and brightly coloured boats, lobster creels and fish boxes, and nets hung up to dry. Some of the villages he painted were in Fife, some were in Cornwall, and others were in France or Spain, but the thing was, after a while they all looked the same. He had to start putting in clues, like signs written in Spanish, or a Cornish flag. But they still sold. In fact he couldn't paint them fast enough. I visited him once in his studio. He had six canvases set up in a row, and he was going from one to the next putting in red bits, then back in the other direction putting in blue bits. He seemed quite optimistic but it made me despair. Do you feel optimistic?'

Up until this point he hadn't wanted to engage in the conversation, he'd wanted the critic to take her opinion somewhere else, far away. But this question got under his skin.

'No, not really,' he said. 'Most of the time I don't. There isn't a lot to be optimistic about.'

Her mood suddenly brightened. 'I agree. That painter couldn't see that. I shall have to read these again. Perhaps there is more to them than I'm seeing.'

'Perhaps there is,' he said.

Now here are our main stories again, and I should warn you that some of these are accompanied by flashes of inconsequence:

Latest opinion polls indicate that if a General Election were held tomorrow the result would be a coalition between *Strictly Come Dancing* and *The X Factor*. Politicians from all parties welcomed the findings, saying they were encouraged that so many people were having fun while engaging in the electoral process. The government is considering lowering the minimum voting age to three, or doing away with it altogether.

More than ten million viewers are expected to watch the next series of *Dr Who* when it appears on the nation's television screens, to find out if anything interesting happens when one doctor is transformed into another. The world-famous time-travelling medic is not a real doctor, which may surprise some viewers.

It has emerged that while some people find twerking, the sexually provocative form of dancing which involves thrusting, bending and squatting movements, distasteful and demeaning to women, other people don't.

The retail sector has received a welcome boost, with plenty of crap in the shops and plenty of customers willing to buy it. Some shoppers are so keen to snap up bargains that they have queued overnight in order to have the best chance of being interviewed on this programme about queuing overnight for the bargains they hope to snap up.

Millions of people are desperate to know how Sherlock Holmes survived after leaping off a roof at the end of the last series of *Sherlock*. The world-famous detective is not a real detective, which may surprise some viewers.

The arms trade, state surveillance, environmental destruction, global inequalities, even a serious story or two about culture? Naaah.

And news just in, our top story is . . .

Well, we thought it was going to be the one about voting intentions but overwhelmingly you have texted and tweeted us to say that it was too complicated so it has been dismissed from the show by our expert panel of judges, and the winning story tonight is . . .

. . . the one about twerking!

Congratulations, twerkers everywhere. And remember, you can't fool all of the people all of the time. Good night.

'Now, you know about clootie wells, do you? These are wells usually with a tree growing beside them, and the water from the well has special healing properties. People come from far and wide to get the benefit. They come with all kinds of ailments and they dip a cloot or rag into the water and tie it to a branch of the tree, and perhaps say a prayer or perhaps not, and as the rag dries and fades and reduces over time so the ailment goes away. Or if a person is too ill to make the journey a friend or relative may bring something of theirs to dip into the well and then tie it in the tree, and the illness diminishes. Sometimes a clootie well is associated with a saint or a spirit, and sometimes no one knows why the tradition grew in this or that location, but the site is always very ancient. And where the tradition survives there is no sign of it coming to an end, not even in these enlightened times!

'You may laugh at what I am telling you, but just as they say God is not mocked neither is the clootie well. I know of someone who visited one such well. She showed it respect but she came neither to be healed herself nor with a cloot from anybody who was ill, and maybe that was the problem. She took photographs of the tree festooned with cloots, because without question it is a curious thing to see by the side of a road, and before she could leave something picked her up and flung her on her back, and cracked her camera off the tarmac, as much as to say, *Don't think you can come here and take those pictures away without an offering*. Well, that tumble gave her a fright and when she got home she checked to see if her camera was still working, and it was, but did she even look at the pictures of the clootie well? She did not. She deleted them. She had been warned, and she heeded the warning.

'I believe that was a wise decision, whatever you think.'

Death, the Shapeshifter

I don't know beforehand how I will appear to anyone. This time, next time, sometime, never. He or she? Giver or taker? The English say, 'He took his own life.' The French say, 'He gave himself death.' It's a grey area, the English Channel.

That famous encounter in Baghdad, I was a she, according to common tradition. Or was I in drag? I don't, honestly, remember.

Sometimes I feel as if I am going about a big country house, its outbuildings and gardens, snuffing out candles. As fast as I snuff, some other character is off lighting new ones. I look up from a lawn covered in tea-lights and see the silhouette at a window on the upper floor, illuminating an entire corridor with new flames. It isn't a race, it's a balancing act, something I often think the lighter of candles fails to appreciate. In this game one should not get ahead of oneself. We have never met.

I dance a little giddily across the dewy grass, applying my snuffer here and there. Tea-lights flicker. Some recover, others succumb to the draught of my gown. To anyone watching from the house my dance probably appears haphazard. It isn't. To choreograph randomness takes aeons of practice.

I am a peck on the cheek, a mild cough. Three ducks on the wall over the fireplace: one falls off, for no apparent reason, and shatters on the hearth. Bullets, blades, gas, bombs, yes, yes, I've used all those methods of collection. It's the details that fade.

I am a painting by Brueghel, a casual remark by Hume, an unfinished symphony, an unread novel.

Here's one I do remember. I am a postman. I have a parcel too big to go through this particular letter box. I ring the bell and half a minute later a woman of about seventy opens it. I hand her the parcel. There's a clear view down the corridor to the kitchen. Her husband is sitting over his porridge.

As soon as I see him I know it's for him I have come.

By the time she gets back he's away.

The parcel was for her. I've no idea what was in it.

It wouldn't have been acceptable for me, a man, to do what was done. It would have been misinterpreted, my motivation questioned. The woman herself would probably have seen me as suspect, even predatory, and so perhaps she should have. Thus I was only a witness, not a protagonist.

I was on the bus. So often on the bus everybody is guarding his or her personal joys or tragedies. Not this time. The woman was sitting several seats in front of me on the top deck. She had a scarf over her head. I couldn't tell if she was young or old, I didn't know what, if anything, the scarf signified. All I could see was that her head was covered, she was alone and she was crying. It wasn't to draw attention to herself. She couldn't help it. There she was, on the top deck of a bus, crying her eyes out.

Five of us were up there with her: myself, a young lad, two women sitting together with various bags of shopping, and another woman by herself. We must all have been aware of the weeping woman's distress. How could we not have been? I wanted to go to her, ask her what was wrong, but I didn't go. Her sobbing continued. I looked to the boy: if I couldn't help her, how could he? I looked to the other woman by herself, willing her to act. She stared out of the window, perhaps nursing a hurt in her own heart. The two shoppers were talking, glancing. I knew they were talking about the one in distress even though they were whispering.

Then, as if they had reached a joint decision, one of them stood and went to her. She sat down and put her arm round her. That was all. A total stranger. She put her arm round her. And it wasn't going to stop the tears but it was certainly something.

My stop was coming up. All our stops were coming up. For a minute, though, it was as if time and travel had stopped. As if there was something shared among us, a possibility, a hope. Yet nothing was said.

The Return of Simon Stoblichties

Even in December a few tourists still came to see the shrine of Simon Sto-blichties. For thirty-seven years the hermit had perched on his platform atop the blasted tree on the peat bog moor, and during those years, and ever since, the village had thrived. The hotels and restaurants did particularly well, especially in the summer months, but there was also a healthy trade in books, postcards and wee figurines of Simon standing in a loincloth, arms outstretched in the teeth of a gale.

Mrs Kincardigan kept one of the souvenir shops. As she was opening up she saw a man staggering down the street who looked very much like the figurines she sold. He had no shoes, was leaning on a staff and was attired in matted sheepskins. His hair was like six crows' nests jammed together and his beard was nearly tripping him.

Now I've seen it all, Mrs Kincardigan thought. *A tribute band's one thing, but this is taking a liberty.*

The stranger tottered over and asked for directions to the shrine. 'I've been gone a long time,' he quavered. 'That way, am I right?'

'Straight along the road,' Mrs Kincardigan said. 'There's no shuttle bus today. When you get to the car park, follow the path another quarter-mile.'

'And is my old tree still standing?'

Really, she thought. 'It fell over,' she said. 'There are bits of it in the museum. The new one looks just the same though.'

He gazed at her through rheumy eyes, as if his mind were elsewhere.

'He wouldn't be impressed, you know,' she said. 'He couldn't abide flattery. If you want my opinion, you're insulting the memory of a good man.'

Now he stared at her with what was presumably meant to be incomprehension.

'But –'

'But me no buts,' Mrs Kincardigan said. 'He died long before I even had this shop. Shame on you.'

She turned on her heel and went in, then moved quickly to a side window to watch him lurch off with his exaggerated limp. She'd a good mind to report him. He almost certainly wouldn't spend any money.

Honour without profit? A mug's game. They'd never catch her at it.

I had been walking a long time. I sat, dozed a while, then I heard the water and was awake again. Water was everywhere, the cavern roofs dripped with it and my feet splashed through salty shallows, but it was a deeper, threatening roar that got me on the move. First came soft, gelatinous tissue, then bony protuberances I had to clamber over. I suppose I kept heading towards the light, a yellowish glow that seemed always to be dimming but never quite went out. It was like walking through constantly parting, pale curtains.

I entered a long dry section, rising gently. A sweet voice floated down the tunnel. The tune seemed familiar but not the words:

Frankie and Johnny were lovers,
So the story goes if it's true,
But Frankie got hurt and Johnny got worse
For breaking that old taboo.
He was his man,
Never done him no wrong.

A guitar was being strummed, simple, slow, bluesy. The tunnel turned and I came on a curly-haired boy bent over his guitar in the curve of the wall. He looked up and smiled but didn't stop singing.

Frankie went down to the corner	Johnny went looking for Frankie,
To buy his Johnny a hat.	Found him under a tree.
The people disapproved of his attitude,	He held his head, 'Frankie,' he said,
They beat him and hurt him bad.	'This don't look good to me.
He was that kind of man,	You are my man,
So they done him wrong.	And they have done you wrong.'

There was something irredeemably sad in the boy's voice. I had no money for him. I smiled back but he kept on singing, so I walked on up that tunnel, his voice fading behind me. I wondered if the light would ever get brighter, if I would ever get out. I wondered how that boy had got in. I heard the water roar, even as the last verse of his song pursued me.

The people came back for Johnny,
Hung him high in that tree.
Frankie never died, but he cried and cried,
'Johnny come back to me.
You were my man,
You never done me no wrong.'

There was trouble at the automatic exits. A woman trailing a large suitcase had repeatedly been feeding her ticket into the slot and the barrier had repeatedly failed to open. She moved to the only gate operated by a human being. To this fellow sufferer in the transport system we call life she handed her ticket, and was surprised when he too did not let her pass.

'Your ticket isn't valid for this station, madam,' he said.

'Yes it is.'

'No it isn't. It's valid for the next station, Arbroath.'

'And this is Dundee,' she said. 'Arbroath is further on. A longer journey. I'm leaving the train seventeen miles early, not to mention reducing wear and tear on the seat fabric.'

'Your ticket still isn't valid here.'

'I live here,' she said. 'As it happens I bought a return ticket from Arbroath to Edinburgh, but I actually live here. I'm saving the railway thirty-five miles.'

'Madam,' the man on the gate said, 'you bought a discounted ticket valid from Arbroath. The discount doesn't apply to journeys made to and from Dundee.'

'From and to,' she said.

'It's a different journey.'

'It's the same journey, only shorter. I got on the train later and off earlier. What's the problem?'

'Your ticket isn't valid for this station,' he said again. 'The ticket you bought was a special offer for customers travelling from Arbroath, not for customers travelling from Dundee.'

'I am not a customer,' the woman said. 'I am a passenger. I bought the best-priced ticket available but chose to get off before my final destination. It's not as if I'm trying to get to Aberdeen on the cheap, is it? I'm not a fare-dodger.'

He gave her a challenging look.

She relaunched. 'Now look. I can't get back on the train – it's gone. Are you going to physically prevent me from leaving this station?'

The man hesitated, then returned to the fray. 'You'll have to pay the full return fare to Dundee before you can leave.'

'I refuse. Let me pass.'

He shook his head.

She sat down on her suitcase.

'I have a siege mentality when it comes to this kind of thing,' she said.

The Fairy Knowe

A boy went to the village shop but there was nothing he wanted there. He walked home through the woods, past a grassy mound known as the fairy knowe, and this reminded him of an old legend about the place. He was standing thinking about this when a girl came along the path towards him.

'Hello,' she said. 'What are you doing?'

'I'm looking for the door into fairyland,' he said, laughing.

'Oh,' she said, 'I know where that is. It's hidden away. It's not here.'

'Show me,' he said.

So she took him round the other side of the grassy mound where nobody could see them and she showed him the door into fairyland.

The next day he walked the same way, and there she was again. And again she took him away to fairyland through the hidden door.

Days became weeks, and weeks became months, and nobody but themselves knew about their meetings in the woods.

One day the boy did not appear. The girl waited. She returned the next day but he did not join her.

On the third day she was coming out of the village shop and the boy was there on the street.

'Where have you been?' she asked.

'What is it to you where I've been?'

'I waited for you at the fairy knowe, but you didn't come, not today, yesterday or the day before.'

'Then why did you wait? Do I have to see you every day?'

'Do you not want to see me?'

'Perhaps. But you are not the only person I know.'

'Do you not want to go with me to fairyland?'

He laughed. 'Oh, fairyland! What's that?'

'Do you not believe in fairyland any more?'

'No. It's just a story.'

'But I showed you the door and let you in.'

'That was a long time ago. I've grown up now.'

'The first time we met, you laughed,' she said. 'You were happy. I made you happy.'

'I'm happy now,' he said.

She hurried away, to hide her tears from him. She thought, *I will never take another boy to fairyland.*

She did, in time. But she did not expect him to believe in it.

The film was preceded by a warning that it contained some moderate vio-lence. Twenty minutes in, Thomas was still trying to work out what this meant. Already there had been sounds of explosions and artillery fire, and a panoramic shot of a city under bombardment. The setting was the Second World War: surely violence didn't get much more immoderate than that? Presumably what concerned the censors – only they weren't called that, they were called a film classification board – was what the audience was exposed to in close-up, or whether the violence depicted was delivered at a personal level. A bomb exploding twenty miles away might, in this context, be deemed not very violent at all, compared with someone being punched in the face.

Every time a new scene opened, Thomas was unsettled. Was this when the moderate violence would start? But if it did, when would it be over? The warning had not indicated how much moderate violence there would be. Suppose people went on punching one another for the remainder of the film? Was there a point at which such violence would be reckoned to have escalated beyond the limits of moderation? And if so, did the director know when to call a halt, so that his film could acquire the desired certifi-cate? Or suppose one character was on the receiving end of *all* the punches? Was that different from the punches being shared out among the entire cast?

Could you really moderate your violence? Beat someone to within *two* inches of their life? Could a band of soldiers fight to, say, the *fourth* last man, then call a halt? Could an air force carry out *rug*-bombing?

Stupid questions. After the film, Thomas walked home, still confused. A team of heavy-looking men was approaching him, so he crossed the street, to be on the safe side. In fact the men were off-duty policemen, so *of course* he would have come to no harm, but he didn't know that.

Further down the other pavement, he was confronted by a man suffering a mental illness, who assaulted him, but not so seriously that Thomas was entitled to receive a payment from the criminal injuries compensation board.

Soup

The rain was on again. Three o'clock and dark already.

He had half a white loaf in the cupboard, six tins of tomato soup. He was sick of soup but it would have to do. He opened a tin, emptied it into a pan on a low flame, took out two slices of bread.

While he waited, he thought about getting two heats from the soup. One: pour it into a mug and hold the mug in your hands. Two: when it's cooled enough not to burn your mouth, drink the soup.

Three heats, if you counted standing over the gas, stirring the pan.

He'd never been one for conversation, but he spoke now, to keep himself company.

'When we were kids,' he said, 'all we wanted was to escape from this. Boys played football to escape. They went to the gym and boxed. Joined the army. Girls went to be nurses. Folk emigrated. Half our street went to Canada, first one couple, then the cousins, then the neighbours. I don't remember anyone coming back except to get more folk to leave.'

The orange soup bubbled round the edges. He gave it a stir.

'We had an electric fire. One bar or two bars, that was the choice. So long as you didn't fall into it you were okay, you could sit over the one bar and get a heat even if the rest of the room was cold. You could give yourself a quick two-bar blast, then switch it back to save on the cost. Now it's all central heating. What are you supposed to do? Turn all the radiators off except one and stand against it all day?'

He could go to bed after the soup, but he'd only just got up. His spine was sore from lying too long.

'How did this come back to us, eh? For a while we had it on the run. The population had thinned out so there was enough to go round. Now it's back.'

Four heats, if you counted imagining it before you felt it.

Five, if you counted imagining it again later, after the soup.

By that time he'd be in his bed.

The Woman Who Fell to Earth

for Jim and Jane Swire

We felt she belonged to us, although she was only here for a while. She came, she stayed, she left again.

A man walking his dog found her lying in a field, her pale body covered in bruises. He thought she was dead, the victim of a murderous attack, but when he touched her face she opened her eyes. Covering her with his coat, and leaving the dog to guard her, he ran for help.

We carried her to the inn, where her wounds were tended and she was clothed and fed. For weeks she was ill. We all contributed to the cost of her care. It was a miracle that she had come to us.

She signalled her gratitude, but never spoke a word. Nobody knew who she was or how she had arrived. We tried her in many languages, without success. Given paper and pencil, she folded birds and shaded in their grey plumage.

In time her bruises faded and her health returned. She now repaid us with kindnesses of her own, helping and caring wherever she could. We grew to love her silence, her beautiful smile. Sometimes, however, someone would find her standing under a winter sky watching the skeins of geese and listening to them call. In spring, when they left for the north, tears would run down her cheeks.

She used to stand among the geese where they had settled in the fields, and they were not afraid of her. The farmers wanted to shoot them, but out of respect for her they put away their guns. She gathered goose feathers and kept them in a sack. We thought she wanted them to make a pillow.

While she was among us peacefulness was in the village, and a generosity of spirit.

One spring day, when the geese were especially loud overhead, she was not to be found. The sack was: it was empty, and folded away in a cupboard at the inn.

We have not seen her since.

This is still a good place to live, but we feel her absence every day. We think she went to be with her own folk, and this gives us a little comfort.

Sometimes I wonder where I've been all my life. There is an absence, a disconnect. I have been in the dark for years, watching a film about myself. Why do I feel like this? Why do I hardly feel at all? I am struggling here, trying to make sense of something senseless. I am sorry.

That's the last thing I should say. Actually, it's the last thing anybody should say: *I am sorry*. That, and: *I love you*. If you could reach the end and say them both – *I am sorry; I love you* – that would be something. To feel those two things, and say them, and know what they meant. To mean them, truly mean them.

To weigh up all you regret, all the hurt you caused, and offer that recognition. You wouldn't be looking for absolution. You wouldn't be apologising just so you could walk away. You would be acknowledging: *There is nothing I can do about it now, it is done, but I am sorry*.

And then, to weigh up the kindness, the passion, the selflessness, the sacrifice, and offer this: that you loved. To say to someone, *You were not the first, you were not the only, but because you are here now you are the gifted, you are the final recipient of the accumulated love I carry from life. Here, take them, my sorrow and my love, distribute them*.

It is of these that human lives are made.

Then how is it that I am asking, *Where have I been all my life?* There is an absence, a gap, a dream. Either my life is the dream or I am. Decades and decades of dreaming. I reach out to touch my life and it is not here, or I am not here. One of us is not real. I have drifted down the river and when I look back I cannot believe the distance I have come. Perhaps I have not moved at all. Perhaps I am still dreaming. Yet the river flows on. If I know it so well, why does it look strange to me? Why is it so full of sorrow and love, and I so empty?

Jack and Death

One day in town Jack becomes aware of a sinister figure lurking nearby, a tall, gaunt fellow in a grey hood and cloak. He gets it into his head that this is Death trying to sneak up on him.

So Jack slips into a close, and when the hooded figure comes by he grabs him and puts a pocketknife to his throat.

'Whit for are ye followin me?' he says. 'I've a mind tae slit yer thrapple here and noo.'

'I'm not following you,' says Death. 'We just happen to be going in the same direction.'

'Well, I've caught ye noo,' says Jack, 'so tell me why I shouldna finish ye aff. The world wid be a better place withoot ye.'

'That's where you're wrong, Jack,' Death says. 'Even if you could kill me, you'd cause more problems than you'd solve. Let me show you something.'

Further down the close is a window. They look in. An old man is lying in bed twisted in pain, with a tearful old woman nursing him as best she can.

'That's where I'm due next,' Death says. 'If you stop me, his pain will go on and so will her distress. That's not right, is it?'

So Jack lets Death go in, and soon the old man is lying at peace and the woman is drying her eyes and sending up prayers of gratitude to God.

Death returns to Jack's side. 'She's thanking the wrong person,' he says, 'but she's glad I came.'

'All right,' Jack says, 'I'll let ye go if ye promise tae leave me alane till I'm as auld as that auld man.'

'I can't promise that,' Death says. 'You might step in front of a horse or be struck down with an incurable disease this very night. You must take your chances like everybody else.'

'But noo I ken whit ye look like, when I see ye comin I'll fecht ye,' Jack says.

'Jack,' says Death, 'if you see me coming you'll know it's time to go. And if you don't, which is more likely, you'll just think I'm the other fellow.'

'God, ye mean?' says Jack.

'No, son, not God,' says Death. 'Life.'

One of Those Traditions

Didn't think I'd make it, did you? Not that you've ever said so to my face, but you've had plenty of conversations behind my back. I'm deaf but I'm not daft. I know what's going on when those low murmurs start in the kitchen. And do you think I don't imagine the telephone conferences you conduct from the safety of your own homes? *How much longer do you think he'll last? He's definitely losing it. Going downhill. Worse every time you see him.* Well, of course I am, I'm old and getting older. I'm hardly going to get better, am I?

Yes, I've been guilty of expressing just that ridiculous optimism. I've used the phrase 'when I get better', and I've watched your faces clouding over as you hear me say it. Got to do something to amuse myself. May as well generate a change in your weather systems once in a while. Wipe the bonhomie off your silly mugs.

The truth is, you didn't think I'd make it to *last* Christmas. Well, here I am, so stick that in your stove and light it. Who's losing it now, eh?

I don't blame you, actually, for not discussing my future prospects with me. Too depressing. And if I get depressed, are you surprised? Can't do much for myself and when I try I make an arse of it and that brings another reading of the riot act: *Don't stand up without one of us there to assist; don't carry things while using your Zimmer; don't stretch for your cup; don't breathe without permission.* With *her* it's like living with the police, then you lot arrive and it's as if MI5 and a vigilante committee have piled in too.

It's not your fault. And I do like it when you come. You're busy people and I appreciate you taking the time to see me. You just didn't expect to see me *this* Christmas, but there you are. Full of surprises, life.

I blame life. One bloody day after another, that's what life is.

Let's have the carol service from King's College, Cambridge. One of those traditions I hate. I've always hated it. And I still can.

Another Child is Born

You sometimes hear it said about a baby, new-born or perhaps a few weeks old. Usually by women of a certain age. Women of a certain age say it of babies of a certain age. They look into the baby's eyes and say, 'This one's been here before.' That's their judgement. The baby looks at them and they look at it – no, they look *into* its eyes, *at* its look – and they consider, and then they come out with this declaration. 'This one's been here before.'

What a burden to place on a baby! She has not long arrived, she has only just started processing tastes, textures, colours, is still struggling to focus on objects and people. Her primary concern is latching on to a breast and feeding. The deeper matters of existence – if that is what they are – have not occurred to her. They are irrelevant. The possibility that she is on a return visit is not on her agenda. It is on the women's agenda. Likewise the unstated assumption: that if indeed she has been here before, she will be here again. Another life in another form in another future – and more to follow – before she has even begun this time round!

And there was that other baby. And you think how – when wise men came from the east saying, 'We have seen his star,' and when priests and scribes spoke of prophecies fulfilled and Herod was troubled, and when those wise men found that baby and gave gifts, including myrrh, the anointing oil of death, and when angels appeared to shepherds who also went to see the child and then told everybody about him – all these were really other ways of saying, 'This one's been here before,' and 'This one will be here again.' But that time these things were said by men, and so were taken seriously. And Herod slew all the children under two, in Bethlehem and all around, and the voice of lamentation was heard, and a religion was born.

And Mary kept all these things, and pondered them in her heart. But how she must have trembled when she heard those men say what they came to say.

The Madwoman

Everything was too much, yet it was not enough.

They needed to escape from the cold leftovers, the empty bottles and the full bottles, the packaging, the piles of presents, the tree, the decorations. The whole family felt this need. Taking the first opportunity, they drove to the mall for the sales.

At the end of the street the madwoman was in her garden, shouting at the crows. The crows were shouting back at her, or perhaps they had started it. They wheeled above her as she scolded them. She did not appear to notice the car going past.

The madwoman was the family's little joke. 'She's crazy!' one of the children had said once, seeing her dancing along the gravel path. To them she was an entertainment. They did not know her name or indeed anything about her except that she lived in that house and was not like them.

The mall was packed with people like them. Everybody moved at the same bumping, clumsy pace. Families were laughing and bickering. Sometimes a mother yelled at a child. Some people smiled, others looked cross.

There were no seats free in any of the food-court outlets. They bought burgers and ate them standing.

It was so good to get out of the house.

They returned to the car hours later carrying bags full of many things. They worked out how much money they had saved by not buying those things the week before, and were pleased with the bargains they had got. The week before they had bought other things without making such savings, but that was different. It was a different time, a different experience.

When they turned into their street they saw the madwoman again. She was still in her garden, standing on the grass in the half-light. For all they knew she had been out there the entire time they had been away shopping, shouting at birds or dancing along her path or just standing as she was doing now. She was looking up at something in the sky, but it wasn't crows. The crows had gone.

The madwoman was the family's little joke, but nobody mentioned her as they drove past.

Jack and the Giant

Jack was no longer a young man. One day he was walking through a forest when he met Death. It was years since they'd last met. She'd changed. She linked arms with Jack and they ambled together along the path for a while, then embraced and parted.

There was a blue door in a red stone wall. Jack went through it.

A gentle, broad, grassy slope led towards a magnificent palace gleaming in the sunshine. The gate was open so in he went. It was the palace of a giant, who came down the marble steps to greet him.

'Jack! Good to see you! In you come. I'll show you to your room. Anything you want, Jack, it's yours.'

Everything about the palace is beautiful, from its ornate galleries to its cool fountains, from the sweet background music to the tables laden with fine food. Jack is impressed, but it bothers him that the place is almost empty: all this wealth and luxury shared by just a handful of folk, each looking down his nose at the others, and at Jack too.

Jack seeks out his genial host.

'Where is everybody?' he asks.

'Why, everybody's here, Jack,' the giant says.

'Naw, naw,' says Jack. 'Where's aw the *ither* folk?'

'Who do you mean?'

'Folk like masel,' Jack says. 'Is onybody allowed in here?'

'Not just anybody,' the giant says. 'You have to sit a kind of exam.'

'Weel, I never sat an exam in ma life,' says Jack, 'so how am I here?'

'You don't really know you're sitting it at the time,' the giant says. 'Only I know.'

'And whit dae ye hae tae dae tae pass this exam?'

'Would you like one of these lovely peaches?' the giant asks.

'Thanks,' says Jack, 'but if ye dinna mind, I'll just step oot for some fresh air.'

'I don't mind, Jack, but if you go out you won't be let back in. It's very nice here. Where will you go?'

'I'll keep walking, and see whit happens.'

'But nothing might happen, Jack.'

'That's true,' says Jack, 'but I'd rather find oot for masel.'

And he passes through the gleaming gate, and continues up the hill.

Fifteen Minutes

So, he was in the room. He had fifteen minutes.

His torturer was strapped to a horizontal frame, just as he had been. Naked, just as he had been. Various implements were laid out on a table. He had been told what to expect. Nevertheless he was surprised at how completely the intervening years vanished.

The man's eyes watched him as he walked over to the table, picked up a baton, felt its weight, put it back down.

He bent over the man. Yes, this was certainly his torturer. There was no forgetting or mistaking that face.

Those bound hands had inflicted on him unspeakable brutalities and humiliations. He still did not quite believe that he had survived.

The choice was his. In fifteen minutes they would return and it would be over, whatever he had done or not done.

'We know what you went through,' they said. 'You have immunity, for fifteen minutes only. Do what you wish.'

What he would do depended on what he saw in his torturer's eyes.

If he saw fear or remorse, he might go in one direction. He would not forgive, but he might walk away.

If he saw arrogance and scorn, he might go in another direction. The impotence, pain and terror he had felt might boil up, and he would use the things on the table with quick, blind fury.

But how could he know what he was seeing?

The man was not gagged. He said nothing.

If he walked away, the torturer might believe himself still victorious. He might despise his victim all over again.

If he did to the man even a tenth of what had been done to him, what would he have become? Into what new hell would he have descended?

The weakest thing was being unable to decide.

The minutes ticked away.

He had two questions.

'Why did you do those things to me?'

'How could you do such things to anyone?'

He looked into the eyes. Still the man did not speak.

'Do you understand me?'

The man nodded.

He thought: *He does not know the answers either*.

When he realised this, he knew what he was going to do.

My Encounter with the President

Not for the first time there were no cards marking the seats for which passengers had made reservations. I had reserved a seat, from Perth, but when I reached it I found it already occupied by a tall, elegant man with short black hair beginning to go grey in places. He was working on a laptop but looked up at my approach and gave me a broad and beautiful smile. To my astonishment I recognised him as Barack Obama, forty-fourth President of the United States of America.

'Don't tell me,' he said. 'I'm in your seat?'

'Yes,' I said, 'but please don't disturb yourself. Luckily the train isn't that busy. Would you mind if I sat here?' I indicated the seat on the other side of the table.

'Go ahead, please,' he said. 'I greatly appreciate your not making a fuss.'

He waited until I had settled myself before returning to his laptop. He tapped away at the keyboard, occasionally pausing to think or reread. I wondered if he was writing one of those speeches for which he is justly famous.

The woman with the refreshments trolley could barely speak, she was so embarrassed to be serving President Obama. He bought a coffee and a Mars Bar, and found her the exact change as she said she was running out.

'Going far?' I said, when he closed his laptop.

'To Inverness,' he said. 'I'm giving a speech to the Gaelic Society there.'

So I had been right! 'Do you speak Gaelic yourself?' I asked.

'Not a word,' he said. 'But they've promised not to hold that against me.'

He took out some papers from an attaché case and began to read them, initialling each page as he finished it. He was left-handed, and had an awkward, upside-down way of writing.

'I'm sorry for the trouble you're having with Congress,' I said.

'So am I,' President Obama replied. He was still very polite, but I detected a slight note of irritation in his voice. He was a busy man, of course, and no doubt had important state business to attend to before we reached Inverness. So I got out my newspaper, and did not disturb him again.

The Search Party

We would never have gone out if we had not intended to return. We left a fire in the grate, banked up with dross, and a light in the window in case we were still out after dark. We left provisions too: tea, coffee, sugar, bread, tins of this and that; the makings of several meals. And there were a few bottles, the contents of which we were sure would fuel stories and songs around the fire when everyone had eaten their fill. Yes, we certainly meant to return.

But somehow we were distracted. It wasn't so much that we lost our way, more that we found a path we weren't expecting, and we followed it. We were seeking something. That was the whole reason for going out. The path might lead us to whatever it was. But what seems to have happened is that after a while the path began, as it were, to follow us: it went where we went, rather than the other way round. And now I am not sure that it was a path at all.

We paused to rest not long ago, huddling together against the cold, and one of us said, 'What is it we are looking for?' Nobody could remember. Another asked, 'Is it a thing, or a person?' So we checked, but we were still roped together and we did not think anyone was missing.

The snow has stopped falling, but everything is white. The moon, though so very far away, is bright. Perhaps we should have left markers, to guide us back. It is too late for that now. We must go forward. We will reach somewhere eventually.

By the time we do, we will probably have forgotten the details of what we left behind – the smell of wood smoke, the lamp in the window – but something will stir in our memories. At the end of our search will be an unfamiliar place, which, nevertheless, we will recognise. And I think then we will discover that some of us did not make it after all, and we will remember their faces and their voices. And we will go into the warmth, taking them with us.

The Miner

All the stories in the world originally came from one source, a mine in a remote and desolate place where only the story-miners lived. The stories came in many shapes and sizes – some heavy and bulky, some smooth and delicate, others sharp and awkward to hold – but they had one common property: something in each one shone, or glittered, reflecting light in its own special way.

The stories were dispatched, unrefined, across the world, to people who had no knowledge of the mine's existence. When they came across one of the stories in their own locality, they assumed that it belonged to them.

Over many centuries the mine workings grew deeper and more complex. When one seam was exhausted, another was opened. Still, it became increasingly difficult to find and extract new stories. As this happened, the miners themselves grew fewer. The older generation died. Younger families left, seeking less demanding and more rewarding work. A time came when only one miner remained – a strong and skilful labourer, but the last of his kind. One day he came up from the mine empty-handed: there were no more stories down there.

Sad though he was to see the end of a long tradition, the miner was a realistic man. He collected his tools and personal belongings, and set off in search of a new occupation.

How long he walked is not recorded, but eventually he left behind the bleak landscape familiar to him, and travelled through a country of thick forests, green meadows, rushing rivers and cultivated fields. He passed through villages and towns and spent time in huge cities. And he began to notice – lying at the roadside, or marking the edges of flowerbeds in parks and gardens, or abandoned in heaps in disused warehouses – the same multiform stories that he had once mined. He collected several of the discarded ones, and used his tools to recut or polish them a little. Then he walked on, discreetly depositing them in pubs, churches, schools, theatres, places of work, places of play . . .

And when people came across one of these slightly altered stories, they picked it up and took it home, assuming that it belonged to them.